The Lands of Dream

Charles Clemons

Portal Press

Soddy Daisy
Tennessee

The Lands of Dream

A special thank you to Dr. Louie Edmundson for his literary advice and expertise.

Published in the United States of America by
Portal Press
8114 Karr St
Chattanooga, TN 37421

ISBN 978-0-578-02318-2

First Printing
July 2009

To my mother, who without my dreams would not be possible.

"All that we see or seem is but a dream within a dream."

- Edgar Allan Poe

Table of Contents

Stories

Poems

Knowledge

The Simplicity of Life

The Sacrificial Rock

A Journey

Glossary of Dreams (A-Z)

The Southern Realm of Dream

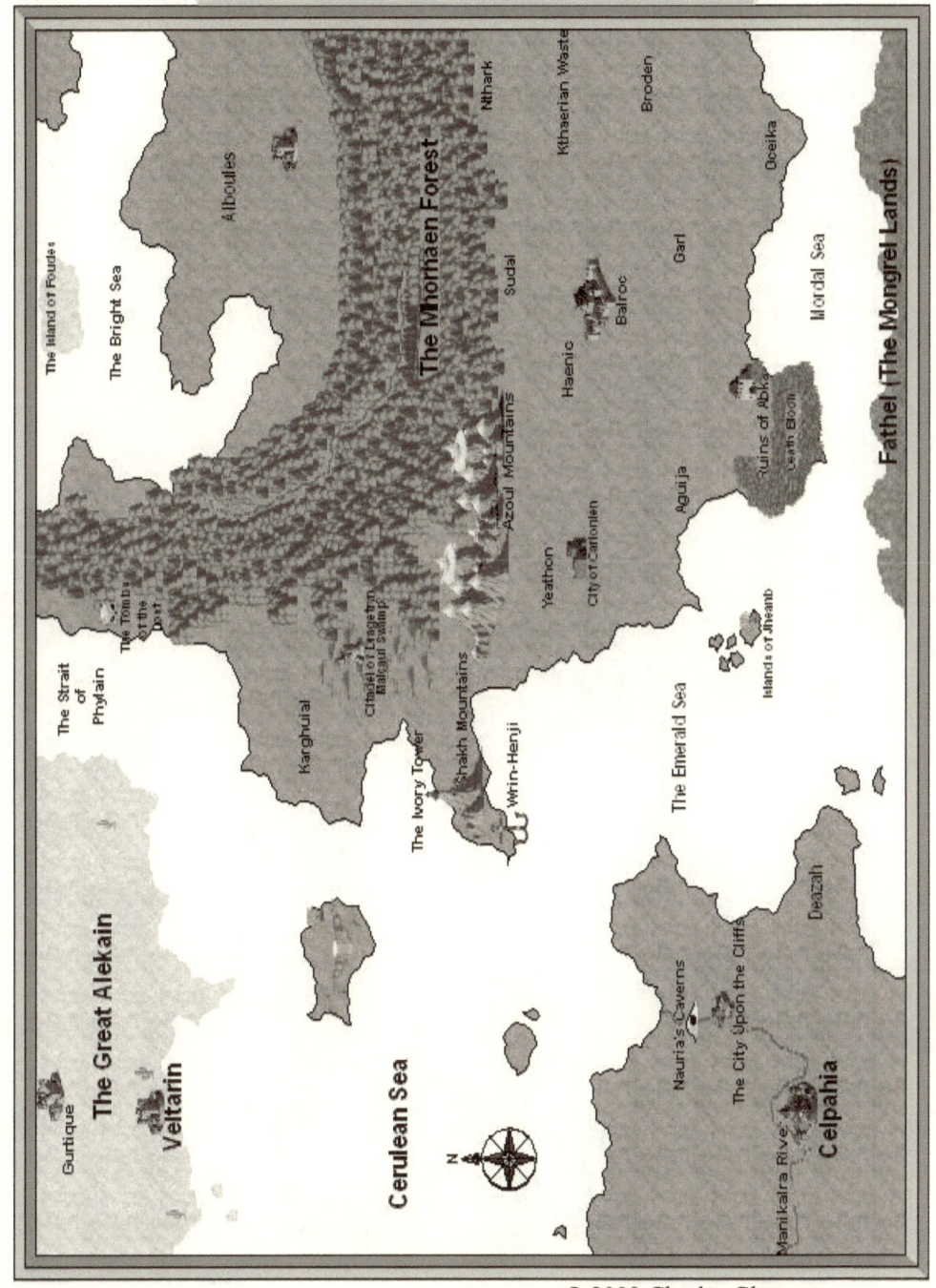

© 2009 Charles Clemons

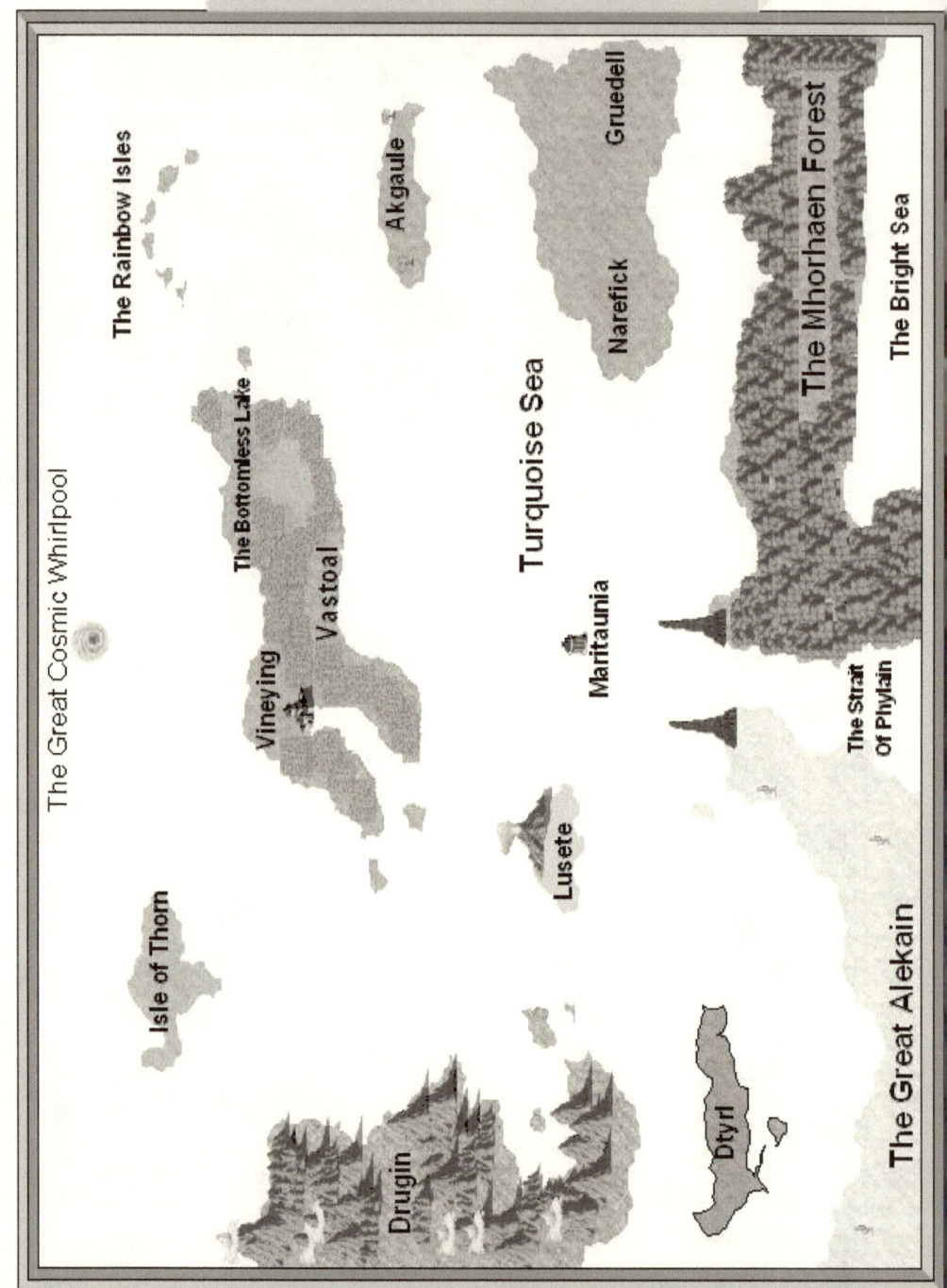

The Quest Knights

Jurlgrann, the youngest and heartiest of The Quest Knights

Jurlgrann was the youngest and the heartiest of the Quest Knights. He had fought in the savage Morlathean Wars, emerging a hero. Even he had forgotten the number of Narefickians he had killed in those wars. It is said that he killed more men than any other ten men combined who fought in the Morlathean Wars. As his legend grew so did his value to King Darl. He was eventually promoted to Captain of the Royal Guard, as the king's most loyal and trusted subject. But now a tragedy of dire proportions had befallen his beloved country and king and now for the first time since his promotion, he wasn't at the side of his king.

King Bubahl, in an attempt to gain the upper hand in the war between Narefick and Gruedell, had commissioned Jewlbard the Assassin to kidnap King Darl's daughter, Princess Siera. Jewlbard, the greatest thief in all the lands of dream, had passed the heavily guarded Plains of Kerra between Narefick and Gruedell without incident. He had scaled the towers of King Darl's palace, permanently silencing seven guards and escaping with the princess. He had covered his tracks so well that no one noticed she was missing until her chambermaid raised the alarm the next morning. Jurlgrann had been sent as the leader of the Quest Knights to find and return the princess before King Bubahl could harm her or use her to influence the war between Narefick and Gruedell.

Marthel, a tracker, was the second of the Quest Knights. He had been chosen for his ability to hunt and track, but primarily for his cunning. If they didn't catch Jewlbard before he reached Narefick, they would need his expertise to sneak into Narefick and out again with the princess. His skills of thievery would surely be helpful in finding Jewlbard and traveling behind Narefick's front lines. If King Darl lacked any faith in Marthel in was in his loyalty, not in his skills.

Riding directly behind Marthel was Aleick, the finest archer to ever raise a bow in Gruedell. As a youth he had won every archery tournament he had participated and was eventually appointed trainer for the king's archers. He had served the king well in his current position as high commander over all the king's archery regiments. It was his archers who turned the tide of the twelfth Morlathean War by stopping a charge of the dreaded Narefick Calvary, turning a rout into a victory. There was only one thing greater than his skill with the bow and that was his devotion to the throne of Gruedell, which was another reason why the king had chosen him for such an important mission.

The last of the Quest Knights was Prince Lasier, brother of King Darl. He had secretly begged his brother to be included in the mission and in turn the king had reluctantly selected him as the fourth Quest Knight. Of all the Quest knights, it was his own brother in whom the king had the least faith. His kingdom and family's future depended upon the success of the Quest knights, which was why he had carefully handpicked each Quest Knight. Their success or failure would determine the fate of Gruedell and its royal family.

Marthel could tell by the dry tracks in the dirt that they would not catch Jewlbard before he reached the safety of Narefick. The young tracker gritted his teeth and climbed back on his horse. From his expression, the other Quest Knights knew that their fate would be determined not within their homeland, but within the borders of Narefick. They would now have to try and catch the crafty assassin in the territories loyal to King Bubahl or sneak into his heavily guarded castle to rescue the princess. This was a task that bordered on the impossible, but they rode on into the desert waste of the Kerra Plains anyway, prepared to do both their king's and country's bidding, no matter what the cost.

The arid desert forced Marthel to ride ahead so he would not lose the tracks in their own dust. He did so with relatively good speed, but with the aging of the tracks they were losing ground. Several times, Marthel had to stop and retrace the tracks as Jewlbard had doubled back to cover his trail. As the sun faded away into the night, so did Marthel's ability to track the cunning Jewlbard. Standing helplessly while Marthel tried to relocate Jewlbard's path, Jurlgrann came to the realization that trying to track the cunning Jewlbard was playing into the assassin's hands. Their only hope was to ride directly for King Babahl's castle in hopes of reaching it first.

They rode on without stopping, using the moonless night to their advantage. The horsemen slipped past several small military camps through the night and their horses did not stop to rest until early the next morning. Narefickian patrols were thick during the day so to avoid detection the Quest Knights hid below a cliff and rested their horses, thus losing any hope they might have had to catch Jewlbard before he reached the mighty fortress of Narefick.

Prince Lasier sat in the cliff's shadows and waited for his chance to make his own name. With his return to Gruedell, along with the princess, he would no longer be known as King Darl's brother, but as one of the legendary Quest Knights. His fame might even exceed his brother's. The four hardened men spent the day mute under the shadow of a gully. With the setting of the sun, they quietly took once again to their horses following the sharp hand commands of Jurlgrann.

The four had been riding for about an hour when Marthel's eyes picked up a small beam of light in the distance. Within seconds several more lights appeared from over the hillside. A small patrol of Narefickian horsemen carrying torches rode into view. With no time to escape, Marthel signaled for the Quest Knights to bridle their horses and be quiet. The patrol was moving fast and might pass by without noticing them in shadows. The four Quest Knights lay next to their horses in silence. The thumps of horse hoofs clanked only a few feet away as the men on the ground waited, hoping their downed horses would not give them away. The light from the guards' torches bounced off their armor and Jurlgrann was sure that they would be spotted, but the men of the patrol rode on peering ahead instead of observing their flanks. Prince Lasier waited in an agonizing cold sweat. He had not joined the Quest Knights to cower in fear, but to slay his enemies. He would not let this become part of his legend. Royal armor rose from the darkness raising a shiny blade. Metal cut through flesh and bone bringing down an unsuspecting rider with ease.

Jurlgrann watched helplessly as the foolish Prince Lasier raised up and brought his sword down upon the first horseman squirting blood from the ambushed rider's neck. The armored horseman fell with the weight of his armor crashing to the ground as Prince Lasier finished him off with the point of his sword. The other seven horsemen of the patrol drew blades that glistened under the light of stars as do fairy wings under a full moon, but these sparkles were not of whimsical beauty, but were born from hard steel bent on death.

It was such a waste thought Jurlgrann. They would have passed without the drawing of blood. He knew that once blood was drawn, more would follow as blood begets blood. Having little choice Jurlgrann picked up his double-bladed axe and ran to assault the men of the patrol. Before he reached the first horseman, Aleick's arrows found their home and dropped two riders. Jurlgrann ran between two of the horsemen swinging his axe in an arc powered by massive muscles born from the jungle tribes of Kalsal. His first blow cut one of the riders in half, while his second decapitated the other rider's horse. The second rider, lying under his horse, was helpless to defend himself and Jurlgrann finished him while he struggled to break free of his downed mount. Spinning around, he parried a blow from another rider but before he could counter, the rider fell from an arrow.

Marthel leaped onto the back of a horse bringing two curved daggers to bear jabbing them into the joints of the rider's breastplate making blood flow from the crack in his victim's armor. In the commotion, one of the riders broke free of the ambush pushing his horse to freedom. Aleick calmly pulled an arrow from his quiver and took aim. The tip of the arrow leaped with fierce velocity, soaring through the night piercing the man's heavy armor and separating his shadowed image from that of his horse. Prince Lasier stood with his bloody sword and smiled with pride. Having been born royalty, he had never killed a man in actual combat and he was proud of his accomplishment. Jurlgrann cursed in silence. He knew from experience that such ambushes accomplished little but to make the road ahead more difficult. The patrol they had wiped out would surely be missed by tomorrow and the presence of their group would be known. Now instead of roaming patrols the entire Narefickian army would be searching. They had lost the only advantage they had, the element of surprise. That night they rode as fast as they could to put as much distance between themselves and the dead Narefickian soldiers as possible.

The next day the four men hid like holed-up foxes beneath a rock formation, thus avoiding the heavily patrolled lands of Kerra. The desert was swarming with armed soldiers. Most of the patrols had been doubled in size and the number of squads indicated that their enemy had a good idea of the Quest Knight's vicinity. It would do their king or country no good if they were caught or killed, so they did the only thing they could do, wait. One thing was for sure, they weren't going to catch Jewlbard before he reached the castle of King Babahl.

With the fall of night, the four Quest Knights took to their horses and began their journey once again. With the skills of Marthel, they managed to avoid the Narefickian night patrols and reached the outskirts of Narefick. The terrain changed almost immediately. Fed by a fertile river basin, the Narefick soil was abundant with vegetation. Strangely enough, to Jurlgrann it seemed as beautiful as the land of his birth. All his life he had hated Narefick and its people and somehow he had imagined their land as harsh and ugly like the Plains of Kerra.

The lush terrain hid the party's movements and under the guidance of the tracker Marthel, they were able to travel by day without being seen. It was shortly after dusk when their luck gave out and the men were spotted by a patrol. The horsemen broke into a full gallop pursuing the Quest Knights who under command of their leader fled through the brush. Jurlgrann ran, not from fear, but because the mission came first. Every skirmish could mean possible failure and he had no intentions of failing his king or country. The Quest Knights rode with all their might, but after traveling through the heat of the day their horses were near exhaustion.

Sitting upon his wheezing horse, Jurlgrann gave his companions the command to stand and fight. Aleick, the eldest of the Quest Knights, jumped off his mount and took his able bow in hand. Jurlgrann stared at death in defiance and gave the command to charge a numerically superior foe. Before the two groups clashed in hand to hand combat, Aleick's bow rained death and four Narefickian soldiers never saw combat. Jurlgrann raised his battle-axe and cut down one horseman as they collided. He swung its blade with the intensity of a madman and the skill of an artist. His strikes were so brutal that his victims didn't make a sound, save for the sound of splitting armor. There were so many horsemen that it wasn't possible for the warrior to block their blows. A sword found his side and another gashed his leg, but his axe never stopped. He kept up his defense by chopping those down foolish enough to get within his range. The force of his axe was so great that the armor and parries of his enemies were useless as blood spilled and men died. The clangorous noise of swords and armor clashing along with the squeaking from the twisting of leather mingled with the grunts and cries of men. All around were the sounds of war and then suddenly there was silence. All that remained was a heap of death. Jurlgrann sat upon his horse covered in both his blood and that of his enemies. Prince Lasier, only slightly wounded in the arm, grinned from ear to ear. Stories of his gallantries continued to form in his head. This was just another tale for his people to recount of his legend, a legend that in his own mind grew from the breath of every moment. It was a thrill that Prince Lasier had never known and one that Jurlgrann wished he could forget. Marthel, who knew a little about field dressings, bandaged both Jurlgrann's and Prince Lasier's wounds before they continued on in their quest. Their horses rode struggled through the night snorting stream through their wide nostrils with failing muscles and on into the next morning before they and the men upon their backs reached the shadow of King Babahl's fortress.

Before the determined men stood their final obstacle, an immense castle with deep black walls and tall pointed towers that actually parted the passing clouds. It had been built deep into the side of a large mountain range leaving only one side of it exposed, making it impossible to perceive its true size and even harder to penetrate. After studying the castle for a few moments, Marthel was confounded by the vacuity of the palace. There were only a few guards scattered along its walls. Aleick dismissed it as good luck, saying that the majority of King Babahl's armies must be out looking for four. The whole situation gave Jurlgrann a bad feeling, but it had to be better than having his adversaries camped in front of the castle awaiting his arrival. They spent the day working their way over to the mountainside crawling on their bellies like snakes, being careful to keep themselves averted from the eyes of the tower's sentries. The proud men, icons of their country, crawled without shame along the mountain's massive base until early that night they reached the edge of the castle wall. Marthel carefully inspected the wall's masonry and found it a stout structure, but his keen eyes found a stone with a slight crack, a fault that showed possibilities. Using tools acceptable to his trade, he began to file the mortar between the blocks. Within hours, Marthel had worked the stone out and the Quest Knights found themselves in the castle of their enemy.

The shadows in the darkly lit castle favored the group as they moved stealthily behind its tracker ,dissolving into its gloomy corners and passageways, but many of the corridors were only narrow enough for a single man and often they would be guarded, forcing the knights to take another route. When there was no other way around, an accurately placed arrow from Aleick's bow allowed passage, a method Jurlgrann avoided whenever possible as each life that they took shortened the time they had left to find the princess. The interior of King Babahl's castle was vast and with each successive vestibule their hopes faded. It was the cunning of Marthel that gave a renewed hope. Upon finding another guard, Marthel knocked the unsuspecting man unconscious and took him hostage. Awakened roughly by the inquisitive Marthel, the man claimed to know where the princess was and promised to lead them to her, if they would spare his life. Marthel walked behind the guard with one hand on his mouth and the other upon a knife resting against his hostage's throat. With a loyalty to his king and country greater than his own life, the man willingly led the group into a trap.

Roaming guards had found one of their victims and now units of armed men patrolled the inside of the palace searching for the legendary Quest Knights. Their captive deceptively appearing afraid led them to a guard post. It was Jurlgrann who was the first to notice that something was wrong. Soldiers appeared from both the front and rear of the group surrounding them in a long narrow corridor. Aleick dropped to one knee and began firing to stop their advance from the rear. Jurlgrann unhooked his axe from his belt and charged up the corridor to reach its end before the Narefickian soldiers could pin them within it. In anger, Marthel used his knife to gash the throat of his hostage and steal his life before he drew his own sword and ran up the corridor behind Jurlgrann and Prince Lasier. Using the small hallway to guard his flank Jurlgrann broke into the waiting crowd of soldiers a man possessed with the molten combination of hatred and loyalty. Sheer strength and momentum he broke their line gaining the Quest Knights a position inside the open hall. Metal and armor clashed along with the cries of men. Prince Lasier and Marthel tore into the room right behind the great Quest Knight and fought like savage dogs. King Babahl's guards, who had so carefully prepared the trap, were surprised by their invaders' aggressiveness and fell back from their position. They were the king's royal guards and years of living in the luxury of King Babahl's palace hadn't prepared them for the fury of the battle-tested Jurlgrann and his fellow Quest Knights. One by one they fell to the blade of Jurlgrann's axe. The impact of his blows sent men in full armor crashing against stone walls. When he had finished, twelve of King Babahl's men laid scattered across the room. Of the Quest Knights, only Prince Lasier's life and legend were lost. He lay a bloody mess with a deep open wound in his chest, but resting upon his calm dead face was a smile.

Aleick had stood firm in the hallway holding off the guards from behind. Screams of the dying and the swishing of arrows echoed through the long hallway as bodies collapsed before the power of Aleick's bow. The bodies of the dead started piling so high that they completely filled the corridor, making it easier for Aleick to kill his opponents as they tried to crawl over the heap of death. He reached for his last arrow and sent it to rest in the heart of another man. Dozens of guards continued to swarm into the hallway and crawl over the bodies of their fellow men. Instead of running and dying a coward with a blow to his back, Aleick drew his sword and died with the honor of a Quest Knight. When the remaining guards made it to the end of the hallway both Jurlgrann and Marthel were gone.

In the turmoil after his last fight, Jurlgrann had surprised and killed several more guards, leaving a wake of death on his way to the court of King Babahl. The throne room he found was built much like a huge amphitheater with the king's throne as the centerpiece. King Babahl sat luxuriating in a plush seat like a fat pig enjoying the pleasures of his country. He was surrounded by a multitude of servants. The many women of his harem, cupbearers, guards, jesters, dancers, wizards, astronomers, and advisors were all waiting to fulfill any command.

Sitting in a small metal etched chair to the left was the infamous Jewlbard, and next to him lay the princess, chained to the court's floor. Jurlgrann moved from corridor to corridor as the king barked orders to his retinue who continuously fanned him, rubbed his feet, brought him food and danced for his pleasure. The courtroom itself was several stories high and lined with balconies looking over into its massive center. It was through these that Jurlgrann checked his progress toward the court's floor. Paying little attention to anything but the whims of their master, Jurlgrann took the entire chamber by surprise when he kicked Jewlbard out of his chair and seized the chain detaining the princess. His huge axe struck the chain, snapping it in two as sparks of metal sprayed from the collision of sharpened metal against metal. Guards scrambled to block the exits and form a wall of men to protect their king, but everything stopped with a booming command from King Babahl. Jurlgrann stood still like a pillar with the princess's arm in one hand and his axe in the other. The king, who never lifted a finger during all the excitement, burst into laughter. Jewlbard picked up his chair and sat down joining in the laughter along with the rest of the king's court. The sly assassin held a small sharp knife that sparkled with rare gems. Ignoring the laughter, Jurlgrann with a stern chin studied his predicament while taking into count every man, every exit and every option.

When the laughter ceased, the king spoke, "A job well done my able friend, but I think you forgot to plan an escape! Surely you don't think my men are going to let you leave this room alive, do you? Release the daughter of King Darl and forfeit your arms and I might show you some mercy. Who knows? I might have a place for a man like you in my kingdom."

Jewlbard, dressed in his usual vibrant clothes, sat in his chair holding his knife ominously with a long smirk on his face. Jurlgrann stood in front of every eye in the room, raised his axe and gave his answer by slaying the princess in cold blood. The young princess died instantly, sliding from his blade to the floor staining the court of King Babahl with royal blood. Everyone including the king froze in utter shock. Jewlbard's grin fell from his face like an apple from a tree.

Jurlgrann had succeeded in his quest as by taking the princess's life, King Babahl could not use her to influence the war between Narefick and Gruedell. At that very moment, Marthel was riding back to Gruedell to tell the story of how they found the princess dead by the very hand of King Babahl. Now King Babahl's daring plan to kidnap the princess had backfired. She would become a martyr and a cause for her people to turn the tide of a war now centuries old. As for Jewlbard, he might as well have died with the same blow. Jurlgrann knew that King Darl would spare no expense in having him killed. He would set a price on his head so high that no assassin in Dream would be able to resist. At the very moment Princess Siera's life ended, so began the count down toward Jewlbard's own death.

Legend says Jurlgrann fought courageously in the courtroom of King Babahl that day and almost reached King Babahl before his men could drag him down. Even in his death, Jurlgrann serves his country for his name still lives on the tongues of his countrymen. Every day since the Quest Knights rode in honor of Gruedell, Jurlgrann's legend has grown and every day King Babahl has fought a hopeless war to save a crumbling empire.

"When the Lands of Dream were formed by those who dreamed in the universe first, the gods created the races of Dream to worship and increase their own power with the major gods creating the elf, dwarf, man and mongrel. The lesser gods, unable to form intelligent races, created monsters to deify themselves."

The Theft of the Dead

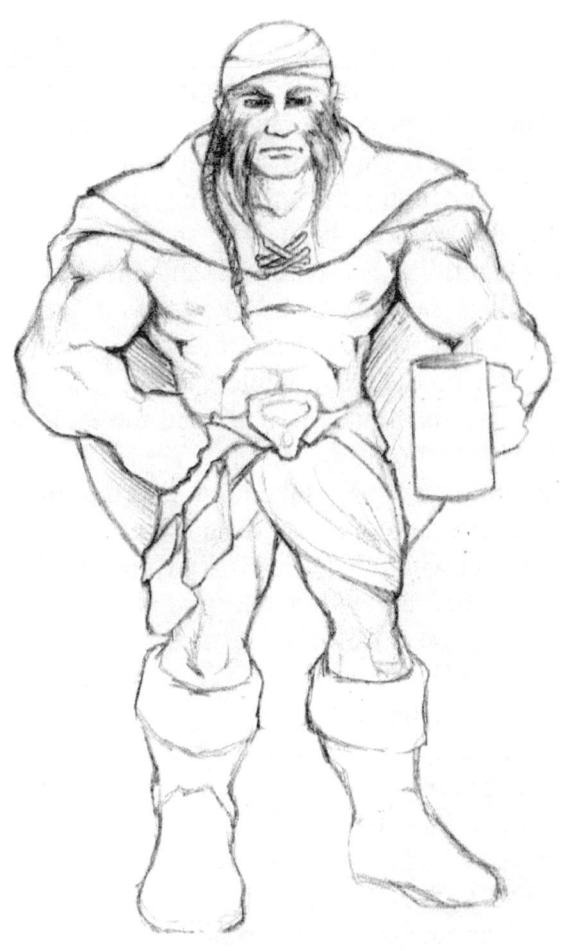

The Mighty Moshgill

Part I
The Plan

Moshgill lifted a warm ale to his lips, draining his mug for the fifth time. He slammed the metal mug hard upon the broad wooden table his comrades sat around signaling the barmaid to bring him another. A filthy woman came to the table quickly exchanging his empty mug for another brimming with more of the thick golden brew. The strong drink rolling over his lips and into his beard had been brewed beneath the Harsahal Mountains by subterranean dwarves who knew a thing or two about breweries. It was known as hearth stout and was capable of keeping a man warm even during the harsh winters of Yeikegu. He pounded his fat belly laughing as his mind softened from the effects of the beer he had consumed. The cost of dwarven brew was nearly twice that of other brews, but no man could make brew like that of a dwarf and besides he and his band were celebrating their last robbery.

A portly man with a bald head, dirty apron and long beard came to the end of their table interrupting their celebration.

"I'm cutting you off till I've seen some coin."

"Oh come on Bauif, have we ever shammed on you?" asked the wily Aguieas of the bartender.

"You four have drunk enough to pay my rent for the month, I don't want you to get into a debt you can't afford to bail yourselves out," he said.

"Bauif, we would never cross you," declared young Kaudot. "We need some sort of safe haven."

"I'm not bringin' you four another drop till I see some coin."

"We don't have any coin right now," proclaimed Aguieas slyly.

"Why you grubby sewer rats!" screamed the bulky bartender whose body was covered in knotted muscle as well as fat. He pulled out a small club which he used to beat deadbeats. "I'll take it out of your hides!"

The young thief jumped from his seat agilely dodging the strong but awkward blow of the bartender's club. The heavy club struck the table in which the four men sat, slinging the mugs of beer on its top crashing against the bar's floor. Suds splashed against the walls and the four men as they danced out of the bartender's way laughing in glee. The bartender swung at young Aguieas missing once again as the young man swiftly leaped backwards laughing wildly.

"Bauif," he screamed trying to control his amusement, "I said we didn't have coin, I didn't say we couldn't pay!"

The heavy bartender stopped laboring to breathe after the commotion of his attack.

"You know the rules, coin or blood!"

"Oh Bauif old friend, what we have is much better than coin."

The young thief tossed a small red ruby onto the table quieting the fury of the bar's proprietor.

"That is enough to pay for every drop of liquid you have in the place," bragged the young man.

The bartender grasped the shiny gem in his hand to ensure its authenticity. It glimmered under the light of candle bringing a sparkle to his gluttonous eye. He placed the jewel in his apron eyeing the four suspiciously before taking his place back behind the bar. The four men laughed as they reassembled their table and chairs to continue their celebration.

"Wench, bring us more brew to replace the ones Bauif splattered upon the walls!" ordered Aguieas happily.

Bauif nodded to the rough barmaid who brought over four new mugs of brew. Aguieas smiled rumbling his hands through the many rubies in his pocket. They were the eyes of Whaie stolen from the temples of Leasden four nights ago. He and his band of thieves had slit the throats of many priests to possess their sparkle, pilfering enough for the four to live as wealthy merchants without degrading themselves by work for over a year. But the four men laughing and drinking at the table weren't farmers or merchants by trade; they were thugs who made their living in the hard shadowed streets of Veltarin. Built on the southern edge of the Great Alekain Desert near the shores of the Cerulean Sea, the city's high walls harbored the worst bandits, thugs and outcasts in the Lands of Dream. Having failed as a port meant to serve boats sailing from the west to the north through the

Strait of Phylain, the city had been overtaken by huge organized gangs who used the once proud town as a base of operation to rape and pillage the realms of Dream.

Aguieas had been given the gifts of a clever mind and deft fingers, which he had used all too well to survive to the ripe old age of twenty four, making him a type of sage in the harsh alleys of Veltarin. His band of brigands were freelancers, meaning they were able to keep their loot without tribute, but this also made them targets for the territorial guilds that patrolled the streets of Veltarin. None of this scared Aguieas as he had never met a man he could not beat by skill or wit.

He held up another ruby and eyed its brilliance. Their last take was enough to escape the brutal life among the rabble of thieves he had grown up in. The four could move to the south where the land was fertile and order prevailed, but what would they do there? Till the land and grow calluses on their soft and able hands? He laughed at the thought of his comrades doing an honest day's work. They were greedy brigands, each and every one, and the riches they held in their pockets were not enough to quell their lust for treasure.

"So what's the plan?" asked Moshgill, the muscle of the group. He was slow and couldn't steal an egg from a blind hen, but his brawn had served them well over the years especially in their activities of extortion and collection.

"I say we go get a room in the Chale and enjoy the best this town has to offer!" replied Kaudot, the youngest of the group. He was a good thief, fast and as quick as the wind, but with his youth came recklessness. He was always willing to try any theft no matter what the risk.

"We need to get out of this bloodsucking town before word gets out about our score," suggested Omeiku, the conscience of the group.

"Omeiku is right," announced Aguieas.

All three bandits sitting across from him stopped what they were doing in shock at his statement. Aguieas never initially agreed with Omeiku. Things were always done with both having a plan on opposite ends of the spectrum and through tough negotiations they would finally find some medium for the group.

"Where do you think we should go?" asked Moshgill, the physically strongest, yet mentally weakest of the group.

"Yeah Agu, got a good plan?" asked Kaudot rubbing his hands together in excitement and ready to steal an egg from a dragon if need be.

"All our lives we've been small time thugs, it's high time we go big!" he declared with a devious shimmer in his eye.

"What do you mean?" asked the cautious Omeiku, "You saying the four of us breaking into the Temple of Leasden and stealing the eyes of gods from fanatical priests is a little thing?"

A thick candle flickered between the four barely pulling the men from the darkness of the dirty bar within they sat.

"That was a good take, but it wasn't enough," he declared.

"We haven't even spent it yet," reminded the wary mind of Omeiku.

"Yeah, when are we getting our cut?" asked Moshgill suddenly realizing he hadn't seen a single ruby yet.

Aguieas leaned forward into the light, which sinisterly illuminated his face. It was a face that had seen much in its short time: murders, robberies and even the monsters of the Alekain in his short service to the Royal Veltarin Guard. He had deserted his unit, giving up the possibility of ever living a legitimate life after a bloody fight with a lizard creature possessing a long tongue, sharp as any knife forged by a man. The slimy creature had scaled the city's high walls under the light of the moon in mad lust for the flesh of man. The gray shadowed monster, a vile creation of the gods of old, slaughtered every man his patrol and gravely wounded him in a desperate fight to the death. In the end he took its tongue before fading into the gloom of Veltarin's streets to escape his civil duties. Across his cheek he wore a long scar as a badge for his short time as a law keeper, a life to which he would never return.

"We're not going to cut it," he proclaimed boldly, "we're going to invest it."

The three men across from him shuddered in horror of the word that came from his mouth. He wouldn't have gotten a worse reaction if he had mentioned the four jumping into a live volcano.

"Invest in what, someone else's luxury?" asked Kaudot. "Really Aug, are you getting soft on us?"

"If you mean invest in drink and whores I'm all for it!" cheered Moshgill swigging down another beer.

Omeiku looked over at his friend suspiciously. He had been affiliated with the sly Aguieas, who seemed to have nine lives, for two years. In the slums of Veltarin time was harder on a man than in the other parts of Dream. A year in its murky shadows was like living twenty in the rolling green hills of the southern lands or ten in the frost of the great northern continent Yeikegu. He had seen much in those two years, such as the time when Aguieas convinced a band of thieves bent on murder and three times their number to surrender for fear of imaginary reinforcements and even dared a royal arbitrator to put him to death to release him of a burdensome "curse" that would befall the person that was responsible for his death, but he had never seen his partner play it safe. The young ruffian Aguieas sat across from his four friends and peered into the candlelight from the shadows.

"To make it big, we have to think big!" he said with a confident grin.

The impetuous Kaudot leaned forward, ready to sign on before he completely heard the plan. Moshgill, too inebriated to focus, leaned backward to flirt with the dirty barmaid who had been serving them droves of beer and who had suddenly and miraculously turned quite attractive. Omeiku's stomach began to churn uncomfortably before the dreaded words left Aguieas' mouth.

"I saw we take this plunder and finance an expedition to loot The Tombs of the Lost!"

"What do you expect to find there, Aguieas, our graves?" asked the cautious Omeiku.

"I'm not afraid," stated Kaudot, "but what do we want with the dead?"

The hulking Moshgill, unsure how he had gotten to the bar, emptied another mug. Drinks were on the house and he was going to get his ruby's worth.

"There is loot there of incalculable value!" avowed the convincing Aguieas.

"Like what?" asked Kaudot interested once again.

"The Hamse bloodline is buried there. Do you think they buried the past kings of Zeethe as paupers?"

"I have heard horrible things about that necropolis. It is said the dead walk its soil."

"Why is it, Omeiku, that you never hear anything good about any place I mention robbing? We are thieves you know."

"Because you are always taking us to places that have the words temple, crypt or dungeon in their names!" replied Omeiku defending himself.

"What are you complaining about? You're still breathing and you haven't worked an honest day in the past two years."

"What kind of loot are we talking about?" asked Kaudot, more curious about the loot involved than any risk.

"The treasures of kings!" proclaimed Aguieas proudly.

"Are you mad? Spend the wealth we have for the rumor of another?" argued Omeiku.

"We have just enough to buy the gear, the pack animals and charter the boat we will need to organize an expedition to the shores of Zeethe. I swear to you three," he said endorsing the plan, "if we pull this off, we will never have to steal or better yet work another day of our lives!"

"Because we will be dead!" countered Omeiku.

Aguieas eyed Omeiku wickedly before placing his palm flat onto the table. He had set the table to a vote. Omeiku quickly placed his hand upon the table with his palm up, thus voting against the madcap proposal. They were a close knit group of brigands ruled purely by majority. Once a plan was approved or disapproved by a majority of the group, defiance would be paid in blood as all had sworn to murder any who defied the collective's will. Kaudot, fond of adventure, brought his hand from the shadows. His white palm reflected the dim light of the table's thick round candle.

"Don't you do it!" warned Omeiku. "If you think the beasts of the Alekain are dreadful wait till you try to kill that which is already dead."

His hand stopped its dissention upon his words as his two sober comrades in arms watched intently. Its rise or fall meant either the continuation or the death of Aguieas' plan. The young man, barely sixteen, had never left the coast of the desert continent known as the Alekain. To sail upon the crystal blue Cerulean Sea toward fables he had only heard of in tales was too alluring for a man inclined more toward the rashness of the adventurous Aguieas than the cautious hesitancy of wise Omeiku. His palm slammed against the table's hard wood surface to the delight of Aguieas and the simultaneous dismay of Omeiku.

"Ha," screamed Omeiku, "you need three votes and Moshgill must lay down his palm by his own free will. And since no plan can ever be placed to vote again your plan is out!"

The three looked over at Moshgill who nodded in his seat, coming in and out of the cloud of unconsciousness. His eyes opened to find three sets of eyes watching him intently.

"What?" asked the large drunkard.

"Yea or nay?" asked Aguieas to his large companion.

Moshgill was brave but not reckless, and he had sided with the cautious Omeiku as much as he had with the impulsive Aguieas.

The hulky thief stared at the three a moment then passed out in his seat.

A smile came upon the face of Omeiku as Aguieas cursed the drunkenness of the hulking Moshgill. He had allowed his companion, who sometimes leaned toward the logic of Omeiku over his daring strategies, to drink so heavily as to cloud his decision-making process. He had botched the vote by letting him go too far. Suddenly the colossal man began to lean forward as might a giant tree losing its grip upon the earth. His massive body fell forward, collapsing on top the table with a disturbing boom, and before his three companions the palm of his right hand landed palm down.

"I'll make the preparations," announced Aguieas, juggling the rubies in his pocket.

Part II
The Journey

Aguieas sat proudly upon a sheen gray stallion outside the protective walls of his birthplace, the great fortress city of Veltarin. The Alekain spat sand onto his new clothing as if angry at his intended departure. His companions sat next to him glistening under the bright suns of Dream as might great kings all upon great steeds of their own.

Moshgill, being three hundred and fifty pounds of bone, fat and muscle sat upon a short but stout draft horse with a rippling black physique. The big man's round belly protruded from underneath immaculate chainmail which jingled like music to his ears. To the side of his steed hung a two-handed hammer four feet long from its handle to its tip. Muscles capable of wielding such a weapon bulged on Moshgill's arms harboring strength almost as great as the beast of the Mhorhaen. It was rumored his father had been a Kthaer barbarian, but no knew for sure since he was found an orphan in the streets of Veltarin.

Kaudot chose the lighter protection of hardened leather which would not encumber his movements. A broad sword with a blue tang tempered by a blacksmith from the prosperous northern side of town, an area where he normally would not be allowed to visit due to his station, hung from his waist. Although young, he was quick and brave, a combination which had served the group well, claiming many unsuspecting lives in the dark corners of Dream. Born the child of a prostitute, Kaudot had struggled all his life knowing nothing but the bloodthirsty rules of gang life since birth. Although slender, he was hard in mind and body, having abided by the code of the thief never to kill anyone unless it was to your own benefit his entire life, but now he somehow felt different, almost sophisticated, as he sat on top an elegant white steed riding toward the high seas to challenge the dead for the treasures of their afterlife.

Omeiku, a man of reason, had not been blinded by the promise of glory as had his comrades, because he knew all too well the legends of the dead from the Tombs of the Lost. The soil upon which the tombs stood were rumored to be hallowed in the eyes of the gods and guarded in death by those foolish enough to dare robbing its sacred mausoleums. He followed upon his steed out of loyalty and the binding unwritten law of the rogue: "Never betray or murder those of the gang for its livelihood is your own." So he rode on the through the dry wind of the desert behind his comrades ready to test fate once again.

Young Aguieas sat proudly in lustrous silk clothing unhindered by the weight of armor, for he depended primarily on speed to overcome those he opposed. He had survived to this day by his stealth, cutting down those with far more strength and sometimes even skill to live on after the deaths of many a foe. Tightly latched to his waist was a fine rapier which he wielded against his adversaries, drawing blood as freely as an artist painting on a canvas.

Aguieas rode in the lead toward the coast where the ship called the Blood Galley sat anchored awaiting their arrival. It was manned by a vile crew of pirates who would cut a man's throat upon the glimmer of a gold tooth in his mouth. He didn't trust its captain, but in regard to ships, only gunships from the coast which brought in riches for Veltarin's elite and pirate ships called to port in Veltarin and since the former could not be hired on the budget of even well-to-do thieves, the latter was their only option. But Aguieas was as cunning a thief as the lands had known and he knew how to deal with one of his own. He had paid the Blood Galley's captain half the cost of the voyage with understanding upon their return he would withdraw the second half plus a bonus from the depository of Veltarin. The captain, believing him to be nobility and therefore an easy target, handily agreed as Aguieas knew he would, to complete the voyage for the money if they returned empty handed or murder them for their claimed treasures if they returned victorious. What the captain did not know was that Aguieas had no intentions of ever returning to the Alekain or the treacherous Blood Galley once they made the shores of Zeethe. Any stolen treasures would be taken by mule to the just and law-abiding capital of the province Karghuial and sold so they might live as kings.

In the distance sparkled the great Cerulean Sea, and docked at the day use only harbor of Gwasheat was the begrimed hull of the Blood Galley. Its dark frame, built with planks from the black trees of the dark forest Cahkul, rocked disturbingly a dark object inappropriate to the beauty of the sea upon which it sat. Multicolored mules were lined up in front of the large ship being ushered in by its salty crew who looked more like dirty miners than the usual brightly colored sailors of the Lands of Dream.

The four horsemen dressed like aristocrats rode hard to the edge of the docks stopping their mounts at the edge of the sea. A scruffy man who barely looked capable of finding his next meal let alone acting as captain of a ship introduced himself, "I am Captain Curveit, welcome to the Blood Galley. Please let my crew handle your horses and gear. I'll show you to your quarters."

The untidy captain gave the men a dirty grin, which would have sent shivers down the spines of most men, but not to those who had been born and raised in the south of Veltarin. He was a cutthroat and each of the men who followed him into the creaky old boat knew it well and upon seeing its foul innards the men felt as if they had never left home. The interior of the hull was covered in slick dingy mold appearing not much different from the exteriors of its crew all of whom wore soiled unkempt clothes. The captain took the men to a small room deep in the hull which held six beds in a musty cloud of mildew.

"This ship is normally one of labor not transport," he said in a playful lie. "I apologize for the appearance. I assure you, there is no more stout a ship on any sea in the Lands of Dream, for I have sailed them all."

Upon shutting the door, the captain shot a scheming smile to two of his crew who instantly appeared from the invisibility of the ship's dark corridors ready to murder the rich passengers if so ordered.

"Should we gut them now?" asked one man holding a long knife.

"No," responded the captain curiously, "I'm going to invite them to dinner in my quarters tonight to find out more about their intended cargo."

The men grinned in agreement to the plan, for it would be a waste to kill such fancy dressed men in haste if they planned on returning with something or someone of great wealth.

The ripened ship, a veteran of the sea, pulled from the day-lit harbor of Gwasheat in order to escape the night when the harbor would no longer be under control of man, but under the murderous eye of strange beasts. The beautiful turquoise water of the Cerulean Sea gently held up the moss-covered hull of the Blood Galley which raced away under the power of wind from the parched coast of the Alekain. Four thieves watched the sandy coast of their homeland fade away having given up thieving in its shadows to test their skills in the continents of Dream.

As the moon rose, so did the mugs of the ship's crew, who drank wildly as do most men who live lives of risk. The men laughed and danced without a care as the four thieves disguised as nobles came to dinner in the captain's quarters. The captain's quarters were far more elegant than the rest of the ship, being decorated with fine furniture, paintings and riches from merchant ships which now sat at the bottom of the sea.

"Gentlemen," replied a dirty bearded man stuffing his face with food, "good to see you, please seat yourselves."

The four seasoned men had seen the worst dregs of society eat raw meat like dogs, but none had seen anything that matched the repulsiveness of the men at the table before them. At the head of the table were the Blood Galley's captain, master and master's mate. Grease rolled down their stained hands, rotten teeth and smacking gums. Even grotesque by the standards of vile street thugs, the four men sat down at the table, wary of the food that was set for them. Moshgill, a man with an iron stomach, sniffed the mush on his plate slinging the stinking mess upon it aside.

"I'm sorry," laughed the captain, "I'm sure the four of you are accustomed to finer foods. Life on the sea is hard and since we sometimes travel many weeks upon the waters of Dream without docking, our food is sometimes… well let me say, not fresh."

Aguieas eyed the captain sitting smugly across from him chewing his dinner happily. A slight smirk formed upon the young thief's face. The captain also a consummate thief was making the four as uncomfortable as possible in order to exert his dominance. Dominated victims made easy by targets having their confidence broken and therefore their will to resist. This strategy would continue throughout the voyage administered with starvation, bullying and sleep deprivation until the predator felt his prey was ready for the taking. Aguieas only hoped that his bait of treasure to transport back to the Alekain would be enough to hold the captain's greed in check.

"So tell me a little more about this cargo you need me and my men to transport back to the vault of Veltarin."

Moshgill, although appalled by the food presented by their host, had never been offended by drink of any sort and was gulping down the thick red wine in his goblet.

"My family has sold a large tract of south farmland and my acquaintances and I are going to the mainland to collect payment," answered Aguieas in a tantalizing falsehood.

"Ah wealthy landowners," replied the salty captain with fearless eyes. "This be inherited land?"

He and his men laughed as if in on a joke the other four knew nothing about.

"This ship be inherited?" asked Aguieas so to retard the captain's scam.

"Haha!" laughed the captain acknowledging the spunk of his passenger, "I just asked for your own safety, as it is popular among the pirates of the sea to seize wealthy land owners for ransom. That way sailors can claim to make a living off the land as well as the sea!"

In a blind rage from the threat thrown upon him by a haggard sailor, Kaudot stood to his feet slamming his fist upon the table.

"How dare you insult us with threats after we commissioned your service!"

"Please, K sit down," responded Aguieas trying to diffuse a possible confrontation with a superior foe.

Moshgill gulped down another goblet of dark wine responding in a drunken outburst, "We're not nobles or farmers, we're adventurers laying claim to the treasures within the Tombs of the Lost!"

"So that is what this is all about," responded the captain, "some fool's quest for death? Why we'll never see the second half of our payment if the four of you are allowed to leave this ship!"

The captain stood up followed by his aids before yelling a booming command of "Now." Suddenly, the door to the captain's cabin flew open, revealing the murderous eyes of desperate sailors. As the bold captain spoke the command, Aguieas leapt onto the dinner table unleashing his rapier. The thin pointed blade cut through the stale air of the small room with a whistle coming to land point blank upon the chest of the ship's captain.

"If you say anything that I don't tell you to say," ordered Aguieas, "I'll run the point of this sword right through your salty heart."

The point of the blade pierced the top layer of the captain's skin drawing blood upon his stained shirt. Aguieas' band of thieves took up arms with Moshgill standing in the doorway, blocking a rabble of malnourished sailors from entry into the small wooden cabin. His giant shadow loomed over the scrawny men backing down their attack. With his earlier confidence rushing away with pain, the captain stood silent, afraid to speak.

"Turn your greed from physical wealth and replace it with a greed for your life, because if we do not set foot on the coast of Zeethe on schedule, then you forfeit your life to cold steel."

"Tell them to go on deck and continue our course, but before you speak… remember your life depends on this order."

"Back away, continue on with the course to Karghuial, that is all."

The rabble of sailors bearing clubs and knives backed away slowly disappearing into the darkness of night.

Moshgill quickly bolted the door, pushing a cabinet to block its passage.

"Not one of us leaves this room until we make shore," stated Aguieas plainly.

"Agu, I need to talk to you in private," stated Omeiku with concern.

"Mosh, K, keep an eye on our guest."

Moshgill's shadow loomed over the small men as he and Kaudot stood next to the men with weapons drawn.

"We know nothing of navigation," whispered Omeiku to Aguieas. "What if they sail us to some deserted island or pirate port? If they do we're finished."

"We must be sure he is too afraid to do any such thing."

Aguieas spun around from whispers with the very same grin the captain bore earlier.

"My partner believes that you might betray us, but I explained to him that you value your life far too greatly to attempt something so foolish," he stated walking over to the captain and his men. "Your plan to rob us failed purely out of avarice, because you underestimated us by believing us to be easy targets."

He brought his sword up, laying it gently against the chest of his master's mate, "I assure you, my heart is as cold as your own."

The grizzled man upon which his sword's tip set, stared into his eyes nervously. He had learned to smell fear, dealing with it daily as a thief and the man before him reeked of it. With the ease of a killer Aguieas ran the man through, piercing his heart with cold-blooded ease. The tip of his rapier protruded out the back of the man dripping blood before it withdrew leaving the man a still lump on the cabin floor. The ship's master, fearful that he might suffer the same fate, reached for a knife on his belt, but before he could unsheathe its blade, the tip of Aguieas' rapier had punctured his eye and entered his brain. The man's body slumped to the floor, leaving the captain standing alone at the mercy of the men he had originally assumed were rich nobles, but in actuality were as ruthless as any cutthroats he had ever seen upon the seas of Dream. The captain cowered in front of those he had a few moments ago, intended to murder and rob.

"I offer you an honest offer, finish the transaction to which we originally agreed by delivering us safely to the coast of Zeethe and I shall let you keep the money we paid you and your life. Who knows? After doing something legit for once, you might turn to an honest life and herd or grow something.

Now it was time for his men to laugh, and laugh they did for it was funny to believe that any man of thievery might ever give up the excitement and ease of robbery for long days of honest labor. The captain would die as they would one day, with a cold grip upon some alluring treasure.

The Ten Laws of a Rogue

1) Only trust someone as long as you need them.
2) It is foolish to die when you can live to steal another day.
3) Never betray or murder those of the gang, for its livelihood is your own.
4) The poor work, the rich do not. Emulate that which you would prefer to be.
5) The only requirement to ownership is possession.
6) With regard to escaping, it's everyone for themselves.
7) No life but your own is worth that of great treasure.
8) Never defy a guild vote.
9) Do not murder unless it benefits you to do so.
10) The final law supersedes all others: Do what thou wilt.

Part III
The Tombs of the Lost

The four thieves safe upon their horses and miles from the coast let the captain go as agreed, giving him a donkey for the long trip back to his ship. The captain sitting upon his ass in humiliation turned backward toward the thieves who had bested a pirate captain upon his own ship.

"Not many days pass where I am out-conned by landlubbers," he said humbly, "I'd tip my hat to you if I had one, gents."

His donkey stumbled along the rock trail toward the bright blue Cerulean Sea. The Blood Galley's crew sat at its edge awaiting their failed captain either to take him back or murder him for his failure. Aguieas had not murdered him to keep his word, not for having a soft spot in his heart, but for one of the ten codes of the thief: Do not murder unless it benefits you to do so. The four thieves turned adventurers led their train of donkeys through the grasslands toward The Tombs of the Lost lay nestled on a tract of land useless to the living as they were surrounded on three sides by the dark Mhorhaen Forest. The fourth side was held in place by the waters of The Strait of Phylain which led to the cooler waters of the northern realm of Dream. A forbidden place of burial formed during the first coming of man into the Lands of Dream; it was rumored that a god of Dream killed by a man in his own temple witnessed by his priests had been buried there by the gods making the ground sacred. As the kings of men died, their servants brought them to the sanctified necropolis to be one with the gods, turning the burial ground into a treasure trove of unimaginable wealth. The word of its great wealth had lured many to its borders, but if any returned, none had met them. What beasts, curses or guardians the stone mausoleums hid was unknown to the men that rode toward it, but the magnetism of its riches drew them toward it like moths to a flame.

They rode hard through the rocky hills until nightfall, then set up a small camp under the stars. A bright fire sheltered the men from the bitter winds that blew across the Azoul Mountains. Because they had spent their lives under the hot suns of the Alekain, the frigid wind cut through them like a knife, bringing the four to a shiver.

"I need a big woman to keep me warm!" declared Moshgill who favored women of girth.

"I saw a jenny back there that might keep you warm tonight," laughed Kaudot. "If you think she could handle a portly man such as yourself."

"I have seen the cows he sleeps with and that jenny is too much a looker for him," joked Aguieas.

"You scrawny bags of bones can bed with those skeleton girls I see you with all you want. There's nothin like a big woman to squeeze onto after like a warm pillow!"

"Mosh squeezed em a regular woman after once and it killed her," replied Kaudot.

"Laugh all you want, but the fat on me is like a blanket. You'll wish you had a little more later on tonight when those winds are blowing against your bones."

"What are you, Mosh, a land whale?" asked Aguieas poking fun at his large friend.

"I'm a man-bear!" he laughed rubbing his long stringy beard in jest.

"Your mother might have been a bear!" laughed Kaudot.

Moshgill jumped up from his spot and playfully sat upon Kaudot trapping him against the ground helplessly.

"If my mother was a bear, then yours was a snake, you stick!"

"Okay, okay, my eyes are popping out!"

As the three men laughed carelessly, Omeiku sat quietly behind the heat of orange flames pondering the tales he had heard about the dreaded graveyard. It was said that tortured souls in the form of black ghouls crawled from the caverns of the earth to roam the graveyard under the dim light of the moon. The bite or scratch of a ghoul passed on its curse dooming its victim to die painfully over several hours before rising again to hide from the sun and wander nights in an eternity of slow decay. It would do no good to complain as they had spent all they had for this venture and to abandon it paupers was not in the nature of thieves.

The next morning the men continued their journey toward the blasphemous tombs until they saw their dazzling white monuments shine from a distance under the bright suns of Dream. Mausoleums that looked more like temples than gravestones stood high and wide in intricate architecture glorifying the remains of their occupants to sustain their memory till the last click of time. From a distance it appeared a brilliant white city sitting quietly against the black Mhorhaen, encircled by a tall wall of polished marble. The men stopped, mesmerized by its splendor.

"Such expense just in its construction, imagine the riches that it must hold!" asserted the young zealous Kaudot.

"We should rob it during the day before the creatures of the night roam its boundaries," suggested Omeiku, hoping to avoid a life-and-death struggle between the living and the dead.

"Agreed... the light of day will be our ally," pronounced Aguieas.

The four finely-dressed men moved like the thieves they were toward the sparkling walls of the ancient burial ground, slithering like snakes through the brushy hillside, crawling to the edge of the brush surrounding the aged but meticulously maintained perimeter. High glossy white marble walls sloping outward, to deter its scaling, ascended twenty feet high obscuring the graveyard's smaller monuments and tombs from curious eyes. Aguieas fingered the wall's smooth surface admiring its fine construction. Having lived in the worst of slums since a child, he had an eye for things of magnificence as most thieves, but his was one of admiration as much as desire. Being ambidextrous, the astute young rogue shifted through his side pouch with one hand as he felt the wall before grasping a long coarse cord in his bag. He quickly unraveled the fiber made from tough twisted mongass root onto the ground before tying its end to a long barbed hook. With the precision of a master rogue, the hook landed over the top of the wall, biting into its target with a firm tug. Four forms mounted the defensive wall with the ease of experience, landing in an immense lush parterre. Tall curved bushes and bright colorful flowers lined the cheerfully decorated graveyard in perfect astronomical symmetry. Although creative of mind, even the ingenious Aguieas stood astounded at the unimaginable beauty in which he found himself. A long pool of water glimmered in the center of the graveyard as might a reflecting pool surrounding the palace of a great king. The painstakingly preserved garden warned the four intruders that were not the only ones within the tombs among the living. Quickly regaining their composure the four thieves slumped behind a large tomb.

"Someone is here," warned Omeiku.

"It looks more like we're trying to rob the palace of the great King Hamse the fourth than a cemetery," replied Kaudot.

King Hamse the fourth was an honest man of the people who had taken unkindly to rogues during his reign over Zeethe. Aguieas crouched quietly studying their situation. He would have preferred to have entered an overgrown and forgotten crypt than a well-kept garden as the former meant desertion. He had never feared rumors of supernatural legends because he wasn't a superstitious man, but he did respect what was real, and whatever had maintained the isolated graveyard in which he stood was real.

With assurance from the light of the suns the hopeful thieves scurried through the graveyard twisting through a maze of tall hedges toward a magnificently built mausoleum which stood taller, more elegantly designed than the others and therefore more appealing to the eyes of a thief. The tall domed structure stood prominently under the light of sun serving as a final resting place, and hopefully to the thieves that stood outside its structure a tomb of wealth.

Aguieas although brave, wasn't rash, and instead of rushing out to break into the large burial chamber, he chose to study its structure from afar. The edifice was round on the top forming a dome made of vivid bronze, which still shined untarnished as if recently polished. The lower portion of the tomb was square and supported by four tall granite pillars equally spaced around the structure's base. In its center stood two massive bronze doors made of long thick bars spaced equally at about half a foot apart. At the top of the door was a large inscription reading: Tomb of Hamse, King of Kings.

Upon seeing the name, the keen eyes of Aguieas swelled open as if the actual image of the tomb held some monetary value. The tomb of a commanding king who had wielded power over an entire continent would not be without great treasure, but what guarded such a sacred structure? If it were unguarded, some grave robber would have stolen its valuables long ago, but in all his years on the streets of Veltarin, he had never heard of anyone doing so with or without success, almost as if those that had attempted to do so were never heard from again.

As he studied their options, a man with a bald head which shined under the sun as did the dome of Hamse's tomb walked around the back of the tomb wearing a bright white robe and carrying a gourd in his hand. The four bandits instinctively pulled back into the shrubs watching the man like a pack of wolves ready to strike at any moment. The man peacefully began to pour water from the gourd upon the various plants surrounding the mausoleum gently touching each of their flowers as if they were his children.

The serene man was a monk of the Mauoeif sect dedicated to the preservation of their dead god's tomb positioned in the center of the extensive Tombs of the Lost. The gods of Dream deal not with duels of mortal creatures, but on one occasion a sly warrior challenged the god before his followers within his own temple. The young warrior Seurāope cut the great god down centuries ago in cold blood before he himself was dismembered viciously by the bare hands of the priests of Mauoeif. Since the death of their god, generations of priests continued to maintain his temple as a tomb awaiting his second coming.

The man seemed docile enough and would be an easy target for four bloodthirsty thieves with their minds set on obtaining loot. Aguieas signaled for Kaudot to perform a quick assassination. The young assassin had done many over his career quickly stealing the lives of his victims before they could blink an eye or gasp for air. Silent feet touched the ground softly slipping up behind the tranquil man as he dug around a small plant with his hands. As if a weaver of time, the small man spun around on the ball of his foot while planting his other into the soil firmly. Before the swift Kaudot could deal his blow of death, a dirty palm struck his neck pinching a nerve. Kaudot's eyes rolled into the back of his head before he collapsed to the ground in paralysis.

Aguieas' blood boiled with rage as his comrade dropped as though lifeless to the ground. His muscles tightened, propelling him through the brush with a tight grip upon his swift sword bent on murder. He charged toward the monk bringing the blade of his weapon down toward the man's heart. With a speed unseen by the young rogue the monk pushed his blade aside with the palm of his hand snapping its long thin blade. A knee under cloak exploded into Aguieas' waist bulking him over as a palm struck his neck sending the rushing bandit against the side of the tomb unable to move. Aguieas tried to leap from his awkward landing but to his surprise his body was limp… numb.

The massive Moshgill seized the priest with a single hand lifting the small man into the air by his clothing. His second hand reached out to rip the tiny man apart, but before he could grab the nimble man the monk swung down his palm down across Moshgill's arm slapping a nerve. The gorilla-like grip of Moshgill buckled into a weak clasp freeing the agile monk who almost simultaneously somersaulted up Moshgill's arm onto his back. Both palms of the fanatic priest struck the neck of Moshgill who tumbled to the ground like a tree turned to mush. As his giant partner tumbled to the floor in a misshapen heap Omeiku aimed a small hand held crossbow at the priest who stood no farther than six feet away. The projectile instantly cut through the air as the steady hand of Omeiku tugged against the trigger. The priest spun toward his attacker flipping his head aside dodging the bolt effortlessly. Upon missing his target, Omeiku reached for his sword as the monk pounced into a flying kick. A hard heel bone struck Omeiku's face pummeling him back into the brush unconscious.

As the last man fell in defeat the formidable monk blew a bone whistle hanging from a string about his neck. A long riddling shrill shattered the serene tranquility of the graveyard. The monk took a second breath but it released from a slit in his neck instead of passing his lips.

Aguieas, quick of mind and body, had almost dodged the open hand strike of the monk avoiding its full force and therefore the complete effects of its paralysis. During the ensuing fight, he had the slightest of feeling in his left arm allowing him to wiggle it and regain sensation. As Omeiku flew into the bushes from a flying kick, he had awoken his legs and cut the monk's throat with the tip of his broken rapier.

It was Kaudot who had fallen the hardest and therefore it was Kaudot he assisted first. The young thief's eyes sat limp and lifeless in his arms. Aguieas smacked the young man's cheeks, desperately massaging his neck so to return him to life. The young man's eyes blinked as he regained control of the nerves disabled by the monk's startling attack. Aguieas began to work on his comrades quickly, awakening their limbs and senses, when his own senses warned him of incoming danger. Footsteps of a group far larger than theirs were coming toward their position. Warily, Aguieas slid around the side of the tomb to see a dozen or so monks dressed identically to the one he had killed rushing toward him. His first instinct was to escape into the giant hedge maze and run until he could run no more, but his friends were still recovering from temporary paralysis which would make them easy prey for the zealous monks in pursuit. Breaking a sacred law of the rogue, he rushed over to Moshgill and helped the bulky figure to his feet.

"Hurry into the tomb!" he commanded forcefully.

Omeiku saw the panic in Aguieas' eyes. He had traveled and fought by his side through the thick and thin of thievery over the years and if something instilled terror into Aguieas' heart, it was something to fear. The four thieves hobbled to the tomb's entrance tugging on its gates madly. They held tight under lock of key and in a terror Moshgill attempted to rip the barred door from its hinges. His hulking muscles swelled with blood and his teeth gritted, but the massive door held firm. Aguieas pushed his friend aside knowing a broken door would do little to shield them from the fury of mad monks bent on protection of their lost god. He pulled a long thin metal pin from his boot and began to wiggle it through the tumblers of the ancient lock. He agilely maneuvered the thief's pick, lifting and setting tumblers in place, before giving the lock a twist. The gates creaked outward and the four rogues rushed inside slamming them shut before the wild eyes of infuriated priests. A dozen or so priests began to tug wildly on the barred door like mad dogs lusting for blood. The stout Moshgill set a wide stance holding the gate in place as his comrades searched the dark burial chamber for something to bar the gate. The small men across from the grand Moshgill might be more agile of body and mind, but they would not be able to match his brute strength. Kaudot rushed back to the door carrying a long six-foot metal candle holder barring the gates tightly. With the might of a barbarian deep from the Kthaerian Waste, Moshgill raised his hammer high and with three monstrous blows hammered the metal candle stick into the stone wall, thus sealing the living with the dead. The four thieves stepped back as the monks tugged relentlessly at the gate in vain.

Eyes of determined men ready to shred the four brigands apart for glory of their dead god Mauoeif, bore in the darkness. The men sighed having for the moment avoided the fury of the feral monks. Aguieas had never encountered man or beast that fought like the monk who had so easily dispatched a group four times his own number. He knew they stood no chance in a battle with a dozen of the monks that stood outside the door. If they were to get out of this situation alive, it would require some sort of escape.

"What are we to do now?" whispered Omeiku terrified of the mad eyes staring at them as if they were animals in a zoo.

"I'm not fighting that group of monks is all I know," commented Kaudot, still shaken from the earlier fight with the single monk. "We'll have to wait them out."

"Those insane men will never give up!" asserted Omeiku. "They've been waiting for centuries for a dead god they've never met to return. Even if we could live a hundred years in here, their grandchildren would be standing right there waiting us out!"

"Monks don't have children, they brainwash others to take their place." corrected Kaudot. "Don't you, you little mindless worms!"

"Either way," replied Omeiku upset at being corrected during such a dire moment, "we'll starve first!"

The thought of starvation got the hearty Moshgill's full attention.

"I may die here, but it won't be from starvation, I'll tell you that. I'll eat every one of those little men before that happens!"

Aguieas, unsure of their next move, sat down quietly in thought. He could have run leaving his three partners to suffer the fury of the mad monks, but somehow he had chosen to die with them instead. His closeness to them had weakened him as a thief he thought. He had lost his edge by breaking one of the laws of a rogue: "it is foolish to die when you can live to steal another day" and now he might lose it all.

"You're quiet Agu," stated Kaudot.

"I'm thinking."

"Of the inscription you want on your tombstone?" asked Omeiku.

"There is an answer to everything."

Omeiku threw up his hands and sat down to stare back at the many eyes watching them with malice.

Part IV
The Theft of Kings

Kaudot, the youngest and most curious of the four tomb raiders, struck a flame from his tinder box and lit a candle sitting in the corner of the ancient tomb. He walked around the large tomb's entrance carrying the candle high before stumbling upon a burial chamber. Above its door hung an inscription elegantly carved into polished stone: King Hamse the First, the Builder. The young rogue slid his hands along the thick stone door of the vault finding it sealed with some form of granular mortar. Excited about locating the tomb of a king, the thief's young hands retrieved a long pointed file from the bottom of his versatile kit of thievery. He quickly filed at the grainy sealant turning the once-solid mass into a powdery dust. The sound of sawing caught the attention of his fellow thieves.

"What you out to steal K?" asked Moshgill.

"I've requested an audience with the king."

"Mind if I come along?" asked Moshgill, coming to his aid.

Aguieas and Omeiku sat with perplexed stares toward a gate holding back dozens of enraged monks with blood in their eyes.

"Do they even speak?" asked Aguieas curious about those who had him trapped like a rat in a cage.

"I do not think the servants of the dead Mauoeif have taken any vow of silence, but since the death of their god they have withdrawn from the world doing who knows what for centuries in their temple," advised the wise Omeiku.

"Do they believe he will come back?"

"More than you and I lust for gold," replied Omeiku, "I don't know which one of us is a greater fool, them for worshipping a dead god or you and I who risk our lives for plunder."

Omeiku stood and faded into the shadows of the tomb's rear chamber to avoid the many eyes watching him intently. Aguieas spit at the men hitting one between the eyes.

"He's not coming back you know," he stated, standing up to see what Kaudot and Moshgill were up to.

He found his two comrades covered in mortar dust filing away as if their lives depended upon opening the door.

"Any luck?"

"We're not too far away, big Mosh here can already wiggle it a bit," stated Kaudot working at the sealant diligently.

Although thieves hate hard work, they don't mind working hard to steal. It was still early in the morning and nothing would do better to get his mind off the eyes watching him than to turn his attention toward his favorite pastime, theft.

"Omeiku, watch the gate to make sure those little midgets don't try anything."

Omeiku looked at his friend in frustration, "Sure, we'll just worry about getting out of here later I guess."

The three rogues dug at the ancient tomb, filing, tugging and digging for hours before the door finally fell inward crashing into the darkness of the room beyond. Candles loomed into the gloom and dust lighting a room which had been encased in darkness for hundreds of years. Cobwebs and thick dust covered the ancient chamber built to glorify the death of a man who glorified the great Kingdom of Hamse in his life. The dark chamber was circular like the main chamber of the tomb, only much smaller, barely having enough room to hold the sarcophagus which sat in its center. Spaced equally around the room creating corners in the round chamber, were four tall statues etched into the walls. The first statue was of a barbaric king with a long beard wielding a longbow, who looked more like a common hunter than a member of royalty. At its base was an inscription: King Hamse The First, The Builder. The second statue was that of a sophisticated king clean-shaven and holding a scroll of diplomacy over that of a weapon. At its base was the inscription; King Hamse The Second, The Conqueror. The third statue was that of another bearded king, but this one's beard was shorter and neatly trimmed as though a blended combination of the first two. This statue held a small knife in one hand and a scroll in the other. At its base was the inscription: King Hamse The Third, The Liberator. The fourth statue was different than the others in that its face was a block without chiseled features. At its base was the inscription, King Hamse the fourth, leaving a blank space for a title to later be determined by the actions of the current reigning king.

Kaudot eyed the tomb of the once-great king speculating what magnificent treasures it might contain. Rubies, emeralds and diamonds sparkled in his mind as walked around the burial monument in wild imagination. Lacking the patience of his fellow rogues, Moshgill reached out to lift the massive stone lid, but the quick hand of Aguieas got in his way.

"It's too easy," Aguieas said surveying the room, "the rich never give up what they have easily… even in death."

Moshgill, suddenly aware of a potential death trap, backed away from the large stone coffin with slow nervous eyes. Aguieas studied the ceiling and the walls for anything that might drop or strike the men upon opening the ancient tomb. He had been given the gift of observation, a tool he had used many times, to steal, escape, murder and live to tell about it. Upon finding nothing of apparent danger within the dark chamber, he began to study the sarcophagus itself carefully running a candle along its edge. The lid was rounded and ended in a lip that hung over the base of the burial container. It would be where fingers would grip it to lift it from its base. The flicker of a candle shone underneath the corners of the lid to expose tiny sharp hooks covered in glistening grease. Aguieas knew its scent and mustard yellow color. It was a rapid poison extracted from the venom sack of the Gjnuk spider, a two-foot long arachnid that was a natural predator of western Fathel's yawning caverns. The quick acting toxin hardened the smooth and skeletal muscles of its victims once it entered the bloodstream, hardening the arteries and turning the heart muscle into a cold rock. Aguieas knew not these conditions, but through his profession, he did know the look upon the face of its victims as their body stiffened in agony and their skin turned blue before painfully falling into the grip of death.

"Mosh, lift this up with your hammer."

The half barbarian hooked the stone lip with his massive hammer. Veins and muscles strained in his arms and neck raising his skin as the might of man struggled against the weight of stone. As man won, through strength and leverage, the large stone cover ricocheted off the floor with a loud bang freeing whatever it hid within. The three men curiously peered into the black open tomb squinting to soak in the image within. As their eyes adjusted to the inner darkness of the stone vault the image of white fur lined its interior. Aguieas grasped the thick wiry fur in his palm squeezing it between his fingers. He pulled it aside to find the rest of the tomb empty. The men pulled two seven foot tall furs from the tomb before staring at the empty tomb in disappointment.

"Who builds a grand tomb, yet doesn't place the body of the man for whom it was intended?" asked Kaudot obviously thwarted by the lack of the king's body and the treasure he had expected to find along with it.

"Bah!" screamed Moshgill angrily. "All that work for nothing!"

Aguieas held one of the furs shifting it between his fingers.

"This obviously meant more to this man than material wealth," said Aguieas in deep thought.

The king's tombs were like riddles, with each man being buried with or replaced by something that they valued in their life. Aguieas walked around the chamber, ignoring the complaints of his comrades examining the statues. King Hamse the First was dressed like a forester, someone who valued the simple treasures of the forest than the sparkle of precious gems and metal. The statue of King Hamse the Second was far different, being that of a man dressed in the luxuries of a merchant. He had a crown, a necklace and rings.

"The tomb of the second king will have the treasure."

"What?" asked Kaudot. "How do you know that?"

"I just do," stated Aguieas confidently.

"Ah we'll end up doing all that work for nothing," replied the lazy Moshgill.

"What else you got to do, monk wrestle?"

Moshgill unconsciously reached up and grasped his neck which was still sore from the last encounter he had with a monk. The three walked back into the main center chamber to find the reliable Omeiku watching the front gate carefully. Aguieas walked up behind his old friend.

"How's it going out here?"

"That little one on the end keeps trying to slip through the bars, but when I go over there with my sword he slides back out," replied Omeiku.

"Stay sharp, we have tombs to rob."

The three thieves set back to work filing away at the second door putting in the only time a rogue devoted to a hard day's work when thievery was the end result. The sun crawled along the sky as the men toiled within the tomb, removing the door from its stubborn hold upon the stone vault. The thick stone door fell inward collapsing under the brawn of the great Moshgill who grunted like a wild beast as he thrust it loose. Dust boiled out of the dark crypt adhering to the labored sweat of the men covering their hands and faces in a fine grime. Upon entering the dark chamber, the men found it to be identical to the first with a sarcophagus in its center and the exact same statues spaced equally around the circular room. The impatient Moshgill brought forth his hammer to lift the thick stone lid as he had done in the first tomb but was stopped once again by the wary Aguieas. The kings had died many years apart he thought in reason of a puzzle that might or might not exist in tombs that had been sealed by different men. The secrets of burial tombs were rarely passed on from architect to architect for fear of grave robbers. His eyes studied the old room, moving along it while slowly adjusting to the dim light. The walls seemed solid and without openings, and the roof appeared one sturdy piece. The stone sarcophagus' lid had the same raised lip around its top for lifting, and upon closer inspection Aguieas found it to be without the poison hooks of the first tomb's chamber. He was missing something… something that might mean the difference between unimaginable wealth and certain death. It was moments such as this when the lure of treasure and the fear of death clashed, requiring the professional thief to have a keen intellect. It was the wit of the architect against the puzzle-solving skills of the rogue. The young Aguieas who was up to the task slid his fingers patiently along the walls and the stone tiles on the floor searching with touch as might eyes along a riddling painting. Whatever lay in wait for them would require some sort of action on their part to stop that which had been waiting for decades to waylay any would-be robbers. His fingertips gently caressed the rough stone coffin coming to rest on a small round hole which had been filled in with a fine sealant. Something had been put in it and then sealed off. Whatever lay in wait was inside the ancient sarcophagus.

"K," he ordered breaking the silence he had been immersed, "give me your rope."

The young rogue, having been quietly watching his mentor, unraveled a long rope he carried upon his hip. Aguieas wrapped the rope around the stone lid's lip tying it into a long loop surrounding the top of the ancient burial casket. Under the watchful eyes of his companions, he pulled the end of the rope into the center chamber of the mausoleum next to Omeiku who looked at him strangely.

"Mosh, would you please?" he asked his large companion.

The brutish Moshgill knew exactly what his friend wanted and without asking he seized the thick rope and began to pull enlarging the bulging muscles in his arms and back. He strained against the huge slab placing his foot against a raised stone in the floor tugging with strength, in regards to humans, known only by the warriors of Kthaer. Seeing their friend struggling without success, the other three men took their place along the rope and tugged with all their might. With bulging eyes and contracting muscles they wrestled with the weight of broad stone sealed to the massive coffin base with thick ancient sealant. The sealant cracked as the tension of the rope tugged the stone lid from the resting place upon which it had sat in decades of darkness. The scraping of stone dragging upon stone echoed through the ancient tomb giving the failing muscles of the men at the end of the rope the inspiration to continue against the pain of muscle and limb. The dozen or monks outside the chamber watched helplessly as the giant stone lid collapsed to the floor with a loud thud. As the lid struck the stone floor, bright red smoke rose into the burial chamber engulfing it in a dense scarlet cloud. The red smoke began to filter into the main burial chamber coming toward the men like an angered ghost awakened from its eternal rest.

"Into the first tomb!" cried Aguieas with wide eyes.

The four thieves rushed into the burial chamber of King Hamse the First. Moshgill's muscular hands gripped the thick stone door raising it from the ground behind the scrambling hands of his fellow rogues fitting it back into its place. Small emanates of milky red gas curled into the small chamber through the cracks of the door. Wisely the men held their breaths as they shoved the door against the entrance. The stone door fit snuggly into its old place, sealing the burial chamber from the main chamber of the tomb.

"Damn this forsaken place of the dead!" screamed Omeiku in fear of what lay beyond the door he held nervously.

"What was that?" asked Moshgill curiously. "Some sort of spirit?"

"A poison in the form of air," answered Aguieas rationally. "With time it will pass out the tomb."

The four men, exhausted from their struggles with the weight of great stone slabs and doorways, sat down to wait out the ancient toxin. Several hours passed before the men were willing to pull the door aside and reconnect the tomb of King Hamse the First with that of the burial chamber's entrance. As the men reentered the tomb's main chamber they found it free of the original menace presented by the ghostly red smoke only to discover an even greater peril.

After the lethal smoke had cleared the smallest of the besieging monks had used another weapon in the arsenal of the fanatical servants to the memory of Mauoeif, contortion. He had painfully collapsed the cartilage in his chest, sliding into the inside chamber of the tomb entering it simultaneously with Aguieas and his fellow thieves. The monk's small determined hands took hold of the iron candlestick barring the door and tugged at it in a mad obsession to serve his lost god.

Weapons unleashed by desperate men glistened under dull candle light to counter the mad discipline of the fighting monk. It would be a fight to the death as the four thieves desired to live almost as much as the devoted monk desired to send them to death. Kaudot, being the youngest and most zealous of the four, struck first, confidently rushing across the dim chamber and thrusting the point of his sword at the chest of the waiting monk. The monk's white robe fluttered past the young rogue as his limber body dodged the swift lunge with ease collapsing his enemy with a rapid palm to his neck. The young rogue fell limply to the floor into a semi- conscious state. Moshgill came to the aid of his friend, wielding his mighty hammer of crushing iron. He slung the brute weapon with ample strength wielding it as easily as a smaller man might a thin pole, cutting the wind and smashing stone. The monk dodged three such strikes, which found the walls and floors of the stone tomb instead of their intended target before running up the wall, pushing his foot off the ceiling and landing behind the powerful Moshgill. One hand strike to the massive warrior's back incapacitated his motor functions and he fell to the ground helplessly stunned.

Upon the fall of Moshgill Omeiku fired an arrow from his crossbow almost in unison with the collapse of his friend only to see his arrow cease its flight into the palm of his target's hand. Both Aguieas and Omeiku stood astonished at the godly speed possessed by their adversary. The three stared at each other for a moment in an awkward silence before Omeiku rushed to reload his crossbow. As soon as he reached for an arrow upon his sleeve, the monk moved to action, building up so much speed he passed the wall in a white streak, propelling himself from it to kick the crossbow from Omeiku's hands. The little man, nearly a foot shorter than Omeiku, who in no way was considered tall, stared up at him from a fighting stance almost as if toying with his adversary. Omeiku himself by no means a slow person, unsheathed a small dagger heaving it at the unarmed monk. The monk dodged it and unleashed a flurry of blows to Omeiku's neck, chest and arms which immobilized him so quickly that his body locked in paralysis before he fell to the floor with his two other fallen comrades.

Aguieas struck from behind the monk thrusting with his broken but still deadly rapier only to miss his target miserably as the small bald man in his bone-white robe spun to the side striking at his neck. Aguieas being as keen of mind as swift of body had learned from his first encounter with the monks and this time he anticipated the monk's counterstrike. As the monk gyrated by him he raised his arm up to his head blocking what would have been a final blow to himself and his thieves-in-arms. The monk stood across from him in a low fighting stance waiting to counter his last foe's every move. Aguieas met the small man eye to eye wondering why the fleet fighter had not followed up his last attack. Their eyes met giving Aguieas time to analyze his opponent. The monk was counterstriking. Every attack he and the other monk had made had not come first, but after theirs. They were faster and more disciplined than any man or creature he had ever encountered, but they had one flaw, they were predicable. The previous two times he had struck at the two monks, they had reacted exactly the same, dodging to the side at which he held a weapon so as to avoid his other hand during their counterattack. Trusting his gut feeling, Aguieas leaped into action, plunging his sword at the monk's heart and spinning the monk into another counterstrike that would end the life of one of the two combatants. The monk easily evaded the fleet assault turning to

Aguieas' right side and bringing down a would-be paralyzing blow to his neck. Aguieas' arm met the monk's above his neck as he spun backwards, stabbing his adversary in the chest with a hidden dagger in his left hand. Blood splurted up the monk's throat pouring out his mouth onto his white robe as he took his last breath, finally entering the shadow world of dreams to meet the god he had served so fervently.

Aguieas turned to the monks at the gates who stood watching intently almost as clones with their identical bald heads and white robes.

"Don't worry," he said huffing and puffing while eyeing them from the corner of his eye, "each one of you will have your turn."

With help from Aguieas, Moshgill, Kaudot, and Omeiku awoke from their conscious slumber vigorously rubbing their muscles to return blood flow to their tissues. It had been another humbling experience for the proud group of thieves who had nearly been defeated once again by a single unarmed man almost half their size. Moshgill stood back to a massive six foot five towering over the men watching him through the tomb's front gate like tourists at monkeys in a cage. Embarrassed by how quickly the monk had taken him out of the fight, in frustration the mighty Moshgill stomped over to the barred gate unfastening his pants.

"I'll get you little runts away from the door," he declared urinating through it.

The monks danced aside, dodging his bodily fluid as he laughed loudly.

"There you go," he yelled angered by his imprisonment, "look at mighty Moshgill, it's about the size of your puny arms no?"

Aguieas, ignoring the antics of his companion, cautiously walked into the second burial chamber stepping around the stone lid lying in its doorway and peered into the open sarcophagus. Inside lay a nearly perfectly preserved corpse of a king. The man had a long stringy beard having grown from a neatly trimmed one after his death and wore lavish clothing and fine jewelry. Aguieas' eyes glimmered like jewels as they beheld the necklace around the once great king's neck. A brilliant asterism sparkled under the light of his torch in a deep blue hue. It was the great sapphire Star of Sky, the largest sapphire without flaw to ever be mined within the Lands of Dream.

Upon its mining from the depths of Deaylium's northern mines, hundreds had died to acquire its wealth before it was finally given in tribute to King Hamse the Second as a gift from the king of Deazah as part of a peace treaty to end the Emerald Sea Wars. But now he, a minor thief, possessed it. His hand shaking as if it was his first theft pulled the precious stone from the neck of its rightful owner and held it up high in admiration. This was the gift of an unselfish son, reasoned the thief, for there could be no other explanation for someone to bury such a treasure. It was worth a hundred times the rubies they had invested to come to the Tombs of the Lost, and now all that remained was for him and his men to find a way out of the tomb in which they were now trapped for them to sell it and know the riches of lords and kings. Kaudot came up behind his friend mesmerized by the blue rock hanging from Aguieas' hand like a puppy watching a dangling steak.

"What is that?" he asked gazing into the blue alluring sparkle.

"It is the Star of Sky."

"How much is it worth?"

"More than you can imagine," answered the astute Aguieas weighing its value in comparison to that of their lives.

The great jewel's sparkle summoned even the full attention of the level-headed Omeiku who stood next to Moshgill awestruck by its brilliance. The four thieves had spent their entire lives dreaming of such a score and for it to be finally within their grasp left the four silently enthralled. Although each had come for such loot, none had actually believed that four thugs from the slums of Veltarin would ever obtain the treasure of a king.

As might children who discovered a cookie in a jar, the four thieves thought of the possibility of more such treasures as if the wealth of one lifetime was not enough. Kaudot quickly turned toward the third tomb extracting his file and prepared to put it back to work. Its fine point and jagged edge sawed assiduously at the sealant releasing its grip upon the stone tomb. He worked in silence until Omeiku spoke.

"The monks are gone."

Aguieas and Moshgill stared through the barred gate astonished not to see the dozen or so short bald headed men in long bone white robes.

"Where did they go?" asked Kaudot suddenly having lost his focus.

"I don't know," replied Omeiku strangely.

Aguieas stood near the barred gate careful not to get within arm's reach or to expose himself to some sort of missile fire before peering through the gateway. The sun was fading casting a dull shadow upon the once vibrantly colored graveyard. A cool chill suddenly seized the men's bodies. Omeiku stood next to Aguieas watching the darkness engulf the vivid colors of the graveyard's gardens as if blanketing them in the ash of dusk.

"They have left because of the night," stated Omeiku ominously.

"They might be around the sides or on the roof waiting to ambush us," suggested Kaudot.

"No," replied Aguieas confidently, "that's not their style. Whatever reason, we have to seize it now!"

"What of the third tomb?" inquired Kaudot fearful they might leave something of value behind.

"We have to get out of this cemetery before whatever ran those monks off arrives. Mosh, get us out of here."

Part V
The Night Belongs to the Dead

The bulky Moshgill gripped the candlestick he had pounded into the wall and tugged on it. His muscles tightened and enlarged, calling upon the strength of his forefathers to release its hold. Stone cracked until giving way to the great barbarian's will releasing its hold upon the iron candlestick. Aguieas slung open the barred gate standing suspiciously just outside the tomb's entrance. His eyes keenly scanned the tombs, flowers and headstones for movement as an uncanny peripheral vision watched the sides of the tomb. A cold darkness with the properties of black ice fell upon him chilling his heart to the core.

"Back to the wall!" he ordered.

The thieves skulked through the shadows with a skill invisible to the common eye, using shadow, cover and speed to elude observation. Aguieas who led the way paused upon seeing something along the horizon. The thing moved strangely, rising up and down almost in a slinking manner like giant snakes rolling upon the ground. His hand rose signaling his comrades to cease movement. The four pondered the strange shadowy phenomenon as it shifted furtively toward the group like a wave upon the sea. Aguieas' eyes tightened at their lids, focusing through the sudden dark that had fallen on the men like a drenching rain. The black rolling mass had arms, legs and eyes… yearning dead eyes. Glistening black bodies pouring over one another in lust of flesh seethed toward the men in long smooth glides.

"Ghouls," whispered Omeiku in terror.

Ghouls were the guardians of the dead, infected souls cursed to roam their nights lusting for the flesh of the living and their days huddled beneath the earth. The only way to kill a ghoul was outside a burial ground, for within its boundaries they were immortal. The sleek bodies tumbled unnaturally toward the men, who would have been obscured by the night to mortal eyes, but to ghouls who owned the night, they were as visible as if standing in broad daylight.

"Run," screamed Aguieas.

The men burst into full retreat zigzagging through gravestones and tombs wildly rushing from the mob of black dead who followed in close pursuit. In the lead, Aguieas stopped quickly as he found himself surrounded by greasy black faces. The glossy fiends came crawling from holes in the ground leading up from their day lairs to hunt the living. The rubbery creatures began to swarm upon the men as if forming from the shadows. A black wave of teeth, claws and eyes poured upon their small defensive formation like black sludge over a stout wall blanketing it from the dim light of night. Weapons unsheathed and cut through skin and bone dismembering the hands and heads that reached out toward the four skilled rogues. Moshgill raised his hammer pounding the slender dead back into the ground from where they came, calling upon the berserker rage of the Kthaer Warrior to increase his strength to that of the beasts of the earth. His hammer flattened the dead within his reach crushing their skeletal structures and leaving the creatures seemingly immobile. Black rubbery forms surged toward the wild barbarian clawing and tugging at his muscles to drag him into a pile of bodies and snapping teeth. Moshgill's hammer tore through the ranks of the dead clearing a hole in the encirclement of night ghouls.

"Now!" screamed Aguieas leaping through the break in the dead's ranks.

He cut down a ghoul leaving his rapier protruding from its eye using the weapon to push it aside. The hilt of his broken rapier still protruding from the black ghoul's head slid from his fingers as within the compound of the graveyard it was little more than dead weight. His fellow rogues followed bringing along a mob of black infestation clawing at the fleeing men to pull them below ground and feast. Moshgill came last dragging half a dozen dead who clung onto his back and legs ripping at his flesh with teeth and nails.

"Agu!" screamed Omeiku. "Mosh is falling behind!"

As the words vibrated through the bones of his inner ear Aguieas' first thought was to run even faster, so he too would not fall to the might of the black horde in pursuit, but something that rogues were not to possess took precedence… loyalty. Although his path of retreat appeared clear, he stopped and spun around to see his brother, the great Moshgill, being overwhelmed by a black mass of flailing arms, legs and heads. The giant warrior ripped the slender monsters from his body, dashing them against the ground, but with each he plucked free from his flesh, two more would take hold. The mighty warrior under the weight of dozens of flesh-ripping ghouls fell to one knee.

"Go!" screamed Moshgill unselfishly.

His form, covered in ghouls like a wasp ambushed by ants, fell into the darkness doomed to roam the properties' boundaries for eternity as a restless guardian of the dead.

Upon the fall of the giant Moshgill, ghouls began to swarm over the heap of feasting dead to bring more courses to their late night meal. Fear gripped the men once again and the three sprinted from the madness that haunted them wildly in the night. A glossy hand came from the earth seizing Omeiku's leg causing him to tumble to the ground. He fell to the ground face first against the ground. Stunned from his tumble, Omeiku began to lift himself up when hands appeared from the surrounding soil, gripping his arms, legs and neck. He fought to stay above ground, digging his hands into the soil ignoring the teeth that began to tear the flesh from his legs below the ground. He seized a root and for a moment he held fast half above ground, half below. He saw the shadows of his two friends, Aguieas and Kaudot, run away into the darkness unaware of his disappearance. Teeth and hands tugged frantically at his flesh desperate to devour the life they no longer possessed. Omeiku held his breath as he was pulled below the dirt dying in silence within the hands of the dead in order not to deter the escape of his comrades.

The legs of the remaining two rogues pounded against the soil nimbly dodging failed grave robbers from the past that rose to the chase. The surrounding graveyard was pitch black, dimly lit like smoke from reflection of the moon. An illuminated temple brightly cut the obscurity ahead offering the last hope of shelter as the black night materialized into the dead. Using a basic skill of his occupation, Aguieas leapt onto the wall like a toad painfully forcing his fingertips into the grooves between its stony outer layer scaling the tall tower with the ease of a spider. Kaudot followed in tow disappearing through a third story window behind his mentor. The ghouls below clumsily tried to follow howling into the night in vain.

The two surviving rogues found themselves standing in a long hallway brightly lit by torches secured along its wall in brass holders. In their desperation to escape the swarm of black dead below, the thieves found themselves inside the temple of the priests loyal to the lost god Mauoeif, known as the Shrine of Waiting. It was kept brightly lit day and night by its keepers to be a beacon for the second coming of its god. A sect thousands of years old, its monks lived in isolation from the Lands of Dream maintaining their faith, constantly training their bodies and minds to guard the tomb of their god and be worthy of his return. Its followers were taken in as orphans, given food and shelter, and raised in the faith of Mauoeif to die of old age in his service or share in his glory upon his second coming.

Fearful of the wrath of the lost god's priests for entering their sacred temple, Aguieas moved gingerly even for a thief apprehensive of any sound made that might make their presence known. Kaudot followed down the long hallway with nervous eyes, for there would be no escape from the fanatical monks if they were discovered within their temple. The hallway turned left straightening out for twenty feet or so before coming to an abrupt end at a wooden door. Soft toes touched the stone floor almost caressing its surface as the two tip-toed down the corridor toward the door. There were no shadows for a rogue to disappear in such a brightly lit hallway and finding a place to hide till daylight might be their best bet thought Aguieas as he pushed the door open. The door swung open quietly as Aguieas lifted up on its heavy hinges to lighten its load and exposed a half-oval stairway leading up to an altar. Two large candles about two feet thick and five feet tall stood on each side bearing flames about the size of grapefruit. Stone tiles stained yellow in some unusual manner decorated the stairs leading up to the altar which in its center showcased a large statue of the god Mauoeif chiseled from white marble. It glistened bone white having never been touched by the hands of man since its creation by the loyal monk Nerkuagi who struck the death blow upon the warrior Seurāope, considered in his time the greatest human warrior to ever raise a sword in the Lands of Dream. It had been Seurāope who had cut down the great goblin king Eb-Atoyle in the beginning as man began to dream into the realm of Dreams helping to carve a place for himself among the many beasts from across the universe who had dreamt there first. It had been his many victories and lack of comparable opponents that led him to hunt a god and therefore seal his own demise.

Kneeling at the center of the altar were three monks in white flowing robes praying to the statue which looked like a man but bore three arms with the third in the center of his chest. It was with this arm the god Mauoeif carried a shield to protect his chest during combat while with his left and right arms he wielded curved swords to cut down those that opposed his will. In a meeting with the other gods of Dream the battle driven god once boasted he was by far superior to all in armed combat, and it was these words that had led Seurāope to his temple to slay him before his own followers.

The unaware monks kneeled forward with their foreheads touching the cold stone meditating "the call", a prayer given nightly by the temple's priests before start of the next morning. Earlier when the four rogues had been manhandled by the monks it had been on equal footing, but this was where the rogue excelled over his adversaries when his art allowed him to remove his victim without a fight. Aguieas nodded to Kaudot to assassinate the farthest monk to the right. Kaudot pulled forth his curved dagger sneaking up slowly behind his victim. Aguieas, responsible for the other two, pulled two long needle-like daggers from his hips specifically designed to pierce the heart of their targets whether they struck them from the front, back or left side. The points of his daggers struck the worshipping monks in the back simultaneously penetrating their hearts as Kaudot drained the life of his target, concurrently stealing the lives of the three without them ever seeing their assassin. Blood poured out onto the yellow stone turning it a dirty orange as the three monks became little more than sacks of dead tissue finally joining with their lost god.

"I told you each of you would get your turn," replied Aguieas to the murdered bodies of the dead.

They stood little chance of seeing the light of the next morning, but at least inside the temple the foes they faced could be killed unlike the horrid horde outside. They would spill blood till the suns of Dream rose or until they themselves entered the unknown darkness of the dead.

The profession of thief stole everything money, identities, valuables and this night lives as daggers cut into the throats of the sleeping and meditating. That night before the suns of Dream rose, sixteen Mauoeif monks were put to rest with their god.

As the suns rose the black horde of ghouls lusting for flesh outside the temple crawled back to the darkness below the Tombs of the Lost to wait out the day as they could never see the light of day or sleep a single moment while they served their eternal curse. Crawling into the dirt and mud to escape the pain of light were two new ghouls, who had once been proud thieves.

Just as the first sun broke over the horizon of Dreams Aguieas and Kaudot slithered out the Shrine of Waiting scaling the outer walls of the perimeter and thus escaping the horrors within the Tombs of the Lost. Knowing the wrath that would be set upon them once the remaining priest of Mauoeif discovered the murders of the members their brotherhood, the two men ran like hunted prey feeling the invisible eyes of their hunters upon their backs. They ran until their hearts could pump no more falling into the weeds gasping for air like fish out of water.

The keen eyes of Kaudot peered through the blades and stems of their foliage hideout watching intently for danger. A slight breeze blew in through the swaying brush bringing its leaves and branches to a rhythmic dance under the warm morning sun. The once anxious eyes relaxed under the stimulus of the soothing rustic locale. The young rogue lay back onto his back breathing heavily while staring into the sky. They had done it, thought the young rogue calming down from the exhilaration of their escape. They had robbed the Tombs of the Lost and lived to tell about it, something no thief in all the Lands of Dream could claim. But before he could fully enjoy his peaceful daydream, the interrupting sound of rustling grass brought him back to reality. His eyes once again gazed through the brush. Men in bright white robes and glossy bald heads came out of the underbrush carefully searching the area. He leaned back into the seclusion of the weeds to quietly warn Aguieas. Aguieas peered through the tall foliage before turning back around to his comrade.

"Listen to me carefully, Kaudot, because I'm about to do exactly what I'm going to tell you," he whispered acutely. "It would be suicide to try and fight, our only chance is to run. Once we run out of here, don't stop for anything. Run until your heart stops because these men will never give up.

He rose up ready to sprint, "Remember don't stop for anything… not me… not anything. I won't stop for you."

Kaudot understood the laws of the rogue and once the rule of each man for himself had been established, it stood supreme and he knew his friend Aguieas meant every word as it was the law. Although it seemed a selfish or cowardly decree, its application bothered neither of the men as each had known the risk of the theft when they had placed their palms face down onto the table that night in the bar. The two figures leapt from the weeds like foxes in the hunt rushing from the small men in flowing white robes. The mad monks, bent on retribution, took chase through the brush and thorns in silent and unrelenting pursuit. Aguieas who was no stranger to flight after a theft ran hard agilely dodging the natural obstacles of the wild terrain, hurdling fallen trees and low lying ditches. His feet never missed a stride as the slightest misstep could bring him down to the ground and ultimately to his grave. Kaudot followed, shedding anything and everything of weight upon his body to increase his speed. He unlatched his thief's kit dropping it to the ground with a jingle along with his side pouch of hooks and climbing ropes. He then shed, without missing a stroke, his leather armor to equalize his weight with that of the thin-cloth clad priests in pursuit.

The two thieves ran methodically for their lives through the wild brush that grew from the deep Mhorhaen in the distance followed by a streaming growth of blood-driven white robes. Aguieas broke through the thick vegetation upon a long rocky field leading downward to the coast of the bright blue Cerulean Sea. Anchored along the coast was the greasy black hull of the Blood Galley. Without slowing down, Aguieas ran toward the murderous crew of the old ship to what little hope he had to live another day. His legs struggled to keep him upright as he rushed down the hill followed by dozens of devote priests in frantic chase. Suddenly, green sails lowered on the old ship catching the wind and slowly pulling the old ship out to sea. It sailed further away leaving the two rogues to suffer the vicious justice of the Mauoeif monks in pursuit. Aguieas stopped at the edge of the sea grasping his knees hectically panting.

"Hurry!" screamed a voice.

A small rowboat paddled from behind a patch of bushes along the coastline revealing the Blood Galley's captain and two rowers.

Following the first law of the rogue, he jumped into the boat trusting the captain's intentions because he had no other choice. As his feet touched the small boat's wooden planks, the men within it began to row to sea. Kaudot waded out into the water crawling in barely a few feet from outstretched arms. The experienced sailors in the boat rowed with long strokes in perfect sync jetting the small craft across the water like a sled on ice. Dozens of enraged monks piled into the water's edge in futile pursuit. Its captain proudly stood at the front of the small vessel taunting the failed monks.

"Ha Ha!" he laughed in excitement of their escape. "Later landlubbers, you have been thwarted by the sea once again! Now run along… what if your precious god shows up while you're all out here playing in the water?"

The black ship sailed safely into the horizon leaving the green coast of Zeethe as nothing more than a memory. The shrewd captain came over to the two men speaking with authority in a closed end sentence.

"A life for a life, that is all."

As the captain walked away to command his ship on its return to the Great Alekain, the rogues understood every word. He had spared their lives to pay back the debt he owed for sparring his own. The next time he saw them, no such further formality would be given.

Aguieas fingered the giant Star of Sky in his pocket soon to be a rich man if he could survive his trip back to Veltarin aboard the treacherous Blood Galley. Although the sapphire between his fingers held a wealth unlike any he had ever dreamed, he would have thrown it to the bottom of the sea at that very moment if it would bring back his lost friends Omeiku and Moshgill breaking the law of the rogue which stated, "No life but your own is worth that of great treasure." The laws of the rogue had served him well, keeping him alive in times where many others had died, but at that moment as the suns of Dream turned the Cerulean to a vast prismatic rainbow, he swore off the life of a rogue, never to steal for personal wealth again.

The Mhorhaen Trilogy

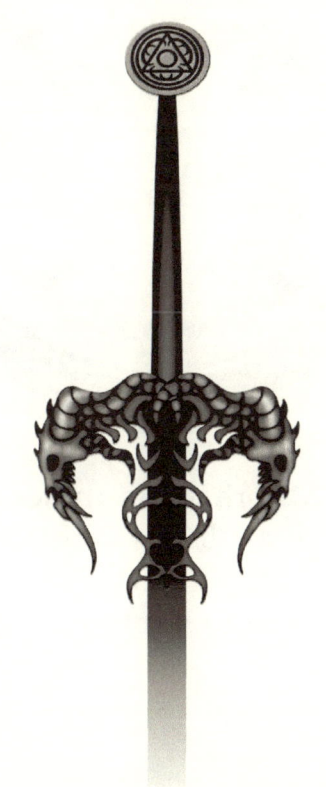

King of the Hunt
Past the Depths of the Mhorhaen
The Last Drop of Evil

"Most claim the Mhorhaen is endless, while others say
its depths separate the lands of men from those of hell
and that jejirs are simply demons who have wandered
out to hunt men."

King of the Hunt

The Rare and Elusive Jejir

King Hamse and his two royal guards rode quietly behind their diligent tracker. They were in search of the rare and elusive jejir, a large and dangerous beast that exhibited qualities of conscious thought. Some hunters even claimed that jejirs had learned the secret of fire. King Hamse may have doubted their ability to make fire, but he didn't doubt their intelligence. He had hunted the creatures all his life and had seen their cunning first hand. He had seen them use primitive weapons, ambush hunters, cover their tracks and even build crude structures, behaviors similar to man, but one thing they were not was civilized. They were solitary hunters of the worst sort. They had been known, particularly during harsh winters, to kill man for food. King Hamse had the hides of two jejirs hanging in his courtroom, a feat that no one in all the lands of Zeethe could claim, and now he hunted for a third. The jejir was blessed with a keen sense of hearing, so neither his tracker nor his bodyguards wore metal of any kind. The slightest ping or clank could warn a jejir of their presence. Only the leather-wrapped tips of King Hamse's arrows were made of metal. His bodyguards wore thin leather armor and carried wood cudgels as weapons. His tracker wore nothing but thin cloth armor, while the king carried only a bow as a weapon. A heavily armed hunting group would never be able to keep up with a jejir if it were to break into a run.

They had been tracking one particular jejir for over a week in the lands north of Sudal, a land troth to his kingdom. The tracks were fresh and open indicating to the king that this particular creature didn't realize it was being tracked. The tracker signaled his king through the use of his hands, explaining that they would catch up to the beast within the day. Through hand gestures, the king commanded his servant to move ahead of the group and continue tracking on foot. The jejir was very sensitive to sound and neither he nor his men had spoken a word in three days. The king and his bodyguards would stay behind until the tracker had spotted the jejir, then the true hunt would begin. His two guards would ride out to flank the beast and keep it from getting away, while the king would move in for the kill. A well-placed arrow would save them from chasing a wounded and hostile beast in the darkness of the forest. King Hamse had seen many a jejir escape or evade hunters for days after they were wounded and he had no intention of returning empty handed.

His tracker, who trailed their prey, left small markers of cloth for him and his men to follow. The king, with his bow in hand, slowly rode along the trail of cloth being careful to guide his horse silently. Up ahead lying by a patch of bushes was his scout who had obviously made visual contact with their prey. He motioned for his guards to stop and wait for the signal of his scout. Every muscle in his body was clenched in anticipation of the impending chase. He had become bored with the luxuries of his kingdom, and now only the excitement of the hunt could make his heart pound again. As he waited in silence, he noticed that something about his scout didn't seem right. The king motioned for his men to stand ready and he slipped off his horse. As he crawled over to his motionless scout, he noticed that his scout seemed to be lying in a peculiar manner. Reaching over with his cupped hand, he raised his servant's head from the ground. It flopped as if it wasn't connected to his body. His face had been torn off and his body had been broken and twisted unnaturally. The king jumped to his feet and ran to his horse. The beast couldn't have gotten far. He and his men had been out of contact with his scout for only a few minutes. In hopes of catching the beast before it could get too far away, the king and his men rode as fast as the forest's trails would allow. The king knew that once night fell all hope would be lost. One of his guards spotted something ahead in the distance and the king had the guards split off to both sides to surround it. The king pulled out his bow and rode straight to the area pointed out to him by his guard. He pulled on his reins and stopped, being careful to watch for movement. He could see one of his guards riding to the left but his other guard had ridden into a depression out of sight. His horse snorted and tugged to continue the chase but the king held it at bay; the creature couldn't have outdistanced him on horseback. It had to be hiding amongst the trees and rocks of the surrounding forest. He pulled an arrow free and unwrapped its tip. Leaves rustled in the wind and the sun above the trees made shadows dance along the forest's floor but the king's eyes never flinched or gave way to a blink. He began to slowly ride around the area watching for any signs that might have been left by the beast. Suddenly, a crashing sound came from behind him and the flesh on his back gave away to blood. He fell from his horse and rolled to the ground gripping his bow and a single arrow. The jejir must have been hiding above him in the trees. In front of him stood the sanguineous beast on two legs tearing his horse apart with its large raccoon-like hands. It moved with such quickness that there wasn't time to think before it had butchered his horse. The king instinctively fired his arrow at point-blank range. It struck the savage beast with such force that it knocked it off its feet and sent it tumbling to the ground. Before the king could get back to his feet, it ran off into the forest. If it had come back, it would have slaughtered him for he had nothing but a bow and his bare hands for defense. He retrieved his arrows from his slain horse and ran in the direction of the fleeing jejir.

The king cursed upon finding his arrow. It had gone clean through and unless he had hit a vital organ it would not make enough of a wound to hinder the huge beast. He ran in full sprint dodging trees and brush in search of his wounded prey. One of his guards spotted him, picked him up, and they took to the chase on horseback. They searched for it the rest of the evening without success. With the fall of night they set up camp and gave up on the hunt. King Hamse damned his run of bad luck. They couldn't track the beast at night and by morning it would be too late. They went ahead and built a fire for warmth and to signal his other guard who had not yet returned. His hunt was over and he sat down in utter disgust. Tomorrow they would look for his lost servant and then ride back to his kingdom empty-handed. His guard took first shift as the king lay down in frustration.

A piercing noise startled King Hamse and awoke him from his deep slumber. He wasn't sure how long he had been asleep but the cold night had shrouded him in darkness. The flames of his fire had died out long ago and the coals emitted little more than a red glow. The cold wind blew across his face and a chill ran down his body. The king wondered why his guard had allowed the fire to burn so low and called out his name. Only the crackling sounds of the campfire and the rustling of trees answered his call. Panic ran down the entire length of his body. He reached outside the warmth of his blankets and pulled his bow towards him. The sound of breaking twigs struck his ears once again and the king rolled up to his knees pointing his bow towards the sound. Nothing but the cold darkness and silence greeted his senses. He called his servant's name through the cold bitter air, but only silence answered. He couldn't see clearly beyond ten feet for the parsimonious trees wouldn't even allow the light of the stars to reach the forest floor. Rising to his feet, he began to slowly back up from the direction of the sounds. King Hamse was a keen hunter, and even though he couldn't see his prey he picked out its location from the sounds of its movement. Again he heard the sound of breaking twigs. He pulled back the string on his bow and released an arrow. He could hear the thump of his arrow as it hit its target. It fell hard unseen in the darkness collapsing with a thud. He immediately ran towards his shot to eye his new trophy. He had hit his unseen target but it wasn't what he had anticipated. His skilled shot had felled one of his royal horses.

The next morning the king found his loyal servant with the rising of the sun. It was a sight that even turned the stomach of a war veteran as experienced as the king. If it were not for his ensanguined clothing the king wound not have recognized his own bodyguard. His body had been beaten beyond recognition. Upon closer examination he found that his guard's club was missing. The king kneeled slowly to the ground and cracked a smile. It was hunting him. The damn thing had come back to hunt him. King Hamse was a proud man and the thought of some animal tracking him on the very land that he owned infuriated him. He was the King of Haenic, the most powerful kingdom in all of southern Zeethe. He would not be hunted like some wild animal. The hide of this creature would hang in the halls of Haenic where he could drink and eat beneath it and laugh out loud as he told the tale of its capture.

Instead of retreating, the king continued the hunt out of stubbornness, anger and pride. Upon finding the jejir's trail he followed it deeper into the secluded forest of Mhorhaen not caring that he was now alone and without a mount to outrun his prey if it found him first. The trail twisted over rock and hill ending at the edge of a steep tor. What he found was beyond his wildest imagination. Below him in the darkness of dusk sat the lair of his intended trophy. It wasn't a hole in the ground or a secluded cave as he had expected but more abstruse. It consisted of crude structures in all shapes and sizes. They were made mostly of wood and rocks but they all seemed to have been carefully placed as if by some strange plan. They didn't appear to offer any form of shelter or mark anything in particular. In fact, to the king, they all seemed quite useless. In the middle stood a large wooden gateway similar to that of a torii. It was this structure that interested the king most. Once again it didn't seem to serve any purpose, but the king knew that the jejir would eventually return to it. Whatever purpose it had originally served for its creator did not matter, all that mattered now was that it served him. After taking a few moments to study his surroundings, the king chose a favorable spot and waited. Hours passed and nothing moved without the help of the wind, but the king waited with the sedulousness of a hunter. The creature was out hunting him and would eventually return once it could not find him. All the king had to do was be patient.

It was late that evening when the beast's form appeared from the walls of the woods. The king cocked his bow and was about to send death on its way when something made him hold his release. It had returned dragging something that interested the king. He slowly let the tension out of his bow and lowered his deadly aim, but his eyes never left their target. It had returned with the bodies of his three men. Holding one leg of each man, it dragged their misshapen bodies through the dirt and tossed them into a distorted heap. It was humiliating to see his men being treated as common animals, but his curiosity was great enough for him to hold his shot. So he sat motionless and watched the thing's strange behavior. After it discarded the bodies of his men, it began to collect dry branches and grass and pile them under the primitive torii. Then to the king's amazement, it sat down and began to bang two rocks together. Occasionally a spark would jump out from between the stones and the beast would immediately throw them into its pile of brush. It did this over and over until a small flame grew out of it efforts. As the flames grew, the monster began to dance wildly around the torri and chatter loudly in a tongue unknown to the king. He had never heard a jejir make a sound, not even when they were wounded or killed, yet this one was pounding the ground with its great fist and babbling at the stars. Then as swift as a bolt of lightning, an arrow from the king's bow caught the unwary creature in its chest while in full dance stride, causing it to tumble to the ground and roll violently. The jejir immediately leaped to its feet as if unscathed and ran off into the forest and the chase began once again. The king took to the chase but stopped when he saw the stream of blood covering the ground before him. The creature would be dead in minutes and finding it while it was still alive and giving it a chance to strike back would be foolish, so like a true hunter, he let his prey run itself to death. The trail of blood left by the jejir was immense and it wasn't long before he found his trophy carcass. He inspected the location of his shot and it was perfect. On any other animal there would not have been a chase at all. Even though he had a great hatred for the jejir, he greatly respected their raw power and sly cunning. This particular jejir had fought with bravery equivalent to any man King Hamse had ever met. He would display it in his royal courtroom with the honor it deserved.

The next day King Hamse set up a small camp and gave his men a proper burial. Then he skinned the great beast and prepped its hide for the long trip back to Haenic. He estimated the trip back on foot would take about three weeks and with only two arrows left, he expected it to be a hard and lean one. He supplemented his diet with nuts, roots and berries he found along the way, and on the second day he fell a large bird with a good shot. It wasn't his lack of supplies that made his trip so hard, it was the harshness that nature can show a solitary man. On the fourth day, the sky opened up drenching him and his meager supplies. The weight of his trophy soaked hide increased three fold and the soft ground gave way with every step. The cold northerly winds from the mountains of Azoul froze his damp gear forcing him to delay his return. He found a small hillside which gave a little protection from the wind and rain, and by using his prized hide as a small tent, setup a temporary camp.

The next morning, with the rains over and the warmth of the rising suns, the king broke camp and began the rest of his long trek through the immense forest of Mhorhaen. No one knew exactly how far the forests of Mhorhaen stretched or to where they led. Most claim its depths are endless, while others say they separate the lands of men from those of hell and that jejirs are simply demons who have wandered out to hunt men. Many had ridden off into them before to find their end, but either returned in failure or were never heard from again. Whether they had gotten lost and died or found something and never returned, no one knew. It was something he had wondered about since he was a child. The king continued to walk in deep thought, when a familiar track broke his concentration. They were the markings of a jejir! Most men spent an entire lifetime never seeing one and now he had found two on one hunting trip. Having the spirit of a hunter, the king couldn't pass up the opportunity to bring home two jejirs in one hunt. He immediately stashed his rigging and prized hide beneath a large tree and took up the new chase with only his bow and two remaining arrows. The previous day's heavy rains made the tracking easy. The mud not only made the tracks deep and well defined, but impossible to hide. He followed its trail throughout the day and on into the twilight. Being aware of the jejir's ability to back-track and set up ambushes, the king stopped his hunt with the fall of night. He waited through the night in the branches of a large ancient tree and started the hunt again with the first break of light. It was just a little after meridian when the trail of the jejir led the king to the remains of what been a small camp. Strewn through the camp like rag dolls were the bodies of three knights and one horse. All of the men were wearing panoplies with the king's royal regalia on them. They undoubtedly had been sent in search of him. They must have been caught completely by surprise because not one had even drawn a weapon. He quickly foraged through the wasted camp being careful not to make any noise in hopes of finding more arrows. He found nothing of use. They had been sent out to find him, not hunt jejirs. Afraid that he was losing ground, the king didn't spend much time at the camp before he continued on his latest hunt. From the items left around the camp and the spacing of the jejir's tracks, he could tell that it had left in haste, more than likely in pursuit of the remaining two horses.

Less than five miles from the camp he found the remains of one. It had been a fine horse, one from his royal stables. "Such a loss," he thought looking at the beautiful creature. Making sure not to take his eyes off the terrain ahead, the king kneeled down and felt the warmth of its body. While using his eyes and ears to search the area for danger, he shoved his hand through a wound deep inside its corpse, and found it to be still warm. This creature seemed to be highly aggressive even for a jejir. Most jejirs killed out of fear or hunger but these returned to kill even though they had escaped or had already killed. The king had never heard of jejirs being territorial but these seemed to deliberately hunt down anything living, whether it was man or beast. He was close, very close, maybe within an hour of catching it. He freed an arrow from his quiver and continued to follow the deep markings of his prey. The trail led the king further into the deeps of the Mhorhaen, deeper than he had ever been. The thicketed forest began to tighten and the daylight drew away from the earth and retreated up through the treetops. Small spears of light pierced the trees and struck the ground giving him just enough light to see after his eyes adjusted. In front stood a forest unlike any he had ever seen. Every tree in every direction was covered with patches of dried blood and riddled with long claw-like markings. The king had never heard of such behavior in jejirs, maybe they were some type of territorial markers or warning. The air was thick with flies and a stench that was almost unbearable. Ignoring both the stench and the bites of swarming flies the king concentrated on his task at hand. The beast's trail continued on through the trees ahead, all with the same markings on their trunks, until it came to a clearing and the mouth of a large cave. Outside the cave stood another torii similar to the one the king had seen before but this was made of stone and far more elaborate. All around the cave hung the skulls of men, horses and dogs. The skulls were not clean as one might expect but covered in the dried blood of their previous owners. Piles of broken skulls that would not hang lay around the strange torii, some almost waist high to a man. The king kneeled down quietly and touched one of the skulls removing a layer of soot from the pile of bones. Those that lay upon the ground were black from having been burned by fire. This particular jejir must have killed over a hundred men from the looks of the piles around its cave. The king sat down behind a large square stone and made a call into the still air. The king's call melted into the deep forest but a distinct echo came from the dark cave ahead: the echo of fist pounding. Out came the beast in a frenzy pounding its huge hairy chest looking for anything to dismember. Within seconds its keen eyes spotted the king and it bellowed out a roar as it leaped towards him. The king's arrows caught it inside its mouth and pierced its skull from below, instantly killing it. Its huge seven-foot mass landed on top of the stone just in front of the king. The king stared down at the huge specimen that lay motionless before him. One of its hands could've wrapped completely around his head. It would be his fourth and largest jejir, a feat beyond that of any man. He kneeled down for a closer inspection when a shadow from within the cave ahead caught his attention. Something had crawled into the shadows lining the cave's entrance. He drew his final arrow and waited. The immense pull of his powerful bow strained the muscles in his arm and a bead of sweat froze on his face as he waited in silence. His keen eyes spotted another movement in the shadows but this one was much further to the right. It was the next shadow that froze his heart in mid-beat, jejirs! There were several of them! They knew he was outside somewhere and so were moving around to try and spot him. He slid down behind his massive trophy and began to slink across the ground like a snake in hopes of putting some distance between him and his new foes. Once he got out of sight of the cave, he took to a full run. Fear had taken his heart and he was no longer a great steady king, but a common man afraid for his life. He ran through the forest of blood trying to step where he would leave little or no tracks. Now the mud and rain worked against him leaving tell-tale signs to his hunters of which way he went. Mud splattered against his legs as he ran with fear, an emotion he had rarely known as a king. If he could get far enough away before they took chase they might lose his scent. He ran across rocks whenever he could and avoided soft soil whenever possible. He knew that once they lost his scent, they would search for his trail and chase after him in that direction, so he was careful to change his direction several times in hopes losing his pursuers. He finally cleared the bloodstained thicket of the jejir and found the sparse trees in front of him comforting. He ran until his legs unwillingly collapsed underneath him and he tumbled to the forest floor. He rested in the very spot that he fell and lay motionless listening to the sounds of the forest. His heart beat in every part of his body and the cold bitter air stung his gasping lungs. The forest began to spin around him and he closed his eyes. He could still feel it moving and swirling all around him threatening to swallow him up and never let him out. He sat up and opened his eyes. They were coming! They were doing what all hunters do to their prey, let them run themselves out. He jumped to his feet and found a large tree, being careful to not leave a trail or scent, and climbed up it. He hid behind a long thick branch and waited. Within moments the ground was swarming with jejirs. Some ran on ahead in the direction that he had been heading while others crawled around on all fours sniffing the ground. They chirped to each other in a crude manner and some even pointed at things as if trying to give directions. One began to sniff around the base of his tree. The king held on and was so still that he didn't even dare to breathe. Its huge eyes stared up into the treetops and met his. It began to scale the tree with the skill of a cat and almost reached him before he could kill it with his final arrow. Its heavy mass crashed to the forest floor spiraling a gush of leaves into the air. Three jejirs down on one hunting trip, it was a feat no one would believe and he now feared he would not live to prove those skeptics wrong.

The other jejirs began to bounce around and howl in excitement with the finding of their game. Two more climbed up the tree after him, but the king used his bow to keep them from reaching his branch. After several attempts to ascend the tree without success, they began to heave rocks at him in frustration. It was the same game that he used to play with his prey as a child after he and his royal hounds had treed some small helpless animal. Now he was the helpless one on his own. He was able to dodge most of the barrage but each time one missed, they would pick it up again and use it against him. His only hope was to climb higher where their throws wouldn't have enough force to hurt him or even worse, knock him loose. He put his bow on his back and began to climb higher. As he tried to climb, the throwing got more intense as his hunters began to get excited with his movement. Stones began to strike him all over his body causing blood and welts to rise on his skin. He scrambled from one branch to the next mimicking his earliest ancestors. Ignoring the pain of the rocks hitting him as he climbed up, he made sure he had a tight grip on each branch before he went to the next. His grip was so tight that he was still holding on to the branch that broke when he hit the ground.

The cosmos is but a weave of space and time that curves with mass. Dreams can warp this fabric expanding the holes within it and therefore create doors to new worlds.

Past the Depths of the Mhorhaen

King Hamse the Third leading a rabble of men
against the armies of the dead

Part I
Call for Death

Young King Hamse the Third sat on his massive throne surrounded by the riches of his great kingdom, Haenic. He inhaled the rich aroma of incense rising from hand carved pillars spaced around the large round throne room, staring quietly at the exotic furs covering its smooth polished ivory walls and the thick rugs on its marble floors that offered warmth to the soles of bare feet. The throne below him supported his weight with thick lavishly feathered pillows supported by a gold and silver etched frame sitting high upon a granite pedestal. Thin voluptuous maidens, the most beautiful in all the lands of Zeethe, stood scantily dressed at his side ready to fulfill his every whim. Succulent meats and luscious fruits graced the bowls upon his table, accompanied by fine wines floating within precious goblets. Jesters, dancers and musicians were at his command, but in spite of all these fancies, he found himself weary.

Unlike his father who had been a statesman expanding the empire of the Hamse's royal bloodline three-fold during his reign, he cared little for politics and like his grandfather, he craved the hunt. He stood up from his throne, pushing away the advances of his concubines and thundered into the royal trophy room. Upon its walls were the skins of great beasts from across the Lands of Dream. Immense cave bears, saber-toothed cats, blood wolves, and frenzied boars had all been put onto the wall by his hands, but hanging in the center honored above all else in his kingdom hung the furs of two jejirs slain by his grandfather the late King Hamse the First. He had disappeared during a hunt before his birth and although his father never told him the legends of his grandfather's hunts, he had heard every last one from the soothsayers and the other children of the court, romantically soaking them in throughout his childhood. His own father, King Hamse the Second, had become king at the young age of seven after his father's strange disappearance and had developed a great fear of hunting from the experience, never raising a bow during his life. To only have been there, thought the young king, clinched in a death struggle with such a great beast! Just imagining the scene of his grandfather bringing such a trophy down with his bow made blood race through his arteries and brought life back into his normally emotionless face. He gritted his teeth and clinched his royal fist staring up at the seven-foot tall hides the sight of which brought life to his muscles as he thought of his impending hunt. Jejirs although rare in his grandfather's time, were now even more uncommon and until three days ago, an attack had not been reported for nearly eight years. As soon as the news reached him by rider from Sudal that three villagers had been killed and taken by one of the beasts, he had thought of nothing else and by his command, his kingdom spared no expense to prepare for the hunt. He had done nothing as a young man by order of his father during the only other reported attack in his lifetime, hoping every day since that he would get another chance at hanging his own jejir in the royal trophy room. Tomorrow morning he would leave for the Mhorhaen to enter its depths vowing not to return without the monster's hide.

The sun rose above the distant mountains of Azoul illuminating the slanted eyes and stern face of a determined king. He had not slept a single moment the entire night waiting for its emergence. His steed grunted as he kicked it forward with wooden spurs leading an entourage of three guards, a tracker and a flag bearer carrying the official Hamse seal. Peasants kneeled down in the fields and along the roadside as they passed gladly soiling their clothes to show respect of their great king. The party rode hard, stopping only to rest and water their horses in order to make the edge of the Mhorhaen forest in three days. The king inspected the site of the attack finding a ravaged home and misshapen trails of blood that disappeared into the depths of the forest. He met the family in person and publicly, over cheers from the local villagers, vowed to bring back their bodies so to lay them to rest as well as the dead beast itself to end its terror, knowing as he spoke the words, he was doing so primarily to put his own heart at rest.

Night crawled over the small village in the northern province of Nthark swallowing up the border between the wild bestiary of the Mhorhaen and the domain of civilized man. Honoring the lost, the king took lodging with the distraught family choosing peasantry over his customary royal accommodations with the local noble waiting out the night. Having poor senses in regard to the nocturnal creatures of the Mhorhaen, it was at night that man was at his most vulnerable, and therefore the king and his men waited to travel within its boundaries during the light of day. A ball of fire rose above the thick treetops of the forest illuminating the king, his four huntsmen and the plowed fields of northern Nthark. His small hunting entourage, which included three guards and a tracker, sat on their horses ready to begin the hunt. The king wore a light tanned-leather vest, more typical for a simple woodsman than for the most powerful king in Zeethe, sheathed a long sword, which he prided himself on its usage, and held a longbow of his grandfather with great distinction. His bodyguards were direct descendants of Kthaer barbarians each standing over six and a half feet tall and bearing well over three hundred pounds of rigid muscle and solid bone. They were powerful brutes of men who followed the traditions of their ancestors by forsaking the protection of armor for free strength and the speed of light furs. It was said that most men could not match the strength of a Kthaer woman, yet alone one of their warriors. They wielded giant two-handed battle-axes that stretched five feet from tip to tip, which were heavy enough in the hands of a Kthaer barbarian to decapitate an ox with a single blow. His lone tracker, a wild tribesman from the islands of Jheanb, had been captured during the great Emerald Sea Wars between Haenic and Deazah and although he barely spoke, his knowledge of the wild was unrivaled. The thin clad tracker, barely five feet tall, kneeled down at the edge of the forest sniffing the blood lying in the dirt, as would a common animal. The elder tracker paused, listening to the buzz of flies thick upon the trail of blood; this creature had no fear of man, he thought, as it made no attempt to hide its tracks. He jumped upon his light horse leading the king and his men into the shadows of the Mhorhaen. Sunlight turned to darkness in an instant upon entering the wood. Thick gnarled trunks rose from the forest floor disappearing into the foliage above giving leeway to sharp thorns and light underbrush. A path of flattened brush twisted through the colossal tree trunks disappearing into the depth of the wood. Dried blood and flesh hung on the branches and thorns, feeding a swarm of flies and blood-sucking insects that felt free to taste the live flesh of the hunters as well. The men ignored the stings of the pests, so not to be distracted, as they were in the beast's world now. The king's fingers held tight around his longbow as he rode quietly behind his assiduous tracker acutely observing the shadows and sunspots throughout the wood in quiet anticipation. The creature had passed into the wood with six days lead, normally an insurmountable time with respect to a hunt, but with the speed of their horses, and considering the weight of its three victims in hand, the men expected to catch up with it within a week if all went well. Comfortable that the beast was not near, the tracker pressed his horse and the men rode agilely through the thick forest swerving around giant trunks of wood in following the blatantly visible route of their prey. Patches of sunlight cut through the thick treetops piercing the men's eyes as they rode through the dark forest on panting steeds. Smoke bellowed from the nostrils of the stallions running through the icy air like muscular steam engines through a dark mountain tunnel. The men held tightly to their reins, cutting through the frost of the morning and riding until late afternoon before resting their horses. None of the men spoke as they silently chewed dried meat and berries during the only break they would allow themselves that day. The men rode hard during the light of day finally coming to a stop as the sun's radiance began to fade away giving way to the bitter dusk of night. The men hunched into a deep ravine enduring icy temperatures abetted by thick furs and the warmth of a small fire.

  Shimmering light trickled through the pores of the forest's top illuminating the smoking embers of a fading fire and the alert eyes of a king. This year's winter had been harsh, blowing in great snowdrifts from the Azoul as well as the stirring hunger of the jejir. His men roused from underneath their warm furs mounting without a grumble for the daylong ride ahead. The bitter air cut through their furs like a knife slicing into their flesh during the hard ride. The five horsemen rode like mad-men in fur through the wind, trees and snow, their minds bent on the destruction of the beast they pursued. They rode through the day riding further into the depth of the Mhorhaen than most men of Zeethe dared to dream. No known man had ever passed through the Mhorhaen and returned to tell the tale. Many believed the wilderness had no end, while others claimed they were the edge of the world and to find their end meant doom. The king cared little for the rumors or legends of the forest as his grandfather, the first king of

Hamse, had traveled further into their depths than any man in his quest to hunt the mysterious jejir. He had seen the paintings of his grandfather locked in battle with the giant white beast fighting tooth and nail, using only a bow and his wit to slay the beast. He aspired to match or maybe even surpass his grandfather's accomplishment in his own lifetime even if it meant the exhaustion of his great kingdom's riches.

The men traveled without complaint through the unforgiving ice and snow, breaking its grip upon the forest with the full strides of their powerful stallions. The king's royal stallions were fierce beasts in their own right, with direct bloodlines from the stables of the horse riders of Broden, ferocious plainsmen from the west, boasting the swiftest cavalry in all the lands of Zeethe. His young stallions were not allowed to breed in order to harness the fury of their raging testosterone, making them wild temperamental creatures of ferocity. The men rode relentlessly eight days in pursuit of the elusive beast through the northern coniferous forest stopping only for short rests and to wait out the frigid nights. On the ninth day of the hunt, the keen eyes of their tracker saw a break in the trail. The small man signaled for the others to stop, nimbly slipping off his horse to study the trail. A wide pile of brush lay flat while a smaller trail led off straight ahead. The beast had left the bodies here before dragging them off one at a time. The perspicacious tracker stood up, cautiously examining the area. In his experiences with wild animals, such actions meant the creature had a lair nearby. The men drew arms by the tracker's command and followed him quietly stepping around the beleaguering clinging twigs and leaves along the trail. The small tracker softly shifted the brush aside squeezing through as silent as a mouse, signaling for the larger men to stand quiet as he explored ahead on his own. He slinked ahead carefully avoiding objects of noise maneuvering around the forest's undergrowth so as not to alert the beast. He stopped inaudibly staring at a large wooden arch made from knotted, twisted tree branches. Dangling from its center where the corpses of a man, woman and a small child. Their bodies were covered in dried blood that had oozed from cuts and bruises sustained from their being drug across the Mhorhaen Forest. The lithe tracker scampered up to the cadavers wary of the beast they sought. They were suspended by crudely tied vines with their throats cut to allow for the drainage of their blood. He turned from the dirty faces that were still gripped in fear even in death. How horrible a death it must have been he thought to himself as he returned to the hunting party. He gently whispered into the ear of the king of the scene he witnessed clandestinely hoping the king would choose to return with the bodies without attempting to engage the beast. The king's heart soared in excitement of the news. He had never even seen one of the beasts alive; now he would have the opportunity to kill one as he had dreamed to do so since a child. He instinctively drew back an arrow in his bow leading his men to the crude structure from which his people were suspended. His men quickly cut the corpses down, wrapped them in soft burial cloths that they had brought along with their gear and fixed them along the backs of their horses. For a moment as the king's men placed the bodies on top the horses, a ray of hope beamed in the tracker's eyes that they might return home, but it quickly faded as he saw the king's intentions of returning with the body of the beast or not at all.

The men returned to the raw arch and began to search the area for traces of the beast's whereabouts. They wandered the area in a close-knit group as their tracker stalked the monster. The area rose onto a large formation of pointed rocks and old knotted trees encircled by small crevices in the earth. The men of hunt carefully maneuvered around the small cave openings as they stalked their quarry. The creature's tracks led to a large crevasse that split into huge rock formations dropping down into the earth. A cold darkness oozed from the dark fissure chilling the men standing above it to the bone. This was perfect, thought the king, raising his bow toward the cold shadows of the earth. They had trapped the beast leaving it no way escape without him getting in a shot at pointblank range. He held his grandfather's bow proudly. He had used it to drop mammoth deer and bear from over a hundred yards distance with its raw power. He drew his heaviest arrow, which had a one pound tip and large barbs intended to cause maximum damage upon impact, and readied it in his bow.

Now it was time to call out the beast and his destiny. He screamed with all his might emitting hot steam from his lungs into the cold air using his diaphragm to carry his voice deep into the cave. As he ended his scream, birds rustled from the trees above escaping into the tree-covered sky above. The five men stood silent and for a moment it appeared nothing would answer his call for death. Then a cavernous rumble rolled from within the gloomy cleft, shaking the ground at the men's feet. The beast burst out of the hole with the speed of a creature a third its size holding out its colossal arms in a seven foot stretch with long white claws four inches in length. Its white and gray matted fur dangled from its body as it rushed from the cave intending to shred the hunters apart. With the reflexes of his grandfather's bloodline, the young king cocked his arrow, took aim at the beast's heart and unleashed his mighty arrow. The heavy iron arrow gyrated through the air drilling into the flesh of the beast's chest digging into its thoracic cavity and missing its heart by less than half an inch. The beast tugged at the shaft of the arrow breaking it in two as the arrow's head refused to release its grip upon its flesh. The king drew another arrow from his quiver swiftly placing it within his bow to take a second shot at the towering creature. The large fiend's hand seized the king's bow and snapped it like a dry twig at the same time knocking the king onto his back and down into a small cave hole below. He fell ten feet below the earth to the base of the cave's entrance landing hard on his side against a pointed rock.

One of the Kthaer barbarians, accustom to wrestling bears in strength rituals, seized one the jejir's arms with the steel grip of his two mighty hands and pulled it back from the rolling king. In anger, the beast lifted the man up into the air with its arm and seized him with its other to lock him in a bear hug. The barbarian's torso collapsed under the weight of the powerful grip as his lungs and internal organs were pierced with the broken shards of his ribcage oozing blood from his eyes, ears and mouth. The other two king's barbarians drew their axes and charged the beast. The beast moved aside avoiding the blow of the first barbarian's axe, but the second found its mark, slicing deep into the creature's abdomen. It howled in pain as the sharp iron sunk deep into its flesh, but it forced the two men back by slinging the dead body of their brethren like a club. The slung body of the dead barbarian crashed against the two men with a power unlike any they had ever felt, tumbling them backwards into the forest. The crystal white eyes of the large rabid creature then fixed upon the small tracker. It slung the body of the dead barbarian at him like a three hundred pound limp mace crashing its bones against the ground as the nimble tracker pounced out of the way barely escaping its wrath.

The two barbarians recovered from the beast's first blow and rushed in again with the spirit in which Kthaer barbarians were known, striking at the beast once again with their battle-axes. Both struck their targets from behind as the beast swung his first victim at the elusive tracker, but one paid dearly as the creature spun around to seize the barbarian's throat and engulfed his head with its wide hairy palm. It crushed the helpless man's throat collapsing his trachea and esophagus, separating his spinal cord from the base of his skull. The heavy barbarian's body tore from his skull flopping to the ground lifeless at the massive creature's feet. The king, recovering from the force of his fall, rose to his feet as the battle raged above him unsheathing his shiny long sword. Blood leaked into his fine furs from a long inguinal gash. He crawled through the rubble of the cave crushing the bleached bones of man and animal as he moved toward the light of the cave's entrance a dozen or so feet ahead. Stepping out the mouth of the cave, he found himself behind the beast as it battled his last surviving barbarian. Raising his sword upon his head with both his hands, he ran toward the beast with the point of his sword pointing at its back determined to pierce its large pumping heart. The blade's point drove into the beast's tissue sliding off its broad scapula bouncing off target and missing its heart once again. The mammoth beast spun around, feeling the sting of his blade, before flinging the king into the air and crashing him against the trunk of a tree dazing him.

The king fell to the ground without the grip of his sword as it protruded from the dorsal of the violent monster and struggled to stay conscious. The beast and barbarian locked in struggle slowed down to a messy blur as his consciousness threatened to leave him. He shook his head vigorously attempting to clear it from the haze covering his failing eyes. This was what he had waited for his entire life and he would not let himself fail now. He rose to his feet straining to revive himself. The last barbarian screamed with streaked battle paint across his face and seized the creature's neck attempting to steal its life with the might of the Kthaerian wastes. The beast turned its fury upon the barbarian gripping his neck and locking the two in a struggle of life and death as the strength of man failed before the strength of wild beast. The last barbarian fell lifeless before its conqueror lying at its feet in a mass of the dead following after his countrymen.

The giant creature fixed its clear eyes onto its next victim and stomped toward the waning king with blood seeping from the arrow wound in its chest, the axe wounds that tormented its body and the sword protruding from its back tangling crimson blotches into its white matted fur. The king stood helpless looking for any object he could use to repel the lumbering creature. Then the king's last surviving man, his tracker, sprung onto the back of the beast gripping onto its fur like a monkey stabbing it with a short knife as if chopping at a block of ice with quick blows following each other in lightning succession. The large creature tried to swat at the tiny man as he crawled around its massive body dodging its powerful hands and sharp claws while stabbing it at every opportunity. Taking advantage of his tracker's assault, the king dashed to an arrow that had fallen from his quiver during the scuffle and held it with the tight grip of a determined hunter. The colossal beast seized the leg of the tiny man crawling on him like a parasite and tore him off his body to dangle him out like a prize. The agile woodsman raised up quickly stabbing the beast's hand to break its grip, but managed only to have one of his arms seized by the beast's other free hand. With brute strength known only to the feral, the creature began to pull the poor man apart. The small tribesman let out a deafening shriek as his torso began to separate from his pelvis. A primal instinct took hold of the mighty and civilized king as he ran with all his might leaping on the chest of the substantial beast, gripping its hair with one hand while thrusting the sharp arrow's tip into the center of its left eye with his other. The sharp tip pierced its cornea passing its skull and sinking into its soft brain. The beast's last order from its central nervous system tore the poor tracker in two spewing his bowels onto the ground. The king rode the beast to the ground, as would a falling lumberjack topping a tree, smashing on top of it boiling leaves and dirt into the air. The king heard its last gasp for air as it died beneath him.

He had done it, he had slain a jejir! Pride swelled up into his bruised and battered body as he stared down at his long sought after trophy. It was an accomplishment few had ever known as at that moment only six jejir hides hung in all of Zeethe. In his initial excitement, he had forgotten about those who had died so viciously by his side. Their bodies lay distorted and broken, strewn around the cave entrance encircling the king and his prize hide as grave memorials of the great battle. Languid eyes spattered with blood peered up at him from the grief stricken face of his tracker lost forever in death. The king reached over with his hand and brushed them closed for eternity. Being groomed to become a king since birth and seeing the deaths of thousands during the expansion wars of his father, he saw the deaths of his men as little more than the destiny of their servitude. Unable to return with the bodies of the men that had died in his honor, the king buried the four by his own hand under stones, leaving four unmarked rock mounds deep within the Mhorhaen never to be seen again by the eyes of man.

As promised, the king tied the bodies of the jejir's victims on horseback, placing the body of the man on one horse and the shredded bodies of the woman and child on another. The next challenge was that of trying to bring the beast's corpse back to his kingdom some several days ride away. He could crudely skin the beast with the knife of his tracker, but he dared not do so for fear of ruining the prized hide. The possibility of having such a magnificent beast standing in his trophy room was too great a temptation to ignore. Using a creative pulley system of ropes and tree trunks, the king towed the huge five-hundred pound corpse on top two horses he tied together to distribute the massive weight for the long return home. He slid on top of his horse with failing strength as the river of life seeped from his side turning the fur of his clothing and horse scarlet. He led the string of horses by quickly tying the lead rope to his harness as his vision gave away to darkness and finally unconsciousness.

Part II
Through Death's Door

The king awoke on top of his horse in the mist of hoofs beating along the hard dirt trail. He shoved his long hair and scruffy beard aside to see from where the sound came. Knights in bright gleaming armor with red insignias holding shiny spears into the air rode toward him hastily spiraling dust onto the trail behind. Within his worn mind he rejoiced that his men had found him. He had done it; he had slain a jejir he thought happily. The formation of men halted before the haggard king surrounding him with clanks of armor while sitting upon shuffling horses.

"Who are you, beggar?" asked one of the armored men in a booming voice.

The king looked up the man in bewilderment. Their tabards bore red hawks upon them surrounded in blazing yellow fire. He did not recognize to which of his nobles these uncouth men at arms belonged.

"How dare you call your king a beggar!" said the king slapping the young knight's face startling his horse.

The young cavalier retaliated by slapping the weary king off his horse with the force of an iron gauntlet. The king in a near-death state fell from his horse collapsing onto the ground before the band of knights unable to move. The armored men laughed at the royal king who in his weakened state appeared as little more than a drunkard.

Suddenly the king noticed that he did not have his train of horses carrying the bodies of his people and the body of his prize possession. He stumbled to his feet deliriously ordering the men to search the area. In return to his orders, the men laughed even harder seeing a serf giving staggering commands to the royal guards of King Aeaf. The insolence of the men angered the great king and in response he seized one of the unprepared men with surprising speed, pulling the armored knight from his horse. The heavily armored man fell onto his back landing in a embarrassingly helpless state like that of a trapped turtle. So to gain control of the situation, a heavy iron boot from another knight crashed into the king's face drawing blood and knocking him unconscious.

The next time the king awoke, he found himself chained to a cold dirty floor in a dark stone room lit by a single wall-mounted torch. Confused, he wrestled with his chains to break free, but gave up in frustration as his strength faded once again. A dirty man chained to the far corner missing most of his teeth watched the shabby king struggle with his bonds.

"What you do to get beaten so badly?" asked the ragged man through the shadows.

"A case of mistaken identity!" yelled the king furiously. "As king, I assure you the men that did this will find themselves in here before long."

"Oh excuse me your majesty," said the man in jest. "I meant no disrespect."

The king nodded to the man in amnesty taking the man's comments seriously.

"King Aeaf is it?" asked the man curiously continuing the conversation to break the monotony of his imprisonment.

"I am King Hamse, Lord of Haenic! The greatest king in all the realms of Zeethe!"

"I am in here for eating carrots that did not belong to me and for that I will probably receive a dozen lashes and a month in this foul dungeon, but if you keep that crazy talk up you will never see the light of day," he said in warning to the poor soul that lay imprisoned across the cell.

"As soon as it is discovered who I am, all of this will be resolved and I assure you, although I do not know who you are, you will not be punished in such a way for eating carrots once I am free."

The tattered man looked at the poor wretch in exasperation, "If you know what is good for you, you will drop this whole king fairy-tale and tell the royal arbitrator that you are a simple beggar."

"Beggar!" screamed the king shocked at the suggestion. "No king of Haenic would ever claim to be a common beggar!"

"Haenic... Zeethe," said the man. "I have lived over thirty seasons and wandered these lands since a child and I have never heard of such places."

The king stopped and looked at the man strangely. His kingdom stretched across a continent touching four seas and assimilated fifteen other kingdoms as provinces. To not have heard of such a powerful kingdom was madness! The man was clearly insane and unlike himself, belonged in chains. A heavy set of keys began to rattle outside their cell.

"Listen to me," whispered the vagabond, "you are about to be taken before the arbitrator. Do not mention anything about being a king. Monarchs tend to frown upon such claims. I am telling you, it would best to tell them you were drunk."

A short fat man holding a big set of keys lumbered in to the cell followed by two armed guards.

"There he is," slobbered the scruffy man, "but be careful with that one because he is a king!"

The two men lifted up the feeble king, holding him up as the jail keeper forced himself down into an uncomfortable squat to unlock his chains.

"Take him up!"

The two guards dragged their flaccid prisoner down a long musty hall under the light of smoking torches through the dirt and muck of the underground dungeon. Warm air flowed against the king's face as they dragged him from the cool shadows of his prison to the dry light above. The bright light hurt his eyes and forced him to cover them as they hauled and threw him before the king's arbitrator.

"What are the charges against this man?" asked the richly dressed man from his throne.

"Your honor, this man is charged with assaulting one of the king's royal guards, trespassing, and false claims of nobility," retorted the fat jail keeper.

"I don't think I have ever had the privilege of hearing all three of those charges in a single day, yet alone from one man," he said looking at the poor wretch before his feet. "How do you respond to these charges?"

The king looked up at the man through groggy eyes weak from extensive blood loss and lack of nourishment.

A loud voice rumbled from the frail man awakening the large courtroom, "I am king of Haenic, lord over the lands south of Sudal, north of the Mordal Sea, east of the Cerulean Sea and west of the Red Sands!"

"Has this man been drinking?" asked the arbitrator after hearing all the strange names.

"No your honor," replied the jail keeper.

"How long has he been imprisoned?"

"Three days," said the dirty jail keeper.

The arbitrator looked at the man before him who was obviously not drunk but insane, "From the looks of you, it is a poor land."

The men of the court laughed at the arbitrator's sly comment, a joke at the expense of the fallen king.

"I have passed through the Mhorhaen in search of the mighty jejir and somehow unwittingly wandered into your lands."

The arbitrator leaned back into his chair unfamiliar with the name, "You mean the Dark Wood?"

"I know not what you call it," he responded.

The arbitrator laughed at the possibility of anything being beyond the great black forest.

"There is nothing beyond the Dark Wood," he claimed. "You tell stories as great as any I have ever heard. If it were not for you being mad, you would make the king a good jester."

"I would rather die," spat the king.

"Keeper… did anyone besides the guard he assaulted see the act?" asked the arbitrator insulted by the actions of the man before him.

"Yes," murmured the fat man.

"Was he found on the king's land by more than one man?"

"Yes."

"And I have heard his self-proclaimed right of royalty without documentation by my own ears. I have no choice but to find you guilty of all three charges and hand you down a merciful sentence of a dozen lashes and five years imprisonment in Alboules' prison."

The guards lifted up the convicted man, ready to drag him to his sentenced lashes, when the strength of his forefather's flowed into his failing muscles swelling them to their peak. Startling the unsuspecting guards, he seized the head of one guard crashing it against his knee, bending his helmet in the process and dropping him to the floor out cold. Not finished with the anger of his outburst, he spun around wrapping the second guard's neck with his chains and forced him to his knees by cracking his kneecap with a brutal blow from his foot. The guard's eyes began to budge under the strain of the strangling chains as he fought helplessly for a breath of air. The jail keeper pulled free a leather blackjack crashing it against the unwary king's occipital bone stealing his consciousness.

"How dare he make such an outburst in my court! Take the mongrel out and double his lashes!" yelled the arbitrator. "If he lives through that, then throw him through Death's Door!"

The angry men dragged the unconscious man out by his arms down stairs and through the halls to the whipping post where they beat him while still unconscious as ordered. Blood and flesh tore from his back exposing the bones of his ribcage, before he was pulled through Death's Door and chained to live out the rest of his life.

He awoke in the dim light of Death's Door, the deepest level of Alboules' dungeon, where only the worst criminals were sentenced. He awoke to find himself in the company of murderers, rapists and political prisoners. Death's Door was a giant seven foot tall room about three hundred yards in length and eighty yards in width held steady by stone support columns. Each man was chained to the floor and wall by all four of his extremities with short chains that allowed only enough room to sit or lie down. The prisoners were lined along the walls with two full feet between the reach of each man.

"Hello," said a man chained to his left.

The king looked over at the filthy man straining to see his features through the murk of the deep dungeon. He had a pale colorless face with a dirty scraggily beard that hung over the holes in his mouth left vacant by the absence of his teeth.

"Glad to have a new partner, been four days since Tabby died and the oaf on the left of me doesn't have a tongue."

The king suddenly became aware of the sharp pain crawling over his back relentlessly pounding with its own heartbeat. He unconsciously reached back to feel what caused the pain grunting, finding that the length of his chained would not allow him to do so.

"They deal out lashes with every sentence whether you stole an apple or cut someone's throat," laughed the toothless man. "So what got you put down here?"

Broken in body and heart, the king slumped his head weary of the mockery he had been subjected to over the past few days.

"Please don't tell me you are mute too!" said the man in terror.

"I'm not," answered the king breaking his silence.

"Oh thank you, I don't think I could have lasted another day without someone to talk to. Here in the thick darkness of Death's Door, a man can't see past two men, so the voice of those near you is your only light."

"Why do they call it Death's Door?" he asked from the shadows.

"What?" said the man confounded by the question. "You have to be joking; everyone knows about Death's Door. It is the most infamous place in all Alboules."

"Humor me."

"Might as well since we are going to be best friends, unless you choose Mince over to your right."

The king looked over a heap of a man lying unconscious. He looked to have already seen death.

"Don't think he is going to last much longer refusing to eat."

"The food that bad?"

"No," proclaimed the man quickly, "we get the leftovers from the king's daily banquets! Some of it is half eaten, but it's still better than most men ever see! I guess he figures we deserve it since each meal could be our last."

"Why is that?" asked the king curiously.

"You really don't know anything about Death's Door do you? Where did they find you?" he said looking at the king strangely and then continuing after the king offered no explanation of his ignorance. "Every evening they bring in hundreds of meals and hand them out randomly, with one being poisoned. That's why they call it Death's Door because no one put in here gets back out through that door except through death. Most men when they first come in here, fast from fear, but they either give in to the food lotto or they die like poor Mince is doing over there."

The king looked over at the poor man slumped unconscious, "How long has he been in here?"

"Two or three weeks I guess, I've been in here for almost two years now myself." He leaned toward the king and with a proud look on his face whispered, "I know that makes me seem lucky, but I have a system in place. I only eat every other meal to double my odds of survival and tonight is an odd night, I sure hope I get a big piece of meat!"

The king listened to the man's lunacy, horrified by the lot he had been cast. He would not eat scraps he thought angrily. No king of Haenic ate the charity of leftovers.

"That's what I recommend you do too. Everyone who lives any amount of time in here has a system. Like Lucky over in the far corner, he just passed four years, making him the senior man in deaths' door." The strange man leaned over as far as his chains would allow and whispered, "What I wouldn't give to know his system, but he passionately guards it." He screamed so to carry his voice over the large room, "Hey Lucky, say hello to the new chap!"

"Shut up Pot, I'm not tellin you nuthin!" echoed a voice from the damp darkness.

"You mean ole bastard, you're going to take your system to the grave with you!"

"I'll be here the day they carry you out!" he screamed back.

"See I'm not selfish like that louse, feel free to use my system if you want."

The king nodded to the man, too tired to carry on the conversation. He couldn't believe the nightmare he had found himself in, chained and beaten like a common thief, and worst of all, he had lost his prized hide. He would get out of this place he told himself and return home, bringing an army with him that would bring this insignificant kingdom to its knees. They would suffer for the humility he had endured at their hands. As thoughts of revenge filled his head, guards shuddered in Death's Door swinging it open and rushing in warm air from above. Two men hauled a long cart covered with fruit, vegetables and meat into the musty cell, causing the men within it to salivate like dogs being fed scraps from their master's table. The fat jailer led the food cart handing out plates of food to the men dropping plates into their laps as they reached out for the mercy of nutrition or poison, whichever fate chose to deal.

"Life or death, which shall it be?" asked the fat man loudly in good humor.

The cart came to a squeaking halt next to Mince, who laid motionlessly disregarding the call for food. The jail keeper kicked the man to rouse him then dropped the plate of food with a loud clank next to the man when he failed to respond. The squeaking continued rolling up to the king who lay in chains ignoring the disgusting man.

"Ah your majesty, I have a special plate for you," he said teasing him. "This one came directly from the king's plate. I thought you might appreciate it more than the commoners in here."

He handed him the plate and walked on leading the cart down the long cell laughing as he handed out plates to desperate men like a grotesque Santa. He knew each of their nicknames calling them out as he had them the day's only sustenance. Most of the men engorged their food ripping meat from the bone and tearing into its skin chewing it like wild dogs. The king lifted up his plate examining a half-chewed bone and the bundle of fruit sitting on it. His stomach rumbled from its aroma, but the king's pride held firm and he threw the plate, down refusing to eat the slop of others. Pot, adhering to his system, happily ate his food, excited that he had received a large helping of roasted meat on his platter. His few remaining teeth ripped the meat from the bone making clear grease flow on his hirsute chin. He smiled from the delight of nourishment and a full stomach clearing his plate before he noticed his new best friend was not eating.

"Hey, why'd he call you that?" he said picking food out of his gums.

The king didn't say anything.

"If you want to use my system, you should eat today so we can support each other on off days."

The humbled king slumped down quietly closing his eyes, not to speak the rest of the day.

The next morning to his dismay, his lungs filled with the breath of life and his eyes opened reconfirming the nightmare of being thrown into a foreign dungeon to rot.

"Good mornin'," said Pot looking at the king through the diminutive light seeping under Death's Door.

"Is there any such thing in this forsaken hole?"

"Not for some," he said quietly, "friar passed through Death's Door last night."

"Was he sick?"

"He drew the lot," he said sadly. "No one wants to spend their life in chains below ground never seeing the light of the sun, but most men still strive to live against all odds, even when things seem as if they couldn't get any worse; and to see the gift of life stolen from a man and carried out that door under the grip of death foretells all of our futures."

The king listened to the eloquent philosophy of the grubby man next to him, "Mind if I ask you what brought you to Death's Door?"

Pot raised his body up as if his spirit had been lifted, "Of course I am sorry. I guess best friends should make proper introductions. My name is Pot, they call me that because I was a potter… a damn good one too." His eyes flickered like a flame as he began to remember his life before the black corners of Death's Door. "She was beautiful, as fair as a maiden as any I had ever seen. I loved her from first sight. I asked her father for her hand in marriage, but he had higher hopes for her than I, refusing to give me his consent. Being a pretentious young man I went against his will and asked her to marry me anyway, and to my heart's delight, she accepted! To this day, I draw on that feeling to lift my spirit every time someone passes through that door. What I didn't know was that her father had already selected her another suitor, an eastern noble who could do more for his family than my clay ever could. Upon hearing of my proposal, her father or the noble, I'm not sure which, had me charged with sedition," he said pausing. "I haven't heard from her since, I still don't know if she ever married him or not."

The king listened to the man's poignant tale as moved as he had ever been by a personal story. Being a king, he had never confided in anyone and he couldn't bring himself to do so, even with a sentence of eventual death hanging over his head.

"How did you get in here?"

"By being a fool," he said plainly.

"That's fine, if you're still fuming over your imprisonment, we've got the rest of our lives to learn about each other."

The food cart squealed into the cold room, admitting the light from beyond searing the men's eyes as the jail keeper pulled the cart in with a cruel smile.

"Life or death, which shall it be?" yelled the portly man who delighted in mental torture.

The fat man offered a plate to the collapsed form to the right of the king.

"What is it Mince, life or death?" he said kicking the motionless body. He leaned down and touched the carotid artery. The overweight jail keeper was an expert in the recognition death and it hung low upon the man beneath him. The artery laid flat without a pulse confirming his presumption. "Death it be," he said under his breath. "Guard, unchain this man. His punishment has been served."

A guard came into the room unchaining the lifeless limbs, dragging the corpse through Death's Door. The cart rolled on to complete its round, stopping before the king. An evil grin accompanied his platter with a light clank against the stone floor.

"Your majesty."

The cart squeaked on.

The king lowered his head against his shoulder and began to stare at the food on his plate. His body craved it, as he needed it to carry on, to nourish his flesh. Death tugged at his soul, cultivating it, preparing to harvest his flesh. His starving tissues pleaded for him to seize the plate and feast, while the pride of his lineage held his hands like invisible chains. He began to drool like an animal at the sight of the delicious victuals. Man and beast fought within his consciousness as primal desire struggled against civilized thought.

"If you don't partake, you will surrender to Death's Door as Mince did," whispered his friend. "Don't give that fat bastard the satisfaction of dragging you out that door."

The king closed his eyes, so not to see the loss of his own dignity, as he snatched the plate and began to stuff the food into his mouth, madly filling it to its capacity. Being of royal blood, the king had tasted the finest cuisine of his realm, but none of it compared to the taste of the cold scraps he voraciously consumed. Water came to his eyes as disregarded decorum, eating like an animal on the floor in filth. His friend thought nothing of it, as pride had no place in Death's Door. Behind Pot written in blood etched by a fingertip from an earlier prisoner were these words, "All men are equal in the eyes of death. There are no kings, no peasants… only men."

Time passed as the two men came to know each other as well as any two men had known each other since the beginning of time. Through the strength of his relationship with his best friend Pot, the king managed to avoid the lot of Mince and the anonymity of being carried out and burned with Alboules' trash. His heart sank with every man that was carried through Death's Door and rose with every time he beat its lot. Days turned into months, which translated into a year under the shadows of Death's Door. A once strong and proud king fell into that of a pale and humbled man. His beard hung to his chest, tangled from being uncombed and unwashed. Although humiliated by his captors, he remained determined to outlast his punishment and see through his pledge to avenge his imprisonment. In one of his most eventful days under lock and chain, his keen hunter's eyes caught a slight movement in the center of the dark room. It moved quickly, shifting back and forth as it collected morsels of food that had fallen from the food cart. Its drab gray fur glistened in and out of sight as it wandered through the center of the dungeon's floor just beyond the length of the prisoner's hands.

"That's Wee, smartest booger in this joint, I'm afraid to say," admitted his friend. "Ain't been a soul in this place that has ever caught him. He moves around this place like a ghost coming and going as he pleases."

"I can catch him," said the king assuredly.

"King," said his friend in compliment, for he had confided in him about his past, "this little fella is far more clever than any beast you have ever hunted."

"He's no more cunning than a jejir."

"I told you, there is no such beast, just old wives' tales. Besides your jejir uses strength for survival, this creature is one that survives purely by its wit."

The sparkle of the hunt returned to the king's tired eyes. It was a challenge he had an entire lifetime to complete. His pupils soaked in its movements and daily patterns, all the time assessing his best course of action. It moved in and out of Death's Door through a small crack near a pillar in the center of the room. He could see its red eyes gleam through the darkness as it waited patiently in its hole for dinner every night. As he observed its behavior he pondered how the creature had managed to live so long under the same conditions as the men in Death's Door. Did it not share the same risk as they being apart of Death's Door's lottery? Why had it not died from poison as the men in Death's Door did almost every day? Maybe its keen sense of smell allowed it to avoid the poisoned food! As the days dragged on, the King played a game of cat and mouse, but to its credit, the small creature knew the range of his chains and always stayed safely beyond. Even when he left scraps of food within his reach, the adroit rodent never gave him an opportunity to capture it, avoiding his trap completely. After failing to get his prey within an arm's length, he continued to amuse himself and his friend by contemplating his next course of action, capturing the rat beyond his reach. He slowly pulled a long thread from his pants being careful not to tear it as the seam along his pants leg gave away separating all the way down to his ankle. He carefully tied a loose snare loop in the tread stretching it out about a full inch in diameter. His nimble fingers carefully ran the thread along his tongue so to strengthen it before flipping it out several times to get it exactly where he wanted it. Then with the skill of a hunter he tossed little pieces of food he had saved from his plate around the tiny noose and waited. The thin fiber held tightly between his fingers as he waited patiently for a chance to spring his trap. Hours passed as the king waited in earnest for the small rodent to work its way toward him and his trap.

Two tiny red eyes peered through the hole near the pillar as the creature slowly came out into the open in a cautious crawl. The excitement of the hunt returned to the king's blood regenerating the strength he had in him before his capture. His muscles lay in wait ready to contract within milliseconds of mental command. The mouse crawled over to his food nibbling at it from the safety of his chains watching the king from the corner of its left eye. Then the king sprung his trap with the stealth and speed of a pouncing panther tightening the snare around the small rat's foot dragging and then seizing it with a firm grip. His friend clapped in excitement at the spectacle, it being the greatest event he had witnessed in over three years. The king held his prey proudly holding it up to praise its capture. He was alive again. In his outwitting of the small creature he had revived his desire to live. He gently loosened his grip on the small mammal and began to stroke its course hair.

Over the next few weeks, he came close to his new pet, letting it sleep in his pocket and teaching it new tricks, with its first command being "come." He had trained hunting dogs as a youth in his zeal for the hunt, learning how to control them like an extension of himself. Within just a few days, he could let the tiny creature loose and by giving the command come and offering a treat, the rat would eagerly return to him for its reward. Every day after the dinner cart had made its rounds, Wee would poke its head out of his pocket ready to test the food for its new king. Daily the king would give it a sample of each food type on his plate and watch it carefully for an hour or so before he would eat it himself. Being much smaller, the king assumed an hour would be more than enough time to kill it if it were exposed to poison lethal enough to kill a man. After a year, he had found his system. Whether it was as good as Lucky's or not only time would tell.

The excitement of his pet's capture awakened his mind, setting it into motion a plot to escape from Death's Door as no others passed, alive. The men were never freed from their chains, which were casually checked on a daily basis, as the jailer would reclaim their plates a couple hours after their dispersion, so as not to allow the king and prisoners long enough time to wait out the man who had been poisoned. The only other visit they received was once a week when the jailer mercifully switched out their waste buckets, which stunk the enclosed prison in a horrid stench unknown to the men who had grown accustom to its smell living within. The king's mind spun within problem solving, inventorying every item on him, around his location and on everyone that walked within his range. He studied the obstacles of his chain, the dungeon's door and the jailer who never came into the room with a set of keys. As best he could tell through the dark murk, the large man always left the keys with the two guards at the door, who left it slightly open to light the dark room enough for the jailer to complete his food rounds. When he was not contemplating his escape, he spent the rest of his time speaking in earnest with Pot and training his new pet. The rodent was a quick leaner and craved his praise, standing up and clapping for its treats.

Four more months passed leaving the king chained in darkness still unable to solve the problem of his escape, when something occurred to change its equation. In one of his meals, which seemed mushier than normal, he shifted through the mash when the flash of metal struck his eye. He cleared the food aside, raking it off onto the floor, and quickly sat on it so to hide it from the jailer on his return. He dared not bring it out until the jailer returned a couple of hours later to retrieve the men's plates. He held up the thin knife to his eye so as to judge its quality. It was thick and dull, being made primarily for the tender food of the king's royal table, but it set his plan into motion. He stroked it across the damp stone floor grinding it mercilessly against the hard stone shearing metal from it to a fine edge. After hours of sharpening the dull blade, he took to the task of filing away at his stubborn chains. It took him three days to separate a link in the chain to his left arm. He tugged at the links, finally separating them to allow himself to stretch his arm out with pride. He worked diligently on each chain, taking another week to completely break his bonds. Fearful of being found out, he kept his break of bondage secret from everyone save Wee and Pot. During the week to pass the jailer's chain test, he re-linked his chains and never moved beyond the spot where he had sat for nearly two years. He planned every aspect of his escape, watching his captors' every move, studying their patterns as he had his last prey. Including his best friend Pot in his plan, he carefully tossed the worn knife to his friend in the dark to let him start on his own bonds. Another week passed full of hope as Pot chafed at the links in his chain throughout the night, working with the purpose of a four-year veteran of Death's Door. The king sat idle going over his plan to eradicate any possible mistakes, deftly working his muscles to give him and his friend their best hope of success. The king's muscles and mind held tense with excitement as Pot worked on his last chain. Once his plan was set into motion, he wasn't exactly sure what success meant, but he was sure that failure meant death.

The night before their planned escape, the king sat quiet as the jailer entered Death's Door and rolled his cart into its gloom. The man entered with his normal jovial sense of humor, handing out plates with a comment for each of its recipients. As the cart left the dungeon, Wee poked out his head delightedly ready to test his dinner. It would be a source of fuel he would need for the next day's escape. Wee nibbled away at the luscious food bringing saliva to the king's mouth as he patiently waited to eat after the small mammal like a dog at his owner's table. Wee gleefully did his duty and then began to play during the hour long wait by bouncing from one of the king's knees to the other to please his master. The master treated it for its efforts, hardly paying attention to his pet's actions being distracted by the plans of the next day's escape. Although well thought out, the plot had several elements of risk and while difficult, the king felt in his heart that he could and would succeed. He went over its every aspect numerous times before he looked down and noticed Wee had stopped playing. Its small gray body lay limp on his leg. Tears swelled into the king's eyes as a lump formed in his throat and he grasped his vocal chords to prevent himself from making any noise as he wept for its loss. He had never cried harder in his life, not even for the men who had died by his side in battle as king. The small rodent had saved his life the night before his escape. He pledged to himself in the darkness of Death's Door never to take things for granted again as he had as a king and to appreciate those around him all the more. He placed Wee's body in his pocket where it had slept over the past months to take it out through Death's Door with him. He signaled for Pot to return the knife and he sat ready to spring into action holding it tight throughout the long night.

The next day the door to Death's Door creaked opened as it had hundreds of times before letting in the jailer and his meal cart, but this time things were going to be different. This time, it would be its prisoners that walked through its door, not its keepers. Pot knew his role, as the jail keeper steered the large cart toward the king to hand him down a plate, while making jest of his imprisonment.

"Here you go Your Majesty," he said with a smirk. "How long has it been since you were put in here anyway my lord? I guess your army of rescuers got lost somewhere."

The king looked at him differently this time, with confidence.

"Aye they have left me to rot. I guess it is up to me to get out of this place."

The jailer looked at the man queerly as seeing poise in a man lost in Death's Door took him off guard. The king's left hand sprung out like a striking snake seizing his arm beyond the reach of his chain's usual boundary. The fat man's eyes enlarged to their maximum capacity as he panicked to break free. The king's other hand came from the shadows with lightning speed thrusting the sharp blade underneath the man's mandible, sealing his mouth shut and draining salty blood down his throat. Blood poured onto his hand below as he quickly threw the corpulent man to the hard floor straddling his waist and covering his mouth with his hand as he slit the jailor's throat draining his life onto the stone of Death's Door. Pot leaped to his feet, standing fully erect for the first time in almost four years. His muscles ached and his joints creaked as he forced his body to comply with the actions of their escape. He cared not if he lived or died, as to die by the hands of another man held far more dignity than to waste away in the darkness unseen by all but the eyes of death.

The two men crept past the astonished prisoners toward the dungeon's open door. Two guards waited patiently outside as they had done hundreds of times before ready to lock the doors up upon the jailor's return to be away as soon as possible from the damp cold of Death's Door. The king and Pot came out the door like wild beasts, surprising the men as they sprung onto them entangling them with their fury. Although weaker than the guards, the king managed to cut the first guard's throat so quickly that the guard never had the chance to bring his strength into the fray. The second guard was able to quickly overcome the bony body of Pot, throwing him to the floor, only to receive a knife in his back for the effort. He fell to the floor as the king stabbed him ruthlessly, shredding his internal organs with a flurry of strikes. Pot mindfully recovered from the scuffle and seized the guard's key ring to quickly run back into the darkness of Death's Door and free the rest of its inhabitants. Hundreds of men, hungry as starving wolves, flowed into the halls past Death's Door, breaking its mystical history of no one alive ever returning from its bowels. The king and Pot shuffled up with the madness through Alboules's notorious prison as angry men beat its scanty guard placement to death with bare muscle and bone to burst from its gates into its province as free men.

Upon hearing of the escape, Alboules's king issued orders to kill any escaped prisoner upon sight. The king's men dispersed in every direction, running into the town's deep twisted streets, the surrounding forest and the fields beyond. King Hamse's plans were to escape back into the Mhorhaen with the slight hope of navigating its depths to find his own kingdom once again, when the pallid hand of Pot held him back.

"This way," said the king motioning toward the Dark Wood with his head.

"I can't go," said Pot sadly.

"What do you mean? If you stay here, then you are sure to be captured and killed or, far worse, returned to Death's Door," pleaded the king.

"Remember when I told you about Celestie?"

The king nodded, remembering the story of his companion's lost love. Pot had spoken to him about her almost daily over the past year and a half. Although he had never met her, he felt as if he knew her better than any other woman he had ever known.

"I have to know if she married him or not."

"To go back into the capital of Alboules is madness! Guards will be swarming the streets! Nothing good can come from this plea," argued the king. "Even if she chose not to marry and die an old maid, you could never be with her... not now."

"Please my friend, I beg you, if you help me do this, I will follow you to the ends of the earth as your humble servant."

The king stared into his pale eyes and his heart pleaded for his friend, "I am no king in this land, if you must do this, then I will be at your side no matter the cost."

The poor man's face lit up in excitement as the two men slinked into the capital of the country that hunted them like wild animals. They passed through its streets under the cover of night finding Pot's home exactly as he remembered it. The two men quickly slipped inside through the front door shutting it behind them to cower in the dark. It was exactly as Pot had left it years before. The main table was exactly where it had been, not a chair had moved. An elderly woman came into the dark room carrying a small lantern bursting into a scream upon seeing their shadowed forms.

"Mother!" whispered the albino man. "Mother, it is I your son the potter!"

She squinted to make out his figure in the darkness, then rushed up to hug him in joy.

"I had heard about the escapees from the prison and I secretly hoped you had managed to be one of them, but you must leave at once," she pleaded with her son. "Guards are searching the city house by house killing all those they find. Why, they have already been here!"

"I know mother, but before I left, I needed to see you one last time," he said hugging her tightly. "Where is father?"

Her eyes slumped upon hearing his question. "You know you were everything to your father." She began to cry and before she finished her reply all three within the room had tears in their eyes. "He couldn't handle your loss."

"What do you mean mother? Where is he?" he beseeched.

He saw the look in her eyes and without her saying a word he knew what she meant. He fell to the floor crying wishing he had died in Death's Door. His heart ached as he lay with his cheek pressed against the dirt floor, pressing tears into the soil where he had been raised by his father. His mother collapsed to the floor with him holding him tightly.

"What of Celestie?" he asked slowly regaining his composure.

"She married Lord Alarice and has bore him two children."

Pot spat at the news, angry with the woman he had loved with all his heart.

"My son, as a woman she had no choice but to marry him. She was told that you took a bribe and left for the west with the money to live out your life in luxury. We were warned not to tell her differently lest we suffer the same fate as you."

"We must leave immediately so not to put you at further risk," King Hamse said quickly.

"To the north, your uncle lives as a blacksmith. It is distant from the capital, you will be safe there."

"Mother, they will never find us, we're going into the Dark Wood."

Fear violently gripped her face as she worried for her only child.

"What madness is this?" she said in horror. "Those woods will offer you nothing but death!"

"Mother, this man saved me from the fate of Death's Door, he comes from beyond the wood."

"What is he, a demon?" she asked nervously.

"He is a king!" he declared proudly.

The serf woman glanced over at the pitiful figure standing in the corner who looked closer to a corpse than that of royalty. Not to challenge her son's statement, she turned from the image of the haggard man and pleaded with her son once again to not trek into the unknown pits of the Dark Wood. When he insisted on leaving, his mother filled a harvest sack full of vegetables, fruit and bread to help them upon their journey. Pot hugged and kissed his mother one last time before the two men returned to the streets, slinking through its shadows like vermin. The men traveled east as the king followed his friend so to fulfill his promise and take him to see Celestie, even though doing so meant their possible capture and death. They walked the dirt roads of Alboules at night, while hiding like scared dogs through the light of day. Knights in full battle dress scoured the roads and every corner of the kingdom in search of its prison escapees. The king hid as they passed, using his skills as a hunter to evade those that hunted him. On foot, it took the two men four days to reach the eastern noble's lands. As most powerful nobles in the Lands of Dream, Lord Alarice's land had a royal forest that served as his wild game preserve, a pond and pasture for his cattle, fields and fallows to fill the tables of both the noble and his serfs, exotic vineyards, thriving orchards, homes, trade skill buildings and finally the lord's manor house. Two shadows crawled up to the large lavish home under moonlight and peered into one of its lower windows. Fresh meat pies steamed in its window as its servants prepared dinner for their lord. Seeing the home of a tract baron brought back memories of King Hamse's own kingdom under the darkness of night. How he missed its rolling hills and proud people. The aroma of fresh meat pies filtered down to the two men. The idea of tasting such a delicacy without fear of poison relaxed their stomachs, but while on the run they had little time for such opulence.

"Servants are everywhere," Pot whispered down to his companion. "How will we get close enough to speak with her?"

"That I know not," answered the king. "I doubt many ladies of the manor roam around alone except when they are expected to keep within their chambers."

The gaunt man looked up and spotted a small roofline leading to a small window.

"Lift me up."

The king held out his hand, and after summoning all his vigor, boosted the thin man to the edge of the roofline. Pot seized it, but hung limply, unable to pull himself onto its top. He kicked his leg against the side of the building and with a final effort heaved his torso onto the small crown below the window. The window's shutters groaned in the darkness as he slid through onto the building's top floor. Candles flickered from the wind that rushed in behind him, blowing them out in a gust and leaving him in the darkness of a lavish bedroom. The pale light of a taper glowed from down the hall as he entered the room. Celestie's face lit up the dark room. She had not changed, being as beautiful as the day he asked her to marry him. She screamed on seeing his shadowed silhouette in the corner and dropped the small flame she held in her hand. The fall extinguished its light leaving the two in total darkness. She turned to run down the hall toward safety when she heard his voice.

"My dear, do not fret for it is I, Tyler!"

Upon hearing the voice of her love, she halted in disbelief.

"Why have you returned to me after all these years?" she asked awoken within a dream.

"My love, I never left you."

"Let me bring light to wax so I might see your face," she said through the darkness.

"No!" he said quickly. "My years of imprisonment were hard and I wish you to think of me as I was, not as I am now."

"My father told me that he bribed you to test your loyalty and you took the money never to return!" she responded, unable to see him in the dark.

"I was falsely charged and thrown through Death's Door to keep us apart!"

"Who would have done such a thing?"

"I know not," he said not wanting to place blame on her family or husband.

"Was it my father… my husband?" she asked distraught.

He did not speak.

"Tell me, I can hear it in your voice! Who did this to us?" she screamed.

"I had to see you one last time."

Not wanting to lose him again, she pleaded into the obscurity, "Let me come with you!"

"My love, I am a fugitive, you would not want me now. I look a sickly man and I could not offer you any sort of life."

"My dear," she cried passionately into the dark, "when I accepted your proposal of marriage, I did not accept for your complexion or your money, I accepted only for love!"

His heart hurt hearing the profession of her love. He loved her more than anything he could ever dream possible and he wanted more than anything to accept her proposal and take her with him, but he had nothing to offer her. His future held only death, and although he cared not for himself, he loved her too much to expose her to his fate.

"My love, for some reason the gods chose to keep us apart and I feel to defy them again will only bring the two of us more sorrow. I am what I am today because I refused to accept your father's wishes and asked you to marry me."

"The gods are powerless! They could not punish me more than to take you away from me forever! I have not been happy since the day I saw you last. My husband treats me well and I have much, but my heart does not sing when I am with him as it is singing now!"

They ran together into the darkness and under the light of the moon embraced in a kiss.

"Take me with you!" she whispered into his ears. "I want not to suffer another day without your embrace!

"My love, I escaped from prison. The king's men search for me," he said holding her. "I will more than likely live a short life on the run for I am going where no man goes, the Dark Wood."

"I care not if you are going straight to the pits of Lusete!" she said holding him as tight as she could so not to lose him again. "Take me with you!"

He kissed her one last time and wrestled free from her grip.

"My fate is one I must suffer, I dare not expose you to it again." He said leaping out her window on to the small ledge and dropping onto the ground below.

The King Hamse stood ready, cushioning his friend's drop to the ground.

"Hurry, the servants heard the commotion upstairs and are starting to look around," said the king.

The two men ran across the noble's lands stealing two horses to aid in their escape toward the Dark Wood. As they rode away into the darkness, Pot rode with a broken heart but now fully dedicated to the aid of his new king. He feared nothing, happily awaiting death.

Celestie fell to the floor crying upon the departure of her love. She had always been able to somewhat accept their first separation for she had thought he had done so out of greed tarnishing his memory, but now knowing the truth, she couldn't bear to go on without him.

She lay in the floor crying when her servants found her, lighting candles and lifting her to her feet.

"What is wrong my lady?" asked her servant kindly.

"Nothing", she said recomposing herself. "I want you to go downstairs and finish preparing dinner. I will be down in a few minutes," she ordered wiping her eyes dry.

The servants did as she asked, going downstairs to prepare the lord and lady's dinner. They began to set their places at the table lighting lavish candles and laying out the finest dinner plates and silver. Steam rose from the many fine dishes of food placed upon the long table, which could serve up to a dozen people, but as every night served only two. The lord of the manor sat down across from his lady dressed in exceptional clothing tasting his food as an aristocrat, nibbling at to taste its flavor. He cradled a glass of wine in the palm of his hand using it to wash down his subtle meal. He lifted his knife and began to cut a thick slice of meat on his plate.

"Oh My Lord!" said his wife. "Let me cut that for you."

"I will get that My Lady," said a servant embarrassed that the lady of the home had to do something she herself should have done.

"Now you stay put, if a lady of a home cannot cut the food of her own husband, what kind of woman would she be?"

The lord of the manor dropped his knife, surprised to see his wife rush down to his end of the table to cut his meat. She sashayed down the length of the table holding up her long dress so not to step on its delicately tailored tail and took hold of his long dinner knife reaching around him from behind.

"I would not want my lord to cut swine with his bare hands. Let me do that!" she shrieked bringing the blade to his neck and slicing it all the way across. "You knew of Tyler's imprisonment and you hid it from me!"

Blood poured from the lord of the manor's neck onto his chest and into his plate covering it a scarlet red. The last name he heard was that of the man he thought he had condemned to death. The two chambermaids screamed upon seeing their lord fall face first into his plate dead by the hand of their lady. With wild eyes Celestie held up the blade which now dripped blood onto her quaint and elegant dinner gown.

"You stole the life I was meant to have and now you have paid with your own!" She raised the knife away from her chest pointing it toward her heart and spoke into the air, "I cannot live on knowing I betrayed my love for another all these years!"

Her chambermaids rushed to her seizing her hands, stopping her suicide. She wrestled with the two ladies, but upon losing her grip on the knife, she fell to the floor crying.

"I care not to live any longer!" she cried. "I care not to live any longer, my love!"

Part III
The Dark Wood

The two men rode without constraint pushing their mounts to their limits through the cold night toward the Dark Wood. Their lungs stung as the cold winter air filled their pleural cavities along the dark trail. They became nocturnal riding only at night and hiding through the light of day until they reached the wood's edge. The thick trees intertwined forming a wall of obscurity that separated the realm of man from that of beast.

"So you remember the way back?" asked Pot apprehensively from atop his horse.

"I was unconscious most of the way."

"I'm pretty sure you left that out of the conversation back in Death's Door."

"Look at it this way, if I got here with my eyes closed, think how quickly I can get us back with them open."

Pot looked behind at the rolling fields of his homeland. There was nothing left for them there but death or worse a reunion with Death's Door.

"Lead the way," he said facing what most men would have considered certain death.

The staunch men rode into the forest's shadows with two horses, half a sack of food from Pot's mother, a dinner knife and their wit to match its feral heart. Once inside the Dark Wood, King Hamse slipped off his horse and kneeled to the ground, shoveling out a small hole with his bare hands. He gently pulled the body of Wee out of his pocket, unwrapped it from a dirty piece of cloth, placed it within the hole and covered it with dirt, giving the beloved animal a proper burial. It had played as big a part in his escape as had both he and Pot, and it deserved to die with honor. Pot knew well the fragile mental state of a man who had been imprisoned for years and saw nothing unusual in the quiet ceremony, dismounting his own horse to pay the small rodent due respect. Without saying a word, the king climbed back onto his horse and started toward the heart of the black wood. Not knowing the way he traveled to reach Alboules, the king thought it would be best to travel directly south. Their horses grunted circling immense trees with trunks ten feet in diameter while stomping through the forest's thick brush and leaves. The royal equine used to wide open fields tired quickly struggling through the thick tree leaves, needles and twigs, which forced the two men to rest the beasts several times a day. The nights in the copious forest were harsh, as the men did not have furs to weather its temperatures, which dropped below freezing regularly. Had it not been for their fires, the men and their steeds would surely have frozen to death.

They rationed their food between themselves managing to stretch their supplies for eight days before they were exhausted. Their mounts, having nothing else, were forced to eat the inhospitable vegetation at the base of the forest becoming sick and near worthless to the men as they dragged their panting bodies through the primeval forest. In desperation, the men slew their horses for the value of their hides and flesh leaving their bony carcasses within the depth of the wood barely a morsel for the vultures. Charred by fire, they ate the flesh of their animals, devouring it to keep up their strength as they wandered on foot with no end in sight.

Unable to use the sun or the stars for direction because the sky was shielded from their eyes by the dense treetops, the men used the location of moss and spider webs to keep their bearings, but even though the king was an able hunter and tracker he was unsure of their direction. He kept his misgivings to himself leading on with the purpose of breaking through the unforgiving wild land where no man was king as that title belonged to the beasts of the wood. Many odd birds and other tree-bound prey taunted the king and his friend, as they had no weapons to strike at them from a distance calling at the two with strange sounds as though mocking their plight. They traveled seven more days wandering through the trees like restless ghosts haunting the forest with their faltering spirits. Nothing with respect to landmarks changed from one tree to another bestowing little faith to the men's progress until they came to the edge of an enormous river. It literally cut the thick woods in half exposing the men's skin to the warmth of the sun for the first time since they had entered the wood. It rushed wildly rolling roughly over tall rocks casting a cool mist into the air creating a holographic rainbow that straddled the deep river stretching twenty feet across at its narrowest point. The king pondered, if they were going in the right direction, how could an unconscious man on a horse have crossed such a fierce natural barrier? It was far too violent to attempt any crossing, but through the opening it created in the forest the king was able to use the stars to confirm their bearings. They traveled along its bank searching for a point to cross wading through the thick brush and thorn for three days without finding a single suitable location to make any such attempt. Pot followed the king as thorns gashed his skin with an unwavering demeanor, for his life had little meaning now that he had lost everything he ever loved. His mother and father, his work of clay and his only love Celestie had all been stolen from him. What god had he angered to deserve such a punishment he wailed within his heart. Had it not been for his debt to the king for his freedom from Death's Door, he would have killed himself at Celestie's feet the very moment he realized he could never have her. He looked at the man before him who looked no closer to royalty than a beggar, wearing rags covered by a blood-stained horse skin. But it mattered not to him if the man he followed was insane or a true king, he owned him his life.

The king stopped, turning his head slightly so better to hear the change in the sounds of the rushing water ahead. It got louder as if giving away to a waterfall. They traveled toward the noise stopping at the strange sight ahead. The huge river that slashed fiercely through the rough forest flowed ferociously into a huge cavern disappearing completely from the earth. Water rushed into the immense hole dropping out of sight thousands of feet below.

"I have seen water sprout from the earth, but I have never seen it disappear into it in such a substantial way," commented the king, standing near the mouth of the earth that drank in the giant river with a thirst unlike anything he had ever heard, yet alone seen.

"What cavern could hold the flow of such an immense river?" asked his companion, watching the rage of water vanish below his feet. "It is as if it has ripped through time and space disappearing into whatever is beyond."

"I had to have crossed the river from this side," the king said, getting his bearings.

The strange phenomenon gave him a better sense of direction and hope, as his mount could not have passed such a river except on one side. Although their loads were light, their muscles strained under the heavy burden of their body weight threatening to collapse at any moment during the long rugged march. The men made camp just at dusk before total darkness set in order to be prepared for the fierce cold that set in once the last glimmer of sunlight faded away. They prepared for the bitter nights and avoided hypothermia by digging a hole and then lying in it under the cover of dead leaves and vegetation. It was a primitive method to survive arctic nights King Hamse had learned from Sudal woodsmen as a prince, an effective technique allowing one to lower himself below the wind and provide cover on all sides so hold in the natural heat of their body. The more inhabitants it held the better. As his father would not allow him to hunt with his knowledge, the young prince had learned the secrets of the woods surreptitiously during the times his father was gone during long campaigns of war. He watched every action and heard every word of his teachers, finally becoming a master himself.

It was on the twentieth night of their march through the Mhorhaen that the king and Pot found a threat even greater than the merciless natural conditions within it. The two men were dug deep into the ground fast asleep to wait out the frost when the bloodcurdling howl of blood wolves cracked the night bringing the men out of their hole like defensive badgers. Under the red glow of embers from their dying fire, the king held his knife under the whispering wind listening intently. Blood wolves were huge canines standing near a meter and a half tall and weighing over two hundred pounds with solid black pelage marbled with bright red streaks along their face and body. Although large and fierce, their name did not come from their stature, but from their love of human flesh. A single blood wolf could take down an unarmed man with ease, while a full pack could ravage a small village, dragging off women and children into the night never to be heard from again. They hunted men like foxes did chickens, stealing them in the night under the cover of darkness. Thankfully for man, they never ventured far from the shelter of the Mhorhaen, something that did little to comfort the king and Pot who at the moment were deep within the animal's territory. The king knew if they were found his knife would do little to ward off such vicious beasts.

The pack caught the scent of the men's fading fire, and from past experience they had learned the burning scent of hot cinders was usually accompanied with soft flesh. Fearless of man in their territory under the cover of darkness, the pack swarmed the campsite as the two wary men scampered up the trunk of a large gnarled tree. King Hamse reached down grasping Pot's arm to keep him from tumbling to the ground as the alpha wolf took hold of the potter's leg. The beast's sharp canine teeth slashed the flesh on his leg as they glided along it glancing off his ankle before disappearing in a snap on the way back down to the forest floor. Blood oozed from the wound dripping its scent into the air and bringing the pack to frenzy as they leaped at the two men dragging their claws down the length of the tree's trunk, shredding its bark in frantic attempts to reach them. With each leap, the beasts' snaps came close forcing the men to climb further to the top of the tree until its branches began to sway dangerously. The huge beasts gnashed their long teeth, flinging saliva at the men in anticipation of tasting their bloody flesh.

Unable to scale the tree the pack began to circle its broad trunk as if contemplating a way to dethrone the two men. They growled and bayed at the men throughout the cold night snarling in frustration at missing the kill as they wandered off before the glow of morning light. The men's fingers, frozen tightly around the branches of the tree, throbbed with pain. The king unlocked his stiff joints painfully pulling them free and rubbing them briskly to return their vacated blood flow. Pot looked over at the king from a neighboring branch with a raised brow unsure if the beasts had left or not. The king slid down the frosted tree skating to the ground with the speed of gravity without friction tumbling to the snow-covered ground. After the king searched the area, Pot slid from his perch rubbing his fingers in an attempt to awaken them and avoid frostbite. Being without any sort of supplies, the men resumed trudging through the copious undergrowth trailblazing where no trail had ever been. To be better armed, the king used his knife to turn long branches into primitive spears, so that they might be able to defend themselves from another attack. They doubled the value of their spears using them as walking sticks while keeping eyes and ears alert for signs of the wild fiends.

As the days wore on, the men's stomachs growled as their gastric juices churned without purpose and their bodies pulled free the last of their personal fat stores leaving the men literally with nothing in regards to nourishment. The cruel forest offered little to compensate their hunger during the harsh winter months yielding only a few identifiable roots, some tree bark, grubs and ants as reward for their troubles of digging in its hard frozen soil, looking under rocks and gathering along their way. They stayed hydrated by sucking on ice and kept their minds clear by staying engaged in conversation. Four weeks had past and the men knew not it they were any closer to their journey's end than when they first began. On a good day, they could call it that because they found something to eat, the two men found a nest high within a tree full of eggs and dined on them like wild animals sucking out their innards removing the seeds of life from them to nourish their own. The king's sharp eye's brought them many a meal, spotting edible fungus and a mess of toads, which they feasted on carefully so to avoid the toxins from their parotoid glands.

Another day broke over the Mhorhaen marking the forty-third of their trek. The men meandered with diminishing hope as days passed and their bodies broke down from malnourishment. The small animals, insects and vegetation they foraged throughout the journey and the weather they fought along the way did little to raise their spirits. Their beards hung as low as their fortitude as they dragged themselves on, fighting nature with the last of their strength. A powerful blizzard blew down from above dropping onto the forest floor slowing down the men as they drudged through it with shuffling feet. Pot's leg wound from the blood wolves' attack had swollen from infection and finally collapsed from underneath him as he fell face first into the snow, ready to die. The king rushed to his aid and after seeing they could not continue through the mounting snow, took to building a permanent shelter. If they were to make it through the Mhorhaen, they would have to weather its winter first. He began the process of building a stout wigwam by bending long live tree branches to create a framework and then finished the structure by using grass, bark and weeds as roofing material. The assembly had a small louver on the top to allow smoke to escape and a draft channel in the side to sustain a warm fire. Leaving his friend inside to stay warm and heal, he trekked into the deep snow in search of food. With the coming of snow, the fungus disappeared, while the toads and insects went underground leaving him empty handed. He dug up frozen roots and peeled the bark from trees boiling them into horrid stews so to keep up their strength. The winter wore on engulfing the men with its swirling fury. The king fought the fury of winter with all his might for two more weeks until he no longer had the strength to hunt firewood, collapsing next to his friend welcoming death. He had cheated death in Death's Door, but death always collected its debts and now it demanded payment. King Hamse pulled Pot close to him as the flames of their fire disappeared into smoke. His friend had fallen unconscious the night before and at the moment only expressed life through shallow breathing. He had been a great king, living with the luxuries of lush fur, warm stone palaces and obedient servants, but of all the men he had the pleasure of knowing, he knew of no other he would to prefer to die beside.

A shadowed form flipped aside the wigwam's door, finding the two men unconscious and at the point of death. After examining their vital signs, the man drug the two men out into the snow and threw them upon a hinny before covering them with thick furs. He led the stubborn hinny and his new-found cargo back to a longhouse built into a hillside on the opposite side of the winter wind. The dark figure covered in thick furs dragged the two bodies inside, slamming the door behind him, trapping out every aspect of the wind, including its long cold howls. His muscular arms dragged the two bodies through the silent interior of the hillside stretching them out in front of a stone fireplace. A metal rod stirred its coals crackling a fresh flame before the shadow clad arm added dry wood to the fire. The man returned back to the ice and snow to lead his hinny into a small barn tightly insulated with caked daub to repel the outside elements. He returned to his small home bolting the door for the night with a large wooden plank three inches thick. Once inside, he thrust thick rawhide into the crack under the door successfully sealing the three men off from the rage of the Mhorhaen. The mysterious form removed a long cloak revealing a sharp hand axe hanging from his hip and a long bow slung across his back. Muscular hands pulled aside heavy furs revealing strong knotted arms as firm as the knots of the trees he fell for firewood daily. A thick matted hunter's beard covered his firm jaws set below weathered green eyes. The hunter examined Pot's wounded leg, wrapping it in a large green leaf he pulled from a wooden box, tying it in place with string. He wet the leaf with warm water and massaged it, forcing the leaf's juices into the open lesion. He stretched out onto a mound of furs serving as a divan, having done all he could for the near-frozen men. Their fate was now in the hands of the gods. May they not forsake them as they had him, his country and people he thought before drifting off to sleep in the warmth of his hillside bungalow.

A stream of smoke poured from an isolated hillside into the cold Mhorhaen winter as the wild hunter's home defied the forces of nature. King Hamse's eyes opened to find a much larger residence than the primitive wigwam in which he had lost consciousness. Furs thicker than the shabby horsehides he had worn lay beneath him and his friend. A robust fire flickered bringing benign warmth to his skin. He rose up to examine the interior of the hunter's cabin. Bear, wolf and giant elk hides covered its walls, as well as the many weapons and tools of an avid hunter. Bows, swords, whips and all sorts of traps and snares hung ready to be commanded. His hand reached across to feel Pot's pulse, and to his relief he found him alive. The door to the cabin burst open spitting snow and wind into its interior as a black image of a man covered in leather and fur stood stalwartly staring at him. The only part of his body the king could see was the piercing stare of his green eyes. The form slammed the door behind it and bolted the thick wooden door shut before dropping the corpse of a snow hare onto a stout wood table. The thing removed its veil exposing to the alert king that it was a man as himself and not some primordial monster. The two men, both hunters by nature, spoke their initial greeting not with words, but with a simple nod. Silence was a sign of respect between hunters as they were solitary folk appreciating a man for his silent presence over the noise of his voice. When a hunter spoke it was necessary, for such men did not engage in idle chatter.

"I am Werthhard the forester," he said, sitting down at the table to skin his kill, for even the hide of a small hare made good boots or gloves.

"I am Alvirik the woodsman," said the king giving his first name and a commoner title so not to divulge his last name.

In the Lands of Dream, the title of forester meant a man was a freelance huntsman who lived solely off the land with no allegiance to any country or king, while a woodsman was a commoner who hunted as a trade. Foresters led solitary lives as it was a crime to be caught hunting on the lands of king with whom you paid no tithe. The king himself had always seen the law as fair for it was the king that protected the land and preserved its forest. Now he found himself aided by those he had once convicted.

"Things must be bad in your country as well to bring a woodsman so far out into the Mhorhaen during the heart of winter," said his host peeling the skin from the hare.

"We seek the borders of Haenic," King Hamse answered simply.

"Are you from there?" he asked curiously.

"It is the land of my fathers."

"Have you been there in some time?" asked the hunter concentrating on his work at hand.

"Not for many years," replied the king.

"I know not about the time of your fathers, but I myself was once a woodsman of the northern province of Sudal, coming out here to be a forester by choice. Haenic has fallen upon dark times, being ruled by black magic and sorcery."

The king's eyes opened wide hearing of the blight upon his land.

"Sorcery?"

"Of the worst sort," he replied with a disapproving grunt. "The land no longer has a true king, but that of a black wizard who rules through fear and death while practicing blood rituals upon his own people."

"What happened to the king?" asked King Hamse curious of how he supposedly found his demise.

"Lost during a hunt," he answered quickly recounting what he had been told, "and as he left no heirs, a power struggle ensued between the nobles bringing the kingdom's many provinces to war. While the nobles fought, a mage who served as one of the king's astronomers ambitiously rose to power wielding the powers of the dead having many of the nobles assassinated under the cover of night by his minions from the grave."

The king held his silence so as not to reveal his identity to his host. He was a proud man humbled by his position and until he reclaimed his throne, he would not claim to be a king again.

"I was surprised to see the smoke from your shelter. The two of you are the first men I have seen out here in the Mhorhaen since I relocated here early last year."

"We ran into trouble with some blood wolves a few days back."

"Ah, fierce creatures they are, lords over these woods and higher on the food chain than I!" he boasted in respect of the beasts.

"What of the jejir?"

"Never seen one of those!" he replied in laughter. "Merely myths if you ask me."

The king held his tongue once again to respect the man's beliefs in his own home and also not to steer the conversation toward his true identity. The conversation, long-winded by hunter's standards, ended as the man threw the hare's body into a bubbling pot and slammed a lid on top of it. Being hand-fed by the king, Pot slowly made a full recovery with the aid of the hunter's food and herbalism, being able to stand normally in just over a month in his care. Both men's muscles grew under the endless chores of a forester in the course of chopping wood, hunting game, tanning hides, cooking and sewing. Holding a bow again restored the king's strength of mind, and with it in hand he was without fear of man or beast. After two months with the proficient hunter, the two men took their leave for Haenic, never revealing the identity of the king to their host. The fireside stories of his lost kingdom forced him out into the winter wind to set the wrong he had unwittingly set into motion. According to the solitary hunter, they were no more than ten days from his kingdom's borders, and with the help of some donated gear and a few supplies, the men would have little trouble making it unless foiled by the forest's beasts.

It was a harsh trek through knee-high snow and brush, but with his homeland so close, the king fared toward it without complaint. The picturesque image of its fields and rolling hills carried him forward. Hearing of its existence from another besides the king brought a thousand questions to the lips of Pot who bombarded the taciturn king. As a king, had this been a hunt and had Pot been his servant, he would have smacked him to shut him up, but this was different as Pot was his friend and being away so long, he enjoyed discussing his kingdom as much as his friend enjoyed hearing about it. He discussed its vast territories, which were more than twice that of

Pot's own country Alboules, the strength of its people and the fecundity of its lands. It was a proud nation where although the men of the land were vassals of territorial nobles, they were free to choose their profession whether it be that of farmer, artisan, merchant, trade skill or huntsman and all paid a flat tax upon their goods to their reining noble. The travelers spent their nights under a lean tent made of olien pelt, which was highly water resistant keeping the men dry in the freezing rains that mercilessly showered down upon them. Being generously equipped as hunters, the elements became little more than uncomfortable nuisances as they trekked forward unyielding to the forces of nature.

The thick forest threatened to squeeze the men to death between its tightly woven trunks, vines and thorns until abruptly it disappeared as they stepped outside its dark border into open land. The king stood aghast at the broken land of his birth which now to his gaze seemed almost unrecognizable. The once-plowed fields were overrun with weeds and tall grass, its houses in the distance appeared unkempt and although just after noon, not a man women or child stood outside working or playing. Of everything the king had endured over the past two years, it was the impoverishment of his lands that hurt him the most.

Ashamed of its appearance, the king treaded ahead through the tall grass saying nothing to his friend, who followed him looking at a country that appeared nothing like the stories he had been told. An unwelcome king and his friend walked past orchards with broken trees, long-untilled fields and abandoned cottages. The once vibrant community had somehow evaporated along with his absence. The king walked to a familiar home, finding its door swinging with the rhythm of the wind. It was the home of the family he had stayed with the night before his departure into the Mhorhaen over two years ago. Everything sat as he remembered it, but unused and covered in dust as if abandoned in the wake of some unknown catastrophe. Plates and aged pots sat upon the room's center table, waiting for the ghosts of the manor to return for dinner. The man of this home had lost his son, daughter-in-law and his only grandchild to a beast of the Mhorhaen; now it appeared he had lost everything else in the king's absence. The king kicked over the table in frustration of finding his kingdom in shatters. Those responsible for such reckless abandonment would pay as terrible price, he promised in silence, they would pay with blood. The king stormed out of the small home with fury in his eyes. He desired to rip a man apart like the beast of the Mhorhaen with his bare hands.

"King," said Pot following him outside, "where do we go now?"

The king stopped and turned toward him with anger bleeding from his eyes, "We journey to Balroic the capital of Haenic!"

Having cheated death once before Pot was already living on borrowed time and he knew it. It was of no consequence to avoid it now. He would welcome it with open arms to end his own misery, so that maybe the gods would allow him to at least spend the afterlife with his precious Celestie.

The two men searched the remains of the village's forsaken homes and barns for anything of use for their long journey to the huge empire's centrally-located capital. Upon searching a barn, a voice surprised the men.

"Move along, thieves!" said the voice coming out of thin air. "There is nothing left to steal!"

The king and Pot, unsure of where the voice was coming from, froze using their eyes to scan the large interior of the barn.

"We are not thieves," said the king in response.

"What do you call entering a building and taking things that are not yours?"

The king's finely-honed ears focused upon the voice trying to locate its origin among the echo of the barn.

"I am lord of this land," proclaimed the fur-donned hunter, "everything within it belongs to me!"

An elderly man stepped out of the shadows clutching a crossbow.

"I should run you through right now for speaking like that!" he pronounced to the king. "This land has no king and is rotting away under the rule of black magic!"

The king recognized the old man as the man he had stayed with before entering the Mhorhaen to return the bodies of his lost kin. A smile appeared upon the face of the worn king upon seeing a countryman he knew.

"Stand back you worthless dreg," warned the old man upon seeing the king move closer. "I knew the once-great king of this land, and he had too much honor to pillage those with nothing!"

"Rillait," said the king speaking the old man's family name, "it is I. I have returned from the wood to take back the land that was once mine."

The old man looked at him suspiciously eyeing him with his one good eye.

"Move closer so I can see you, but keep your hands down or I will end your life rogue."

The king took the order of his own vassal walking closer until the man signaled for him to stop. The old man looked at his face covered with a thick beard far wilder than the neatly trimmed beard he had seen him with some two years before. The old man stared deep into his eyes. He had loved his one-time king for the compassion of his personal loss some time back and would have died in his defense if ever asked. The face was sunken from years under the cover of darkness in the dungeons of Alboules, but his eyes were the same. Upon recognizing his own great king, the old man fell to the ground begging for forgiveness of the way he had spoke to the king.

"My lord, please forgive me for the words I spoke! I knew not that it was you!"

"It is I who begs your mercy for the blight upon the land."

"When four horses came out of the forest carrying the bodies of my family and the slain beast with no one to guide them, everyone believed that you were dead and that your ghost must have guided them back to honor your promise to your people!" cried the man weeping into his hands while upon his knees.

"I have returned to take back the throne of my father and return Haenic to its previous glory!"

"My king, you must be cautious," said the elderly man speaking from his knees, "Zespheous has brought the lands of Zeethe into dark times in your absence by worshipping evil gods and sacrificing those that defy his will to Eidolen, the watchful eye. He practices black magic behind the walls of your fortress sending out the dead to hunt and destroy men who have not pledged their never-dying loyalty to him. Those that will not serve him in life will serve him in death."

"Zespheous!" yelled the king remembering the man as an astrologer in his court. "It is he that has brought such affliction on the land?"

"Yes my lord. He has used black magic to rot the land and steal its dead to serve him unconditionally. The men here stood against him and as punishment, an army of the dead marched to our borders, raping the land and murdering all those that did not flee into the forest. Those that fled into the woods surely died themselves from the beasts within," he said sadly. "I hid in the top of this barn not allowing that foul warlock to run me off my land until the stink of the dead roamed on to other parts of the kingdom to bring it all under his rule."

"Where are all the bodies?" asked Pot curiously.

"The dead drag the corpses of the slain away so that Zespheous might use them to fill the ranks in his army of the dead."

"Does any part of our country still stand free?" asked the king.

"Before the attack on our land, only the barbarians of Kthaer and the horsemen of Yeathon stood independent."

"Then we shall travel to Kthaer and Yeathon to raise an army to free Haenic and its people."

"My lord, I mean no disrespect to you, but the weapons of men are no match for the dead. When they attacked our village, men shot them in the heads and pierced their hearts but they kept coming overwhelming their victims by tearing their flesh apart with their teeth and hands like wild animals. The only way to stop them is to behead them and even then their bodies move about blindly trying to kill."

The king listened to the old man carefully. For at the moment he was his only knowledgeable advisor.

"If we cannot kill the dead, then we shall kill the one who controls their black hearts."

"My lord, I no longer possess the strength of my youth, but I can still shoot straight. If you would take an old man with nothing left to live for but to serve you, I will pledge you my life."

"My dear man," said the king grasping the old man's hand, "your fate as mine is tied to the land of your birth. No one, even I, have the right to refuse you your birthright."

Part IV
Two Kings, One Kingdom

Three shadows moved through the countryside with vigilance avoiding roads, open fields and the broad daylight like ghouls slinking outside the watchful eye of Eidolen. Dead roamed freely cavorting along the landscape searching for living to consume in the defense of their resurrector. They stumbled and fell as they roamed like drunkards lusting to consume all forms of life. The men avoided their lifeless eyes moving as do hunters using the terrain for cover even crawling through tall grass fields like snakes on their bellies to stay out of sight. They traveled through the northern province of Sudal staying clear of mindless zombies, stopping upon the sight of a large fort unlike any the king or the old man of the land had seen. Its walls were made of tall tree trunks stacked tightly together side by side nearly twenty-five feet in height. Its walls were painted a horrid purple with random drab yellow crests in the shapes of a large eye, the symbol for the dark watchful god Eidolen. Tall plumes of smoke poured from the top of the fort's opening, their fires providing warmth against the cold winter wind for the flesh of the living, as the dead's flesh needed neither nourishment nor warmth. The men were unsure whether it was a fort or a prison, but either way, the king's curiosity was too great to pass the strange structure without at least examining it first. If men were being forced into imprisonment, then they might fight with the king, and if they were men from his country that were allies of the evil Zespheous, then they should die even if he had to do so as might a common thief and slit their throats while they slept.

The three men waited until the cover of night before crossing the large field surrounding the immense fortification. They listened outside its thick walls, but were unable to hear a sound beyond the whistling of the severe north wind. Traveling along its wall, the three men cautiously found its front gate strangely unguarded. The gate was ten feet tall made of large split tree trunks firmly bolted shut from the inside. The agile king leapt onto the large double door and shimmied to its top dropping down into the inside of the stronghold without making a noise. Muscular hands quickly slid open its main gate letting in the king's two companions. Inside the tall fort's walls were hastily built homes of mud, clay and straw, a far cry from the carpentry skill of his people who normally built beautifully strong homes of polished wood and cobbled stone. The men ran alongside the fortress's inner walls using the back of the homes to hide themselves from view. Not a soul stood outside in the open under the light of the moon.

A door opened to a cabin a few homes down as a young boy threw some water into the street. The king slipped up behind the child on the tip of his toes seizing his mouth and waist pulling him behind the flimsy built hut. The boy bit onto the tough calloused palm of the king, drawing blood. The king barely winced when the boy's teeth dug into his flesh as he carried the helpless child into the shadows of the fortress wall and threw him down onto the ground looking deep into his terror-stricken eyes.

He pressed down onto the boy's mouth holding his head tight. "If you scream, I will kill you," warned the king.

The boy quit struggling as the king removed the palm of his hand from the youth's lips.

"Thank the gods!" praised the boy in elation. "I thought some of the dead had gotten into the village."

"What type of village is this?" asked the king.

"It is a farmer's commune," answered the boy as if the men should know such a common thing.

"One that serves Zespheous?"

"Yes of course, who else is there?" answered the boy from his short inexperienced memory.

"Son, you speak with the true king of this land," declared old man Rillait holding his crossbow. "Show him respect before I let you serve Zespheous in death instead of life."

"I did not know kings kidnapped boys in the night," responded the boy. "I took you for rogues."

"How dare you speak to the king like that!" yelled the old man in anger of the insult against his king. He grabbed the boy's hair entangling it within his fingers attempting to jerk him from the king's grip and throttle him.

"Rillait, please remember you also insulted me upon first sight; he does not know what he says."

"I am sorry, my Lord, I knew not," replied the frightened boy.

"You have done no wrong, boy," said the king reassuring the startled youth. "Tell us about this place and how it came to serve Zespheous."

"Talein!" screamed a woman's voice from the front of the hut.

The king quickly covered the young boy's mouth and signaled for Rillait to hold the boy still while he and Pot slipped around the side of the home to see who was calling to the boy. A woman dressed in dirty peasant clothing spotted their movement and screamed as the two men pushed her into the candlelit interior of the hut. A man jumped up from a small table in the room as the two men pushed the terrified woman in the cabin only to be knocked to the floor by a punch from the king. Rillait followed in from behind with the boy, slamming the door to the small shelter sealing them inside.

"Stay calm," said the king holding out his hands. "We are here to help you."

"Who are you?" asked the man holding his jaw while lying on the floor.

"This is King Hamse the Third!" replied Rillait as if announcing the entrance of a king into his court.

The man and woman nervously looked at the invaders without speaking.

"We are not here to harm you, but to help," stated the king to ease their fears.

"Take what you want, just let us be!" cried the lady of the small home terrified.

"We are not here to rob you, but to ask you a few questions," said the king in a soothing tone.

The man rose to his feet and offered a chair across from him at the table, "Please."

The king sat down across from the man and looked into his eyes, "Tell me about this place."

"This is a farmer's commune, we grow food for the dining halls of King Zespheous."

"How dare you call that vile sorcerer king!" screamed Rillait. The king signaled for his loyal servant to calm down.

"Please continue."

"While Zespheous doesn't need live men to fight for him, he needs us to grow his food, make armor for his armies, sew his clothes, build his compounds. For men who agree to serve him, they are placed in protective communes where some grow food as ours, while others are artisans or blacksmiths. The forts protect us from his dead that roam freely across the land killing anyone living not Zespheous himself."

"And you agreed to this madness?" yelled Rillait.

"What other choice did I have? The trained knights of the nobles could not stop his armies. What chance did I as a farmer have?"

"You could have fought like my countrymen instead of cowering in here like a dog with his tail between his legs!"

"And where are your countrymen now? I do what I do to keep my family safe!"

"Please, Rillait, not another word," ordered the king. "Zespheous has no garrison here?"

"He does not need one since we cannot leave without being killed by the dead."

"How does he get the food from you?" asked Pot.

"During the harvest season, men dressed in long purple cloaks come leading wagons pulled by the dead chained to it like sled dogs. As long as we fill the wagons, they leave us alone."

"And if you don't?" he replied.

"I do not know. The gods have blessed our crop yields to now, leaving enough extra food for us to scrape by during the winter."

"Does Zespheous have a stronghold close to where he has men that could work against us if he knew of our presence?" asked the king.

"I know not of anything beyond these walls," he stated sadly.

"I would like an audience with the people of this commune. Can you arrange it?"

"Yes."

"Go then, tell them their king has returned and wishes to speak with them."

"Talein, go to every house and tell them to meet in the square."

"Yes sir," said the boy, running outside.

The men watched the man and woman, leery of possible trickery, until the boy returned huffing and puffing.

"Everyone is gathering in the square."

"Let me go speak with my people."

The king walked to the square followed by Pot and Rillait finding a rabble of men women and children covered in the dirt of the land waiting to meet the man who claimed to be their real king. King Hamse climbed onto a wagon and spoke.

"My people, I am King Hamse the Third, rightful lord over these lands!" he declared loudly above their heads. "Our land has become infested with the dead. I ask you to rise with me so we can cast them back below the earth where Zespheous and his servants belong!"

"Where is your army?" asked a man from the group.

"You shall be the first, but not the last! We will travel across the land liberating other communes on our way to Balroic to cast Zespheous from power!"

"The nobles with armed knights could not defeat his armies. How can farmers with hoes and pitchforks do what trained warriors could not do with sword and shield?" screamed a cynic.

"You cannot kill that which is already dead!" screamed another.

"We need not kill the dead!" he stated. "All we need to do is overrun the palace and kill Zespheous, once he is dead, the dead will return to their graves."

"Overrun his castle… with what?" asked another man. "We have no siege weapons, no artifacts of war!"

"Who says you are our king? I have never seen you before in my life and I was born here!" screamed a disbeliever.

"If we rise against Zespheous he will send an army of the dead to eat us!" shouted another.

"Shut up you fools!" roared Rillait. "I was born in this land before most of your fathers bed your mothers, and to see my own countrymen cower behind walls built by our enemy as the dead defile your lands sickens me! You are not men... no wonder Zespheous didn't kill you, you weren't worth the time!"

The men in the assembly began to grumble among themselves, angered by the insults thrown at them. The king tried to regain their attention, but the crowd, broken in spirit, had already turned against him and began to disperse back into the village. Once it had dissolved, not a single man had taken up his call to arms leaving the monumental task of killing Zespheous to the king, Pot and Rillait.

The king left the compound with a greater insight of his enemy, but low in spirit seeing his own people lacking the courage to help him free their land. The men traveled under darkness setting up a camp in a small wooded area to hide from the roving dead during the day. As the weary men slept, they rotated on single man guard shifts to be wary for wandering dead. Pot sat the first shift sitting outside their lean-to tent fighting fatigued eyes that threatened to close on him at any moment. His head began to nod as he struggled between the worlds of consciousness and unconsciousness. He fought the cloud of sleep with all his might as it engulfed him, gently caressing him as his passed beyond the Wall of Sleep. Suddenly with the speed of a hawk, he was past the far distance of the Mhorhaen and once again in his home country and to his delight he was no longer a fugitive but free to sit at his potter's wheel and mold with his hands once again. He smiled softly feeling the pleasure of creating something from nothing, placing the fine objects in his stove and stoking up its heat with a prod. When he returned to his cottage, Celestie greeted him at the door with a hug and small peck on the lips. The aroma of a fresh pie baking in the oven filled his nasal passages as his eyes opened to the sight of a man with flesh rotting on his bones.

Suddenly he found himself back in the cold woodlands of Haenic with a hungry zombie starring into his eyes salivating for his flesh. He fell over backwards from the horrid creature as the half-man half-skeleton figure tried to seize him. Pot screamed as he kept the creature at bay by kicking it backward with his feet to wake his sleeping companions. The decomposing man snapped at his legs and feet trying to tear his flesh from his bones as the king and Rillait tore through the top of the lean tent slinging it out of the way. The king pulled a forester's axe from his belt and ran to the aid of his friend who was keeping the zombie a leg's length away.

Upon seeing the king, the zombie turned upon him running toward him with raised arms and gnashing teeth. The king's axe caught the base of its neck at a forty-five degree angle dropping its head from its stalk leaving it dangling onto its chest as it persisted clumsily to try and find him. A second blow from the axe took its head completely off leaving the body without sight bumping into trees and brush in search of its intended victims. The three men commenced to chop the perverted creature into little pieces, which continued to wiggle no matter how small they hacked it under the control of Zespheous' magic.

"What black magic is this that will not relinquish its control over the dead even when in it is in a hundred pieces?" asked the king in bewilderment.

"The black heart of necromancy," spit Rillait in disgust.

"How could they fight such things?" thought Pot, gazing in terror at the bloody squirming mass.

It took three men to disable it completely, and if they encountered more than one, they would not stand a chance. The sound of a twig snapping broke the beguiling allure of the shifting dead fragments upon the three bewildered men swinging their attention to their back. Rillait released an arrow from his crossbow with a thump firing at a darkened silhouette barely missing it as his arrow embedded into a tree.

"Please don't kill me!" screamed a voice.

The three men held back their attack as a young boy's face peered around a tree. It was the young face of the boy from the fort.

"What are you doing here, boy?" asked the king at the sight of the child's young face.

The boy, carrying a sickle as a weapon, ran up to the king kneeling before him while holding down his head in respect. "My Lord I came to serve you and help you rid the curse upon the land."

"Do you realize what would have happened to you if one of Zespheous' servants had found you alone?" reprimanded the king.

"I care not, my Lord, please do not refuse my service!" pleaded the boy with tears in his eyes.

"Your parents will be distraught in your absence. You must return to them," replied Pot in the best interest of the boy.

"My parents were killed during the Dead Wars, and my guardians only took me in, because their own children were taken away by the servants of Zespheous," answered the boy sadly. "Please do not send me back! I can fight as hard as any man! The black sorcerers of Zespheous keep coming and taking the children away. None come back, please don't send me there."

The king had a sharp mind, as keen as his hunter's reflexes, and he never forgot a name of anyone who made an impression upon him.

"Young Talein, by the laws of Haenic set down by my grandfather, a king cannot refuse a man the right to defend the land on which he was born."

"But he is just a boy!" declared Rillait in protest.

"Aye, but he has the true heart of a man!"

The sovereign leader lifted up his newest recruit who smiled with the pride of acceptance. Now the leader of a rabble including an old man, a young boy and a foreigner, the king without a land wondered if they were Haenic's last hope to rid itself of the disease placed upon it by the black magic of Zespheous and if so, what chance did it and its people really have?

The small group packed up camp as the sun faded away in order to travel under the cold blanket of night. Their human retinas did little to reflect the pale light of the moon, exposing only shades and shadows of images leaving the men vulnerable to attack. Unwittingly the men stumbled into a group of dead roaming through the night. The creatures brought back to life by dark arcane magic swarmed in on the men trapping them within the surrounding trees. The king swung his axe chopping into the flesh of his assaulters decapitating them as a lumberjack would trees separating their limbs from their torsos as heads, legs and arms dropped to the frozen earth. The young boy in a panic dodged his slower attackers shifting between the trunks of trees to avoid the grip of their hands and the bite of their teeth. Pot, unskilled with a blade, fell back unable to stop his attackers only to be saved by the king who stood above him not allowing the dead to overwhelm his best friend. Rillait fought behind the king defending his flank, but lacked the strength of his youth and was unable to decapitate his assaulters falling to their fury in a torrent of shredding teeth and fingernails. The king began to chop at the dead upon his servant sinking the sharp blade of his axe into the back of their skulls and pulling them away, but as the dead smelled the blood of the fallen, they swarmed upon the helpless man tearing him apart before the desperate king. They engorged themselves on his tissue covered in blood down the length of their arms, smearing it across their faces as they shoved his entrails into their mouths.

More dead, hearing the cries of battle, began to roam toward the three remaining men as they ran from the onslaught into the unknown dark ahead. The dead chased after them clumsily trying to overwhelm the men with their seemingly endless numbers. King Hamse swung his axe at those that opposed their flight, dropping them in single blows with its razor-sharp blade. The churning legs of the living quickly outdistanced the deteriorating legs of the dead separating the two factions into the obscurity of night. The hearts of the three survivors pounded in their chests as they ran without constraint pushing the will of their muscles to their breaking point until the young boy began to falter behind the strength of the two men.

"Come on boy, lest you feed the dead!" urged the king.

The youth, strong in heart, pushed his body until it would respond no more plunging face first into the tall grass. A hand seized his arm lifting him up into the air dragging him through the swaying grass. He spun around onto his back helplessly watching the stars in the sky streak by, as he was drug across the field and into the cover of trees. The fleeing men collapsed along with the boy into damp leaves and gasped for air to refill their bodies' exhausted oxygen supply. The king wasn't entirely sure if they had lost their blood-thirsting pursers, but it mattered not, as he could go no further. Neither of the three could erase the memory of Rillait being consumed alive before their eyes as they gathered their strength while hiding like foxes on the run. Even the king, who had stood against the wild beasts of the Mhorhaen, was shocked by the ferocity of the dead in their attacks. They attacked without restraint and in numbers so great as to overwhelm even those who might be superior in skill or strength. Slightly raising his head, King Hamse looked out across the great field they crossed finding it empty. He fell backwards in relief for the preservation of their own lives but in quiet remorse for Rillait the Faithful.

The three refugees rested with the fear of discovery hanging over their heads for they knew they did not have the energy to make another such escape from the walking dead. It was still early in the night when they rose to continue their march, giving them several good hours of travel time before daylight. The night hid them from the roaming eyes of the staggering dead as they moved across the land toward its great capital. During the king's reign, Balroic was the finest city in all of Zeethe with giant towers of marble and manmade rivers that intertwined into the city irrigating the people's crops and forming beautiful gardens throughout the marvelous city. His citadel was majestic in nature built with stone carved by the land's greatest artisans brought over by ship with extreme cost in life and riches from the ancient rock quarries of wild Mauklica, where man still did not reign supreme over strange races of humanoids that held it firm from the expansion of mankind. These same stones had been used to build the great ruins of Abka, the first human city that rose in Zeethe, stealing its territories from the beasts and humanoids that now had been pushed across the great southern sea. The naturally smooth stone glittered like the stars at night in the bright sun creating a glowing aura around it as if heavenly in nature.

The men moved slowly so as not to make the same mistake which almost placed them within the stomachs of the dead, when the king signaled for his companions to stop with the silent palm of his hand. A fire flickered in the distance. The king smiled because only the living needed warmth and if it was living, he could kill it. The men slinked through the darkness, creeping up upon the glow to see what stood near its warmth. At first glance the king leaned back shocked as he saw the blank eyes of the dead gleaming under its light, but at a closer glance he found that they were chained to a large stake in the ground. Sitting far from the dead huddled up next to the fire were men in long cloaks staring into the fire. The strange men laughed as they spoke in tongues unknown to the men, adding fuel to the fire growing it as they did their magic. They were conjurers, capable of bringing forth objects, elements and beasts from the thin air to aid them in the heat of battle and overwhelm those they opposed. In all there appeared to be five of the mystical men along with thirty or so dead under their command. If they were to kill the men, they would have to do so quickly, for if they freed the dead or got off one of their spells, then the king and his untrained companions would be sure to fall before their might. The king pulled forth a hunter's arrow and placed it within his bow. He whispered for Pot and the young Talein to move to the other side of the camp and be ready to attack upon his first shot. He waited as the two figures of his faithful companions crawled through the tall frozen grass inching toward their targets. The talkative conjurers with little to fear from the people of Zeethe sat next to their fire oblivious to what was about to befall them.

A black arrow soared through the night invisible to even the man who released it piercing the skull of its target sinking deep within its brain. A second arrow fired quickly hitting another of the men in the chest directly in the center of the yellow symbol of Eidolen upon his robe. Blood flowed from his mouth drowning out the magic, which began to pour from it. Another of the sorcerers stood erect flinging his long purple cloak aside to chant dark words of the past which formed a floating white figure before him. It spiraled from the mist of the night into a solid form with red eyes and long claws hovering gently above the ground. The ghostly form vanished as young Talein leaped from the weeds decapitating its creator with his sickle as he had reaped wheat hundreds of times before during his daily chores. Pot chopped the fourth wizard to the ground with a fierce blow from his forester's axe sinking it deep within the conjurer's chest splitting his sternum wide and expelling his bowels.

The dead, chained to the ground, began to go wild trying to reach the enemies of their creators, tugging at their chains and moaning madly in the darkness. The king raised his bow to kill the final wizard, but lowered it as his two companions crossed his line of fire, taking away any possibility of a clear shot. The last of the casters spoke ancient words from the humanoid gods of old giving him power over the elements of the mind, spewing fire from his fingertips which engulfed the pair as they leaped into the darkness rolling in the cold grass instinctively attempting to put out the intense flames on their flesh. The hot flames scorched their skin painfully burning the tissue from their bones before their eyes. The king's arrow took flight gyrating through the cold still air boring into the back of the caster's skull dropping him to the ground in silence. As soon as the final caster dropped dead, the searing pain of fire extinguished itself from their skin leaving the two men without even the slightest burn. Even with the death of their masters, the dead continued to try and break free from their bonds to engorge themselves upon the flesh of the living.

"What of the dead?" asked Pot rubbing his arms as if they were still burning.

"Burn them to dust," replied the king.

Flames rose upon the dead from the tips of torches growing and feeding upon their dry flesh like oiled wicks. The dead fought at the flames crazily trying to put them out as they collapsed one by one to become smoking corpses upon the ground.

"It appears that fire alone can rid Zespheous' hold upon their souls," declared the king gazing into the fire. "If that is what it takes, then we shall burn Balroic to the ground to steal it from his grip of death."

Crossing the border of southern Sudal in the freezing rain, the king pondered what assignment the five wizards were on in the heart of winter in a land they already subjugated? For what reason would they roam the countryside unless men within its borders still resisted their black will. The men traveled through the land as nocturnal beasts, hiding from the light like vampires fearing its brilliant exposure. They foraged along the landscape surviving by consuming mussels, small mammals, roots and insects. It was a hard diet shrinking the traveler's stomachs, which rumbled constantly sometimes so loudly that the man walking in front could hear the man's in the rear, and yet not one of the three complained along the way.

It was daylight as the king moved in on a large male grantalk, a huge gray migrant bird that fished the rivers of Zeethe and was considered as a feast by any tables' standard. The alert hunter slinked through the weeds of the woods peering through its blades of grass raising his bow for the kill. The substantial bird shifted through the rocks in a small creek bed feasting on tiny minnows unaware of King Hamse's intentions. Suddenly before the king could take aim, the bird spooked and flew high into the air out of the range of the king's mighty bow. Horse hoofs pounded against the frozen soil throwing clods of hard dirt into the air with the combined force of horse and armored rider. Men dressed in thick plate armor rode on top of the grunting steeds guiding their path with determination and wielding long powerful spears. The king recognized their crest and stood up from the weeds. They were cavalry from the province of Yeathon, rugged horsemen raised in the saddle from near birth, sitting upon their mounts as extensions of the animals instead of riders moving with the sleek creatures in gliding strides. One of the riders noticed his image appear from the wood line and with a long ivory horn signaled the other riders who quickly came to his side. They formed a line keeping their horses still as they rumbled to charge the sole man.

The sharp tips of the riders' spears glistened in the morning sun as they broke into a charge. Frozen mud flew behind the spirited charge as the wild horsemen barreled toward the man who walked out into the open seemingly without fear. They lowered their spears and leaned forward into their saddles stabilizing for the impact. The lone man raised his bow aiming at the men. The lead rider saw his action and rose from his saddle slowing down the charge of his men as they lifted their spears into the air to stop before the stoic man. He looked up at the men on horseback with a stern face and long hair blowing in the icy wind.

"You are trespassing on Yeathon land," stated a burly man on horseback. Wild hair grew from his face, neck and arms making him appear more a bear than a man. "State your name and affairs before I run you through."

His horse spun around in excitement kicking its hoofs into the air ready to fight.

"The province of Yeathon is over a hundred miles to the east of here," replied the king remembering the borders of his kingdom before his departure some two and half years ago.

"Yeathon is no longer a province, but a kingdom in its own right expanding hundreds of miles east during our wars with the foul king of Haenic!" he declared upon his cavorting black horse.

"So noble Enstagan has declared his independence from me?"

The man on horseback looked down at the strange man, unsure what to think of a single man challenging a group of more than a dozen fully armored riders.

"You mean King Enstagan, as he no longer hails to anyone below the gods of war!" said the man correcting the once king.

"He no longer hails to King Hamse?" asked the hardened hunter.

"Why, have you got him in your pocket?" replied one of the men in jest, bringing many of the horsemen to laughter.

Fury built up within the royal muscles of the king, but he quickly calmed down, having learned humility from his encounter on the other side of the Mhorhaen.

"I request an audience with your king," he said simply interrupting the amused horsemen.

"Bah," grumbled the horseman at the suggestion, "you might be a minion of Zespheous sent to use black magic upon the king."

"I have returned to free my kingdom and need to speak with your lord. He would not refuse me this basic right."

The tough Yeathonian admired the courage of the man standing firm against him and his fellow warriors.

"I'll take you to the king, but we will have to bind your hands and cover your mouth, so you can't cast spells."

The king, with little option and putting aside his pride, agreed to the men's demands leading them back to his camp hidden within a nearby thicket. The three men walked behind the riders, gagged and bound at the wrist like prisoners as they followed the riders back to Carlonien, the capital of the Yeathonian plains. Wild Yeathonian horses roamed the open plains as the men trudged forward in exhaustion of their three-week journey. Upon seeing the tall stronghold in the distance, the men sighed as a detachment of horsemen met them and carried them to the castle. It was worn and battle-scarred, having repelled numerous assaults from the dead armies of Zespheous. Men coated its walls with a black flammable grease that bubbled from the ground south of the kingdom to assist in fending off assaults from the lumbering dead.

The captured king walked slowly tied like a criminal through the shadows of the great castle gate under the watchful eyes of its people, who saw few strangers in their kingdom who were still alive. The inside courtyard of the fortress stank with the stench of besiegement as stale pails of water and piles of animal and human waste littered its interior. Men slung the waste of their horses and comrades onto wagons to haul them out between sieges. The active castle's occupants hustled about in stocking its supplies of food and firewood as the three men were led through its center as prisoners. In the center of the large stone-walled fortress sat the palace of King Enstagan, one of the last human kings to defy Zespheous' armies of the dead. A Yeathonian horseman, who appeared clumsy when not on a horse, walked bowlegged through the long halls leading the men into the hall of his king. A weary king sat upon his throne drained from many days of war against the dead.

"My Lord, a man found roaming our borders by one of our patrols and has requested an audience with you."

"I did not know men roamed the lands of the dead anymore."

"My Lord, he claims to be King Hamse!"

The expression on the king's face froze upon hearing the name of his former lord. He stood up slowly stepping down from his throne and walked over toward the bound and gagged man, squinting his eyes so to see through the man's long shaggy beard and hair, which lay limp onto his broad shoulders. The old king knew the Hamse bloodline well as King Hamse The Second had defeated him in the some of the bloodiest wars ever to be waged on the continent of Zeethe. In result of his defeat, the king became a vassal to the Hamse bloodline and his kingdom became a province of the ever-expanding Haenic. Now he had the son of his conqueror standing in his court helplessly bound and gagged like a criminal. He turned to the guard who had brought in the king and his followers like cattle to the slaughter and slapped him down to the ground with the might of an angered king. Although he had been conquered by this man's father, in his defeat, the wise king of Haenic had sparred his life, leaving him in charge of his own kingdom all in return of a single vow of loyalty. He had taken that vow seriously never considering breaking it since its conception decades ago.

"Untie these men," he shouted enraged at seeing his king treated like a thief in his own court, "and hope the great King Hamse spares your miserable life once you do!"

The man, stunned from being unwittingly struck by his king, stood up and quickly untied the three men in desperation for his life.

The great king of Yeathon kneeled before the haggard hunter lowering his head to concede his power.

"Forgive my men my lord. Times have been hard since your absence. They know not what they did. Nearly every day the dead, sometimes those of our kin, rise against us and try to drag us to our graves."

Two years ago before his imprisonment, the king might have had the men's heads for such insolence, but he had been humbled in Death's Door.

"Stand my friend," said the king. "You are the king here, not I."

The old man rose from his knees and two kings embraced, gripping each other's arms firmly forging a new alliance.

Part V
The Continent of the Dead

The king sat at a royal table for the first time in years feeling its smooth marbled surface as if for the first time.

"How many men do you have left?"

"Three hundred good riders and five hundred peasants to defend the castle. Every month those things come up the slopes to this castle and every month we grow weaker as Zespheous' armies grow stronger from our own fallen!"

"Who else stands?" asked the king of his lands.

"A year after your disappearance and with no direct heirs to your throne, the fifteen nobles of Haenic met to discuss the kingdom's next leader. No one was willing to champion one king, so all fifteen returned to their lands and war tore across the lands. The wars carried on for months as the armies of fifteen provinces converged upon one another leaving hundreds of thousands of dead on the battlefields. Zespheous waited patiently as we unknowingly played into his hands building him a vast army with our dead. No one knew who he was or that he secretly studied the black art of necromancy worshipping the ancient gods of those before man. He dispatched his assassins to the fifteen provinces with the orders for all to strike at the same moment. Only four kings, to include myself, survived the assassinations. The rest of the provinces crumbled once their lords had fallen being unable to organize quickly enough to repel the thousands of dead that marched upon them raping the land and its people. I know not who else stands free today. I dispatched riders to all the borders of your former provinces, but the dead either consumed them or forced them to return. Now my riders, once brave warriors, are few and ride as scouts charging only roaming dead, retreating back to the castle upon the sight of an army. If it were not for the speed of our horses in the open field and the fortitude of this castle, we would all be in the bellies of the dead."

"How large is this army of the dead?" asked the king.

"In the thousands at my best guess, but as no large force opposes him, Zespheous has his armies spread across the continent roaming its borders murdering the living so there will be no one left to oppose him. He will not rest until Zeethe becomes the continent of the dead."

"It will be the lack of resistance from our people that will be his downfall. My friend, what I ask of you will undoubtedly place an even greater hardship upon you and your brave people."

"Ask me for my life and it is yours my lord," stated his loyal servant.

"No army of men could stand against one that is so large and that will not die. To stop it, the spell weaved to conceive it must be reversed with the death of its creator. I mean to take the head of Zespheous from his body and let him rule his army in the pits of hell," declared the king without a kingdom. "I ask a heavy price from you and your people for the last chance of Haenic to once again be ruled by the living. I request gear and horses for me and my two men, thirty strong bows and all your riders to escort me to the gates of Balroic."

"My lord, these things shall be done," claimed King Enstagan slamming his hand upon the table between the two men. "Let me ride with you to help you reclaim your throne or to die by your side, so that either way I will be done with these foul dead!"

"Your people are still here for your leadership, I dare not take it from them now."

"Yes my lord," pronounced the king of Yeathon, rising from the table ordering that his best men be readied at once.

The next morning, a new king rode from the castle of Carlonien with a trimmed beard, fine armor and fur as garments, now leading an army of riders with glistening lances, swords and shields. Their horses, well maintained from grazing upon the prairies of Yeathon, grunted fiercely in anticipation of the ride ahead. For his plan to work, King Hamse and his men would have to ride with haste and make the palace of Haenic before Zespheous and his wizards could call back their armies to defend it. The men galloped bravely into the bitter morning wind as the last hope of Zeethe. What King Hamse did not know was that the eye of Kednuik had been focused upon Yeathon long ago so Zespheous and his black-hearted sorcerers were able to watch its men and their doings. Its black icy crystal showed the men through the haze of black magic that had formed it under the conjuration of its master. Zespheous had paid dearly for such a power from the black void, calling it forth at the cost of his first-born.

"Master, King Hamse has returned to Zeethe!" cried the watcher of the great crystal eye.

"So my Lord and master has returned from the obscurity of the Mhorhaen to take back the land of his fathers."

"My Lord he rides with the speed of the Yeathon horsemen. Our necromancers in the field will not have enough time to recall our armies to defend the city!" the watcher declared nervously.

The dead, although nearly immune to the weapons of men, were slow and moved at a tenth of the speed of men on horseback. The cunning necromancer deliberated on his options as he only had a few thousand dead within the city's walls as pawns, not enough to overwhelm Yeathon horsemen, since up to now in the wars against his dead, they had shown they could easily charge through a throng of dead and run down their weak and unarmored overseers before escaping the slow pursuit of his dead armies. Without the commands of their overseers, the dead did not work in unity, a weakness that the men of Yeathon had exploited to break up Zespheous' attacks on their kingdom and so avoid the icy grip of his rule. The walls of Balroic housed an immense city with lots of space for the riders to maneuver if they got past the gates. He and his court of robed magic-users would not be able to defend the castle looming over the city from armored cavalry. To survive such an assault, he would have to strike a deal with those whom man had stolen Zeethe from long ago. The powerful sorcerer rose from his plush throne, clearing his five closest apprentices from his path by brushing them aside as he had the people of Zeethe during his conquest of its land. They followed him as groveling servants would a god for he had the favor of the all-knowing Eidolen. The cloaked man kneeled respectfully before a great stone statue of a closed eye lowering his face against the cold stone floor.

"Oh great Eidolen, I your humble servant requests your aid in a time of need," he pleaded to the inanimate object.

Before the cowering men in purple robes the vast stone's eye opened with grinding stone revealing the swirl of the void from whence the magic of the dead is conceived. A booming voice projected from the darkness of the eye pouring from its empty center as would smoke from a chimney.

"Who dares contact me through the emptiness of time and space?" bellowed the eye blinking its eyelid with the scraping of stone as it spoke.

"It is I, Zespheous, the one who has returned your lands to you, glorifying you once again as you were in the conception of Dream."

"Tell me what you require before I claim what is mine to take as I choose!" ordered the stone eye, speaking of Zespheous' life.

"Great one, the old king of this land has returned to reclaim your kingdom for man. He is in strong favor with the gods of men and I fear without your blessings he might succeed."

"What you ask will come at a great price. Bathe the floors of my temple in the blood of one hundred children of man and I shall call forth aid from across the southern sea."

"My Lord, this shall be done immediately!" the self-declared king pronounced before his dark god. "In what form should I expect this great blessing?"

"Boats from the shores of Fathel shall land at the southern tip of Zeethe belching forth those of mongrel blood. Use your dead to bog the gates and hold this human king back until they arrive. They are fierce greedy beasts, and once they complete what I ask, they might not leave of their own free will. It will be up to you to expel them from your lands… dead or alive. May the strongest rule and serve!"

Zespheous kept his eyes averted until the great eye closed with the clash of stone.

"Go to the communes and bring me forth their children! They must protect my empire with their blood!"

His black sorcerers ran from his chambers to fulfill their lord's command without the hindrance of moral dilemma for they had given their hearts away in their quest for the power of ancient black magic. Sorcerers tore babies from the arms of weeping mothers, carrying off their bodies to the great castle above Balroic to serve their evil lord. The men of the land broken of will, did not rise against the power of their subjugators, watching their sons and daughters disappear past the gates of the commune that protected them from the armies of the dead. Children begged for their lives as their blood was drained without mercy onto the temple's floor rushing upon it like the ocean's tide upon the beach to stain its once bright white color crimson red.

Zespheous watched with imprudent eyes as his sorcerers squeezed the limbs of their victims, draining the last of their life onto the floor. Blood soaked against the stone eye, which opened slowly and drank it from the floor. Zespheous smiled when he saw that the deed had been done.

The king and his men rode with haste across the great continent of Zeethe. The mounted knights mowed down the dead that roamed across their path, setting their bodies afire, leaving long streams of smoke rising into the horizon. They rode as nomads upon their own land hardly sleeping as they bore through the wind toward the central capital of Balroic. It would take them months to cross its territory even with the swiftness of horses in hopes of surprising their foe. Meanwhile far to the south, dirty foul goblins bearing rusty spears and wooden shields landed on the southern coast of Zeethe riding atop hairy boars with wide tusks snorting for the clash of battle. They beat their mounts with cruel metal knotted flails growling like dogs as they rode through the land. It had been centuries since the expulsion of humanoids from the lands of Zeethe by the hands of man and now they rode with determination to take it back. Eidolen knew that calling forth his servants from the murk of Mauklica might threaten his human servants as they saw it in its weakened state, bringing forth armies of mongrels to reclaim it as their own. Orc footmen, ogre barbarians, troll sieges and goblin riders would be sure to follow in vast hordes, but the evil god cared not, for the sacrificial blood of humanoids fed his strength as well as humans. As long as the land belonged to those that served him, even the battles between his own servants nourished his strength giving him more control over the Lands of Dream.

The men on horseback rode too fast for Zespheous to monitor their progress through the eye of Kednuik. He threw raw magic from his fingers in frustration, shooting acid against the walls of his throne room dissolving its smooth polished surface. He was unsure if the forces of his god would arrive in time or if his army of the dead, already returning to his castle, would arrive in enough time to vanquish those sent to strike down his enemies.

Months passed as the three forces of man, mongrel and dead converged upon the capital to make war. The king's men, after riding many days, finally arrived within site of the glimmering palace that once stood as his great capital. It shimmered magically under the brilliant light of the sun, and from a distance it appeared as he had left it many years ago. The gates of the large city below the palace were bolted shut, effectively stopping an order for an all-out charge. King Hamse and his riders would have to devise a way past the defense of the great wall if they were to assail the palace above it.

Zespheous being a man of magic, knew little of the art of war or the strengthening a fortress, so in defense of his giant city, he had his apprentices huddle the dead in front of the city's many gates to clog it in battle if it were to be breached. Both king and necromancer knew not that five thousand goblin boar riders streamed toward the capital just ten days' ride away. The adept necromancer had managed to huddle ten thousand dead within the walls of his city before the king and his riders arrived, but in fear of being outmaneuvered in the plains around the city or letting in his enemies, he and his sorcerers watched as the king and his men chopped down great trees to form battering rams. The sound of their axes hewing resonated against the mountainside in which the palace was built echoing into the city below. The men worked feverishly to create their siege weapons, as the king knew more dead would soon arrive to defend their creator by pressing him and his small force between their ranks and the city's walls. His men sharpened the long tree trunks into battering rams, making two separate ones which took thirty men each to wield. They completed the simple but powerful siege engines in one day, waiting until dawn to deploy them on the battlefield. Being far inferior in numbers to their enemy, King Hamse and his men would not be able to break down the gate and overrun their foes. To succeed, he would have to be cunning, a trait of every Hamse King to date. He relied heavily on his days as a young prince sitting before his father as he explained the art of war. Position meant more than numbers he had learned or the army with the larger force would always win. Under the guard of his men, the king formulated a plan that would fulfill his destiny whether it be to reclaim his throne or die a pauper.

The shape of the king emerged from the shadow of darkness as the sun rose warming the face of him and his three hundred and two men. Pot sat next to him on his horse ready to die, not for his country, but in the name of friendship. The king detailed his men into four formations. The first formation consisted of sixty one men and two battering rams, with the sole purpose of breaking down the city's mighty gate. The second group, which included Pot, Talein the young and twenty eight more men, made up his army's archers, who were to keep the defenders from assaulting the first group from over the walls with missile weapons, magic and boiling oil. The third formation, all riders, totaled seventy five men who were to stand ready behind the first formation and feign attack upon the breaking of the gate to bring the dead out into the open and expose their overseers to be targeted by the archers. The last and most important formation consisted of one hundred and thirty six men, all mounted, who hid around the corner of the wall after riding up to the gate to rush in behind the dead once they were drawn out. This formation was to be led by the king. For his stratagem to work, each formation had to do its part so the next could do theirs. It worked on building blocks, and if any part failed, the whole design would collapse. The king looked down to the leader of the first formation and nodded.

"If the gate starts to crack early, hold back your men long enough for the dead from other parts of the city to migrate toward the main gate. The more we bring out, the fewer Zespheous will have to defend him in the castle."

The commander nodded his bronze-colored head signaling his compliance with the order given and signaled for his men to march. The king's formation drug the battering rams so as not to tire their wielders with their horses dispersing at the gate along the wall unseen by those hiding inside. The moans of the dead could be heard behind the city's grand main gate as the commander of the battering formation ordered his men to hoist the great trunks. The rams began to beat at the gate in rotation, one striking the gate as the other pulled away, which allowed each ram to crash into the gate as it bowed backwards, never allowing it to flex back to its original shape.

"Do they have more battering rams than the two at the main gate?" asked Zespheous of his watchmen upon the balcony of his palace.

"No my Lord."

The city's walls towered over its besiegers so that Zespheous' watchmen could not see the king's fourth formation so they assumed that the horsemen were awaiting to assault upon breach of the city's gates.

"He is going to make a direct assault. Signal for the overseers to pull half the guards from the rest of the city's gates and reinforce the main gate," the evil magician ordered high upon his balcony watching the battering rams stroke back and forth like relentless pistons. He was a direct man thought Zespheous, attacking in a no-nonsense formation, coming straight at him.

The thick gate held firm for thirty minutes of unyielding pounding before its structure began to splinter from the force of the exhausted men. The hands of the dead began to reach through the splintering holes only to be crushed by the massive wooden trunks beating relentlessly against the gate. As the holes widened, the dead began to crawl through to ravage their enemy. A final blow from one of the massive trunks tore one of the doors from its hinges crushing it into the city on top of the dead. Decayed men and women swarmed out the shattered gate toward the men who threw down their siege engines and ran toward the third formation of horsemen. The horsemen lifted the exhausted men onto horseback to aid their escape, falling backward from the city's assaulting dead. Seeing their plan, the overseers began to call back their dead as a hail of arrows rained down upon the cloth-wearing casters. The long arrows sunk deep into the unarmored men piercing their thin cloaks protruding from their bodies like needles in pin cushions.

The horsemen dropped off the men of the first formation and made a counter attack, chopping down those that were not the dead in order to lure the dead outside the city's walls. Dead began to pull riders from their mounts and devour them on the ground, oblivious to the arrows and weapons that struck their bodies. The third formation took heavy casualties, and as they drug the dead out in the heat of battle they lost half their men in minutes of the assault. Thousands of dead streamed onto the battle field forcing the remainder of the formation to retreat along with the archers of the second formation drawing Zespheous' forces further away from the shattered gate. The king peered around the corner watching the multitudes of walking dead stumble away from the shadows of the great wall hungrily pursuing his fleeing men. At his command, the men of the fourth and final formation drew their weapons, leaped onto their mounts and rode around the wall's edge at full speed whipping their steeds into a frenzy as they burst through the demolished gate dredging into the dead that continued to swarm out. Ravenous hands tugged at the king's armor trying to pull him off his horse and into the rocking sea of dead below. Teeth sunk into the exposed flesh of his horse which reared up in defiance. King Hamse's shining blade hacked off the hands and arms of those that tugged at him using steel boots to crush the faces and dislodge the dead from their feet. His black steed stepped onto soft bodies crushing organs and appendages as they fell to the ground, disabling their ever swarming heads and limbs. Spurring his horse through the horde of clawing hands and teeth, the king and his first line of men who had not fallen broke through the dead riding into the streets of the city, quickly losing sight of the broken gate and its defenders. The king knew his capital by heart having roamed it as a child leading his men through its maze without flaw. Nothing had changed, not a road or a house, he reflected, riding through it in a whirl.

"My Lord, they have broken through the main gate!" announced one of the necromancer's watchmen.

"How many?" asked the ruler concerned with the tide of the battle.

"Fifty or sixty riders!"

"Signal for the remaining overseers to abandon their dead and pull back to the palace!" he ordered angrily. "We shall see who will triumph, the might of the sword or the mysticism of magic."

Zespheous led his remaining sorcerers to the palace door and ordered his servants to extinguish every torch and candle within the palace and to stand ready to engage the enemy in the darkness. The barred palace door shook as the men on the other side tugged at it with the might of their horses. The door ripped out of its frame and the light of day mixed with the darkness as the forces of good rode into the large palace on horseback to engage the might of evil in its shadows.

"May death find you, so you may serve me willingly," bellowed Zespheous in the darkness, signaling his followers to attack.

A horseman turned to stone sliding from his saddle and bounced onto the hard stone floor from the mere touch of Zespheous. Fire, acid and ice shot from the fingers of his apprentices engulfing the armored men from all sides. King Hamse's horse succumbed to an enchantment crystallizing into ice before tipping over with the king and shattering into pieces. The king fell into the darkness rushing unseen behind a tall pillar gripping his bow and a handful of heavy arrows. Unable to see his targets in the surrounding darkness, the king fired arrows at the sources of the bright magic that filled the room. At that same moment his men rode into the palace's front chamber slicing the unarmored casters crushing them under the weight of weapon and horse.

Unseen arrows brought down the followers of Zespheous forcing the once-prevailing ruler from the chamber in flight with two of his neophytes. They hurried through the dark palace shuffling through its twisting halls and spiraling stairwells distancing themselves from the might of the sword. The cunning necromancer knew that the men coming after him could not see in the dark without the benefit of magic and this would give him the time he would need to make his chambers ready and unleash his last hope, the Devourer. He swung open the door to his royal chamber rushing to his great book of ancient incantations. He flipped through its pages quickly, placing his finger on his spell of choice. A shiny blade swung in the darkness decapitating the first of his servants awaiting his master's will before finding the heart of his other. They both died abruptly as not a word left their mouths to warn their master as he spoke the summoning of the great Devourer, a demon that once called, would consume every drop of his summoner's enemies before turning on him, his entire family bloodline and those that followed him. A shadow rose above Zespheous' head as he bent over his great thick book rattling his concentration. The necromancer king spun around to find King Hamse the Third looking into his eyes. Fear gripped his soul, the same fear his conquest had placed upon the people of Haenic, the fear of what he controlled. The old wizard hastily began to cant an enchantment upon the towering figure only to have it fail with muddled words. The tight grip of the king's gauntlet held his throat tight stealing his only weapon, his voice. The king, having lived in the palace from birth, knew its halls inside and out, easily beating the old wizard to his chambers.

"Your reign of terror upon the lands of my fathers is over," he said, lifting the thin man into the air like a rag doll dangling him with his tight grip like a noose. "Now it is time for you to become what you control."

The king held the dangling sorcerer in the air crushing his esophagus and trachea with the might of his gauntlet. The old wizard's eyes rolled back into his head as he took his last breath. As his life left his body, his magic failed, undoing the control he had over those he animated. Across the continent of Zeethe hundreds of thousands of walking dead returned to the grave. One hundred and seven of the king's men remained alive at the moment of Zespheous' death bringing them to shout in victory as the dead pursuing them suddenly dropped to the ground as still carcasses. The king dragged the body of the vile sorcerer, who had defiled the land of him and his people, onto the balcony of his palace and threw his thin limp body over its edge. The purple-robed corpse flapped in the wind, sailing to the ground crashing onto the street of the great dead city below. King Hamse's men cheered the king standing high on his royal balcony with his cloak blowing in the wind once again the king of Haenic and its people.

A great stone eye within the palace opened exposing the death of the great sorcerer. Fire fueled by hatred welled within its glassy cornea. The all-knowing god knew something the celebrating men did not. His mongrel army from across the southern sea approached the capital riding furious rapid boars with the conquest of Zeethe on their minds. The blood of the land would belong to him once again.

The men on horseback rode through the city in victory trampling the bodies of the fallen dead. The peasants within the great commune of Balroic came out from their protective walls undaunted by the walking dead for the first time in years, emerging into the great city of their homeland to share in the celebration. The number of King Hamse's people remaining were few, but they would be enough to rebuild and for man to start over in the Lands of Dream. But as the people gathered in the streets below the palace of their reinstated king, a black line rose over the far plains blotting out the horizon in the distance. The king walked to the edge of his balcony and watched the black horde surge over the hills in feral formations toward his celebrating city. Goblins held onto the razor manes of their mounts gnashing their teeth and shrieking in delight at the prospect of human prey. The rumble of thousands reached the fortress's walls shaking its thick foundation and halting the men's merriment as they stared into the distance at the stream of dust. Flag bearers hoisted the purple and yellow flag of Eidolen into the air signaling a full charge as it snapped in the swift wind. The great army moved too fast to be one of the dead, thought the king watching it flow toward the castle with the force of a tidal wave which threatened to drag his reclaimed city back into the sea like a sand castle on the edge of the ocean.

"Mongrels!" yelled a rider from outside the castle riding through the shattered front gate. "Hordes of mongrels approach!"

The words baffled the men, as no mongrel force had come across the great southern sea since man had cast them across it some three hundred years ago.

"Pull back into the city!" screamed one of the king's commanders. "Bar the gate with anything you can find!"

The remaining men of the city, some five hundred peasants made up of men, women and children, and one hundred or so horsemen took to the defense of the city under harsh commands from Yeathon commanders.

The king turned to Tidus the Yeathon general who answered only to him and King Enstagan, "Tidus, do any of Zespheous' apprentices remain alive?"

"Yes, my Lord, two were captured outside the gates."

"Bring them to me and organize the men to defend the city at all cost! Do not allow one of those filthy mongrels to enter this city!"

"Yes my lord!" answered the stoic general turning and leaving the chamber.

The general mounted his horse and rode out into the street to coordinate the city's defense. Stout warriors rolled wagons, dragged wooden beams and pushed rubble against the main gate to obstruct the break in it. The few archers that remained took positions along the top of the wall guarding the vulnerable portal to their city. Horsemen lined up behind the gate ready to expel those that might enter. Peasants who once cowered in fear of Zespheous and his dead took arms ready to die under the stalwart leadership of their king. While frail in body, the wizards dragged into the king's chambers were robust in mind and were bound and gagged so to prevent any attempt to harm the king with their magic. Fear loomed in their eyes as the great king they had defied seized one's cloak and dragged him to the great spell book left open by Zespheous. He pulled out a long knife and cut the gag from the man's mouth keeping it close to the man's throat.

"What is this abjuration?" asked the king pointing to the arcane book.

The wizard eyed the words placed to page by quill with the blood of innocent children. Sketches of an anomalous demon and the words that must be spoken to bring it forth met his eyes. Fear seized his body weakening his mind and muscles as he saw what the spell before him would materialize. The color from his already pale face drained away leaving him white as a sheet as he backed away in terror.

"What is it?" demanded the king loudly.

"It is… it is," said the horrified man stuttering nervously, "it is the conjuration of the Devourer!"

"What will it do?" he asked the ghost-like figure locked in a trance upon the book.

"It will summon an enormous demon with bowels as ravenous as hell that hungers for the souls of the living!" he screamed back, full of dread.

"Can you control it?"

"Once it has consumed our enemies, it will turn upon us… I am not sure if I will be able to send it back."

It was their last hope, as the king knew his men would not be able to hold off the goblin horde outside for long.

"Bring it forth, but I swear to you, if you try to betray me, I will gut you like a pig!"

The man turned to the king in a panic, "No I dare not… to conjure such a fiend will incur a cost too great!"

The king raised the point of his knife to the frightened man's throat. "Call the creature!" he said with determination his eyes.

The terrified man faltered and before his court the king slit the cowering man's throat draining his blood onto the floor and tossing him aside like trash. He seized the other wizard dragging him to the book forcefully ripping out his gag.

"Speak the words and bring it forth as I will not ask you twice!"

The terrified sorcerer gazed at the book chanting the words slowly so as not to fail. Once he had spoken the words, he backed away from the book terrified of what he had done. Red smoke rose from the thick book's pages swirling high into the air. It slowly fell to the floor forming an immense figure before the King, his three guards and the reluctant conjurer. The imposing demon stood fourteen feet tall, had three horns upon its head and had a large hinged mouth much like that of a toad. The being's eyes gleamed malevolence streaming blood from their corners as they stared at the pitiful creature that had called it from the void. The king inched closer to the wizard and unsheathed his short sword ready to cut the conjurer's head off with its razor sharp blade if the giant fiend attacked. It read the mind of its conjurer seeing its enemies. It tore through the arch leading out onto the palace's balcony and leaped to the street below crumbling the stone street with its immense weight. Thousands of goblins swarmed against the city's main gate pushing it backwards against the weakening strength of the inferior defenders inside. Arrows rained down upon the grimy creatures, but were insufficient to reduce their great numbers enough to slow their attack. The monstrous form of the Devourer treaded through the city toppling houses and buildings with the force of its unstoppable body. Its shadow loomed onto the interior of the main gate dispersing the men defending it. Hellfire ripped past the men bowling them aside as the demon crushed through the gate splintering metal and wood into the horde of advancing goblins. The fierce force of mongrels shrieked in fear of the great monster unleashed upon them, unable as they were to retreat from the weight of their own numbers pushing toward the gate. The beast shoved whole goblins and their swine mounts into its mouth sending their bodies to its infinite digestive tract and thus condemning its victims to a slow digestive eternity. Long whips of fire that propelled from the beast's hands entangled its prey and drew them to its mouth for consumption. The mongrel's small spears broke within the demon's thick hide leaving the force helpless against their devouring foe. Broken in spirit and weak of heart, the army of mongrels broke before their enemy and fled for their lives, retreating back to the great sea. The monster continued to feed upon those it lassoed until the might of the goblins was gone. Then as quickly as it had pursued the enemies of its conjurer, the giant beast turned upon those it had saved and burst back into the city chasing down those who had summoned it as payment for its evil deed.

"Flee!" ordered a commanding horseman to the people.

Whips of fire blazed into the distance dragging victims to the monster's great mouth. The king pulled the wizard who had called forth the beast and threw him over the balcony to his death. As life left the wizard, so did his magic, dissolving the giant creature from which it came in a cloud of smoke. The king's men regrouped at once in the wake of the great battle and began the process of rebuilding. The first commands of the great king burned away the knowledge within Zespheous' cryptic book in a great fire, which he used to rid his land of the knowledge of magic so that it would not plague its soil again.

The men of Haenic used grand hammers to pulverize the stone eye of Eidolen into dust, taking away the evil god's last foothold upon the continent of Zeethe leaving him defeated but not conquered since his mongrel priest and other human priest far from the border's of Zeethe still lusted for his power. Pot came into the king's chamber with blood running down his arm smiling proudly at their victory and their transformation from prisoners to free men.

"You have reclaimed your land, my king!"

"No, the land has reclaimed me!" King Hamse declared humbly. "I strayed from it once, I will not do it again."

"I always knew you were telling the truth about being a king back in Death's Door," he said, smiling with a mouth nearly void of teeth. "I could tell because you had nice teeth."

The king laughed at the remark as a peasant came into the chamber under lead of guard with his head bowed.

"My Lord," announced the guard, "this man requests an audience."

"My Lord, when Zespheous ordered your trophy room destroyed and its contents burned, your loyal servants stole the jejir hides of you and your grandfather to honor your family's memory as they fled the city."

"Where are these trophies?" asked the king curiously.

"Buried in a chest deep within your royal forest."

"Do as Zespheous commanded," he said carelessly. "I have no time for such things. I have a Kingdom to run."

The man looked at the king queerly unsure what to do.

"Go do as I say now, so we can forget the past and move toward the future."

The man ran from the chamber to fulfill the will of his king. It would take decades for Haenic to return to its former glory, but of all the resources available to the king and his country, time was a resource they had in plenty.

Part VI
The Second Rising of Haenic

The word of King Hamse's return to power spread across the land with the speed of horses uniting the kingdom of Haenic and its people under his rule once again. Thousands of people came out of hiding descending from the icy peaks of Azoul and emerging from the depths of the Mhorhaen. The king reinstated the fifteen provinces of his kingdom selecting nobles where none remained before handing over the centralized province of Garl to his trusted friend Pot. Using his real name, he became known as Tyler the True, and in his own right, led his province to prominence within the kingdom of Haenic, turning it into a trade skills center which produced the continent's finest artists, blacksmiths, tailors, brewers, bakers, carpenters, engineers and of course potters.

Trackers were sent into the south of the Mhorhaen in search of the solitary Werthhard the forester, who had saved the lives of both Pot and the king, bringing him back to ennoble the northern province of Sudal. The young orphan Talein, who had joined the king when times looked bleak, was adopted by the king and took on the royal name of his adopted father to become known by all as Prince Hamse the Fourth. The lands grew, burying its dead and reforming under the rule of a king who now reigned for the benefit of his people. The nobles were given greater power in governing the kingdom, meeting twice per year in equality to their peers to vote on the policies of Zeethe. As the provinces grew in wealth and power, so did the king of Haenic who became greater than all of its past kings combined. His army grew from a rabble to hordes of fleet horsemen from Yeathon, throngs of heavy foot soldiers from Kthaer, multitudes of precise archers from Nthark, masses of agile light footmen from Aguija, formations of sea-worthy ships from Oceika, stealthy hunters from the woods of Sudal and massive siege weapons from the workshops of Garl.

In his great power, the king never lost the humility he had learned in the prisons of Alboules or forgot his pledge to return to its borders and bring it to its knees. A huge campaign was forged to pass an army through the great Mhorhaen and besiege the unsuspecting kingdom of Alboules. A mindful king returned to the edge of the great forest, but no longer as the naive hunter he had been the first time he entered its depths. Eighty thousand men riding horses and dragging supplies to weather the elements of the Mhorhaen marched behind the great king. Of the nobles, only those of Garl and Sudal rode along. One having lived in the wood would prove an invaluable asset to their journey, while the other returned to his homeland to help conquer those that had wronged him.

The passage was a long one taking the large army over three months to navigate past the forest's core with negligible casualties as even the great beasts of the Mhorhaen recognized the power of the force that marched through. The massive army came from the wood unseen by the forces of Alboules since its borders were left unguarded in belief that nothing but the end of the world was beyond its thick foliage. Massive ranks of men marched through the countryside expelling the common folk who migrated in a panic toward their country's capital looking for protection from a hostile and foreign invader. Word of the invasion reached King Aeaf who quickly secured his castle and sent for reinforcements from his nobles. A giant army encircled his castle three days later cutting the King off from his kingdom and isolating him within his castle's walls unsure where or how such a large force came upon his country so swiftly.

"Who are these men?" asked the bewildered king staring through the safety of a window in his palace's center tower.

"No one recognizes any of the strange crest worn by the men or the flags they fly my Lord," answered his advisor. "It is as if they are ghosts that appeared out of thin air."

"Their weapons appear to be very real," commented the king.

"A single rider approaches the gates, my Lord!" cried an observer.

"Give the signal for the men to hold their fire and let him in," ordered the king. "Now maybe we will get some answers to what this is all about."

Flagmen stood high on the balcony of the city's centered tower waving brightly colored flags signaling the commanders below to not harm the rider. A man finely dressed in sleek leather rode somberly atop a glossy black steed eyeing the men that surrounded him without fear. A commander dressed in shiny ornate gold armor stood firmly in the way of the foreign rider barring his passage.

"I seek an audience with your king," replied the confident messenger.

"Let me see if my lord will consent to your request or ask me to behead you for such insolence."

Men holding flags turned toward the tower of their king signaling the request of the rider for an audience. The king's flagmen responded to the shiny commander who read their answer before turning to the rider.

"It appears as if you might live today. my king is feeling generous and has agreed to speak with you."

"The rider nodded to the commander, slipping from atop his horse to be examined for weapons.

"I will thank him for his mercy," answered the man, "I am not so sure my king will be as merciful as yours."

He followed behind a detachment of men who led him hastily through the town to the tower of the king. As the solemn messenger entered the king's chamber, the curious ruler wasted little time cross examining the envoy of the army that besieged his castle.

"For what reason does your army lay siege upon my kingdom?"

"King Aeaf, pardon my intrusion, but my king has sent me to make you an offer in this war."

"It seems I am at a disadvantage here as you know who I am, but I know nothing of you, your king or his lands."

"My king is lord over all Zeethe commanding the forces of fifteen kingdoms that have united to create the great empire of Haenic."

"How can it be that I have never heard of such places?" asked the king of the messenger.

"I know not," answered the man, "as it is because of your actions against our grand king that he has returned to conquer you and your people."

"Actions?" replied the king strangely. "I have done nothing to your king!"

"You claim to not have a dungeon known as Death's Door?"

The king knew the name, but had not thrown any kings into it to his knowledge.

"And you deny throwing a man into it some ten years ago for claiming to be King Hamse?"

The king turned to his royal court, which consisted of guards, jesters, advisors, arbitrators, magicians and generals, "Does anyone know of what this man speaks?"

The memory of such a man came to one of his arbitrators, but it had been so long ago he had almost forgotten it.

"Answer me!" screamed the king.

The man who had condemned King Hamse to Death's Door for minor crimes stood silent afraid to answer in fear of receiving the same possible sentence for spurring such a great war.

"No one including myself knows anything of what you speak!" declared the king. "This must be some mistake."

"There has been no mistake," replied the man vehemently. "My king's terms are as follows. Lay down your arms and confess your loyalty to him and my king will allow you to continue to rule your land as a province of Haenic. He wishes not to kill those that he will soon rule."

"Those are outrageous terms! As we speak my nobles are amassing armies to come to our aid and your men have no hope of breaching our walls before they arrive! Your army will be crushed between the two!" boasted the king arrogantly. "I'll never swear loyalty to another king because I have right to my throne from the gods themselves!"

"We have no need to batter down your walls as you will willingly open them to us one way or another. You have until tomorrow to make your decision known… at dawn if your men continue to resist, the forces of Haenic will flatten this castle and all those within it."

The king, stunned by the terms, let the man go and rejoin the army that camped around his beautiful castle. His advisors argued incessantly among themselves on what course of action they should pursue as his generals prepared for the worst. Night quickly dropped on the isolated castle, and while the most of the men outside slept confident of their impending victory, very few inside slept, fearful of what would occur with the rising of the sun.

A ray of sunlight fractured the horizon lighting the encampment of tents, horses and long travois. The smoldering fires of the besieging army streamed white smoke into the air fouling it as it blew over the walls of the castle's defense. The people of the city waited anxiously almost expecting an onslaught at the very crack of dawn, but to the contrary, the men of the besieging camp rose slowly in the cool morning dew taking their time in their assault. The echoes of wood chopping and falling trees could be heard off in the distance as the king's engineers carefully pulled out gear they had dragged through the Mhorhaen in long travois. Men and horses hauled massive trunks to the camp assembling them into great siege weapons while the people within the city watched helplessly. King Aeaf's garrison consisted of twenty thousand men, a quarter of the force that camped outside the gate, and to make things worse, of the twenty thousand only eight thousand were cavalry or heavy knights with the remainder being mere armed peasants. It would be a war of one province against the specialties of fifteen. The besieged king's only hope was to wait out reinforcements from his nobles. These forces came one by one but were quickly repelled by fierce arrows from Nthark regiments and then mowed down while in retreat by swift cavalry from Yeathon. The besieged king would have no help from the outside. If he was to stand against the strange force outside his gates, it would be by the fortitude of his grand castle alone.

On the morning of the twentieth day the sun rose once again, but this time its rays brought to light tall looming catapults. As soon as the sun's rays glistened off the basalt-walled castle, huge clay balls sealed with corks soared through the air over the castle's high walls crashing into the city splattering into a black sludge. The people of the city examined the strange substance, unsure of its purpose. It smeared as they rubbed it trying to remove it from the streets, walls and rooftops. The strange clay balls continued to burst throughout the city to spill their black innards sporadically and dot the city with runny black spots. For two days the clay structures relentlessly exploded into the city baffling its wise men and king as to their purpose, since up till that time no one had been seriously injured by the weird phenomenon. On the third day King Hamse's archers marched toward the well-defended wall of King Aeaf's city stopping and pulling back their arrows. The defenders on top of the wall leaned behind the defense of its thick stone waiting to counterattack. Suddenly men ran along the lines of outstretched arrows with torches, igniting their tips. Hundreds of flaming arrows took flight in unison with a "whoosh," sailing over the defending soldiers and harmlessly passing over their heads and disappearing into the city. Immediately smoke and fire spread through the city ripping across it in an unmanageable blaze. King Hamse and his generals had planned the siege of Alboules years in advance of the actual attack, harvesting a strange black liquid that bubbled in the south of the kingdom and burned mercilessly when set to flame. The artisans of Garl had spent months firing the clay containers that held the liquid in place until launched onto the unsuspecting city. The substance burned hot, igniting on wood, stone, metal and even water. Within minutes black smoke engulfed the city rising from fierce flames and smothering its inhabitants. Even the men on the city's walls turned to battle the smoke and fire that raged at their backs ignoring the huge army at their gates.

"Why do the people not extinguish the flames?" asked the king as he watched his beautiful city burn from his tower.

"My Lord, it is a magic substance as even when you throw water on the flames it spreads!"

"We are lost," responded the king as the walls of his city contained the flames like a giant campfire threatening to turn his people into hot coals.

King Hamse sat on his horse with Lord Tyler, Lord Werthhard and his generals at his side.

"We should attack now, my Lord, as they are fighting the flames," advised his general sitting proudly glistening in the uncontaminated air outside the burning city.

Huge pillars of thick black smoke rose into the sky forming an ominous black haze over the city.

"Patience," responded the tranquil king, "let the flames do our fighting."

The people within the city powerlessly fought the mighty flames feeding upon its structures unable to stop the fire's swift growth. Men, women and children began to succumb to smoke inhalation as flames bit at the king's mighty central tower. Within hours nothing could be seen within the city from outside its walls, and for a moment, the mighty king from Haenic thought its people would go down with it in ashes. Once the hopes of its people were lost, the city's giant gate slowly opened pouring out its people caked in gray ash. The once proud knights in bright shiny armor unwilling to surrender alive a few days ago stumbled out, unable to fill their lungs with the oxygen they needed to feed their muscles and fight. The city smoldered two more days out of everyone's control, even to those that set it, until nothing remained to feed the flames, which finally vanished with the wind. Only those that surrendered outside King Aeaf's tower survived the raging fire leaving the king and a few hundred of his court to resist the colossal army of thousands outside.

His once proud tower of picturesque stature now stood in shame covered in black soot. Its king, the lord of a mighty country just a few days ago, was now imprisoned in his chambers powerless to stop the might of the mysterious force at its gate. The wise king from beyond the Dark Wood yelled his final demands to his rival king.

"I shall give you one more chance to submit before my might to receive what is left of my mercy!" he screamed into the air. "If you refuse, I shall topple your tower as I have your great city!"

The battle had been so one-sided that even the stubborn king of Alboules knew he had been beaten. The defeated king, along with his court, solemnly came out of the tower with their heads down placing their final hopes upon the mercy of a strange and unknown army.

"Kneel before the king!" yelled a Kthaer commander demanding respect of his lord.

King Aeaf reluctantly lowered himself to one knee in obeisance to a conquering rival.

King Hamse had studied the conquests of his father and had learned from those conquests that his most loyal provincial lords were those he had spared. People always abhorred a foreign ruler and were more likely to follow their own king over another. He had overcome the impulsiveness of his grandfather and in turn, gained the diligence of his father.

"Lord Aeaf, I offer your life in return for your service to me. Take an oath to me, before the people of our lands and the gods of man to serve me without falseness and you shall retain your lands as a lord subservient to the kingdom of Haenic."

"The genuflecting king remained quiet under the bright morning sun, the focus of all eyes both Haenician and Alboulian as he chose his answer, "I swear allegiance to you, your lands and our people."

"Then let your kingdom be the sixteenth province of Haenic!" announced King Hamse proudly.

Both sides rejoiced for the bloodshed of war had passed and now the reconciliation of peace could take hold of both lands. The remaining armies of the nobles sent to free the city, finding no war, used their muscle and bone to build instead of destroy raising the great city to a prominence it had never known before the annexation of Haenic and its wise king. The lord of Garl rode with an escort of one thousand men to his Alboulian homeland to greet his mother with open arms. Word of the great conquest of the army from the Dark Wood had spread across the land quickly, but she had not identified her son with the news in fear of breaking her heart once again. He stood before her having left a fugitive, but now had returned a noble of great power. He hugged her with tears in his eyes wishing only that his father could have been alive to see the turn of events that had taken place so strangely by turning a simple potter to a powerful noble.

"Tyler, you look wonderful!" she said looking at his fine armor. "I thought to never see you again!"

"Thank you mother, I have come to take you back to live with me across the Mhorhaen in Garl my kingdom," he stated proudly as although he was born an Aboulian, his heart was that of a Garl.

A look of concern overtook her aged face for a moment as since a child she had been taught of the dangers within the Dark Wood, but they quickly faded as she looked at her son proudly.

"Come in and let me fix you and your men something to eat," she said, not thinking.

Her son laughed, "Mother, while the women of Garl's cooking could never compare to yours, I have brought a thousand men with me. You could not possibly feed them all!"

"When should we leave?" she asked unsure of his plans.

"Why now, mother, we are to return to the capital as soon as possible! I have many people I would like you to meet!"

She wiped her hands on her dirty dress nervously, unsure what to take with her or where to start packing.

"Let me gather my things."

"Mother you need not bring anything, everything you need will be furnished by the kingdom of Garl! You are a queen now!"

"What of my clothes?"

"You shall have new ones made. The greatest seamstresses in all of Haenic hail to me."

She had saved every piece of pottery her son had ever made lining her cupboards with them.

"What of your pottery?"

"Leave that junk here," he laughed at his mother who had become accustomed to scrimping and saving all her life to make ends meet.

"I will do no such thing!"

"Please mother, thousands are waiting on you."

"On me?" she asked not fully comprehending the stature she now occupied.

"Yes mother, on you," he said following her into the house to help her gather her things.

She ran around the small cottage packing clothes and her remaining food stores as food to a peasant meant everything. He smiled as she handled things she would never need living in his palace under the care of servants.

"I only wish this could have all happened before the loss of Celestie."

He had not asked about her since he assumed she was still married. He had planned on returning to Garl without seeing her to let the mighty Mhorhaen keep apart his longing for her. His mother saw his confusion.

"I have not spoken to her since I escaped the prison of Alboules."

"You have not heard?"

"What mother?" he asked, fearing the worst of his love.

"Upon seeing you last, she murdered her husband and tried to kill herself and has since been banished from Alboules."

"Banished to where?"

"To the island of Foudes."

He stepped back, shaken by the thought of the dreadfully distant island. It had been used as a prison island for those considered undesirable such as the insane, diseased and politically banished. It was an immense island of badlands unsuitable for most life and therefore served its purpose of ridding surrounding kingdoms of their unwanted, but its exiled had adapted to its harsh environment and had become a rogue kingdom of cannibals ruled by a giant tribe fearfully known as the skin peelers. Their king, a madman, ruled over the giant island feeding his masses upon those dropped upon its shore. The thought of his only love in the hands of such wild men was more than he could bear as he rushed his mother out the door of her lifelong home to ride back to the capital of Alboules. The noble stormed into the chambers of King Aeaf finding the two kings and advisors from both countries speaking of the newest province's future within its mother country Haenic.

"My dear friend," said the king seeing the concern of his friend and noble, "is something wrong?"

"Celestie has been banished!" declared Lord Tyler in a passionate rage.

King Aeaf's figure stiffened as if being charged with some misdeed.

"Who is this Celestie?" asked King Aeaf curiously.

"Banished where my friend?" asked King Hamse quieting his noble.

"To the horrible island of Foudes!" cried Lord Tyler angrily.

"My arbitrators know to send no one to its shores unless the devil is in their heads!" King Aeaf yelled in his defense.

"She is not mad!" screamed Tyler stepping toward his fellow noble with blind rage.

"My friend, you are a lord now with a great number of responsibilities. Your country and people come first now, we cannot have internal bickering or wild accusations among our nobles," said the king of Haenic holding back the fury of his friend. "Lord Aeaf, can you explain to me about this island?"

The king and his lords studied the maps of Alboules and its outlying areas as Lord Aeaf explained what he knew of the island.

"I have ships along the coast that can take you to the island if you wish, but as she has been there for near a decade, I fear she is dead from either the environment or worse, its people. I cannot imagine the state of mind a person would be in living in a land of insanity for such time. For her sake, I hope she died long ago," said lord Aeaf pausing.

"I have to know what became of her. If she is dead, then so be it, but I cannot go on wondering till the day I die if she is alive or not," replied Tyler to his fellow lord's warning.

"As time passed and kingdoms along the great sea that surrounds the island of Foudes continued to deposit their undesirables on its coast, an empire of cannibals rose from the wasteland led by a madman known only as the skull crusher. Unable to grow food, the people lived off the only resource that was readily available, human flesh. Everything they have comes from man. They nourish themselves from human flesh. Their clothing is made from human skin and their weapons are fashioned from the bones of man. It is said that through devouring men, they have gained a strength two to three times that of normal men and ravish those that land on its beaches."

Celestie's lover, unwilling to listen to the reason of anyone, including that of his own king, prepared to leave for the coast the next morning. Lord Aeaf promised that three seaworthy vessels, capable of carrying seventy men and their steeds, would be ready upon his arrival of the seaboard. Having duties far too great in merging the two empires, King Hamse was unable to journey with his good friend, but offered him his personal guards to aid him in the dangerous voyage. Lord Aeaf offered his last bit of advice as the determined man left to begin his journey.

"Remember their great strength."

"I assure you, they do not have twice the strength of a Kthaer barbarian," boasted a Kthaer warrior before leaving.

Lord Tyler and his detachment of men rode through Alboules receiving bows of respect from its people as they passed through its countryside flying the colorful flag of Haenic. The men he led were hardy men, the best Zeethe had to offer, but even with their strength, they found it difficult to keep up with the determination of their leader's love. Lord Tyler rode on without sleeping until he and his men reached the coast, exhausted and worn near collapse. After handing Lord Aeaf's orders to the head commander of the shipyard, his men were given three ships as promised with full crews of seamen. The ships left the familiarity of land to disappear into the horizon floating on a giant sea of blue. Many of the men on the ship, especially those of the inland provinces had never been to sea and became seasick yearning for the sturdy foundation of land. Unable to sleep, Lord Tyler stared over the ship's bow as it cut through the waves in the light of the sun and the moon watching for his island destination. He would either find Celestie or discover what had happened to her if he had to strangle it from every soul on the accursed island. He stood in the cold air shivering under the twinkling stars and prayed to the god he had sworn an oath to as a child.

"Ljegh, god of love and art!" he screamed. "I never blamed you for my unjust imprisonment in Death's Door or even when Celestie, the only woman I have ever loved, married another and bore him children, but if you do not lead me to her, then I shall kill myself and instead of serving you in the afterlife, I shall gut you!"

Their sea voyage took twelve days of hard sailing through rough waves, blazing days and frozen nights. On the morn of the twelfth day a man cried from the old ship's crow's nest.

"Land ahead!" called out the sailor.

The men aboard the ship clamored to the stern watching the small speck grow with anticipation. As it grew in proportion to the horizon, the first thing the men noticed was that none of the island's land, hills or mountains had any vegetation on it. It was dead, an island of the dead or so they would wish upon landing on its shores. Rowboats ferried men and supplies to the shore as their mounts were made to swim in from the boats. The waters off the shore were fierce cutting over jagged rocks drowning eight of the men's horses in their fury. Before all the equipment arrived ashore, men began to appear in the distance watching them curiously. They were too far away to see any more detail than their shaded human-like silhouettes. The seamen quickly returned to their ships upon seeing the distant figures to await the return of the expedition from insanity, if such a thing ever occurred.

Lord Tyler, fearless in his love, drove his men toward the shadowed images, finding that they were able to disappear as if invisible when approached. The hot desert sun beat down on him and his men in their heavy armor, parching their throats mercilessly. How men survive such an arid region without some source of water bewildered Lord Tyler as his horse drudged through thick sand. And where were these men hiding? Their forms kept appearing upon the horizon, but as the horses reached further in, the shadows seem to fade away as if mere mirages. The terrain showed little change, save for hills and mountainsides, made purely of dirt and sand without any signs of beasts or vegetation. Sweat ran out the pores of the men and horses evaporating into the arid sky to be lost from the dead land forever.

Two men appeared in the distant heat running through the thick sand as the formation of riders picked up their speed to close the distance. They disappeared over a small hillside barely twenty feet before the riders. The agile horses sprinted over the large dune coming to a halt by command of Lord Tyler who saw the men had disappeared once again like they were swallowed up by desert. Two long hillsides ran on both sides funneling the expedition's advance down into a long sandy gorge. Lord Tyler knew that no mortal man could have scaled the high ridges before they had reached the top of the dune without being seen. Unless they were ghosts or delusions, the only place they could have vanished was into the long twisting ravine. Desperation took hold of the Lord Tyler, as he knew that under such extreme conditions, his men would not be able to navigate the desert for long and would eventually be forced to return to the ships once their supplies were exhausted. His arm raised to signal his men to move in the shaded ravine when a hunter from Nthark pulled his horse in front of Lord Tyler's to stop his advance.

"My greatest apologizes for interrupting your command, but I feel to enter that canyon is a grave mistake," he declared as his horse danced in the sand to get a firm foothold. "The appearances of these strange men, although appearing sporadic, have been leading us to here for some reason. I believe they are part an ambush."

"And what if they are?" Tyler answered carelessly. "What other choice do we have? If these savages want a fight, then we shall show them the might of men from Haenic!"

His horse shunted that of the hunter pushing him aside so as to lead his men into the dark gully. The bright heat of the sun rose up the men's faces chased by a line of shade from the hillsides which engulfed them in its cool air. The clatter of horseshoes ricocheted against rock and hard-baked earth echoing ominously through the long ridge and bouncing off walls of rocks that ran along both sides of the men high over their heads. The path that cut down into the earth turned around a corner where the lead riders came face to face with a wild man. He stood firmly in the middle of the passageway holding a long bleached femur bone in one hand as a blunt club and a sharpened humerus bone in the other as a short piercing weapon. His hair was long and nappy reaching the curve of his acromial. A long beard entangled in dry braids hung down his chest covering his naked upper torso. A thin kilt made from sun-dried human flesh hung from his waist covering his groin. His skin was dark brown from years under the harsh desert sun being even darker brown in spots where splattered with dried blood. The lone savage had wild piercing eyes which showed no fear or respect of the large force before him.

The men on horseback drew their weapons as he screamed into the air exposing blood-saturated teeth and gums. Shadows cast down from the ridge top above as men leaped airborne over its crest landing onto the men below. As the men on horseback battled with the wild men biting at their ears while trying to pierce the chinks in their armor with stone-sharpened bone, a mass of skin peelers rushed from the corridor ahead and charged into the ravine bringing down horses with long piercing weapons of bone. The heavily armored men initially beat off the attack, slaying the unarmored men with the might of metal. But the fanatical attack continued as the assailants persisted in fighting as iron cut through their muscle and bone, stopping only when a weapon struck a vital organ or loss of blood stole their life. Hundreds poured into the gorge pulling the men of Haenic from their horses, weighing them down to the ground and unarming them with the superiority of vast numbers. Nearly half the men who rode into the ravine died within its shadows that day as the remainder were taken prisoner and dragged before the mad king of the insane land Foudes.

Ranting and raving deliriously the islanders spoke to each other, themselves and the wind as they led their prisoners into a large cave further inside the canyon. Within, human bodies hung from the ceiling without their skin, draining blood in crimson pools which dripped ever so slowly from bodily tissues. Lord Tyler had survived the attack, something he would soon regret, as he was led before the mad king of the skin peelers. The man sat in the center of the large cavern on top a throne made of bones covered with stretched and dried human skin.

"What is this that comes from the mainland so finely dressed?" asked the madman, who wore a human skull as a crown.

"We have come from Haenic in search of a woman," replied Lord Tyler, while being forced to his knees by one of his captors.

"Times are so bad in your land that you had to come and steal from those that have nothing?"

"I search for a woman wrongly exiled to this island some ten years ago."

"Then you search for us all!" laughed the self-proclaimed king hideously.

His men began to laugh with him, jumping up and down like monkeys wildly feeding on the excitement of the moment. As the men hooted and yelled strange words for no apparent reason, Lord Tyler's men sat helpless at the mercy of the ruling madman. The captured lord watched the man as he finally calmed down with tears in his eyes from laughter. No amount of reason would get out of this one; to succeed he needed to be as crazy as those before him.

"This woman you seek, what did she do to get condemned to this island of paradise?"

"She murdered her husband."

"Eww, I like her already! A woman like that keeps things exciting, because you never know when she might try to kill you too. You can't close your eyes without imagining her drawing a knife on you in your sleep! Gets my blood pumping just thinking about it!" the mad king said, energized. "What a woman!"

"I failed her in my love and have sacrificed all I have for the slightest hope of reclaiming her."

"What is the name of this woman?" asked the bloody king.

"Celestie."

"Do we have a woman in the caves by this name?" the cannibal shouted to his people. "Is she the wild red-headed woman of my harem that bites when I make love to her?"

"No my King," answered one of his men.

"Have we eaten a woman by this name?" he asked again in a serious tone.

"I did not ask," replied another.

The blood-stained men of the cave began to laugh hysterically at the joke.

"As you can see, she is no longer on this island and your risk has become nothing but loss… but no one except those I have eaten can say Skull Crusher is unfair, and I offer you and your men a deal."

Beaten and demoralized by the loss of his love and surrounded by a force of crazy men and women five times the size of his own party, Tyler had little option than to listen to the proposition.

"I want your ships sitting off the coast," he said peering madly through unnaturally bulging eyes. "Lure them in for me and I shall let you and your men live. Refuse and we shall pick at your bones!"

Lord Tyler knew that he could not trust the insane blood king and that to make such a deal was a bad as making one with Vaguk.

"You have my word, I will not harm them as I will need them to sail away from this accursed island and you and your men shall have all this!" he said holding up his arms as if offering his dirty cave as incentive, laughing viciously while igniting more laughter from his followers.

Lord Tyler said nothing, unwilling to betray those on the ships for his own poor decision-making. Seeing the man before him showing no signs of accepting his deal, the blood king intensified his efforts.

"Do know why we are called the skin peelers?"

His captive did not answer.

"Because we peel the skin from our victims and eat their flesh while they are still alive!" he claimed proudly. "Eating the flesh of the living gives strength and longevity to those that consume it!"

The horrid thought of such a ritual caused Lord Tyler's stomach to become nauseous. The king seized his throat and forced his victim to look into his horrid eyes. As Tyler gazed into them he saw putrid death. .

"Look at me!" the blood king screamed madly. "Has anyone not wondered on the mainland how I could still be alive after all these years? I am over three hundred years old and yet I am as young as you! This horrid island of death offers one thing that no other place in the Lands of Dream can, everlasting life in a dry arid hell! I have lived long enough scraping at the earth so to squeeze water from its dry soil at the bottom of this cave and long for the sight of plants and trees, and by the gods, free-flowing water! You will give me all this or I will eat your men one by one before your eyes until only you are left. And do not think I do not have a special death just for you."

Lord Tyler jerked his eyes away, unwilling to betray the people of his country by unleashing an army of madmen upon them.

"Answer me!" screamed the insane man.

"No, the reason the gods have given you this eternal life is not to exalt you, but to make you suffer for the unnatural deeds you have done."

"Bring forth one of his men!" ordered the angered king.

Five skin peelers seized a random man from the group dragging him against his will to the king.

"Strap him on the dinner table!"

The five men dragged the man to a long stone table stained with blood, as the people within the cave chanted and strapped him onto it, stretching his arms and legs out helplessly.

"From the flesh comes strength," chanted the people in the cave, "from the flesh comes life."

A man wearing the skin peeled face of a former victim slowly walked to the table looking through the eyes of the flesh mask while carrying a long sharpened bone knife. He raised it above the man and spoke as the priest of the blood ritual.

"May this man's strength and life flow into those that devour him so that we may live another day in this harsh lifeless land."

Upon reciting the words, he began to use the sharp curved bone knife to carve the man's skin away. The poor man screamed in horror as the priest peeled his skin from his fat and muscle exposing his bones, joints and organs. Blood rushed from his body onto the great stone table as the people quit chanting and rushed to him tearing at his flesh and stuffing it into their mouths. Their teeth gnashed at him painfully ripping the meat from his bones. Lord Tyler and his men looked on helplessly watching what would become their own fate if they didn't escape from the skull crusher's control.

Understanding the human anatomy, the skin peelers were able to eat half the man's body before he mercifully died on the table. The king gripped the man's heart in his palm as it still beat while using a sharp bone to cut away his aorta, vena cavas, pulmonary arteries and veins before ripping it from his chest and raising it to his mouth to drink from it like a cup. Covered in blood, the king and his men looked toward their prisoners laughing at them wildly in a hysterical manner. The men were forced to watch until the people finished leaving only a carcass of bone and shaved skin. Lord Tyler and his men were led further down into the cave and lowered one by one into a deep dark pit with high smooth walls of stone.

Hardly able to see, the men helplessly listened to the skin peeler's king taunt them from above.

"Tomorrow another of you will suffer the same fate, unless your leader chooses to do as I ask."

Then the blood king, his followers and their light faded away leaving the men in the utter darkness of an unknown pit deep within the earth of Foudes. Although his men were at risk of the cannibal's lottery, not one them rebelled or complained to their lord because they were Haenicians and if death was their fate they would meet it with dignity. Three days passed and as the king of Foudes had promised, each day a man was taken from the pit and eaten alive. Their fate seemed sealed until a voice awoke the men in the darkness.

"Psst," hissed a voice in the darkness above, "can you hear me?"

One of the men awoke Tyler from his sleep so he could also hear the voice.

"Hello, can you hear me?" it said, echoing in the darkness.

"Yes."

"Are you the one they call Tyler?"

"Yes," he said repeating himself to the strange voice.

"Listen, we do not have long," said the anxious voice. "I wish to strike a bargain with you and your men."

Lord Tyler's eyes lit up in the darkness, "What are the terms?"

"I can get you and all of your men out of here, but you must take me with you back to the mainland."

"Agreed, now get us out of here."

"I also want a parcel of land once we get there, so I'll have a fresh start."

"Agreed."

"And no one is to know who I was," the voice demanded in a loud whisper. "Swear to these terms before me, your men and the gods!"

"I swear to all these things."

As soon as he spoke the words, a heavy object dropped down into the pit smacking against the stonewall. The men quickly climbed to the top of the cave pit still unable to see within the cave's interior.

A hand gripped Lord Tyler's shoulder leading him and his men through the abyss down a long chamber.

"Hurry, everyone is asleep at the moment," said the voice leading the men down a long tunnel. "There are thousands of tunnels under the island that were formed by a large fresh water spring deep at the bottom of the cave, but every year the water recedes farther and farther down into the giant cave network. When I first arrived here twenty years ago, it was free flowing, but now we have to dig in the mud and squeeze it from the earth. Once it is all gone, so shall be the skin peelers. That is why Skull Crusher wants off this island."

Light poured into the cavern striking the men's retinas and enabling them to see for the first time in days.

"It is through these passages that we move so to avoid the heat of the desert. It is also how the men led you to the ambush, by popping in and out of these caves."

The man's long woolly hair and beard flapped behind him as he ran ahead leading the men through a network of multiple twisting tunnels. Suddenly he stopped as if remembering something and gripped Lord Tyler's shoulders.

"We don't have long, but what Skull Crusher told you about your woman not being on the island may not be true."

Tyler almost fell to his knees upon hearing his statement as his fingers took hold of the man with a tight grip.

"What do you mean?"

"On the other side of the island there is a tribe of settlers who have resisted the rule of the Skull Crusher. It is possible she could be there."

Once again hope gripped the longing lover.

"Lead us there now!" he ordered.

"To do so shall put us all at a great risk! As soon as your absence is discovered, Skull Crusher will send a force to the ships. If we do not head straight there, he may cut us off," warned the man.

Lost in his desire to find his love Lord Tyler was prepared to take any risk for without her he had nothing.

"Take us there now!"

The man took the order of his newest lord and led the men quickly under the earth of Foudes to the settlement, which defied the might of the Skull Crusher and his skin peelers behind high walls of stone. The dark-skinned man poked his head out of a hole peering into the blazing sun above. He popped back below like a prairie dog signaling to Lord Tyler to look above. Tyler's head rose into the scorching desert taking a moment for his eyes to adjust to the great change in light. As his eyes focused, a huge monument of stone rose from the flat desert winding into a circular formation. The thick crude wall was not smooth or finished, but rather little more than large rocks stacked on top of each other. Lord Tyler began to lift himself out the hole when the tight grip of a hand seized his ankle pulling him into the darkness below.

"Although far more civilized than the skin peelers, these people are protective and use giant boulders to protect their fortress," warned the man.

Lord Tyler and his men, about forty in all, crawled from the tunnels below standing out in the wide-open desert surrounding the great primitive fort. Men on top of the giant wall spotted them, crying out into the desert.

"Skin peelers!" the voices screamed loudly.

The figures of men began to rise upon the great wall standing firmly behind giant round boulders that they had somehow rolled to the top of the wall. Lord Tyler walked to the base of the massive wall standing below the looming shadows of boulders ready to be pushed down upon him.

"I am Lord Tyler, a noble from the kingdom of Haenic!" he screamed announcing himself.

A weathered man ripe with age stood up from behind a boulder and shouted down to the tiny figure, "I care not who you claim to be, leave before I order you to be crushed!"

"We have traveled a long way and have lost too many men to turn around now!" Tyler declared to the top of the soaring wall.

The leader of the settlers looked at the men who were too finely dressed to be skin peelers.

"One of you may come up, but if more than one of you attempts to climb the wall, we will crush you beneath the rocks of the earth!"

Lord Tyler began to mount the large wall climbing from stone to stone as they were arranged almost in a stair fashion leading to the wall's crest. At the very top huge rocks the size of men were strategically placed all along its rim, manned by men ready to unleash them over the edge at a moment's notice. An old man met him at the top of the wall leading him down the other side, which cascaded down just as the outer barrier of the rock wall. The interior of the fort was lush green with grass and plants, the first he had seen since arriving on the island.

"I am Masious, the leader of this small settlement."

"How did you and your people get here?" asked Tyler to the man who seemed at first impression as sane as any man he had ever seen.

"All of us are here for something, whether it be insanity, injustice or a crime, the only difference between us and the skin peelers is we have chosen to try to reform ourselves instead of embracing insanity," he replied walking with him down the wall. "I found this place quite by accident, or so I thought when I wandered upon it some years ago, but now I believe the gods led me to it so that those of us who renounced our crimes and behaviors might have a second chance. The fort is built over a natural spring, and without it, we would wither up and blow away as does all life on this loathsome island." The man paused to look at his uninvited guest. "You do not have the look of someone abandoned here by their country and people."

"We have not been abandoned, but instead I have come in search of a woman."

"A woman, what is her name?"

"Celestie."

"We have about six dozen men, women and children, but I do not recognize that name."

Tyler lowered his head in disappointment, once again he had failed her and this time it appeared he would never have the chance to right the wrong he had done.

"Do you have ships?" asked the man curiously.

"Yes we do."

"From where are your people from?"

"We serve the King of Haenic."

"I have never heard of this land, is it far?"

"Yes, further than I care to travel again," Tyler replied without heart.

"I ask because although the blessings of the gods have been upon us sprouting food in the middle of the wastelands, the past few years the spring that nourishes us and our crops is receding into the ground. I fear before long this place shall become our tomb."

Lord Tyler did not respond.

"Do you have room for us to return with you? I assure you those with me are not dangerous, for the bad ones have joined up with the skin peelers. My people are peaceful and fight only to defend themselves from the Skull Crusher and his lot."

"Yes," replied Tyler hoping to find some good in his loss, "there is room for all of you."

The man's face shone with excitement of the news.

"Then we must gather ourselves and prepare to leave. Where are your ships?"

"I'm not entirely sure, but we have someone with us who knows the way."

"We must leave as soon as possible, before the skin peelers discover your presence."

"They already know."

"You have encountered them?"

"We escaped their caves."

"Does the Skull Crusher know the location of your ships?"

"Yes," replied Lord Tyler simply.

"We will never make it. Outside these walls, the skin peelers are the predators, and we stand no chance out there if they know where we are going. They have attempted to overrun our fortress numerous times without success. But without our boulders and high walls their sheer strength will be too much. "

"My heart has little reason to continue its labor of life," said Lord Tyler sadly. "If it were not for my men, I would lie here and waste away underneath the might of the sun. We are leaving for our ships now. We have no weapons and little hope to make it, but if you choose to do so, you and your people are welcome to come with us."

"We have spears which we have made from gifts out of the soil. I shall have my people ready to go in a matter of minutes," the old man said running to the wall to address his people. "My people, the gods have smiled upon us once again. We leave now for a chance to return to the mainland. Bring nothing but your weapons and the water you can carry."

People began to run wildly around the compound with both expressions of fear and glee as the rush placed upon them turned the hardened people of Foudes to a frantic state. Women gripped the hands of their children as men collected their weapons and slung gourds of water over their backs. A woman sat in the middle of the commotion staring at the ground seemingly oblivious to the excitement of her own people. The old leader, seeing her doing nothing, gripped her shoulders and helped her to her feet asking another woman to help her along. The woman began to lead her away when Tyler caught a glimpse of her eyes. They were as deep and crystal as the blue sea glaringly directly into his heart. Tyler ran to her, pulling the oblivious woman into his arms and holding her closely.

"My dear Celestie, I cannot believe that you are finally in my arms to stay!"

She leaned into his arms with blank eyes failing to return his affection.

"She has not spoken since she wandered up to our fort some ten years ago," said Masious, "no one here even knows her name, but we accept anybody here as long as they are willing to contribute."

"My love… please speak to me!" Tyler pleaded, falling down to his knees. "I cannot carry on without your love!"

He began to cry holding the shell of the woman he loved so dearly. What further cruelty could the gods place upon him? He squeezed her with all his might so not to let her be taken from him again. At that moment he wished he could have died in Death's Door with the image of her in his heart forever. The palm of her hand stroked his hair as he cried so to soothe him.

"My love," she said consoling him, "Your tears have brought me back."

He rose up and they kissed passionately holding each other so tightly that even the power of the gods would not be able to separate them again. They cried with joy as their hearts burst with the fulfillment of lost lovers reunited.

"My dear, we must hurry to return to the mainland before the skin peelers discover our absence."

"I would rather live here with you on this wasteland till the end of my days than risk returning to the mainland where we might be separated again."

"My love, if we make the mainland, we will be able to live out our lives as we please!"

She did not question his statement or even deliberate it, for he held her utmost trust. She would jump off a cliff onto jagged rocks if he told her they would be together after doing so. She took his hand ready to follow him to the end of the world. Armed with crooked and flimsy sharpened sticks grown from the barren dust of the island, the men ran through the dark tunnels behind the skin peeler who had rescued them in hopes of reaching the shore where their ships were anchored before the Skull Crusher and his cannibals found them. The small tunnels widened and suddenly the men recognized the pit from which they had been rescued.

"What is going on here?" asked Tyler, unsure why they had been led back to the cave of the skin peelers.

The man who had freed them stepped backward into the darkness lighting a torch. The faces of Skull Crusher and his tribe appeared from the darkness surrounding the rabble of poorly armed men.

"My poor king, it appears you have been outwitted by a madman," declared Skull Crusher. "Did you not think if I only wanted your ships I could not have had my men dress in your clothes and ride to the beach upon horses to bring in the rowboats? I knew if I had one of my men pretend to rebel and help you escape with the information that your woman might possibly be alive, a man who has crossed the great sea would surely go there to retrieve her. I also knew that the people of the settlement would want to go back to the mainland with you. I'll have to admit I didn't think you would really find her, but I have to thank you, Lord Tyler, I have been trying to capture that fertile spot of land for over a decade now and it's finally going to be mine!"

"You have what you want! So let us go and there will be no more bloodshed!" said Lord Tyler trying to strike up a bargain out of desperation.

"Oh, but you have so much more that I need. I want your ships and for that I need your clothes!"

"We shall give them gladly," offered the outnumbered general trying to salvage the life of those he had put into harm's way.

"Ah, but I want it all. Your clothes, the fortress, your ships… your flesh! My madmen, we have new men to skin!" he shouted in a feral war cry.

Lord Tyler pushed Celestie behind him holding out his spear, he would not lose her again. His heart beat within his chest not willing to acknowledge defeat, not until it was in the hands of a skin peeler. He rushed directly toward Skull Crusher like a wild animal maneuvering through charging Skin Peelers to face the blood king in hand to hand combat.

Skin Peelers seemed to appear from the walls attacking the men from all sides throwing themselves at lifted spears and madly trying to tear their victims apart with the fury of wild beasts with nothing but blood on their minds. The thin spears pierced the attacker's ribcages impaling the first round of assaulters. Almost in unison of the falling of the first wave, a second wave of bloodthirsty men came upon the small group scattering their crude formation.

Lord Tyler found himself locked in battle with the great Skull Crusher blocking his weapon of choice, a bludgeoning petrified femur bone from the hip of a giant that lived on the island long ago. Its massive weight cracked his spear as he held it up with two hands, one on each end, to stop the weapon from crushing his head. He seized the weapon with two hands to wrestle it from the madman's hands but found his opponent's strength to be far greater than his own. The Skull Crusher's hair flung around wildly as he hurled Lord Tyler into the air smashing his body into the wall of the cave. The head of the giant femur bone came down beside Lord Tyler's head breaking off a chunk of the rocky floor and missing his face by mere inches. The man before him, although possessing the strength of three men, was still only a man and bent over in pain as Tyler's foot kicked him in the groin. He seized the man's long hair with a tight grip and bashed his head into his armored knee. Blood poured from the Skull Crusher's face as the heavy metal beat against his skull. With the strength of an ape, the blood king lifted up Lord Tyler like a man a child holding him helplessly into the air.

"Let me show you the strength of flesh!" he said picking up his opponent and thrashing him against the ground.

Lord Tyler's bones cracked giving way to the mad force hurling him repeatedly against the rock floor of the cave. The Skull Crusher lifted his victim high over his head preparing to smash him against stone one last time with all his might when a spear pierced the back of his skull thrusting through his right eye. Blood squirted out the eye socket as its point tore out his eye and wedged into his skull. The strong massive body fell to the floor lifeless ending centuries of reigning terror. Tyler fell on top of his corpse finding Celestie still ramming the spear into the man's skull. She fought with it screaming and grunting as it slid through the Skull Crusher's cranium breaking its sutures like a wedge. With the death of their leader and god, the mighty skin peelers suddenly lost heart and pulled back into the darkness. Dead bodies from both sides were strewn throughout the darkness of the cave having finally found peace on the horrid island of Foudes. Lord Tyler seized Celestie pulling her back from the Skull Crusher's lifeless body to calm her as she tried to stomp at the dead immortal that had nearly killed her love.

"My Lord, I captured one of the heathens," stated one of his Kthaer barbarians holding a skin peeler into the air kicking and screaming by the long hair on his head.

"Set him down," ordered his lord.

The barbarian did as he was told, lowering the skin peeler's feet to the ground while keeping a tight grip on his tangled hair.

"You have a golden opportunity today to save your life by not meeting with Skull Crusher again."

The man looked horrid covered in blood and the dried skin of human flesh. He nodded as if accepting the terms offered.

"Lead us to the beach where are ships are anchored, and if try and trick us I swear to you I will give you to this man as a play toy to do with you as he sees fit."

The much smaller man nodded again pointing in the direction they should follow. The group followed the man through the dark tunnels twisting through corridors and multiple tunnel networks and seemed horribly lost until their captive pointed up to a large hole tilting toward the desert sun leaking onto the cave floor. One of the men poked his head out and to his delight three ships still sat in the harbor awaiting their return. The group made a mad dash to the beach fearful of a possible counter attack by the vicious skin peelers. When the men were spotted rowboats came ashore loading aboard all those save the skin peeler who had led them to safety. He watched enviously as they crawled onto the ship slowly sailing away out of sight.

"What of that man?" asked one of his remaining commanders.

"He has gone over too far, he would never be able to adjust to life off that island without being a risk to himself and others. It is best that he spend the remainder of his life however many centuries it will take for the fresh water below to recede beyond their reach."

The three ships sailed over the blue plain of the great sea cutting its waves as the sun and moon rose and fell in succession of one another marking days and nights that offered little to do but wait. The days of the long ride back were the greatest of Lord Tyler's life as he held his love Celestie trying to make up for the many years of lost time they had endured. Neither of the two could take their eyes off one another in fear the other might fade away as if in a dream. When the large wooden hulls of the three sea vessels docked on the shores of Alboules each man who survived the ordeal stepped onto the soil of the mainland counting his blessings. Some had been exiled from its shores for over twenty years, while others had been exiled from elsewhere and had never seen the beauty of its green lush trees. They marveled at the free flowing water of its rivers and creeks and the giant trees that loomed in the air above their heads. To most it was a wonderland they had only dreamed of ever seeing again. Horses and wagons had been left for their return by order of King Hamse stocked with fresh food, clothes and supplies. The convoy rolled across the fertile land of Alboules amazing its occupants with each natural wonder they passed in the exquisite landscape of the Lands of Dream.

The great tower of Alboules' capital glistened above the burnt city welcoming the travelers from a far distance as they rolled up to its gates amidst a great rebuilding project. Stones rolled by great mule trains filed into the city as its occupants set to rebuild a once great city to even greater glory under the rule of Haenic. Upon reaching the great tower, two old friends reunited with a sincere embrace.

"My friend, it warms my heart to see that you have safely returned from the great sea!" declared the noble king of Haenic.

"I have someone I would like you to meet," answered the noble of Garl, introducing the woman on his arm. "This is Lady Celestie of Garl."

She stepped forward to the king and curtsied without speaking because having been the wife of a noble she understood the tradition of respecting a king by never speaking first.

"My dear, you are even more beautiful than I was told in the shadows of Death's Door."

"Thank you my lord," she replied daintily.

"I am sure your people will adore you as do I," he said kissing her hand gently.

The King and his men stayed three more months in the great province of Alboules, the largest in all of Haenic, setting into motion its reconstruction and future place in his empire. A great project was undertaken to connect the province to the rest of the country by building an enormous road through the once impassible Mhorhaen. The task, which took four years to complete successfully, connected the two by a colossal road guarded from the depths of the wood by guard posts placed within a day's march so that travelers could have safe havens during the treacherous nights of the giant wood.

King Hamse reigned over the great Empire of Haenic for another hundred years, bringing it into a golden age of discovery, wealth and growth unlike any nation before, thriving off the skills of its people who benefited tremendously in their own personal lives being that of free men and women. As time passed the great empire grew under its fourth King Hamse honoring all its kings before: King Hamse the First, the Builder, King Hamse the Second, the Conqueror and King Hamse the Third, the Liberator. Although not of the same blood, King Hamse the Fourth ruled with great honor following in the footsteps of his adoptive father, learning from both his words and actions by taking solitary council in his father's once great trophy room. It was bare now, no longer showcasing the furs of great beasts, having nothing more than a single sharpened dinner table knife on its wall with a plaque below it reading, "The Key to Death's Door." King Hamse the Fourth expanded the empire of Haenic in his own right leading his armies against those of the mongrel nations, but that is another story.

A Female Skin Peeler Shaman

While the seven deadly sins of Pride, Envy, Wrath, Sloth,
Greed, Gluttony and Lust pollute one's soul, there are
five pure pleasures that enrich it:
Eating, Drinking, Sleeping, Sex and Dream.

The Last Drop of Evil

A tall man who was completely shaven from his toes to the tip of his head, including his eyebrows and genitals, stood at the base of a blood-stained altar deep beneath the dungeons of his dark citadel which had been erected in the Malcaul swamp in the dark days of Zeethe's first reign of the mongrel before man dreamed within it. It had originally been the fortress of the great orc king Dragetryn who reigned thousands of years ago over the western continent of Zeethe. Under his iron claw, it had been a torture chamber of horrid repute draining the blood of his enemies as sacrificial tribute to the gods of the mongrel. Having sunk in the swamps nearly six hundred years ago, it now served as a hideout for those men and beasts who opposed the rule of King Hamse the Third whose men hunted the mongrel and their sympathizers relentlessly to expunge them from the great continent of Zeethe. It lay hidden, having once been a seven story structure that stood high above ground, centered in the murk of the vast swamp long avoided by man for its beasts, diseases and the black magic which possessed the very soil, trees and water.

Although a man, the sorcerer worshipped gods of madness who gladly offered power to any who might bring them back to prominence in the new age of man, who now worshipped gods of law and order. He had shaven every inch of his body and purified his skin bathing it in pure mineral salts from the springs of Peazae stolen in the night by his goblin servants. One such servant, a dirty goblin with dull green skin, groveled at his side as he prepared to perform what might be his final spell.

"Master," it said in a vile shrill voice, "our scouts report that men in flat boats have entered the swamps."

The sorcerer's head gleamed under the glow of candlelight sparkling in the dark shadows of the stone room as he prepared his spell. One incorrect ingredient, such as a loose hair or skin follicle could be enough to ruin a spell or far worse alter it. Moss glistened along the walls as the water outside seeped through the ancient stone. The massive fortress slowly sank, dropping beneath the surface by mere inches per year, but after hundreds of years, the bottom four levels had completely submerged returning the ancient rock of its structure back to the earth from where it had been stolen long ago. Its many lower rooms and chambers now belonged to the beings of the swamp.

The sorcerer had not ignored his servant, but only delayed his response as he had more important matters at hand.

"How many?" he asked of the short beast.

"Hundreds of armored men…" the nasty mongrel paused in fear of his master's response, "an army."

He had seen it coming, having been warned by the black rock which spied upon the lands of Zeethe when bathed in the blood of the innocent.

"Where will we run next?" it inquired in a cowardly manner as the mongrel drew upon bravery only in large numbers. "The ships of Alboules sail the southern seas blocking any retreat to the shores of Fathel!"

The bald man ignored the whimpering pleas of his pusillanimous servant focusing solely on his spell. A one-time servant of the powerful Zespheous, the sorcerer had raised the dead unleashing them upon the living to feed a black hunger which never ceased. He had felt the power of the black magic in his blood, pulsating within his brain and sensually addicting him to its call. When he read its words, he felt like a god reaching above the creatures of the earth rising to the mountains of the gods to stand before the sun in their glory. Upon his great master's death, he had escaped into the swamp taking in those who had failed to escape back across the great southern sea to dwell under his reign in the safety of the swamp's bosom. Large ogres, foul orcs, vicious trolls and greedy goblins cowered behind the walls of the ancient fortress as the armies of Haenic came to finish what they had begun with the death of the sorcerer's master. They were superior in number and training because he was a necromancer and not a general and any such conflict would end in his death and that of his servants. All a handful of creatures could hope to give him against such an army was time.

"Send the ogres and trolls into the swamps to turn over their boats," he said thinking of buying time for his spell.

"The men carry long bows," the creature said, warning his master of his disastrous plan. "The swamp will slow the assault… they will be easy targets."

The sorcerer walked over to a dark corner of the room bringing back a glass jar of brown enchanted moss. He had prepared it by soaking the swamp moss in the gills of a Grabzur fish under the light of the moon while holding his breath for two minutes as he signed the enchantment.

"Have them eat this and for a short time they will be able to breathe underwater to avoid the eyes of men."

Grubby hands appeared from the darkness disappearing back into the shadows. The small monster held the shiny container invisibly rubbing its slick surface in the dark. Goblins were masters of hiding, capable of standing in the slightest of shadows unseen by normal eyes. The small gnarled hands held the jug greedily soaking in the radiance of the powerful black magic that oozed from the urn. It seeped into the pores in its skin bringing delight to its evil heart.

"Now!" boomed the sorcerer to the creature he could not see.

Its little feet stomped up the stone stairwell, the sound disappearing into the upper levels of the sinking fortress.

There were not enough ogres or trolls left to stop the advancing men, but it mattered not as his spell would do that, thought the sorcerer, smiling a wicked grin. His eyes gleamed in the darkness enthusiastic of the impending challenge that his next spell would present. It would be his most difficult attempt yet, accompanied with great cost, but a sorcerer was only as notable as his greatest spell.

Madness filled his limbs as he meticulously prepared the stone altar for what would be a stage of power, lunacy, and death. As he closed his mind to the world within he stood rolling his eyes back into his head, possessed by his art and leaving himself completely vulnerable to those outside his own thoughts. Nothing could break his concentration or the magic would fail unable to be retried until the next new moon. In a spell of such great complexity, the mind of the sorcerer could not wander by worrying if his servants would succeed in delaying the army from Haenic. Pain, pleasure, fear… nothing mattered but the incantation he began to perform in a long monotone chant. His body began to shake as the raw power of black magic began to surge in the fluids of his body, changing the chemical makeup of his molecules. His tissues swelled with power rejuvenating his organs and harmonizing his organ systems. His eyes opened smoldering black smoke from dark onyx eyes as superhuman strength surged through his muscles. He had the power to break through the very stone walls that held the swamp from bursting into the ancient chamber, but he held his power within ready to transfer it to his spell at the right moment.

Screams of war clattered above as man and mongrel battled to the death. Metal clashed and blood spilled once again in the ancient torture chamber. The sorcerer tuned out the commotion completing his final spell. A surge of evil magic leaped from his body swirling against the walls, seeping through the mortar and disappearing into the swamp beyond. The dark magic which had formed the desolate swamp untwined from the roots of the trees sinking the muddy soil deep below the water. Trees sank into the swamp pulling the immense treetops below the surface of the water as the swamp bed submerged into the earth. He had undone the magic of the swamp which had been created by his predecessors centuries ago to veil the ancient citadel from their enemies. Now he would take his enemies down with him into the mud of the earth creating a giant tomb that would house thousands. Men clamored in the halls beyond the door to the altar looking for the evil sorcerer who had been hiding within their lands while defying the will of their great king. Axe blades hacked through the dungeon door spraying splinters as the wood split under the weight of heavy sharpened iron.

Water began to burst through the cracks between the stone blocks as the giant fortress sank below the surface of the swamp. Water came running down the stairs behind the sorcerer rushing up his legs as he held out his arms in triumph. The wizard released the last drop of evil from his soul and his body shivered in delight of the power it had held within. A wall of water rushed from the swamp sinking deep into the citadel engulfing man, mongrel and the wizard himself who held a long grin, because for a moment before his death he had possessed the might of the gods.

Four forces operate the cosmos with the men of the waking world believing it to be gravity, electromagnetism, strong interaction and weak interaction, while the men of Dream believe it to be air, fire, earth and water.

The Dreamer Trilogy

The Origin of Dream
A Dream Within a Dream
Search for a Dreamer

The Lands of Dream is a place where a multitude of gods still compete for the worship of men and man is content with the luxuries of their natural surroundings; therefore they do not strive to create new inventions or discover new technologies to better their life, because all is as it should be.

The Origin of Dream

As a child he had dreamed much of the land within which he stood forming in his mind the corners of its realm while asleep under the covers of his bed. He had placed the tall foaming waterfall which cooled his hand in just one night, as simply as might a decorator a table in a tiny room of an enormous mansion. The creation of vast oceans, soaring mountains, peaceful prairies and bustling cities came easily once he had solved the riddle of the mind. The mind was nothing but an array of images with those that were perceived as concrete as those formed. If one perceived death, then death was as real as your own hand, but if one formed life, then one lived without fear of death. Phean, as he called himself in the Lands of Dream, had seen five millenniums pass since his birth and he was still as young as he was the day he left the world he had been thrown from at his birth. Having explored the frontier of his subconscious he had found a way to escape the drab surroundings of his birth leaving the mad creation of another mind behind forever. Its nightmare of murder, religion and greed no longer held his destiny as it did for millions of others. He had severed his ties to it long ago so that he might never suffer its sorrow again.

In the vast Lands of Dream he held the position of a god, having created those that dwelled under its suns and stretching its borders beyond the reach of its inhabitants. In his dreams he had formed territories of great beauty, while in his nightmares he had unconsciously shaped regions of dreadful terror. Giving the Lands of Dream magnificent beauty and vile horror gave the land a peaceful balance in which its people thrived. Sometimes those outside his consciousness would discover his creation, exploring its majestic cities, swaying fields and deep oceans and interacting with its people. Some of these dreamers would arrive by accident finding it nothing but joyful folly, while others hunt it wildly with aspirations to stay.

While Phean loves his creations, he is suspicious of those from outside and shuns them by hiding the secrets for which they search. I know this because he disregards me for my attempts to solve the very riddle he unraveled thousands of years ago.

The first time I dreamt into the Lands of Dream was quite by accident. When I was only a boy, maybe ten or eleven, I found myself standing by a glistening fountain on a deserted cobblestone road. At first I was frightened as most children are when they find themselves suddenly alone, but the fear that had entered my heart from the world of the waking faded away quickly with the gentle breeze that blew upon me from the snow-peaked mountains beyond. My eyes began to search the large field with a single cobble road running through its middle to see where such a road might lead, but both its destination and origin were far beyond my vision. Suddenly my attention turned to a small marble fountain that trickled cool water under the warm suns above. Its touch livened me as if its molecules were the essence of life itself. I played out that beautiful day in the fountain of the wayfarer without care of ever returning to my own world. I believed the brilliant water of that fountain seeped into my soul for from that day on I could think of nothing else.

During the day I would contemplate where I would travel next in my sleep, and at nights I lived life to its fullest visiting kingdoms of wonder and mystery. To the dismay of my parents and teachers, my doctor diagnosed me with attention deficit disorder and in an attempt to stop my daydreaming I was placed on a daily prescription plan. Almost instantly my dreams ceased and although my grades improved I fell into a deep depression. I longed to return to the beautiful realm I had discovered in my sleep, but the drugs I took fogged that part of my subconscious and sealed its door.

As I fell deeper and deeper into despair, my parents took heed of my mood and before long I was taking drugs for depression as well. This continued for nearly a year in which I failed to dream consciously or subconsciously before my father finally threw my medications away. To this day I remember his exact words to my mother as she pleaded with him to give her back my bottles of pills.

"I'd rather see him play and suffer in school than do well in school and suffer through life!" he screamed.

Almost instantly I began to dream again and before long I was climbing high mountains and visiting strange cities of glorious wonder. As my youth in the waking world faded, so did the length and frequency of my dreams. Each night was a struggle to find its borders, and once I arrived I struggled by pushing my physical state to its limits so as to never wake. To do so, I became a hermit of sleep, rarely leaving my bedroom while living in long self-induced sleeps. During this time, my physical health faded but my mind flourished! As the strength of my mind grew I found I could enter the Lands of Dream wherever I wanted and one day I found myself standing in the court of Phean.

It stood hundreds of feet tall in the center like a vast inside auditorium spherically sloped above and below, while the floor that cut through its center was made of hard clear polished quartz. I stood on the sparkling floor looking hundreds of feet above and below weak at the knees from such a splendid sight. I marveled at the hollow world made of polished alabaster knowing no such palace could be constructed by hand, for what I stood within came from the mind of a god. A white throne made of glossy ivory sat at the far end of the chamber and from the great distance of sparkling crystal I could not see if the dreamer I had desired to meet so dearly sat upon it. I shuffled slowly over the vast void distorted through the quartz under my feet, enthralled by the enormous chamber within I appeared. A young man nearly the same age as I with a thick brown graceful beard sat upon the mother-of-pearl throne wearing a thick white fur. It stunned me to be able to stand so close to a god of such great power without permission or guards. My brain began to tickle as the being staring back at me searched my mind.

"Where are my guards, you ask?"

I nodded to him as he had read my mind.

"I am the King of Dreams and need no one to protect me in the very realm that extends from my mind. I could dissolve the floor below your feet with a simple thought and plunge you to your death as I can use the very air around you as my defense."

Instantly a long curved scimitar appeared heavily in my hand nearly pulling me to the ground.

"Throw it," he commanded to me with a booming voice. "Kill me and all this will be yours."

I held it steady fearful to attack one such as he. Upon seeing my reluctance to do as he commanded the same command echoed through my mind. Suddenly as if I were a different person with great skill I slung the heavy blade at the king sitting above me on his massive throne. The shiny blade spiraled perfectly balanced through the air directly at the throat of the great king, but before it could reach its target it stopped in mid air sinking into the air which had instantly frozen between him and me. I reached to touch the wall never having imaged a temperature cold enough to freeze air as solid as a rock. Just before the tips of my fingers reached its surface it unfroze dropping the sword at my feet. As I stared at the blade, the quartz floor upon where it laid began to swell up around my legs rooting me to it helplessly.

"If the crystal rose further your chest would seize up leaving you unable to breathe."

"Great Phean, I did not come to harm you."

"No need for apologizes. I have seen you from within and I know you are sincere."

"Then you know what I seek."

"And you know I will not help you."

"What have I done for you to oppose my desire to be a part of the beauty you created? I have traveled to these lands many a nights and intermingled with its people and have brought no harm."

"You are contaminated by the place from which you come. As was I… once," he declared with the grace of a king on his throne. "I can feel the vileness of it now… seeping from you. It is a disease to want more than you already have, to desire more than the trees and water, to never enjoy what you have because you strive for more."

"I want nothing more than to share the simple wonders of these lands," I pleaded, "The metal machines of the waking world that bellow death hold no charm upon me. Please great Phean, your roots come from the ancient delta kingdom near the first cataract. We are not such distant people."

Memories which had not embellished the god's mind for thousands of years rushed from his ancient memory banks like a tidal wave enveloping his brain with images from the land of his birth. Suddenly he was seven years old with dark brown skin that glistened under the hot sun of the surrounding desert. His toes squished into the rich black soil deposited by the great river Iteru. He played happily as a child along the swelled river banks, without a care in the world, but as he grew older, his happiness faded. He was the son of a peasant, a mere tool of the Pharaoh Djoser. His life had been born to serve, not to live of his own free will. As he grew older and worked harder under the blazing sun building monuments under the cruel supervision of Imhotep high priest of the sun god Ra at Heliopolis, he began to dream wondrous thoughts of fertile lands with nothing but idle time to fill a man's day. He slowly withdrew himself from the heartless forced labor of his born life and finally left it all together by discovering a secret passage to the Lands of Dream in his own mind. So many had suffered and died to please so few in the waking world. A tear ran down from his eye as he remembered seeing his father die from old age at merely twenty five years old. It was the first time he had cried since he entered the lands of Dream some thousands of years ago.

"You are wasting your time," he said callously, "I will not show you the way."

Watching him smugly refuse to show me the way released a rage in me as I had never felt. How dare he refuse to help me. What had I ever done for him to reject me so coldly? I glanced down at the sparkling floor under my feet directly at the shiny gem-handled sword that had fallen to the floor. A glimmer came to my eye, I remembered the knowledge he had instilled in me on its usage. He had stopped me before because he knew what I was going to do, but this time he wouldn't expect it. I could seize it and cut him down with it before he had the time to defend himself. He was the greatest dreamer of all time, quick and agile of mind, but I was an accomplished dreamer as well, having dreamed all across the Lands of Dream. Without thinking, so not to warn him, my fingers gripped the heavy hilt and raised it from the floor without the effects of time. As my hand pulled the weapon back to send it to its mark, our eyes met. They spoke directly to me as a father to a misbehaving child. My eyes welled in terror as I realized the weight of my action. The weapon clanked to the floor falling behind me as it fell from the grip of my fingers. I dropped to my knees, conceding his superiority.

"You are not ready my son. I hold no misconceptions about the residents of the Lands of Dream as there are wars and death much like there are in your world, for it seems these tragedies cannot be removed from the human mind, but what makes you more dangerous than they is that you have the knowledge of science and technology. Those of good, evil and opposed are on a level playing field here, no one will ever dominate the other thus ensuring the beauty of multiple cultures. Your hatred could result in the deaths of all life with global weapons much like those already developed by the madmen of our birth world."

Tears came to my eyes because I knew what he spoke was the truth. I had almost killed a man who had done me no wrong, but simply for declining my desire.

"Continue to search, my son. When your heart becomes true you will find the way. There are others like us who have found the way, expanding the lands with their own dreams, stretching the borders of Dream beyond exploration. Never give up your dreams, for this is where your reality lies."

When I awoke the next morning the world I appeared was louder, duller and more horrid than it had ever been. To this day the Lands of Dream blossom under the dreams of the god Phean and to this day I explore his realm searching for its secret within myself.

Within the mind are conflicts between Good and Evil, Dreams and Nightmares, Truth and Lies and finally Life and Death.

A Dream within a Dream

Alzoond, The Storyteller

Prologue

To awake from a dream and within a dream are two separate and distinct experiences. To awake from a dream happens in an instant and you immediately realize where you are as reality takes its grip upon your consciousness. To awake within a dream happens gradually: although you realize what has happened, you don't really know how long you've been there. You could have been there only a few minutes or possibly even several years. It's as if you blend into the environment of the dream. You realize things are different, but your arrival merges into the setting, as if you always belonged there whether you've been there before or not. To awake within a dream, in a conscious manner, is called dreamwalking. This story is the culmination of such a dreamwalk.

Celpahia is a place that I have walked in many times. Each time I arrive it is a pleasant experience and each trip never lasts long enough, for those in our world never stay in Celpahia for long. I have tried many times to travel to Celpahia and stay but with no success, for the body will always awaken at some point. With great pains, I have attempted to increase my stays through various drug inducements that prolonged my sleep, concerning many of my friends for fear I will one day overdose and die. I have slept for periods as long as weeks, through various drug inducements and other methods not so commonly known, all ending in the same result, to awaken from my dream and Celpahia. Each time I wake from Celpahia, I have a great fear of never returning, and with each new attempt it takes me longer than before to search and find Celpahia so I can walk its streets again. Sometimes I think that the only way to stay in Celpahia would be to die in my sleep while I was there, but when I speak of it to my friends they think that I am mad! Even if I could get someone to help me in this matter, I would have no way of letting that person know if I was in Celpahia and I might awaken before I die and never drink in the taverns of Celpahia again, a risk I will not take. So I must continue to sleep and search for Celpahia and speak with its people so that I might one day find someone with the knowledge or some way to sleep and never return. It is this quest that brings me to my story, "A Dream within a Dream."

The city of Celpahia sits upon the twisted banks of the Manikalra River, which brings many things to the beautiful city. It not only brings in imported hashish from the corners of Veltarin near the great desert of the Alekain, luscious and unusual fruits from the gardens of Buarlia, spices and incenses from the ports of Talicean, but also the mystery and intrigue of the people who arrive upon its ships every day and night. Yes, the appeal of Celpahia comes from its people, such as the sailors and their bizarre tales of mysterious lands, tales that make sense in your sleep, but seem silly in the reality of the waking world. These ships bring in people of all different dresses, accents, traditions, and appearances. Oh, don't get me wrong, the city itself is ethereal! The buildings are made of hand-carved white stone intricately detailed with infinite designs picturing tales of both glorious and horrendous nature. Domes of copper metal, which have turned an emerald green over time, cover their roofs, giving them an elegance and sophistication unlike any city in our world. The buildings are abnormally tall compared to their width and are sometimes four or more levels high, woven tightly together along crooked cobblestone streets. Ivory fountains sit in the middle of the streets with their waters dancing loudly in the sparkle of the sun's light and singing softly under the light of the moon. At night pale white lanterns sit in the windows to light a traveler's way, and the moon reflects off the river Manikalra, which wraps around Celpahia and travels on to other strange cities and docks.

Chapter 1
Walking in Celpahia

When my eyes assimilated the blurry visions of Celpahia that appeared before me, I could not recall for how long I had gazed upon the beauty of the place. My feet had somehow borne me into the center of Celpahia's quaint town square near the Gendar Bazaar. It appeared to be early in the morning for dew still sat upon the marketers' tents and the local peddlers were just beginning to set up shop. I wanted to spend the day amongst the tables and haggle the day away with the rest of the townsfolk and traders, but my dreams in Celpahia were no longer for idle pleasures. I thought it would be best if I were to start my journey with a plan to guide the fury of my blind ambition. I spoke to several people I encountered along its streets without success. Most laughed at me when I explained where I was from stating, "There are no such places" or "I don't care to waste time thinking about such dismal things." With little success on the street, I decided to try my luck in the local taverns near the wharf, where a good drink or a sustained smoke always loosened a tongue.

Walking casually along the river's edge, my senses partook the sweet aroma of Celpahia's West Botanical Gardens, drawing me into them like a helpless child towards a flamboyant street entertainer. Succulent flowers slithered between the joints of my hands caressing my palms gently in the cool morning breeze. I knew that by walking through the tall hanging vines and drooping flora I would waste precious time, but I couldn't resist their mellifluous allure. Besides, it was still early for the crowd in which I hoped to speak and a man cannot live on wine alone.

The garden consisted of copious plants and flowers indigenous only to the Lands of Dream, which present sensations of both sight and smell unlike any known in the waking world. Not only are the colors in the Lands of Dream much more vivid, but there are colors that have never been looked upon by the eyes of waking men, except those that have walked in their dreams.

As I walked along the tight trail before me, I marveled at all the strange plants and insects that swirled around me with odd flutters and buzzes in the still fragrant air. Small almost hidden paths broke off from the main trail seductively luring away travelers to other wondrously secluded sites and angelic visions of magnificence, places where a botanist could spend a lifetime in a simple stretch of track and never lose interest. I lost all perspective of time and space staring blankly at the anomalous plants, wildlife, and brooks that had trickled absentmindedly beneath its bridges and archways since the first dream was dreamt. When the noose of enchantment finally loosened its grip upon me, the sun's rays were beating down directly upon the top of my head as it orbited ever so slowly towards the next horizon. I took one last whiff of the garden's pollen-filled air and rushed down its overgrown paths leaving the shade of the hanging gardens for the damp air of moldy docks.

By the time I reached the harbor, the taverns were alive with activities and strange folk. I chose a pub that was close to the waterfront since it was frequented by disparate sailors and passengers from far lands, in hopes of hearing tales about men from the waking world. I entered the mouth of the tavern, ordered a drink and sat down to survey its dark smoky innards. The bartender returned with a tall wooden goblet weighted down with a thick murky liquor that was sweet to the nose as well as to the tongue. It swirled heavily in the sphere of my cup absorbing into the pores of the wood soaking in its rustic flavor. Drinking, along with all sorts of dice, card, and table games was the norm, and although the focus of its inhabitants was gambling, it was the room's conversation that held my concentration. I strained my ears to listen to the tales of the tavern's storytellers over the laughter and cheers of its inhabitants. I spent the rest of the afternoon and the first part of that evening engaged in conversation, listening to strange and usual tales that would have normally captivated me, but today I was looking for one particular tale, a tale about men from the waking world. Every time I would mention something about men from my world, the subject would always seem to change and nothing I did could bring it back to the table. It was as if everyone were deliberately trying to avoid the subject. I decided to bide my time and stay away from the various wines, liquors, and pipes offered to me by the men I spoke with and hoped as the evening slipped away so might a few tongues.

After much deliberation, I finally set my efforts on one particular man. He had the look of a hardened sailor who had spent many years on the seas and oceans of the Lands of Dream, with leathery skin, a white scrubby beard and tattoos on every inch of his skin visible to the eye. I chose him not only for his age, but also for his habit of chewing a peculiar purple plant that only grew wild in the forest of Axaniagh, a tiny island that hovered at the edge of the great whirlpool in the northern realm of dreams. I had chewed it before and knew very well its intoxicating effects. In one dreamwalk I spent three waking days just gazing at the surface of a leaf as if it were its own universe after having consumed only a small portion of it.

I bought my guest drink after drink of whatever he would gulp down between his chews and listened to him intently waiting for any chance to guide his tales. Whenever his stories would stray away from men of my world I would circumspectly lead him back to stories that might benefit my cause. He knew all kinds of stories about men from the waking world, but none about any who had stayed in the Lands of Dream. Just as I began to get frustrated and lose hope I heard two men arguing on the accuracy of a tale. One claimed that a friend of his had heard it from Alzoond himself and everyone knew he was never wrong. The other man averred that either he or his friend must have mixed up the story for it could be no fault of the wise Alzoond. The argument didn't last long, for both men agreed that they were in no condition to be positive about anything except to have another drink. I immediately regained my ardor and asked the barkeeper if he had heard of the man, Alzoond. He explained that Alzoond was a local soothsayer who told tales for a living and kept records of the utmost integrity. I got directions to his place of business, paid my tab, said good-bye to my motley friends and headed out before it got any later in the evening.

As soon as I left the tavern I was swept up into a crowd of people surging along the wharf towards the center of town. It appeared that I had somehow gotten involved in some sort of festival.

I asked a participant through all the commotion, "What is everyone celebrating?" and he gave me a queer look, for in Celpahia existence alone is a reason to rejoice.

"This is the Celebration of the Stars!" shouted the man while in dance.

"Are you celebrating their beauty?" I asked.

"No, the people celebrating it will be as many as the stars and it shall not end until the stars themselves disappear in the morning," answered the man.

At every corner stood a witty jester or fearless entertainer occupying the crowd with fantastic feats of humor and dexterity. A circus had set up in the middle of the street and appeared to be the center of entertainment for this concourse. I began to push my way through the crowd and reluctantly headed on to my destination avoiding the celebration that had engulfed me. I stopped to listen to a troubadour and asked if he knew any legends of men from the waking world. He paused a moment and sang a ballad that had both poetic beauty and sonorous melody. The music from the Lands of Dream is hard to explain to those whose ears have not felt its softness and lyrical harmony. A young woman glided up from behind and embraced me before asking me to dance through a whisper in my ear. I quickly refused in fear that I might stay until the stars faded away into the next morning. I ended up taking to the back streets of Celpahia to better avoid the distractions of the rambunctious celebration that seemed to have swallowed up the entire city.

Alzoond kept his place of business south of the Manikalra River, near the Temple of Defhj, the god of shifting oblivion. I found it snuggled in among a multitude of other small shops of various professions and retails. Most of the businesses themselves were empty since the majority of the entertainment was taking place on the streets, but to my delight I found his shop open despite the festivities. The sign above the door simply read: *Alzoond the Storyteller*. The shop itself was quite small with parchments stacked everywhere creating mountains, hillsides and valleys of flowing scrolls. In the corner sat an elderly man with a long thin gray beard reading by candlelight. His skin was dark brown giving him the appearance of a well dressed native with a tall oval pointed hat. Although his weathered exterior suggested that of an old man, his mannerisms were smooth and agile like that of a much younger man.

"Yes?" he said peering through his oval spectacle.

"I was hoping to hear a tale," I said.

"Why would a young man such as yourself want to sit and

listen to an old man?" he said. "There is a celebration going on you know. Free drink, free camaraderie, free love… things that have faded from your world long ago. "

"I don't want to hear just any story, but a particular story about a man like me," I said.

"A man like you should be out enjoying himself," he said, "while you can. There are forces working against your return to this land as we speak. Make the most of your time here, don't waste it dreaming within the Lands of Dream."

"That is exactly why I am here," I declared, "I do not want to leave."

He immediately removed his monocle, wiped it off as if to give himself time to respond and said, "Yes, I know of the very story you seek." He rubbed his chin and continued, "Why don't you enjoy yourself while you can. Men from your world usually don't get many opportunities to come here. It is a wonderful place, the Lands of Dream, but there are places…" he paused, "places that are inconceivable to a man from your world. Forget this whim and enjoy the moment!"

"This is no whim and I will not forget it! Please, you must help me!" I begged. "Everyone seems to shun my inquires into this subject."

"The reason nobody wants to talk to you about this is because it is not natural. Men from the waking world might destroy the splendor of the Dream if they stayed, much like they have drained the magic from your own with your one religion," he said sadly.

"But the people of dreams have always been so kind to me and I have done nothing to ever harm its splendor," I answered.

"Of course," he said, "the people of Celpahia don't mind dreamwalkers. For a man to pass through the Gates of Deeper Slumber he must be imaginative and be able to appreciate its brilliance. Men such as this come to escape the mundane surroundings of their world, but they must always return."

"I am only asking for you to tell me a tale just like you would anyone else," I pleaded. "I have done nothing for you to deny me this simple courtesy."

Alzoond leaned back and sighed, "It is your time and I assume I have no right to tell you how to live it. There is a man from your world who lives in the Lands of Dream to this day. I believe he was some kind of royalty in your world." He shifted through his notes and continued, "He resides in an ivory tower that sits in the jagged peaks of the Shakh Mountains above the harbor of Wrin-Henji."

I jumped up in excitement and shouted bluntly, "How did he do it!"

Alzoond replied, "That is something you will have to find out yourself. I have given you the common courtesy that you requested."

I thanked the ancient sage, paid his fee and walked back into the festival, which was still taking place in its streets. The only ships leaving for the port of Wrin-Henji were not sailing until the morning, but I did commission a spot on a clipper ship named the *Sea Dancer* that was to leave at dawn. After everything was prepared for my voyage I went out to see Celpahia for perhaps the last time. I did not know if my journey would be successful or not, but any risk including death was more than worth even the slightest opportunity to stay in the Lands of Dream. On my way back from the wharf, I stopped on one of the bridges that spanned across the Manikalra and peered into its gentle current. Underneath that bridge made of polished granite flowed the great river that is said to start where time began. Numerous fishing boats lined its bank held in check at the end of deeply sunk anchors. What type of fish or creatures they pulled out under the light of their lanterns, I did not know or care for the sparkle of the moon and stars off the current of that legendary river was enough for me. That night I did not sleep, but celebrated with the stars.

Chapter 2
Aboard the Sea Dancer

The sun broke melting the stars away and with that a new day began in the Lands of Dream. Even though I hadn't slept, I felt more energized than I had in my entire life, as the excitement of an impending adventure flowed through my veins. The sprawling harbor came alive as the city's residents and workers emerged with the warmth of the morning sun. Men hoisted cargo onto the decks of ships, while families and friends said their goodbyes with hugs and kisses under the shadows of the ship's crew making ready for sail. The *Sea Dancer* sat anchored near the center of the harbor taking on the supplies that would be essential for the long trip ahead. I spoke with the ship's captain briefly and found that it would take two days to sail down the Manikalra to the mouth of the Cerulean Sea; from that point, the journey across the great Cerulean Sea to Wrin-Henji would take only a few more with a blessing from the South Winds.

The crew worked like organized ants with the ship as their colony and the captain their queen. I sat near the boat as it was loaded and observed its crew carefully finding many peculiar traits, but the feature that stood out the most was that they looked identical all the way down to having freckles in the exact same spot, as if they were clones. Their body stature was much smaller than that of the average man, with none being taller than five feet and all having clean-shaven heads with pale almost translucent skin. Their small glossy heads looked like cue balls shining in the bright vibrant sun. If it were not for their distinct clothing, voices and appearances together, I would have sworn they were all the same man. As the crew made preparations, I finally went aboard and waited for our departure. The captain sent rowers below to take their posts and gave the command to raise anchor and with that, the *Sea Dancer* rode the currents of the Manikalra towards the Cerulean Sea. I stood against its rail and watched the fabled city of Celpahia slowly shrink away.

Our ship floated lazily down the Manikalra with an occasional stroke by our oarsmen to keep us off its winding banks. I spoke quite candidly with most of the crew except the captain who stood at his post behind the ship's wheel. The men of the crew were generally talkative except when I would mention the purpose of my pilgrimage to Wrin-Henji. Most became quiet and excused themselves from the conversation, while others would simply change the subject. One man, when I spoke to him about my intentions, was actually seized by terror and left abruptly with a distressed look on his face, an incident which convinced me to not speak of it to anyone of the crew again.

When I wasn't talking with the crew I spent most of my time watching the banks of the Manikalra. The beauty of the scenery was astounding. Early that morning we passed what appeared to be some type of monastery. The men working in the fields were wearing long robes and their buildings were constructed in cylindrical form much like stupas. What philosophy or god they served I did not know, but I swore to myself if I succeeded in my quest to live eternity in Dream I would one day return and find out. Whatever their purpose, they certainly seemed to live in harmony with each other and their surroundings. The people along the Manikalra thrived upon its shores in small villages and towns. Passing these small communities was always a delight because each village seemed to have a unique architecture of its own. I asked one of the sailors why communities that were so close to each other could have such different cultures. The sailor simply replied that their gods, not their neighbors, were their major influence.

Later that evening we passed a city of immense splendor unlike any I have ever imagined. The city itself was built on the side of a cliff with an elaborate network of swinging bridges connecting its structures to one another. These bridges obviously served as roads for the city and its people. As far as I could tell the city consisted of four major levels in which a person would climb ladders to get from one level to another. The buildings were very large and most were made of glass.

"Why do so many of the buildings have glass walls and roofs?" I asked one of the Sea Dancer's crew.

"That is how they grow their food my friend," he answered.

"And the name of this extraordinary city?" I asked.

"That city has no name," he replied. "It is simply referred to as The City upon the Cliffs."

I waved good-bye to the city's inhabitants standing on the bridges, yearning even more now than ever to never leave the Lands of Dream. That night I lay on the deck of the *Sea Dancer* as her bow cut through the Manikalra and watched the stars. As I looked up at the constellations of dream, I wondered if one of those brilliant planets that lit up the sky was earth. The men of the ship kneeled before their gods and prayed humbly beneath the radiant night sky. I listened to their prayers and longed to pray with them, but knew little of their gods and customs. Most prayed to Mockil Khahe the God of the Depths, for his powers and creatures of the seas could benefit sailors the most. I did not pray, but only listened to their solemn songs and prayers.

The next day I awoke late for I was tired from not sleeping the previous night. The captain assured me that we were still on schedule and would make the Cerulean Sea by nightfall. That day was as lazy and relaxing as any I had ever had in the Lands of Dream. We drifted slowly down the Manikalra without a care in the world. Most of the men on the ship relaxed and smoked their pipes, while others took catnaps. Only the captain stayed alert at the helm of the ship. I leaned up against one of the masts and watched the deep jungle forest as we drifted on. Around noon the captain gave orders for a few of the men to take to the launch. They did so immediately and rowed on ahead of us. When I asked the captain what they were doing he said that they were going on ahead of us to light our way.

"But I thought that we were going to reach the sea before nightfall," I said.

"We will," he slowly repeated, "we will."

As I sat down to ponder the last statement of the captain, a man offered me a smoke and I accepted. We didn't smoke from a pipe but from some kind of a short round bottle that had water in it. Whatever was in it emitted a creamy yellow smoke that swayed my mind dropping me into a deep slumber.

Suddenly, I awoke to the clamor of the crew moving to the prow. I got up and went to the fore of the ship to see what all of the commotion was about. When I looked ahead all I could see was an enormous cave into which the currents of the Manikalra disappeared.

"What is that?" I asked.

"That is Nauria's Caverns," he replied. "It is named after an old captain who tried to sail through it in the dark. He was lost forever."

The tremendous mouth of that great cavern engulfed our tiny ship. Once our ship was inside and my eyes had time to adjust, I could see the immense size of the grotto. Its ceiling must have been three hundred feet above our main mast. Along its walls hung tiny white lanterns lighting our way, obviously lit by our companions in the launch. A powerful wind blew through the cave and the captain gave command to raise our sails. We sailed through the vast passages at a frightful rate and while the captain and the men of the ship stayed calm, I hung onto the main mast with tight white knuckles. As we swept through the dark maze, I understood how Captain Naurias was lost forever. Our lanterns lighted the main cavern, but the river flowed into an endless number of other passages with the same force as our course. How anyone could have hoped to stay on the right course in such darkness without smashing into the walls was beyond me. Such is the price that proud men must pay.

I examined the yawning cavern as best I could by the dull light of lanterns. Dotting the ceiling, I could see thousands of tiny shining objects glowing from the lights of the lanterns. At first I thought maybe they were jewels or some kind mineral reflecting the artificial light, but then I realized that they were eyes! There must have been millions of those eyes. I cautiously assumed they were from some kind of harmless animal similar to a bat and not some horrible creatures bent on feeding upon those that passed through their home. We sailed on through the darkness for another hour before we could see the light of day breaking through what appeared to be nothing but a small hole. The hole grew quickly until it was a huge opening like that we had entered. As the warmth of the suns of Dream beamed down upon my skin, I was glad to be out into the fresh air again. We quickly picked up our mates in the launch and continued on down the Manikalra. It was getting late and I was about to ask the captain about our location when I saw it: the Cerulean Sea. The mighty Manikalra River dumped us into the great sea and I stood unable to speak stunned by the marvelous sight. The captain gave the order to raise all sails and our journey commenced on the open sea.

The clear light turquoise color of its surface was unparalleled by any body of water in our own world, it was if we were sailing on a global size swimming pool. I stood at starboard to feel the warmth of the sun and the cool salty breeze of the sea. The captain opened a cask of wine to toast our previous luck and our ongoing success. The crew rejoiced and the remainder of the day was spent emptying that cask. I was not as accustomed to that type of wine as the rest of the crew and became drunk quite early. We sang songs that I had never heard and many of the men danced between drinks. By the time the rest of the crew was drunk, I had already passed out. When I awoke it was already night, the captain had gone to bed and the ship's master was at the helm. Most of the crew was asleep, except for those that still prayed. Because I felt quite groggy and was fearful I might fall overboard, I decided to spend the rest of the night in my quarters.

The next morning was as bright as ever. The rays of the sun reflected off the clear blue sea creating a wondrous prismatic effect. Bright glistening colors ran in all directions sinking into the depths of the sea. Our ship looked as if it was sailing on a rainbow. It was a sight that I will never forget. This rainbow effect lasted for only a little time and was unfortunately completely gone by noon. Some of the men were fishing from the aft of the boat when the lookout above spotted another boat on the horizon. The captain yelled for a full description when it came into sight and continued with his duties. The rest of the crew continued on with their work and various leisure activities.

Thinking little of it, I sat down to play a dice game with two other fellows, when the sentry screamed, "It's a Tarkian ship!"

The crew of the ship erupted in utter horror. Men began to run in all directions in a complete panic. Only the captain stayed calm. He began to bark orders, but all sanity had left his men. One man shouted: "They will make us slaves in the Tarkian mines!" Another man cried: "They will steal our cargo and scuttle us with the ship!" The captain finally managed to get some kind of order established, and with the help of his master shipman got the crew to change our course. The master's mate took command of a group of men and went below to man the oars. I ran to the stern to watch our progress. The Tarkian ship looked like a tiny speck in the distance. At first I thought we might escape that dreaded ship, but as I watched, it slowly grew larger on the horizon. It would be only a matter of time before it would overtake us. As the Tarkian ship loomed closer the men took to panic once again. I watched the kind demeanor the men of the ship had shown me to this point instantly change and many of the men began to blame me for their impending doom.

A man pointed at me and declared. "His quest is against the god's will! The gods have cursed us for his presence!"

The captain tried to settle his men, but he no longer controlled them as fear took command of them. A group of the men started talking about throwing me overboard. I tried to talk some sense into them without any success. When I realized that they intended to heave me over the side, I stood ready to fight. I was much larger than the short men of the crew and was sure I could give them a good struggle. Numerous powerful hands gripped my limbs and I was hoisted helplessly into the air. Whether their monstrous strength came naturally or was bolstered directly from fear I do not know, but my struggles were little deterrent to their intentions.

The mob carried me over to the side of the ship and a man yelled, "Throw him overboard and the gods may forgive us."

The next thing I felt was the coolness of the Cerulean Sea against my skin. I sank into its depths clawing toward its surface to draw salty sea air into my failing lungs. As I came to the surface, I floated helplessly in the sea and watched the fate of the *Sea Dancer* and her crew.

The *Sea Dancer* moved across the sea with all her available speed, but it was not enough as she was a merchant ship built to carry freight. The sleek pirate ship of the Tarkians easily overtook her slower counterpart. When the two ships collided, the black pirate ship snapped the rowing oars of its victim. There was a minor struggle as the two ships broadsided and the Tarkians boarded, but the crew of the merchant ship was no match for the stronger and more skilled Tarkians. The pirates plundered the ship and took its crew prisoners. I watched powerlessly as they burned that beautiful ship with its yellow sails. The ebony pirate vessel sailed on with its booty and unknowingly left me adrift. The *Sea Dancer* burned the rest of the evening and on into the night. I managed to swim up to her and get several pieces of wood that had not completely burned to form a crude raft. That night, as I floated in the darkness, was the first night I spent in the Lands of Dream without appreciating the stars.

Finally after a grueling night, the chill of the morning was cut with the rising of the suns. It was a welcome sight after floating aimlessly adrift through the darkness of night. I had spent those hours of darkness in fear, not just of falling off my crude raft in my sleep, but also of the unknown beasts that might dwell in the sea's depths. I had heard tales from the local sailors of Celpahia, terrifying tales of creatures beyond a man's imagination in the waking world. For the first time in my life I began to lose faith in my lifelong quest as my situation seemed hopeless. I had no way of getting to Wrin-Henji, and even if I had, I wasn't a seafaring man. I was at the mercy of the sea as might be a piece of floating trash.

My eyes scanned the horizon in the hope of spotting a passing ship, but only the sky touched the sea. Time was of the essence; if I didn't find a way out of this predicament soon I would eventually wake and my search would be over. The time correlation between the waking world and the Lands of Dream is unpredictable. Sometimes a single day or night's sleep can last months in the Lands of Dream. I once lived in Celpahia for over a month and when I awoke in the waking world only a single night had passed. On other occasions the time that passes between the two dimensions is equivalent. I don't know how long I slept before I found my way past the Gates of Deeper Slumber or how much longer I had. I had taken a strong sedative that I had acquired from a Native American shaman which should keep me asleep for at least three or four days. That could give me three or four days, weeks, or months depending on the time relation between the two worlds.

I continued to watch that empty horizon throughout the morning and on into the afternoon. My hopes were fading with each minute that passed, when all of a sudden in the distance there were two black specks dancing in and out of the water. At first I thought that the hot suns of Dream must have bleached my brain and I had gone mad, but as I continued to watch I saw that they were indeed slowly coming toward me. As they got closer, I realized they were not dancing, but jumping over one another. I rubbed my eyes several times to make sure it wasn't a mirage but each time they were still there, slowly coming closer. Occasionally, I would lose sight and I wondered if it had been a vision or if whatever it was had disappeared. But they would always reappear and each time they were closer than before. The two objects began to take form and appeared from the distance to be nothing but large fish. Even though my hopes were down, my curiosity was up. I strained my eyes to get some kind of detail on these fish, when I realized they weren't fish at all, but porpoises. They looked exactly like those from the waking world. As they got closer I watched them play and wondered if they too had passed through the Gates of Deeper Slumber to Dream. When the two playmates got close enough to see my perilous situation, they quit playing their game of leapfrog and swam over to me. They swam all around me, occasionally jumping over me, as though including me in their game. All the while, they chirped as if they were either trying to communicate with each other or possibly with me. Several times one would rub up against me as it swam by, almost as if trying to tell me something. One swam up close to me and started bumping me in a friendly manner. I began to recognize that they weren't playing with me, but trying to help me. I grabbed on to the next one that passed and held on. To my amazement, the porpoise didn't resist in the slightest way. While I held on, both the creatures began to swim in the same direction. I had a hard time holding on and lost my grip several times, but each time they would turn around to collect me once more. My hands started to burn with agonizing pain from hanging on against the force of the ocean and I began to think that I couldn't hold on much longer, when I saw our destination. There it lay in the distance, land! When we got close to the shore I let go and waved good-bye to those free spirits of the sea as they continued their game. Whether they helped me simply because I needed their assistance or because they saw me as a fellow dreamer, I will never know. As the long ride had exhausted all of my strength, I fell lifelessly to the beach, succumbing to the haze of sleep once more.

Chapter 3
A Grand Caravan

When I regained consciousness another day had passed and I awoke under a blanket of bright shiny stars. Not wanting to travel through the forest lining the coast alone, I decided to spend the night on the beach gazing at the stars. While beautiful, the Lands of Dream were mysterious and I dared not challenge what might lie within the shadows of its unknown forest during the middle of the night. Besides, I still didn't know which way Wrin-Henji lay or if I was even on the right continent. These were matters I would deal with in the morning, for at that moment all that mattered were the stars gleaming above. That night the stars seemed much brighter than usual. I suppose it had to do with the darkness of my desolate beach. The constellations of our world are the only things that compare in beauty to the Lands of Dream. Everything else in the Lands of Dream has a deeper, more vibrant color. Before I went to sleep, I prayed to Mockil Khahe the God of the Depths to help those lost sailors from the *Sea Dancer*.

I got up with the first sun of Dream for I wanted to get an early start. I did not know how long it might take to find some sign of civilization, but I hoped to do so before the next nightfall. I did not want to be alone at night in an unknown area of woods without a way to build a fire for warmth and safety.

Deciding to head inland in hopes of finding something or someone that might lead me toward the port of Wren-Henji, I walked along the coastline to find an entrance into the dense forest. The thick forest was inhospitable forcing me to tear through its foliage to pass through its depths. Fighting against thick vines, weeds, trees and bushes, I had barely traveled a mile when I fell against a large rock in exhaustion. The forest around me was full of tempting fruits and berries none of which I had ever seen before, and while most appeared to be edible, I refrained with salivating yearning for I knew nothing of this world's ecology.

I continued to labor through the thick forest for several more hours before the forest's floor began to fade upward so that I could walk without hindrance from its undergrowth. With the new sparseness of the forest I began to cover ground more quickly with far less effort.

Several hours later I came to a twisted and hardened dirt road that had seen much traffic in its time. With my newfound luck, I randomly picked a direction and followed the road willing to go wherever it led. I walked this quiet passage the rest of the evening listening to the soft sounds of the surrounding jungle before camping along its side with the fall of night.

The next morning I got up and continued along the lonely road without seeing a soul the rest of the day. Early that afternoon I began to feel the pangs of hunger and the weariness of my long journey, when the soft sound of jingling bells caressed my ears. Unsure whether I was about to meet friend or foe, I hid behind a tree and listened quietly. The sound of the bells was eventually blended in with what sounded like horses' hooves. More sounds joined in like a symphony creating that of a vibrant noisy caravan. Around a bend in the road came a small cart being pulled by an old mule lined with round dented bells. On the creature's head was a large hat, something like a sombrero, with more tiny bells hanging off the edges. On the cart behind the oddly dressed animal was a tall slender man with earrings in both his ears and long lean agile hands holding thin leather reins. Behind the insignificant cart was a long row of horses, wagons and buggies of all shapes and sizes. It appeared that my luck was continuing to hold.

The lead wagon of the grand caravan halted when I emerged from the woods. I felt honored for a caravan as large as this one to stop for one man.

The driver of the lead cart paused looking at me queerly before speaking, "Do you need some help, stranger?"

"I am traveling to Wrin-Henji and have lost my way," I answered.

"You most certainly have my friend! Why you are taking the long way," he laughed. "Come on… climb aboard! We are going to a town just a few miles from that very port."

"Thank you," I said grateful to have an escort.

The people of the caravan began to climb from their wagons so to get a better look at the newest member of their convoy. All had long black hair, both the men and the women, and most wore some kind of flamboyant headgear whether it was a bandanna, hat or headband. I climbed into the lead wagon and the grand caravan rolled once more. I believe that from my appearance they took me for a poor beggar. My clothes were torn and weather-worn and not having shaved for days made me look quite pathetic, but they treated me with the respect of a human being. The caravan moved very smoothly for such a large group and we made camp beside the road that night. Each wagon in the caravan seemed to have its own family whether they were related by blood or friendship alone. I had never seen a group of people so full of kindness and generosity in my life. Members from almost every wagon kindly invited me to eat and stay the night. I decided to eat and stay with the tall gentleman with whom I had ridden in the lead wagon, for he was the only one who rode alone. For dinner, my host cooked something similar to mutton upon an open campfire. It was thick and heavy and although I ate more than my fair share, my host didn't seem to mind. He actually seemed happy to see me enjoy his food so immensely and after we ate, we lay by the fire and held our full stomachs while in conversation.

"Why are your people so good to a stranger such as myself?" I asked.

"Because," he answered, contently full, "we are gypsies and know what it is like to be poor and not accepted by others. We have always lived on the road because no country or city wants us. The road is our home."

"I am glad to be in your home!" I claimed, happily gorged.

He laughed out loud and patted me on the back, "What kind of business would a man such as you have in a small fishing harbor like Wrin-Henji?"

I reluctantly explained my purpose, unsure of what reaction my host would present. To my surprise he did not appear shocked or appalled at my reply.

"I knew you looked like a man from beyond the Realm of Dreams. I understand your quest. You, just as we, are only looking for a place to belong. I will make sure you make it to Wrin-Henji!"

I thanked him and felt glad to have found someone in the Lands of Dream who did not oppose my dream.

"But first," he said, "I must stop being so selfish and start sharing your company with the other camps. It is a lovely night for conversation!"

We frequented several campfires and received warm welcomes from each. Before I knew it, I was going from campfire to campfire on my own as if I was a born gypsy. That is how I came to the camp of Madam Saenela. She was the eldest of the caravan and dealt in oneiromancy. She offered to read my fortune and out of courtesy I allowed her.

She gave me a strange card reading, placing random cards in structured formation and ended with a grim warning, "The older gods are watching you. Beware of their pawns, for they are striving to make you fail."

Unnerved by her penetrating stare, I thanked her for her advice before apologizing for not being able to compensate her services. She nodded and I moved on to find my friend laughing beside a strong roaring fire. He was gleefully watching a woman dance and asked me to join in. I did so gladly and sat down with those by the fire as if I were family. A woman offered me some warm creamy tea and I joyfully accepted. I queried a man next to me about the tea and he said it was brewed from wild mushrooms. It warmed me to my bones and at that moment my mind settled, as had every muscle in my body, allowing me to me relax and forgo the anxiety of my race against time.

The beauty of the woman dancing before me was clearly evident, but what made her dance so appealing was her singular movements. Her rhythm was one with the sound of her castanets. She swayed in harmony not only to the music, but also to the flicker of the fire. She began to move faster and faster till my eyes could hardly keep up with her. Her every motion streaked behind her and as she spun I could see every color of the prism following behind her. I began to sway with her movements and could see the motion of my own hands float with colors of their own. Then, it seemed as if the dancer was completely still, while we, the spectators and the campfire, were spinning in all directions.

My friend, the wagon master, woke me early the next morning. He found me lying under his wagon wrapped in thick furs that were not his own. My eyes held a heavy weight as if I had been asleep for a thousand years. The other members of the caravan were loading up their carts and wagons.

I rose up and asked the caravan leader, "What happened last night? I don't remember coming to bed."

He roared in laughter and said, "You didn't. We had to carry you over here! Mushroom tea is to sip, not to gulp!"

I got up and dusted myself off, while my newest friend sat on his cart and laughed at me stumbling around camp. The caravan rolled out like a train leaving its station towards a long and grinding trip. Riding alongside my friend, I felt I stood a chance of finishing my quest. I had lost several days with the sinking of the *Sea Dancer*, but finally I had found my way among the gypsies who led me slowly but steadily toward the man in the Ivory Tower. Surely seeing I was a man from his world, he would help me. He of all people would understand my desire to stay.

Late that evening our caravan came to a stop and the caravan leader motioned for everyone to set up camp.

I asked, "Will we reach this town you spoke of tomorrow?"

"We are already there." he continued. "People don't like bands of gypsies rolling into the middle of their town, so we will set up and do business here. Once they know we are here, they will come to us."

We loaded down gear and set up huge tents. What had earlier been a quiet lonely road now became a merchant's camp of immense proportions. The gypsies were skilled businessmen and women of all kinds. Some told fates and fortunes while others entertained and sold mysterious trinkets, but all dealt in one thing or other. The gypsies brought wondrous things from the vast Lands of Dream to their clients. Potions, oils, drugs, remedies, lotions, furs, endless varieties of materials, cloths and goods were just a few examples. The older boys of the caravan were all sent into town to publicize our arrival. My friend gave me a fresh set of clothes to replace the rags that I currently wore and we sat down to dinner.

"I do not mean to sound ungrateful, for you have been very kind," I took another bite and continued, "but I must leave for Wrin-Henji as soon as possible."

"It is too dark for you to climb that mountain tonight, besides you will need supplies and some climbing equipment. We will leave for Wrin-Henji as soon as it gets light."

I thanked him and his friends again for their help and finished my dinner. Later that evening the boys returned in high spirits and the gypsy camp spent the night as it always did, in revelry.

The next morning we got up early and packed for our hike to Wrin-Henji. I put on my new clothes. They were common gypsy garments, but I wore them proudly. My friend loaded our supplies on his mule and we left camp, heading for the port of Wren-Henji. We took a small trail off the main road that was barely wide enough for our mule and followed it through the thick wooded landscape. We hiked for about an hour until we came to a clearing and to my delight I could see my destination! From the bluff I could see the snow-white peaks of the Shakh Mountains and the gleaming white tower in its center.

"How much farther to Wrin-Henji?" I asked in excitement.

"A couple of more hours."

The next two hours it took for us to reach Wrin-Henji were the longest of my life. Each clearing we came to or corner we traversed only led to another wooded trail. Occasionally, I would catch a glimpse of those imperial mountains or the sparkle of the sun off that ivory tower through the trees, which renewed my strength and hunger to climb the mountains upon which it stood. The trail finally ended at a small bluff near the ocean just across from the sleepy harbor of Wrin-Henji.

The bay was filled with a multitude of vessels, ranging from great seafaring ships to tiny fishing boats. The tranquility of this small port nestled against the Shakh Mountains was a welcome sight. The town of Wrin-henji was built for one simple reason, to serve as an entrepôt for ships sailing between the many destinations in the Lands of Dream. My gypsy friend and I spent the morning in town preparing for my impending journey. He financed the entire cost of my supplies and equipment and I thanked him for all his help, not as my financier, but as my friend.

Deciding to have one last drink together before I would begin my climb, we went to a local tavern to say our good-byes. Sitting in the tavern we went over all the information we had acquired in town. Apparently it would take me about three days to ascend to the top of the great mountain's peaks. There was a small trail that led to an obelisk about a third of the way up. This supposedly would be moderately easy, and I should be able to reach the ancient monument before nightfall. When we asked the men of the town if they knew anything about this obelisk, the men would began to act strange, almost as if afraid, before declaring to know nothing of it, but a local boy declared that sometimes at night he saw fires near the precipice of the monolith.

The second day of my climb would be the hardest, for the trail would became thin and rocky as it wound up the cliffs of the Shakh Mountains. I would have to find a small cave or alcove in the cliffs to spend the night and if I was lucky I might make the top by the end of the next day. My friend was giving me a few suggestions when three men in long white cloaks with gold trim came into the bar. They were all dressed and groomed in exactly the same manner looking like clones and carrying no possessions aside from a single dagger that each wore on their belt. Their heads were completely shaven save for a single ponytail and they all wore long goatees.

One of the men made an announcement upon entering the bar, "We are looking for a man from beyond the Realm of Dreams. It is very important that we find him. Has anyone seen this man?"

I was about to say something when my companion firmly put his hand on my shoulder and shook his head to silence me. Whether it was this action or the fact that we looked like gypsies got their attention I do not know, but after no one in the bar came forward, one of the odd priests came over to our table.

"Have you two heard or seen anything about this man? I assure you my god will reward any useful information handsomely."

I watched my friend as he leaned back in his chair touching the scimitar on his belt and replied, "No, but we are gypsies and I know many a tale about men beyond the Wall of Sleep. Pull up a chair and I shall tell you a story."

The man rudely interrupted, "Bah, I do not have time for such gibberish! If you hear anything come to the temple of Eidolen, the watchful god, and tell us immediately or you will suffer the consequences from the god who sees all."

"All but the location of the man you seek," said the gypsy caravan leader smugly.

The priest turned and gave us an evil eye that made chills run down my spine, but as for my gypsy friend, it brought only a smile to his face.

Having little time to deal with heathen such as us, the priests left in haste, and it took several minutes after their departure for the bar to return to its lively form. I didn't have to ask, for my friend could see my question from the expression on my face.

"They are foul high priests from the religious sect of Eidolen. I thought only the dim mongrel and unintelligent beast served Eidolen's vile lusts. The conversion of human servants will strengthen his hold on the Lands of Dream," he said in deep thought. "I do not believe they were here to help you. They are loyal to their god's will, whatever it may be, and they will murder without thought if it pleases their god. We must leave town at once!"

We quietly slipped out of town with the cunning of veteran rogues. I could tell from his slick movements that he had much experience in sneaking out of towns without being seen or heard, and now I fully understood why his caravan held so much faith in his abilities. Once we were outside of town we said our farewells and I began my ascent of the great Shakh Mountains. I waved to my gypsy friend standing in the wind with fluttering feathers one last time, knowing I would never be able to repay the debt I owed the gypsy and with that, we went our separate ways.

Chapter 4
Scaling the Shakh Mountains

I spent the rest of the day toiling up the beautiful countryside of the Shakh Mountains under its cool shadows. I did my best to ignore its flowering paths and calm winds in hopes of making good time in order to reach my destination as soon as possible. While the supplies on my back were necessary, they were also quite heavy and added to the arduousness of my climb. The provisions provided by my gypsy friend included traditional climbing tools such as ropes and a grappling hook as well as other survival items including food, heavy clothes, new boots, a flint stone and a short sword which I proudly wore upon a new belt. With such an array of equipment, I felt assured that I could handle almost any situation that might arise.

That evening after a long strenuous hike I reached the obelisk. It had been built on a flat ledge that was surrounded by large stone blocks that appeared to be used like seats. The base of the black glossy obelisk came out about three feet from its pillar and looked as if might have been used as some kind of altar. Its column was a long rectangular shape about twelve feet tall, being larger at the bottom than the top, with each side being covered in hand-carved glyphs and symbols. The writings on its surface were alien in nature and unlike any I had ever seen, while the top of the structure came to a very sharp point as if to mark a certain location in the constellations. What man or creature worshipped at this marker or which god it glorified I was unsure, but as it was getting late, I hiked further up the mountain to avoid the eyes of anything that might come to worship at its base. I found some shelter from the wind under a fallen tree and burrowed beneath it to sleep out the night. Since it was not cold, I refrained from building a fire and ate salted meat from my provisions.

My muscles ached from the previous day's hike and the chill of the bright new morning made my joints throb with every movement. I built a small fire to warm myself and to heat a modest breakfast. Sitting on a rock, I happily ate my meal and surveyed the part of the mountains below that I had conquered. The harbor of the small town below looked insignificant from my perch, yet the light blue water of the ocean and the white sand of its beaches stretched on into a never-ending horizon. Ships of all sizes and designs were pulling out of the harbor with their precious passengers and cargo. The Lands of Dream would continue on with or without me, and if I were to be a part of its magnificence, I could not fail.

As I was getting ready to begin another day trekking up the mountain, I noticed some movement near the gleaming obelisk. Straining my eyes, I looked at the same spot again and waited patiently. Fear gripped my body when the three fanatical priests of Eidolen I had met the day before appeared on the trail below. They were dressed in the same robes as they had worn in the bar the previous day and moved quickly up the mountain like ducks in a row. They did not speak to each other and from what I could see they were not carrying any food or supplies. In a panic, I began to lighten my load by burning all my excess supplies. I knew that if I did not lighten my load they would catch up to me before nightfall, but at the same time, I did not want to leave anything behind to help them up the mountain. All I took with me was an eolith and my short sword. Frantically, I began running up the trail like a hunted rabbit.

The trail began to wind upward steeply sloping into the mountain cutting through rock and dirt. At many times, the only thing that kept me from tumbling below were the roots and vines growing along the trail. Every so often I would take the time to look back to monitor the progress of my pursuers and every time they were closer than before. No matter how hard I pushed myself, they seemed to push harder. With each passing minute, my straining muscles waned, threatening to give way and leave me at the mercy of the mad priests in pursuit. While I stumbled up the mountain like a drunken goat, the men climbing below moved with the effortlessness of a hunting mountain lion. I knew my only hope was to outrun them for they would not rest until I was dead or gone from the Lands of Dream.

With each step I took they seemed to take two and finally my legs gave way underneath me and I slid backward almost slipping off a cliff and tumbling thousands of feet below. I huffed and puffed, holding onto a small loosening branch which at the moment was the only thing between me living and dying. I tugged at the branch pulling myself back over the cliff as it began to peel from the trunk of the small plant. It split, coming loose as I leapt forward to seize a rock for dear life. Loose rock and dirt slipped over the side disappearing over the edge. I fell against the trail and hugged it giving up hope of outrunning my foes. If I were to escape their wrath, it would be by taking their lives, and with three against one, the odds were not in my favor.

I found a small ledge and sat resting for what would surely be a battle to the death. The small sword in my hands shook as my nerves rattled the metal in my hand. I had never killed a man in the waking world or that of dream, but If they attempted to stand in the way of my dreams, they would have to kill me before I bestowed death upon them. The rise below my ledge was steep and would make any direct assault upon me difficult. I sighed staring over it knowing this would probably be the only advantage I would hold in the upcoming battle.

Lying flat upon the ledge, I waited anxiously with my sword in hand for what would probably be my death. Would I die in the waking world as well or would a death here in my dreams simply seal me off from ever returning? Time seemed to stop as my heart throbbed in my chest bursting to escape its ribcage prison. The sound of sandals scraping on the trail below startled me and I lay further down ready to spring and pass death along before it could pass on to me. I tried to lie still in complete silence, but my heart pounded in my ears and my muscles tightened with adrenaline. My very breath seemed so loud that I was sure my foes would hear it and I would lose my one major advantage, the element of surprise. It took all the willpower that I could summon to lie in complete silence while hands climbed up the ledge where I waited. A hand appeared over the edge of a flat rock followed by a shiny bald head. Shock seized his face as I raised my blade swinging it down upon the top of his head. My muscles flexed surging with raw animal power sinking the sharp blade deep into the round head ending the priest's life and devotion to Eidolen the All-Knowing. Hoping to hold my advantage of surprise for a little longer, I leaped over the ledge and tried to spear a second priest in the face with the point of my sword. The agile priest leapt backwards with an astounding swiftness causing me to miss miserably, but in turn his avoidance caused him to lose his grip upon the earth and tumble to the ledge below the one upon which I landed.

As the priest fell backwards, he took his colleague, the third priest, along in a mangled jumble of arms and legs. The two men jumped back to their feet quickly recovering from their fall staring up at me with mad eyes of murderous lust. I waited in quiet challenge at the edge of the bluff with my sword in hand. A foreign emotion had taken hold of my soul after my first kill unleashing something I knew not I had within me. Trapped by the two priests and unable to outrun them, I stared back at the two men below ready to shed their blood in a carnal rage I had never known. Like a pack of cunning hyenas, they used their numbers to their advantage and instead of assaulting me straight on, they split apart in an attempt to encircle my position. One moved further down the ledge to scale up to my level, while another stood still holding out a dagger to climb up if I moved down after his companion. I watched helplessly as one climbed up and another waited to strike at precisely the same moment as the other. Feeling I had no other option, I waited until the first priest made the ledge, then as he stalked toward me holding out his dagger, I leapt onto the priest below leading with the point of my sword. I tried to impale the priest but he moved with the agility of super-human speed dodging my weapon and cutting my arm with a long gash as I rolled by him. The cut was deep and bleeding profusely down my side as I rolled backwards holding out my blade in defense. Now both priests stood on the same ledge as I edging toward me with their weapons ready to strike. They struck with the speed of possessed shadows coming at me simultaneously in one swift attack. I dodged the first priest's dagger pushing him aside, but the second priest's blade found my side gashing it severely as my sword found its mark sinking deep into his chest. A penetrating pain ripped down my arm from the wound in my side and I lost grip upon the hilt of my sword. It went over the mountain side still protruding from the fallen priest's chest as he disappeared from the ledge out of sight. In a numbing pain, I fell to my knees weak from pain and loss of blood and helplessly unarmed. The priest whose weapon I had missed during his last assault came up behind me ready to steal the life he had hunted so fiercely in the name of his mad god. I spun around to see the face of the man who would take my life, unsure what a death meant to a dreamer in the Lands of Dream. When I turned around I saw his face, but it had the expression of agony instead that of victory. Protruding from his stomach was a long curved blade. His body fell over me like a ton of bricks knocking me backwards under the weight of a freshly dead man. I strained to push the body of the fallen priest from me, but in failing strength I collapsed almost into unconsciousness. A hand seized the lifeless body and drug it aside revealing the face of my gypsy friend in the dwindling sunlight.

Lying helplessly on my back, I held my hand up to block the sun and asked, "Where did you come from?"

He sat down beside me and answered, "I had decided to stay in Wrin-Henji the day you left to keep a watchful eye on those miserable priests." He spat and continued, "Good thing too! They left that very evening to pursue you."

He used some cloth from one of the priests' robes to bandage my wounds with the skill of someone who had done so many times in the past. As he doctored me a sudden dizziness overcame me and I fell backwards.

"Are you all right?" he asked.

"Yes, thank you," I replied.

"Sorry it took me so long to get up here and help," he said, "but they moved with a speed which I could not overcome."

Exhausted, I tried to get up on my own, but my limbs failed. The kind gypsy leader helped me to my feet and suggested that we should camp for the night so that I might rest. I declined his sound advice and insisted that I must continue, for I had a new enemy chasing me and this was one that my able friend could not save me for it was time itself. Climbing that mountain in the dying hours of the evening, I couldn't help but feel sad for the three priests of Eidolen. Although it was unavoidable, I hated being involved in their deaths. This was their world, not mine. It seemed a shame that such a horrible act had to be committed to stay in such a beautiful place. The remainder of our evening was spent climbing, trying to put as much of the mountain behind us as possible, until the darkness of the impending twilight and my fatigue forced us to stop until morning. We found a small niche in the cliffs that provided some protection and safety from the elements and slept that night in moderate comfort.

When I awoke my side was sore and the cut on my arm throbbed mercilessly. The chill of the mountain's altitude and the early morning air bit sharply into us. While stretching to loosen and warm up my muscles, I climbed out of my protective den to survey the mountainside. The fog was so thick that it was difficult to see the ground beneath your own feet. It looked as if the clouds had fallen from the sky and were lying on the mountain like a white fluffy blanket.

We packed up our meager supplies and renewed our climb in the cool mountain air. The abruptness of the terrain made the remaining part of our ascent very difficult. In some places the face of the mountain was so steep that we had to climb back down and maneuver around to find a different way. It was hard work with few places to rest and I was glad when the slope of the mountain began to gradually level out. I still couldn't see the top of the mountain or the ivory tower that sat upon it, but I knew we were almost there. When we neared the top of the mountain the soil became less rocky and more fertile and therefore easier to walk upon. Wild flowers of unimaginable beauty sprang up in all directions while butterflies and bees hovered above their masses. A gentle breeze blew over that ocean of flowers bowing them down in wave after wave of majestic color. The tranquility and quietness of the fields reminded me why one would choose to live among these mountain peaks alone for eternity. And standing on the highest point of the mountain, towering above all else stood the ivory tower.

Chapter 5
The Man in the Ivory Tower

We followed a thin trail through the flowering fields leading to the residence of the man in the ivory tower. Aside from the brilliance of the massive tower itself, the surroundings of his abode were quite common. Around the tract of the tower stood a short rock wall about three feet high that defined the surrounding primitive but eloquent courtyard. Inside the barrier were numerous small wooden fences, some defining pens for livestock, while others served to separate diverse vegetation that grew in all shapes and sizes. The main gate was little more than a small wooden fence attached to a cobblestone wall which surrounded the overgrown courtyard. In the center shot up the immense circular tower that pierced the sky at a good two hundred feet above the ground. The tower wasn't actually made of ivory, but instead of a white polished white-veined crystal marble indigenous only to the Lands of Dream. The spire of the tower came to a spiral point with four equally spaced windows at the top. At the top of the tower flew a flag with a shield-shaped crest in its center. My gypsy friend pushed the small gate inward causing it to creak as if in pain with a loud grinding moan. Upon our entrance into the courtyard two monstrous wolf-like dogs rose to their feet tugging at thick chains which held them firmly to the ground. The huge beasts stood as high as modern day cows snarling at the end of their chains with powerfully bulging muscles. My friend, fearful the creatures might break free from their thick chains, unsheathed his sword and held it outward feebly hoping it might repel an attack, but he as well as I knew if either got loose, there would no escape. We instinctively backed out the gate as the door to the ivory tower opened and an oddly dressed man stepped out to greet us. He appeared to be somewhere in either his late sixties or early seventies and upon seeing intruders on his property yelled as us.

"Have I got a couple of thieves on my hands?"

My gypsy friend might normally had taken offense to such an

assumption in offense, but at the moment all he cared about was the giant creatures staring him down.

Upon seeing us backing away, the man from the ivory tower unchained one of his pets and then commanded it to stay, "You two have climbed a long way to die."

In morbid fear I cried, "We are not robbers. I am a man from your world seeking your noble and wise advice!"

His hands unchained the second wolfhound, which leaped in our direction, but halted upon the word stay.

"Come closer so I can see if I recognize you."

I stepped forward nervously, for I had never met him in this world or our own.

He eyed me for a moment and then said, "I do not recognize you. Were we friends in the waking world?"

" No," I declared, " but I seek your secret of living in the Lands of Dream."

"Ahh, you are a dreamwalker much like I once was!" he said. "Have your companion leave his sword in the ground and the two of you may enter my house as guests."

My friend the gypsy knew that if the old man wanted us dead the sword he carried would be of little deterrent to such beasts, so we did as he said and walked uneasily past the man's pets into the ivory tower. The interior of the structure was lit by a score of candles and embodied by the rich fragrance of burning incense. The first level was one large room with a rising staircase that twisted upward into the darkness above. In the center was a large circular stone table covered in piles of books, charts and maps. What part of the walls that weren't covered by dusty books sparkled under candlelight. The furnishings were sufficient, but were not lavish as I had expected. A stout fire burned brightly in the corner making the drafty tower seem quite cozy.

"Please sit down and I will fix you two a bite to eat," he said.

A thick iron ladle dipped into a heavy black pot scooping out a hearty stew. Our host brought both of us a heaping bowl with a cut of chewy bread then sat down across from us and continued.

"I have lived in the Lands of Dream for some time now and you are only the third dreamer from the waking world with whom I have spoken. You must be a great dreamer, as I once was, to stay within the Gates of Deeper Slumber as long you have."

"I do not wish to dream anymore, but to stay here as you have," I responded.

"Much of my memory of your world has faded now. What I do remember seems silly now. At the moment, I can't even remember my name. I was a lord or king, I think, from a country on an island maybe." He stopped for a second as if to concentrate, "I can't remember the name anymore. Oh well, it is of no value here."

"You look too young to have lived here for very long," I replied.

"Men from the waking world do not age in the Lands of Dream. I am the same age I was on the day I left the waking world."

"How long will you live?" I asked in curiosity.

"I will never age, for time no longer has a hold upon me. I will live as long as there is one conscious creature in the universe with the ability to dream. Dreamers stretch the empire of dreams from all across the universe, the borders of Dream touch every star in the sky," he answered.

"Why if so many are allowed to come, do so many try to stop me from staying?" I queried.

"It is not the people that try to stop you, but the gods," he said. "They fear the one god who pushes out the many. Many were once dreamers and gods from your world, gods of wood and water, earth and sky, but now they are all but forgotten by the men of your world. They fear that your knowledge of this jealous god may spread among the men of dreams and push them out of the Lands of Dream, their last solitude. Now the many gods try to push out the one god."

"Will you help me?" I asked, "I have so few allies in this world. You are the only one I have found with the knowledge I seek!"

He stood up and took our dishes as would a servant before saying, "I will help you, but I assure you that the gods are plotting against you as we speak."

"What must I do?" I asked anxiously.

"You must cut your soul from the ties in your world. This means your body will die, but your soul will live on. Once your body is laid to rest your soul will remain here forever," he said.

"How do I do this?" I asked.

"You must lock the Gates of Deeper Slumber, cutting any link of your soul to your body in the waking world." He paused a moment, took a deep breath and continued, "You must drink from the Fountain of Dreams. This will seal the Gates of Deeper Slumber and separate your soul from the body that holds you in the waking world."

"Where is this fountain?" I asked with ebullience.

"You must travel past the great Alekain Desert to the lost city of Gurtique," he said. "There in those ancient ruins lies the palace of King Parleis and the Fountain of Dreams."

My gypsy friend jumped to his feet and passionately announced, "No one can pass through the Alekain desert and live!"

The old man smiled and said calmly, "I never said it would be easy, but it can be done, for I did it nearly fifty years ago."

"Please forgive my friend. He is only trying to protect me. Tell me everything you know about this fountain and the desert I must pass to reach it," I said, willing to risk everything for even the slightest chance of living in a perpetual dream.

"I will," said the man, "but I must warn you. Thirty years ago another young man climbed the very mountain you climbed to find the secret of the fountain. He had fallen in love with a young girl during his visits to the Lands of Dream. I warned him as I will warn you, but he did not listen as you will not. He left this mountain thirty years ago heading towards the Alekain desert and was never heard from again."

My friend stood up, speaking his mind once again.

"The trip to Alekain would take at least ten days, not to mention the time it would take to cross such a harsh environment! I have heard of the horrors that dwell there! Well-crafted expeditions financed by kings have attempted to pass that desert for the riches of abandoned Gurtique and failed! You have sent him to his death telling him this!"

I grabbed my friend's arm, pulled him back down and apologized for his rashness.

The old man replied laughing, "He is perhaps the sanest man in the room and he is the only one from the Lands of Dream. How ironic!" He stood up, looked at me, and said in an exasperated voice, "I suppose any further warnings would be a waste of time. Come on let's go up to my observatory so I can prepare you for your trip tomorrow."

My legs carried me up a score of stairs straining wearily up the tower's many floors until our host finally pushed open a hatch at the top leading us into the summit of the structure. The spire was circular having four equally spaced windows that faced upward toward the sky like that of an observatory instead of outward as do most windows. Books lined the walls as they do in a public library seemingly having no end in sight as they were stacked in every place possible. Sitting by one of the windows was a large telescope built on a stand with wheels, so as to be able to roll to any of the tower's upper windows.

"I had forgotten that there was only one chair up here," said the man rubbing his head. "I'll be back in a minute. Make yourselves as comfortable as possible."

While he was gone, my friend went over to one of the windows to observe the view. I used his absence to explore the material on his table. There were all kinds of constellation, navigational and terrain maps with enigmatic markings, but the thing that got my attention was a single biographical book entitled *The King of Dreams*.

The man returned in short order bringing with him two more chairs. He pulled them up to the table and kindly asked us to sit down. Then he took a silver censer from one of his crowded shelves, placed it in the center of our table and lit the material within. It burst into a still blue flame that burned without the usual flicker that accompanied fire. His face radiated a deep blue as he peered over the table.

"The weed that burns in the bowl will cover our plans from the gods," he whispered, "and my hounds will keep away any spies."

He unrolled a map, studied it for a second, and continued, "To reach the outskirts of the Alekain will be a long journey, but passing through that desert will be your true challenge. Living among its dunes and hills of sand are creatures that have been placed there by the gods themselves. These creatures have been handpicked from all over the infinite cosmos to guard the lost city of Gurtique and its treasures. They hunger for the souls of men and if eaten, you will lose your place in both the waking world and the Lands of Dream. Your name will be forever erased from the stars in the universe."

Hearing what he said placed doubt in my heart for the first time since I had entered my dreams. If I failed I would not only lose the Lands of Dream, but my entire existence. The doubt did not last long for my sole existence was to stay in Celpahia. I didn't see that giving up my reason for existence to save it made much sense.

"Tell me what you know of these beasts, so I can be forewarned." I asked.

"Well," he said, "very little is known about these beings for few have ever glimpsed one and lived. All that is known is mostly hearsay and myths. Some are said to be invisible and the victim's death is the only thing you can see. Others are said to be flat and the color of the sand, so that when a man gets close enough, they will wrap around him and drag him under, smothering him. I know nothing of the previous two, but one I have seen one with my very eyes. It was black as coal and had the body of a fat pudgy man, but the face of a large toad. It was a little larger than a man and had small bat-like wings. When I crossed the Alekain long ago I had two guides accompanying me. We were all mounted, well armed and equipped, but such matters were of no consequence to this monster. One of these monsters swooped down from the sky in complete silence and ripped one of my guides off his mount. I sat in horror on top my camel and watched it stuff him violently into its hinged mouth, much like a snake eats large prey. The tips of our spears merely bounced off the flying beast as if it were solid steel. All we could do was run as the monster sat holding its belly while it devoured my poor guide." He paused a moment as if reliving the nightmare before continuing. "When you cross the desert move slowly and be observant. Don't follow widely-used trails as nothing actually travels across the desert. These trails are merely traps to lure you to your doom. Watch out for unusual landmarks as well because they are more than likely being used to attract victims. You will be better off if you travel alone or in a small group to make it more difficult for the creatures of the Alekain to see you. It is useless to try to fight these creatures… your only hope will be the swiftness of your flight and the might of your wit. You as the prey must be more cunning than the hunter if you are to pass successfully. That is the only advice that I can give you that is of any value within the Alekain. Your next dilemma will be Gurtique, and of this matter I know even less. It is said that a giant, whose lineage is of both man and god, guards the fountain. He is said to not be accepted by either and lives in the lost city hoping to gain the favor of the gods. He did not live there when I stole a drink from that fountain. Undoubtedly he has been left there by the gods to ensure my success will not be repeated again."

With that he got up from his chair and began to gather up maps and that was all the three of us spoke of the trip. The rest of the evening was spent preparing for my long trip to the Alekain. Most of the supplies and food donated by my host were common items of necessity, but some were of a magical nature and of great importance. He gave me three maps, one being navigational and two terrain, an elemental stone that constantly sweated water, and a pouch full of useful powders and trinkets.

He also gave me a pair of shoes made from a cloth that would not leave tracks in the sand. My gypsy friend and I looked over the maps and charted our impending adventure. After all our preparations were complete, the man in the ivory tower led us to our rooms so we might rest before morning. Even after the long hike of the previous day, I found it difficult to sleep as my mind formed images of the wondrous city of Gurtique. As I lay dreaming within a dream about the lost city beyond the desert of death, I wondered just how long I had been asleep in the waking world. As I dreamed in the Lands of Dream, my body lay locked away in a secluded cabin unknown to anyone but myself, and I could only hope I would dream long enough to reach and drink from the fabled Fountain of Dreams.

The next day we got up before the suns of Dream rose over the summit of the Shakh Mountains. I threw my gear over my back and stood ready to leave as the first light cracked into the dawn. Our host wished us well and we said our good-byes to the man in the ivory tower and began our descent before the sun lifted out of the Cerulean Sea. We had not traveled more than an hour when a large formation of men carrying torches appeared on the mountain trail below. Still being early morning and the mountainside not yet fully illuminated by the suns of dream, it was difficult to distinguish their features and therefore to know their race or allegiance, but the reflecting light from the suns off their weapons told us enough. We rushed back to warn the man in the ivory tower in hopes that he might be able to shed some light on the subject at hand. We found him casually clipping buds in his garden caught up into the soothing harmony of tending his many plants.

We rushed up to him like terrified children to a comforting parent. Upon seeing us he continued calmly with his labors speaking to us while tending his plants.

"One moment, I must pull up these male plants before they can pollinate," he pulled on a green stalk ripping it from the ground then continued. "You must have forgotten something very important to return with such haste."

"An army of soldiers climb the mountain as we speak!" I cried.

He dropped his clippers in the dirt and spun to me with a new sense of urgency.

"Hurry, follow me."

He led us back to his observatory and rolled his telescope to the window facing Wrin-Henji. He removed his eyepiece and squinting mumbled, "It appears that the gods have amassed an army to oppose you."

"How many?" I asked.

Looking up he said, "Oh, two maybe three hundred." He rolled his telescope to the other side of his tower and peered through the lens saying, "Just as I feared. They are all around us."

"What?" I yelled. "Let me see!"

My eye peered through the long telescope focusing upon the men below. They wore bright shiny armor, with long colorful pantaloons.

"There is no way we can fight so many," declared my gypsy friend.

"We will not have to fight," said the old man confidently.

"Do they not intend on killing us all?" I asked in disbelief.

"They will not lay siege to my tower," he declared, "for they fear my inventions. They simply intend on waiting out your stay in the Lands of Dream."

In anger I proclaimed, "I will sneak past them tonight and kill those foolish enough to stand in my way! I will reach the Alekain with or without their blood on my hands!"

"That may not be necessary," answered the old magician. "I am an inventive man and have recreated something that has never been seen in all the Lands of Dream."

I looked to him in earnest, ready to try anything to escape the army that lay in wait, "Tell us!"

"I have constructed an airship."

Those words, like no other words I had ever heard, restored a resounding new hope within my soul.

"An airship, is it readily accessible?" I asked in amazement.

"Well," he answered in a proud voice, "it's more of a balloon, but yes. Everything on it is finished. I have only failed to properly test it."

"Today would be a perfect day to give it such a test!" I professed.

"Come, we must get it ready before the gods can formulate another way to oppose us."

He led us down a dark spiraling staircase into a shadowed wine cellar below the base of his tower. Bottles of glass, wood, metal and stone lay all about, some full and some empty of the various concoctions from all across the Lands of Dream. He kept the balloon disassembled in a small room hidden behind a stack of wooden barrels.

"I keep it well hidden, even when I work on it so the gods would not get wind that I could do what man is not supposed to do... fly. It was built for one man and his equipment, so that I might one day explore the corners of Dream and gather materials for my experiments." he said sadly. "May it serve you well!"

We laboriously drug the heavy balloon outside the tower and stretched it out in the great mountainous field that surrounded the lofty ivory edifice. As we used a great fire to heat air and piping to pump the air into the balloon itself, it slowly rose from the ground taking shape before our eyes. It was not large as hot air balloons go, but if it worked, it would be more than enough to easily pass over the surrounding armies below. After giving me a crash course in its use, the man in the ivory tower bid me farewell. As I stepped into the balloon's basket, he handed me a dirty root which he had only pulled from his garden a few minutes ago.

"Take a bite from it and chew on it when you get tired. It will keep you awake."

I turned to my friend the gypsy king knowing that it was here that we must part. While I knew I would miss him and undoubtedly be less likely to succeed without him, it was all for the best. This was not his quest and therefore should not be his risk. We embraced and as we were about to part, he gave me the name of a man in the city of

Veltarin that might be able to aid me in my quest, if I made it so far. He declared that the man owed him a favor and if I so needed I could cash it in upon reaching the small walled city at the edge of the Alekain. Then to my surprise, he firmly placed his beautiful curved sword into the palm of my hand. Its ruby-encrusted handle sparkled under the light of suns, a loving gesture that touched my soul. I took it happily knowing it was what he wanted to do and that to argue the point would be an insult.

All he said when he handed it to me was; "I expect it back once you return from the Alekain."

With that, I got into the balloon's wicker basket and cast off.

Chapter 6
A Balloon Ride to the Alekain

The balloon lifted off the ground carrying me and my equipment with remarkable ease. Following the directions given to me by its creator, I steered the balloon toward my final destination. The strange airship, which was shaped much like that of a pale egg, used strange brown stones called heat rocks as fuel that once placed in fire would magnify heat tremendously and burn for dozens of hours before finally burning away. To raise the balloon all one had to do was start a small flame and then throw in a single heat rock, simply repeating the process by throwing in a new heat rock before the other decomposed. My first heat rock quickly lifted my balloon into the air immediately dwarfing the mighty Shakh Mountains and its ivory tower. Rising higher and higher, I watched my two friends diminish from sight in a matter of seconds. My diminutive airship drifted across the sky with the leisure of a moving cloud, passing over the Shakh Mountains and the port of Wrin-Henji. The opposing army stopped and watched my unusual contraption in astonishment since men in the Lands of Dream did not fly unless by power of beasts or ancient magic. Archers fired their arrows in vain missing terribly as I flew out of their range and finally out of sight. The lights of the armies' torches disappeared in the haze of distance and suddenly I found myself in utter silence, with nothing in sight save myself, the balloon in which I rode, the sky and the ocean below.

Riding the wind, my balloon effortlessly and smoothly sailed through the sky above the first layer of clouds. The material of the balloon above my head was the color of bleached bones and shone like a light bulb mirroring the sun. It was a clear windy day and my airship skimmed over the great Cerulean Sea making good progress. My heart rejoiced as I sailed in one day what would have taken me many days on foot and aboard ship. My new mode of travel would also be invaluable in crossing the great Alekain desert hopefully allowing me to avoid the unspeakable monsters within its tracts of shifting sand.

That night I stayed awake in order to navigate my airship and keep it on course. Strangely, the wind behind me pushed me along almost as if the ship I rode in knew my flight path, and I had to do little more than raise and lower my altitude by the usage of heat rocks. The root upon which I chewed to stay awake tasted of the earth, soaking into my mouth like mud, but with each chew I took, my eyes widened open to their fullest and I felt refreshed and wide awake. Late in the middle of the night I came up upon a small bark on the open sea sailing gracefully upon its glassy surface. A man standing in the ship's crow's nest stared up at me perplexingly as I passed him like a second moon. We waved at each other peacefully before he disappeared into the fog of night leaving me to desire the tranquility of Dream that he already possessed.

The next morning my eyes were greeted with two brilliant sunrises of blood red. The clouds that I had been following through the previous day and night had completely dissipated, and all that stood before me was sky and sea. According to the flight plan handed to me by the man in the ivory tower, the trip to the city of Gurtique would normally take weeks by land and sea, but through the air, it would require only a few days. To pass time I studied the two maps of Dream known to man, the northern and southern realms, eyeing them with envy. There were many strange and wondrous lands spread across the hand-drawn atlases that I longed to see. I sat back and dreamed within a dream that I might travel across Dream, as does the man in the ivory tower, having an eternity to do so. Having little else to do and forsaking sleep, I split my days and nights over the Cerulean Sea between meals, which consisted of many strangely colored and unusually shaped fruits and vegetables provided to me by the man in the ivory tower. Although astoundingly beautiful, the vast Cerulean Sea offered little to observe besides a crystal blue plate of seemingly endless aquatic plane, until one afternoon when I passed over an enormous coral reef. Its fields of brightly tinted coral stretched for miles turning the blue sea below into a looking glass of spectacular color. It was a glorious sight of soft pastels and florescent illumination that almost brought an end to my quest as I lowered the edge of my basket into the sea as I stared into it hypnotically. I abruptly threw a heat rock into the balloon's hot box streaking back into the sky. The force of my rising violently threw me into the bottom of the basket as I jetted into the air barely escaping crashing into the sea. From my new height, the coral reef below blended into prismatic harmony smearing into a collage of impressionistic art. In the distance stood a massive peak of land surrounded by mist and water emerging from the sea like a mountain atop land. My balloon sailed directly over the lonely island paradise passing over its tan beaches, thick tropical forests, blue lagoons and cascading waterfalls. Strangely, I did not see any signs of civilization, as if the small island had been freshly dreamed and not yet fully explored.

That night I caught up with a formation of clouds and floated along as one drifting quietly underneath a blanket of sparkling stars. Juice from the magic root soaked between my teeth keeping me fresh and awake as if I had slept for several days straight. I held my position in the sky until the next morning when I was greeted by two immense suns rising from the sea. They bore down brightly my balloon forcing me to squint into the horizon beyond which a small shadow appeared. It expanded in the distance, slowly materializing into the black image of a galleass with tall pointed sails and long rowing oars. The huge ship lumbered across the sea plowing a wake through the otherwise perfectly calm sea. I pondered its destination and in effort to feed my curiosity, I steered toward the oncoming ship. The size of the ship presented itself in its entirety as it swelled larger with each moment producing three masts and decks. The fore and aft masts were smaller than the main mast, but all wore the colors of a Tarkian warship! The ship's sails were completely black nearly blocking out the horizon behind the massive vessel with a red skull design in their center surrounded with arrows pointing equally in all directions, a symbol in Dream to represent absolute chaos. Chaos was a religion to the Tarkians and since they were primarily mercenaries by trade, chaos was always for sale. My heart froze in terror upon seeing the ship and in an attempt to outdistance it, I reached down into the bottom of my balloon's basket and freed a heat rock. Before I could throw it into the heat box, the gunners upon the ship's gun deck propelled giant harpoons into the air. Three giant metal missiles about the size of a full-grown man whizzed past my vessel screaming by as they cut through the thick sea air. I immediately threw the heat rock in my tongs into the heat box and pulled on my rip chord with all my might. My balloon began to rise upward, but fearful of how quickly I might rise with three rocks in the heat box at one time, I refrained from throwing in another and looked over the rim of my basket to observe my progress. The man-of-war's gunners reloaded their giant deck-mounted crossbows and fired in quick succession streaking three more harpoons into the air screaming for my death. All three missed, but this round had come much closer than the last, and with Tarkian gunners being known as some of the best in all the Lands of Dream, I knew if I did not pass over them quickly or high enough, my quest might end over the Cerulean Sea.

A third volley of shots fired upon me as I came upon the giant ship. Two ripped along both sides of my balloon barely missing the center, while a third tore through the basket in which I stood. It ripped through the wicker basket streaming by my leg, missing by inches and nearly tearing it off. They had pinpointed my speed upward and I knew that if I continued to rise at the same pace, the gunners below would find their mark and put an end to both my balloon and me. Desperate to escape, I changed my plan of action and released the heat from the heat box hanging beneath the base of the air chamber plummeting down upon the Tarkian war galley.

All three shots of the next round of fire missed widely as the harpoons streaked over me high into the air. I dropped down upon the ship and passed over its center mast by half a dozen feet or so coming in direct contact with the ship's scout standing in the crow's nest. He stared at me with bright orange eyes set into the center of a long face of wrinkled skin with gray splotches. I quickly sealed the heat box before pulling out a burning heat rock with metal tongs. Its heat sizzled like lava melting the end of my forceps before I dropped it down upon the sea vessel below. It rolled down the main mast igniting its sails before crashing to the main deck and burning through into its chambers below. Flames began to surge upon the ship roaring high into the air as the fire from the ship's sails spread across its three decks. Huge flickering flames and black smoke billowed into the air like that of a coal ship out of control. Then out of nowhere, I heard a huge rip. Hot air whooshed out of my balloon and I began to sink toward the sea once again. Even as their ship was burning out of control, the Tarkian gunners had held firm and kept their sights fixed having struck their target even as they burned upon the sea. Terrified of crashing into the sea, I threw a handful of heat rocks into the heat box above and fell backwards as my airship ripped upward like being jerked aloft at the end of a rope. Dizzily, I pulled myself back to my feet and looked backward to watch the Tarkian vessel collapse into the sea a submerging fireball. A burning ship is the worst nightmare of a sailor as it gives its victims two choices of destruction, either a quick painful death by fire or a long agonizing one drowning at sea. As I sailed away from the burning wreck, I could have claimed that I had burned it purely so that I could escape without fear of the Tarkians following me, but in my heart I knew that I had done it out of revenge. I wanted them to pay for the destruction of the *Sea Dancer* and the capture of its crew.

While I watched the ship disappear into a watery disaster, I turned my attention back to my own dilemma. My balloon had a long tear in the fabric that was threatening to give way and dump me into sea at any moment. At the current rate I was using heat rocks to resupply the heat escaping from my balloon, I would run out of fuel sometime by morning. A strong wind gusted at my back and I fell to the bottom of my basket hoping it would be enough to push me to the coast before my balloon collapsed from the sky.

A nearly unbearable heat radiated from the overstuffed heat box above breaking me out into a full sweat. I lay beneath the horrendous heat hoping against hope that it would not collapse above my head pouring scalding rocks down upon me like burning hail. I continued my flight through the night and by morning I threw in my last heat rock. At that moment, there was nothing else I could do as even hope had faded from my heart as my balloon began to sink slowly toward the sea's surface. As I watched the sea rise, the bottom of my basket where it had been torn by the Tarkian harpoon, began to rip. I placed my feet upon the frame of the basket and held on for dear life. As the last bit of heat escaped the internal chamber of the balloon, my descent accelerated to an alarming rate. I struggled with the steering mechanism to curve my decline, but the situation had deteriorated far beyond my control. Suddenly along the horizon, a sandy image appeared ahead and I heart rose ever so slightly at the sight of land. If only I could make the coast, I thought, struggling against the forces of nature, fate and the will of the gods themselves. The bottom part of my basket dipped into the sea ripping in two and scattering me and my equipment into the open sea. The balloon itself continued on for another thirty feet or so before collapsing into the water ending its reign of the skies forever. The maps, food and gear given to me by the man in the ivory tower all sank to the bottom of the sea leaving nothing afloat but me and what I wore. I had managed to save my gypsy friend's scimitar and the water stone in my pocket, but it and the weight of my clothes were jeopardizing my ability to stay afloat.

The sea was harsh, tossing me around helplessly as I struggled to stay above its murky depths. The coast was still far off and I looked out into the distance wondering if I had the strength left in me to navigate it. I fought the waves as I struggled to keep my dream alive. I couldn't give up now, for I knew I might never return to the wondrous beauty of Dream if I failed. My arms ached excruciatingly as I tread through the bouncing sea and my lungs stung gasping for air against the weight of the water surrounding my chest cavity. Suddenly exhaustion took over and my arms failed to heed my mental commands. My legs struggled to keep me above the surface of the water for a moment, but finally surrendered to the sea as well as my head sank with one last gasp for air. I looked through a murky world at the last sight I would see within my failed dream-quest when as if by a miracle my foot suddenly touched the bottom of the sea. I had come down upon a sand bar! I struggled up the underwater sand dune while holding my breath and rushed to reach the air, gasping in life and a new hope. I reached the coast later in the evening and fell to the beach too exhausted to do anything but labor for breath. I spent the remainder of the day lying on the beach soaking in the sun. After having not slept for several days, I fell into an irresistible sleep unable to take another step.

Chapter 7
Crossing the Desert of Death

I awoke the next morning near mid-day lying upon a hot beach with my head drenched in sweat. The wind, the birds, the sea and the beach quietly carried on with their activities completely ignorant of my presence. Getting up, I knocked the wet hot sand off my body and took a minute to regain my bearings. Whether it was the hot sun or the strain of the swim to shore that drained my strength I was unsure, but my limps felt like wet noodles. Although I had lost the finely detailed maps given to me by the man in the ivory tower, I did remember that the city of Veltarin was somewhere north of the coast and it would be there that I could find the friend of the gypsy king. With my ruby-handled sword in one hand and my water stone in the other I began my trek to Veltarin.

The terrain along the way was flat and arid and the further I went inland the more desolate the landscape became. The trees along the beach line slowly became bushes and the grass disintegrated into lifeless sand. The sun became hotter with each step and the only sign of water dripped from the stone in my hand. Before long all that stood around me was sand and an occasional shrub that fought for survival. My journey inward was slow and had I not had my water stone to suck on, I doubt I would have made the trip to the outskirts of Veltarin.

As the city materialized out of the shifting sand, its bronze cupolas and minarets stood glorious in the waste of the Alekain. A great wall that slanted outward protected the city and defined its boundaries from the swirling sands of the surrounding desert. The walls were broken into segments by small guard towers that were strategically placed every forty feet. The outside of the city's walls were covered in a clear grease that ran all the way from the top to the bottom. At the base of the wall stood three foot tall spikes pointing upward toward the wall ready to catch anyone foolish enough to try to scale its exterior.

The main gate served a dual purpose, being the city's only

entrance and exit and was so deep it appeared more like a tunnel than an actual gate. The walls themselves were thirty feet thick making any attempt to collapse them a near impossibility. The main entrance kept the city firmly cut off from the outside by means of three heavy iron portcullises placed about ten feet apart. In the center of the city stood an immense donjon that rose high above the city's outer walls. Three watchmen with pikes as long as men stood on the donjon's ledge staring out into the distance. It did not take long for one of the men upon the tower to see me and signal my arrival with a long bronze horn. The city's gates creaked open spitting out a detachment of mounted soldiers in chain mail covered with white clean tabards with a bright red screaming phoenix branded on their chests. Each was armed with a long spear that could be used as a short lance while mounted and all held giant round shields with the same screaming phoenix on its face, the emblem of Veltarin. It was rumored that the city of Veltarin was dreamed by a great cosmic phoenix many years ago and that it had been the inferno of its mind that had burned the landscape leaving the great Alekain a scorched land.

One of the guards in shiny gleaming armor raised the visor on his helmet and spoke, "I am Odgean, Lieutenant of the Second Royal Veltarin Guard. State your name and business."

Knowing not who served the gods of Dream, I told the man that my ship had broken up on a reef near the coast and that I had relatives in Veltarin. Wary of strangers, the glistening knight tested my story by asking the name of one of my relatives and so I spoke the only name in Veltarin I knew, the name given to me by the gypsy king. As soon as the name left my lips, the men of the guard before me leaned back staring at me peculiarly.

"How are you related to him?" asked the imposing horseman.

"He... he is my brother," I said formulating an abrupt lie.

"Turn around," ordered the lieutenant as if knowing I spoke untruthfully.

I nervously turned around leaving my back exposed to a group of armed soldiers waiting tensely before spinning back around expected metal to pierce my torso at any minute.

"Being the brother of Xanier, I expected to see a pointy tail," replied the lieutenant of the guard in jest.

The rest of the soldiers in the patrol burst into hideous laughter leaving me unsure if my lie had been discovered or not. Then almost as if about to strike me, a hand presented itself to me pulling me up onto the back of a horse and the Second Royal Veltarin Guard escorted me past the city walls. As I rode through the long shadowed entrance, a crew of men labored upon a giant wheel on top of the wall which slowly opened the first gate. It was obviously a complex mechanism with gears and capstans that would allow only one of the three gates to open at one time. Once the first gate had closed behind us, the second gate began to rise letting us stand before the third and final gate. Upon the closing of the second gate, the third opened and I finally stepped inside the nearly impenetrable city known in the Lands of Dream as the city that defies the gods.

The interior of the city looked much more like that of a prison than a township with bars on all the buildings' windows. Its streets were simple dry dirt that had hardened into near pavement strength from the arid desert air. The streets were bursting with people streaming up and down in a hustle and bustle that matched any busy city in the waking world. Once I stepped into the city, my guard detail left me alone, and so to find the friend of the gypsy king, I stopped a man on the street and asked him if he knew where I might find him.

He looked up at me weirdly as if I were from another planet and responded, "No one looks for him... he looks for you."

I tried to get the man to elaborate on his response, but he walked away briskly as if suddenly trying to avoid me. I asked several more people on the street the same question and each time I received a similar response with one woman running away in terror. Suddenly, a small thin man wearing dark dusty clothes came up to me as if trying to sell me something.

"You the one looking for Xanier?" he asked, looking around as if he was being watched.

"Yes," I said excited to finally have found someone willing to help.

He motioned for me to follow him around a tall row of buildings. Once we stepped off the main street into the shade a huge bulking man seized me and threw me up against the wall. He pulled out a thin knotted wire about the thickness of a fishing line and forcefully used it to bind my hands, while the small thin man held a curved knife to my throat.

"So you are a long lost relative of Xanier!" said the man

holding the knife sarcastically.

"He's too fair to be a relative of Xanier!" said the larger man snickering.

"I'll fix that, if he doesn't start singing! Why are you looking for Xanier?" claimed the man with the curved blade.

"Wait!" I yelled, "I'll explain!"

"It better be good," continued the man, "because Xanier doesn't like people looking for him."

"A friend of his referred me to him. I seek only to speak with him," I answered.

The small thin man quickly pushed me against the wall once again and began to search me roughly with his hands. He pulled my ruby-handled sword from my belt and lifted it up to inspect the gems inlaid in the handle.

"What's he got?" asked the big man curiously.

"A sword and a rock," he replied ignoring the small damp rock for the more impressive sword.

"We takin' him to Xanier?" ask the big man of the smaller man.

"Yeah, we'll see if Xanier knows this so-called friend."

The two men led me through a maze of back streets and dark alleys until we came to the town square where the city's secret of survival within the great Alekain was revealed. In the center bubbled a clear spring that gushed a fountain of crystal clear water that rushed outward into four separate stone carved aqueducts distributing fresh cold water to every corner of the city. Its citizens walked along its edge filling clay pots and bowls before whisking them away to their home to drink, cook and wash. A cool breeze lifted from the ice cold spring as though it came from a giant outdoor air conditioner. Fearful for my life, I began to scream for help, but the people of the city upon seeing whom I was with, turned away and ignored my pleas. A powerful hand seized my neck twisting it until it was about to snap signaling for me to shut up. I did so and quietly followed the two men without question.

As we continued past the center of the city, the buildings became older and poorly maintained, almost slumping over on top of us in shadow and space. What had once been a clean beautifully-constructed city had now declined into a haggard tight slum. The two men rushed me through twists, turns and doorways until we paused in front of what appeared to be an old abandoned building. I was quickly pushed into the darkness sunblind passing from the bright desert sunlight into a dim interior. As I stepped into the shadow of darkness a deep voice commanded me to sit down. A multitude of hands seized my body roughly shoving me blindly into a chair I could not see. The room hung in silence as my eyes adjusted to the image of a hulking man across from me. He sat silently studying me over a table between us.

"I don't have family," he said pausing to take a breath, "I'm an orphan from the streets and if I did meet a so-called member of my family... I'd kill him with my bare hands. So tell me how am I related to you?"

My mouth opened and before I could get the words out he slammed his fists upon the table between us and screamed, "Tell me brother, where is our mother? She forgot to introduce herself to me!"

At that moment I wished my gypsy friend had never mentioned this man's name. He sat eyeing me patiently for my response. From his appearance, he was a powerful man with bulky muscular arms covered in wild and lavish tattoos. His head was square as if it had been chiseled from a block of stone giving him a powerful jaw line and stern look cold as ice. His head was shaven and covered in tattoos, while his face was neither. From the evident strength of his gnarled hands and arms, I believed he could easily kill a man with his bare hands, something I hoped to avoid at all cost.

"I apologize for any misunderstanding. A mutual friend of ours said that you might be able to help me," I replied solicitously.

"You lie to me again, because I have no friends, only associates," he said angrily, "Do you see these tattoos on my arm?"

"Yes."

"Each one is the portrait of a man I have killed," he said calmly showing me a dozen or so on one arm. "But I like the way you look so I'm going to let you pick where yours is going to go."

His men began to laugh in the shadows at my expense once again. The thought of becoming a portrait upon the skin of a man from the Lands of Dream paralyzed me in fear and I stared back at the giant man in silence.

"I understand, you've probably got a lot to consider since you're about to die. If you want, we'll handle the details after your dead."

I tried to speak but fear had stolen my voice.

He point toward me and suddenly his affiliates jerked me out of my chair and dragged me towards the door. While clawing and kicking to get loose, I forced out my gypsy friend's name in a scream of terror.

There was a pause and then the deep voice commanded the men holding me to let me go and said, "Yes, now I remember where I have seen the sword you were carrying. Please… get up and sit at my table as a guest."

I picked myself up off the floor and straightened my torn clothing. I wasn't sure if the sound of his voice was that of sincerity or sarcasm, but I sat down at the table from fear of what might happen if I did not. After I sat down he spoke again.

"What did he tell you about me?"

"Well… he just mentioned that you were his friend and that you owed him a favor."

"Did he ever say anything like what kind of a favor he wanted me to return to you?" he asked, with a surprisingly kind demeanor.

"He said that you were an adventurer who could help me in my quest," I declared relaxing a bit.

The whole room exploded into laughter, including Xanier himself.

The room quieted with the sound of his voice, "An adventurer… huh! I see that skinny runt has not lost his sense of humor. I'm more of a cutthroat or thief, but I assure you he is not my friend. He is the only man still living that has ever shamed me. He spared my life in a fight to the death and it is this favor I owe him. It is this favor that keeps him alive! Now finally I have my chance to rid myself of him, his favor and all its shame. This quest, what is it?"

"To reach the lost city of Gurtique," I said simply.

Once again the room burst into commotion.

A man said, "You are a mad man! We would have to be fools to try to take you there."

Another man said that he would not go and several other men agreed.

Xanier's voice broke the turmoil, "All of you are going or you'll end up dead in the street! If you want to call yourself fools, that is fine, but don't tell me what you will or will not do! I will choose who stays and who goes. None of you has a choice in the matter, so quit whining like women and get your gear ready. We're leaving first thing in the morning."

With that, his men became mutes, suddenly working like ants for tomorrow's journey into the desert of death. I learned later that Xanier and his men were little more than thieves who ran the east and south sides of Veltarin but that Xanier was a man of his word. If he said he would let you live, then he let you live, but if he also told you he would kill you, then he would kill you. With Xanier, you got what you saw. Xanier sat down with me to speak of his plan and demands, while his men readied themselves for our trip.

"My men are accomplished archers and if any of the beasts that live within the sands of doom get close we'll make them look like pin cushions. Once we get to Gurtique you are on your own. If you want to waste your time looking for some fairy tale water fountain that's fine by me, but don't expect us to help you. We'll be out looting the city. Since I'm supplying the men and gear for this trip, you'll do as I say or you don't go. We get all the treasure that you or my men find in Gurtique or along the way, as compensation. All that we are providing you is safe conduct through the Alekain. Once this is complete, our mutual friend will soon be dead by my hand."

When he finished, he got up and left not giving me a chance to reply. His men spent the rest of the night sharpening their weapons and packing their rigging. I was supplied with a camel and a saddle, which had two large leather flasks, one on each side to carry water. They gave me my friend's sword back and a long spear that I could use as a lance when mounted. I also got some clothing better suited to the Alekain's environment. Even though these men were the dregs of society, common thieves and assassins, I was glad to have their help. They were hard men born out of the Alekain. Who better to lead me through it than they?

The next day we loaded up our equipment and supplies and rode out of the city. The people of Veltarin avoided our presence in the streets and made sure to stay out of our way. I could see their curiosity about why we were leaving the city, but none would risk a question or even a long look. Even with their nonchalant attitude, I was sure most would pray for our failure, whatever our intentions. We rode through the city's deep dark gates and out into the heat of the

Alekain ready to stand against it as a force of sixteen men counting Xanier and myself. The men were equipped with spears similar to mine and carried long bows as secondary weapons. Xanier rode in the lead upon a dirty brown horse without a trace of armor, wielding a long hammer with a sharp spiked back. Our band rode hard through the dry wasteland trudging through deep hot sand bent on defying the gods of Dream.

The terrain of the Alekain was bare without any type of visible vegetation, save for dry near-dead shrubs struggling against the breath of the phoenix. Where could these beasts described to me by the man in the ivory hide? Everything around us seemed but a lifeless wasteland incapable of supporting any form of life whether it be man, creature or god. We rode the first day without incident and camped the night away between two sand dunes. We used small Bedouin-like tents to protect us from the wind, sand and cold night of the Alekain, but as I lay behind their cloth walls, I felt uncomfortable knowing they would provide little or no protection from the creatures of the night. I shared a tent with three other men and with most of us unable to sleep, I got to know them well, particularly one who went by the name Jarne. From his exterior, it was clear that he had lived a hard life on the streets of Veltarin. He was short, being no more five and a half feet, slender as if he had missed a meal or two, proudly displayed several scars and two missing fingers on his left hand that he had lost as a child against a rival gang after losing a game of body strip dice. It was a popular game among the gangs of Veltarin that only the fearless or insane played as the loser had to give up a body part or be killed by the other players involved.

Of the three in my tent, he was the one who was most willing to answer my questions about Veltarin, so I drilled him with a volley of questions about the city's history and traditions. It seemed Veltarin had two sides, one which was rich and elegant having become wealthy being the only sea port upon its desert continent. The other, the home of Jarne, was dark and seedy, a slum of poverty where only those of the greatest wit and daring survived. It thrived upon pirate's plunder, sex, gambling, theft and murder, for the greatest assassins in all of Dream called it home.

I asked him about the city's elaborate defenses and he explained that they were in place solely to protect its residents from the horrible monsters that roamed through the Alekain as mindless ghouls striving to murder men. Erected by the gods, it was the responsibility of these fiends to protect the secrets said to be hidden within the lost city of Gurtique. Bars had been placed on the windows to keep out those creatures having the gift of flight and grease on the walls to stop those with the ability to climb. Although having been born in Veltarin and having never left the Alekain, he knew little about these brutes, but he did know that to encounter one meant certain death because he had seen the remains of those who had.

The next morning we awoke to find the camp guards missing. Not a scream or clamor of battle had awoken anyone, including Xanier, and the only sign we could find that the men had ever existed was a small ever fading trail that led off into the burning Alekain. A group of six horsemen were sent in the direction of the trail while we broke down camp. They returned to Xanier a few minutes later claiming the trail had completely washed away in a sea of sand before handing their leader a severed hand. He eyed it a moment and then buried it in the sand so not to unnerve the remainder of his men. My first thought was if something could kill and drag off two men without us knowing, it might have been able drag us quietly from our tents one by one.

Jarne leaned over into my ear and spoke of the matter, "The monsters of the Alekain were created to do one thing and that is to kill; it appears Xanier's debt may be more than we all can afford to pay."

That day the men of Xanier traveled in low spirits, but not one spoke against their leader who rode ahead with a proud and defiant jaw. He was man who had been born and raised in hell and no creature of the gods could turn him back once he had made up his mind. Later that day a massive sandstorm struck throwing mountains of sand upon us nearly burying us in a soft grave as we rode through the pounding waste. We quickly set up camp and hid within our tents with wet scarves upon our faces to aid our breathing. The storm continued through the day and it was deep into the next night before it passed. Xanier doubled our guard, but few of us if any slept. The next day the weather treated us far better, presenting us with a clear hot sunny day. While the weather had improved, our lot did not and once again we encountered death. Our formation had been riding about an hour when we came up upon a strange field of dry thorns. They stretched across the desert as far as the eye could see in both directions and thinking little of it our group rode through them toward Gurtique. We had traveled only a few dozen feet into the thorns when the lead rider's leg brushed up against one of the bushes and without warning his body went into convulsions. He began to shake all over and as he turned toward us his face twisted in dreadful agony. Then in a matter of seconds, his body and face hardened as if transformed into stone turning pale blue. Before any of us had time to react, his body slid from top his horse and struck the ground like a statue. Men who defied the cold black hands of death on a death daily basis froze in utter fear trapped in a minefield of blue death. In every direction the dry thorns dripped with a thick syrupy poison that only needed a prick to inject their toxins into the bloodstream. Xanier slowly raised his hand and then ordered us to dismount. I carefully slipped off my horse trying to keep it as still as possible, but the creature jostled me, swiping my arm near a dry patch of thorns. I fell from the saddle just as the beast leaned into the desert brush. The horse jerked wildly as the thorns penetrated its coat, shaking and falling into another horse and pushing both it and its rider into a volley of thorns. All three victims suddenly turned hard with pale blue tint and succumbed to the horrifying blue death before our eyes, as if freezing solid within a blazing hot desert. We tensely moved through the poisonous field of thorn fearful of the slightest misstep and after several intense hours passed through it without further causalities. It seemed death came in many forms within the Alekain and we were but pawns in its mighty grip. "How many more would die before we reached the abandoned city of Gurtique?" I thought to myself as our rabble army trekked into the blazing sun.

With step we took further into the Alekain our morale lowered as if being drained into the very sands below our feet and before long the men began to openly rumble of death and madness. It was only the iron rule of Xanier that kept his men in line and surging forward against the god's will. He sat upon his horse proudly, defiant of the Alekain, savoring the death match in which he had become entangled. I believed he was doing this for the challenge as much as to rid himself of his debt to the gypsy king and for the unclaimed treasure of King Parleis.

If the heat was not enough, the desert floor began to rise up the legs of our mounts until we were forced to dismount and drag them along through knee high sand. It was a strenuous task making our journey slow going, and by the time the suns of Dream began to fade below the dunes of the Alekain everyone was exhausted. Feeling as though we should camp in deep sand, Xanier gave an order for us to continue and a couple of his men groaned at the command. Suddenly furious at the defiance to his command, Xanier jumped off his mount with the vitality of a possessed man as if the ordeal had not affected him at all.

"If anyone disagrees with my authority, then let that man step down and say it to my face!" he screamed, standing in the sand with his bare hands clenched.

There were ten men left, not including Xanier or myself and not one spoke a word. Xanier stood in front of the entire group unarmed for a brief time in complete silence waiting for someone to take his challenge. When it became obvious that no one was going to come forward, he mounted his pack animal and said, "Then I must assume that the men who disagreed earlier were not men at all."

The men remounted their weary horses and followed Xanier who sat upon his mount like a statue ready for whatever fate had to deal. Fate accepted his challenge and once again we drew death. It was late in the evening and we were just about to set up camp to weather the night, when the monster struck! It came over a dune to our left at an astounding rate completely surprising us. Its elongated arms and legs flopped over the hill as it ran toward us striking at the group with its multiple arms. It was large, about eight feet tall and about as wide, and looked like a large octopus with dull gray skin. Before any man could draw a weapon, it seized two men holding its prey with two arms each while standing erect with its remaining four. The men drew their bows, but held their fire so not to hit their own comrades. Xanier ordered his men to back away from the creature's range and paused without ordering a counterattack. Then to our consternation the creature stuffed one of the men into its beak-like mouth and began to devour him before our eyes. The man screamed in agony as his head and body were jumbled into the creature's mouth which broke bone and tendon with the ease of a meat grinder. Terror seized us as we watched our comrade helplessly disappear into the monster's stomach. Then before the creature could eat its other victim or grab another Xanier gave the command for his men to fire. Arrows were unleashed into the air sinking into both the monster and its victim. Strangely those that struck the monster passed through it as if penetrating jelly and vanished into the sand beyond. While not killing the beast, the arrows obviously hurt it for it began to shriek in a deafening tone before taking its final victim and rushing over the dune out of sight with flailing arms. A few of the men leaned forward to chase the horrid monster of the gods, but their feet held firm by command from Xanier. It was getting late and to chase such a ghastly monster in the waning twilight of the Alekain would not benefit anyone but the monster itself, so we rode away from the creature instead of chasing it before being forced by the darkness of night to set up camp. We had lost six men seemingly in a slow whittling down process in comparison to being overwhelmed by the monster's strength.

That night in our tents, I heard for the first time among the men open dissent against the leadership of Xanier. It appeared that their fear of the beasts of the Alekain has overcome their fear of Xanier. Upon seeing that I was near, the men quieted down and after receiving the quiet treatment even from my friend Jarne, I rolled over to get some sleep.

Late that night I was awakened by a thick cloth over my mouth and a sharp knife to my throat. It was my eight-fingered friend who whispered for me to be quiet and not resist. Suddenly I could hear the voice of Xanier damning someone. Men screamed and metal clashed for what seemed like an eon, then silence gripped the Alekain once again. As everything quieted down, Jarne let me up kindly apologizing by firmly stating it was for my own good.

Outside the tents lay the body of Xanier with enough arrows lodged in him to have slain a bull. I almost laughed as he had become the pincushion he had bragged about in Veltarin. The bodies of two of men lay at his side having fallen to the fury of his bare hands which had strangled them as he was being repeatedly shot by his own men. The Alekain had many facets to bring on death and we had become one of its tools as we killed our own in blind disorder. Before I knew what was happening, hands seized me once again forcefully tying me up like a calf at a rodeo before dragging me into a meeting of which I had no say.

The men argued among one another about what to do next

ignoring me completely. First they would immediately return back to Veltarin and explain to the remaining members of Xanier's guild of thieves that he had been slain by a monster of the gods. Secondly and to my dismay they would murder me to ensure the truth would never be revealed. I kicked and screamed through my bonds like a spoiled child until I was finally given an audience thanks to Jarne who kindly removed my gag.

"Please, let me continue on my journey to Gurtique, from which you know I will never return whether it be from success or failure!" I pleaded.

"It's a risk... he might return to Veltarin and tell what transpired here," spoke one of the thieves.

"He ain't got no water, no horse, no chance out here!" screamed another thief.

"What's yur problem? Getting too soft to kill people anymore?" replied the first thief.

The accused thief pulled a knife from his waist and flashed it at his accuser, "Want to see how soft this is?"

"This man has done nothing to us," spoke Jarne in my defense, "I'm all for killin' those that need killin', but if we killed everyone just to kill them, none of us would be here."

"Aye, but his death is an insurance to benefit our own lives," said another.

"Then it's settled, we should kill him."

"Wait," said Jarne with one last appeal, "if this man is meant to succeed then we should not interfere or own fates will become distorted."

The dirty rogues rubbed their chins in deep thought pondering his words as might a philosopher the meaning of life. It appeared the thieves of Veltarin were as superstitious as they were ruthless.

"How do we suggest we test this fate of his?"

"We leave him alone without water or horse. Then if he dies, we did not interrupt his fate or change our own," suggested Jarne.

I looked at Jarne suddenly wondering if he was friend or foe.

"Fine, if this man can navigate the Alekain alone without food or water and defy the beasts lurking in its heart, then he was destined to reach Gurtique."

The men laughed, and when morning came I was left in the heat of the desert to die alone. The bandits being "gentlemen", I was allowed to keep the ruby handled sword for self-defense before they trotted off into the blazing horizon. Jarne managed to slip me my sweat stone as he shook my hand good-bye and I sucked on it as they rode out of sight holding my ace in the hole. Might it be the only card I had remaining?

I traveled in the direction of Gurtique as quickly as my legs would allow through the deep shifting sand of the Alekain. How much time did I have remaining in this dream and how long had my body been asleep back in the waking world? Would I soon awaken with my goal was so close at hand? For the moment, it was not the beasts of the Alekain or the desert itself that was my worst enemy, as time itself held that place ticking away ever so slowly ready to steal me back to the pallor of the waking world. Waves of heat rolled from the horizon like microwaves cooking my flesh as I drudged through the breath of the phoenix with my water stone firmly in mouth to avoid its deadly thirst. Every dune I passed arose only to reveal another and then another until I felt as if I were in a revolving ball of sand dunes with each looking identical to the last. I followed the rising and falling of the suns as had Xanier's men to ensure I was heading in the right direction, and save for trying to keep my path straight, I depended purely upon chance that I would not somehow pass the crumbling city of Gurtique and wander to my death in the heart of the Alekain. Three days and nights passed without incident save the near loss of my mind. During the day, the desert heat beat down upon me mercilessly threatening to bake my mind, while at night strange sounds and wails terrified me with chills to my very bones. My slight uncertainties of the lost city's location continued to plague my mind but my true trepidation was that I might run up upon one of the creatures of the Alekain while alone and be erased from existence for all eternity.

After much labor, I reached the top of a giant sand dune, one much larger than any other I had seen, and hoped from its great height I might be able to see lost Gurtique, but once again all I saw was more dunes and further emptiness. My heart sank as I fell to my knees in both physical and mental exhaustion. As I sat in near defeat upon my knees in the sand, I noticed a small black spot that I had not noticed before, but I quickly dismissed it as a figment of my imagination brought on by the desert sun or by my mental and physical fatigue.

Save for lying down and dying, the only option I had was to carry on taking one step at a time. With the crest of each dune I ascended, the black speck had grown as if gaining ground upon me. Somewhat unnerved, I ran down one dune and up another and as before it was closer than before! Wild thoughts began to wander through my mind, but to ward off panic, I pushed them aside and chose to continue on at a normal pace. Upon reaching the next dune crest, I crouched down and surveyed the object in the horizon and found that it had grown even larger and from the best I could tell, it had a multitude of legs! It had to be the octopus creature coming back to finish off what it had missed during its last attack! I leaped to my feet in hysteria and began to run with all my remaining strength. I ran as I had never run before pushing my body to the peak of its limits. If the horrid beast caught up to me, not only would everything I had accomplished in Dream be lost, but I would be erased from the halls of existence never to be remembered or spoken of by another living creature again. I ran without concern for my direction climbing sand dunes with deep grunts and shaking limbs. Suddenly, my ankle turned and I rolled headlong down a giant dune like a tumbleweed rolling to its base in agonizing pain. I tried to stand upon the ankle I twisted, but it quickly gave way, leaving me face first in the hot sand. Dazed and confused from fatigue, my fall and the unbearable heat of the desert, I crawled to the top of the next dune and lay down in defeat.

I watched the eight-legged speck rise and fall out of my sight with each dune it passed, hoping it to be anything but the monster that had so easily attacked a dozen or so armed men. Because it was such a formidable predator, any attempt to fight it alone would be of little hindrance to the monster and for a moment I contemplated suicide so that I might be saved a cognizant digestion.

When it was only a few dunes away, I slid behind the apex of the dune upon which I sat and hid like a coward preferring not to see what would soon consume my body and soul. Eight feet threw sand upon my prone form as they leaped over me casting me in a cool dark shadow. I spun around to see what had jumped me to find Jarne astride a horse with another in tow. The site of another human being brought tears to my eyes!

"You sure move fast for a man on foot!" he said sitting on his horse and drawing deep breaths as if he had run me down on foot. "You made me wear out the horses trying to catch up with you!"

I rushed up to him and seized his arm like a lost child might cling to a found parent. Jarne helped me up upon my horse and seeing that I was in no condition to ride, led me through the desert toward Gurtique. As we rode, he explained to me that their trip back had not gone well. When they had left me alone in the desert, the group was six in number and by the next morning they were only four as two had mysteriously died in the night. Jarne believed it to be some sort of poisoning having to do with who would control the gang once they returned to Veltarin. After a lifetime in the streets of Veltarin awaiting a death that would surely come sooner than later by the hand of friend or enemy, he had decided to give it all up and start anew, and although joining me might not be the best aspect to begin his new life, he had nowhere else to go. So late the next night, he stole two horses and some supplies and rode back toward Gurtique. I gratefully accepted his assistance knowing that without him I would have assuredly failed.

We rode cautiously between dunes skirting their sides when possible so as not to reveal our presence and traveled two more nights and days without incident. Late in the afternoon of the third day, we came upon what looked like an ancient well. Its circular rim was made of finely carved stone and was almost completely covered in sand, except for about two inches from its opening. I was wary, remembering the wise words of the man from the ivory tower, but Jarne saw it as a good sign.

"Wells don't appear out in the middle of nowhere," he said, "so we must be getting close to the lost city of Gurtique."

I implored him to ignore it, but his curiosity and the possibility of it containing life-replenishing water was too much for him to simply pass it by without a further look. He leaned over the edge of the black hole and peeked inward with his sword drawn. I quickly drew my own sword and stood ready to help. There was no amount of help that I could have given to stop what happened next. With the power and quickness of lightning, a huge snake-like creature about four feet thick rose out of the well and snapped off the upper torso of my friend Jarne. The beast went back down into the well and all that remained of my friend was his limp lower torso and legs. Blood gushed from Jarne's waistline pouring into the dry sand staining it in a puddle of crimson. Tears filled my eyes as I lay on my belly and drug his remains away from the well to bury it in the sands of the Alekain with dignity. A sorrow I had never felt in the Lands of Dream soaked into my soul and I nearly surrendered to a tide of grief and misery. How could a world of such beauty harbor horrors of such absolute anguish? Taking the horses and what gear Jarne had brought, I moved deeper into the Alekain, and unfortunately for poor Jarne, he had been right, for I rode just one more day before I reached the outskirts of the fabled city of Gurtique.

Chapter 8
The Palace of King Parleis

The abrasive desert winds and sands had worn away the city's polished walls and lofty towers leaving behind broken spires and crumbling walls as reminders of its former glory. The swelling desert sands had engulfed many of the crumbling buildings and wide streets as if the city itself was slowly sinking into the depths of the Alekain. It was rumored that the patricians of this once grand and thriving city had incurred the wrath of the gods by denouncing their existence and declaring themselves to be gods. In a blind fury, the gods cursed the city's people, erased their souls and perverted their bodies into the beasts of the Alekain that hunger for the flesh of men. The city's main gate had deteriorated over the thousands of years it had sat dormant leaving nothing but a gaping hole. For fear of the front entrance being watched, I chose not to enter the city through its main gate, but rather through one of the many holes in its walls so as to escape the eyes of any watchful creature that might be lying in wait. Outside the walls I had left my horses tied in the shade of the city's outer walls in case I might need to make a quick escape.

Once I was inside, I cautiously moved from one decayed structure to another, trying to find the palace of King Parleis where the Fountain of Dreams was said to perpetually flow. Whatever catastrophe that was sent by the gods against the city must have struck swiftly and without warning for everything seemed to have been left in place as if ready to be used at any time. Inside the homes sat broken tables with dishware displayed as if awaiting someone for dinner. Fine artifacts along with helmets of gold, shields of bronze and swords of silver carelessly littered the streets, a treasure for most, but useless to me, a dreamer.

Even after hundreds of years of quiet desolation and relentless deterioration, the splendor and beauty of the city's past was still evident in its finely carved monuments, wondrous architecture and magnificent layout. Marble and granite had been as commonly used for construction as is concrete in the cities of the waking world. Immaculately detailed statues of pure jade and opal representing gods and heroes of their time were worn yet still stood triumphant. Then standing before me like a glimmering image of heavenly architecture stood the crumbling palace of King Parleis which towered high above all else within the city. It had a milky smooth exterior as if somehow carved from a gigantic pearl that could have only been dreamed by the mind of a god. I slipped into the glorious palace as would a thief holding my weapon against me in case a need for it happened to arise. The walls, entablatures and friezes paid tribute to the people's gods of their time glorifying the darker gods of the universe such as Ataxia, Emothe, and Oniejk the distant gods of marvelous gifts and horrific punishments. And so by their worship the city had grown to one as marvelous as any in the cosmos and by their wrath it had collapsed into nothing. As I marveled the beauty of the palace's interior, the quick sound of a snake startled me.

"Psssst!"

I froze in place and continued to listen intently, fearing that something was suddenly hunting me. My eyes and ears slowly searched my surroundings nervously.

"Psssst, over here," whispered a voice.

I followed the sound of the raspy voice, which led into a dark room along the hallway in which I stood.

"Hurry up," whispered a shadowed head from the darkness, "he'll see you."

I stepped up to the door with my sword drawn, wary of the beasts of the Alekain and the strange methods they utilized to capture their prey.

"Step out so that I might see you are what you present yourself to be," I ordered into the darkness.

A man about six feet or so with black curly hair stepped out into the light, "Hurry before we are spotted and our dreams are ended."

I kept the man well within view with my sword between us in case he tried some sort of trickery or shape shifting. When we got inside, he immediately peeked out the door down the hallway to where I was heading.

"Who are you?" I asked.

He turned around and in a whispering voice said, "I am a dreamer like you, searching for eternal life in the Lands of Dream."

"The fountain... do you know where it lies?" I inquired.

"Yes, it was within my grasp when a giant the height of three men chased me from it. For seven days I have dreamed here and for seven days the giant has hunted me through the ruins of this city. I have tried to lead him away from the palace, but he will not stray too far."

"Shouldn't we try to sneak by him tonight, when it is dark?" I questioned.

"No, I have tried that. He can see in the dark as well as you or I can in the light. Our best bet would be for the two of us to try to gain entrance to the fountain from two different sides at the same time. Then he will only be able to chase one of us while the other one slips in," he proposed.

I could see he had the same hunger as I to stay in the Lands of Dream. He would not leave until he was dead or until he awoke in the waking world, just as I.

"Isn't there some way we could sneak by or kill him?" I asked.

"A sword cannot penetrate his heart, even if you could get your sword that high and slipping by him is out of the question. He can sense the presence of a man by the scent of his flesh."

"But you know this palace better than I for you have been here for days and I have just arrived. You will have a distinct advantage."

"Then let it be known, whoever accomplishes this goal first will help the other by leading the giant away afterward," he declared. "I can think of no fairer pact."

We agreed with a firm handshake common not to the Lands of Dream, but to the mundane world of our birth. We quickly stepped into the hallway with weapons drawn more for effect than actual use and slowly walked down the long hallway toward the Fountain of Dreams. The ceiling of the hallway stood more than forty feet high, towering above us as would that of a normal home over the head of a small child. As we came near a tall doorway, I saw something that even in my current predicament seized my attention. It was an immense painting of King Parleis, and while strikingly painted, it was not the work of the artist that sparked my interest, but that the king's eyes bled from the painting's surface dripping onto the floor as if the great king was still suffering for his blasphemy against the gods of Dream.

My fellow dreamer pushed open the gate to the center of the palace and there trickling, a crystal treasure beyond any value to a dreamer, flowed the Fountain of Dreams. My admiration of it was short-lived for upon our entry a giant man nearly eighteen feet tall and holding an axe nearly nine feet in length rushed at us shaking the ground upon which we stood. Both of us ran like frightened children as the massive titan burst after us in pursuit swinging his axe like a chainsaw. We burst into the light of the Alekain splitting up once outside the palace in order to free one of us from the guardian's wrath. The giant man came out into the light with us and with long powerful strides rushed after me. I could feel his long legs catching up with me and although I ran with all my might, a shadow loomed over me. I could see the image of his axe in front of me in the form of a shadow and as it swung I leaped to the side barely avoiding its razor sharp blade. The blade streaked below me with a whistle crashing into the side of the palace cracking its stone exterior. Finely carved and polished stone fell down upon the giant separating us for just long enough for me to recover and continue to run. I spun around a corner and with a long pant I noticed a small brass grate in the middle of the road. If I could not outrun my predator, I could do as small prey do and go where their hunter cannot. I ran over to the grate and began to pull against it only to find that it had been sealed with the dust and rust of time. My muscles strained as I grunted against the rust frozen grate when my pursuer came around the corner with blood gleaming in his eye. I could not fail now, my mind screamed… I could not fail now! Suddenly a power I had never known surged through my limbs and I tore the grate from its hold in the road pulling off brick, mortar and metal as if they were mere paper. I threw myself into the dark hole as an iron axe burst in after me raining rock and stone from above. I crashed into a pool of flowing water that cushioned both me and the debris which fell alongside me. A giant eye peered down into the hole before a hand reached down near the water missing my head by mere inches. I crab-walked backwards through the water to escape the reach of the monstrosity that now fumbled through the darkness in an attempt to squeeze me to death.

Once inside the dark tunnel, I found what I assumed to be a large water system that had once served the great city from below. I quickly ran against the current leaving the giant vainly splashing through water for me, hopefully giving the other dreamer I had met enough time to safely drink from the Fountain of Dreams.

The structure in which I found myself was half circular, about eight feet tall and nearly fifteen feet wide. I struggled against the water flow which seemed to slowly rise as I continued up the dark aqueduct. Above my head spaced seemingly almost uniformly were grates similar to the one I had escaped which let in just enough light so that I could see where I was going. It appeared that the grates above had once been able to be opened by the residents of the ancient city and used to bring up water to the surface level. As I moved through the waist-deep water, I hoped that I might be able to enter the city from another point through one of its gates and ultimately find and drink from the Fountain of Dreams. The further I walked, the more options I had as the subterranean canal began to break off into other tunnels giving me a literal labyrinth of choices. I leaped up and tried several of the grates finding most to be frozen by time or completely covered denying me access to the outside.

As I stood in a junction of tunnels, sounds of splashing echoed from ahead, but from which of the tunnels before which I stood I could not tell. The sound continued to grow and having nowhere to hide but the water, I lowered my body into the water to the base of my nose and waited with sword in hand. Maybe the sounds were simply from the current ahead splashing against the walls of the aqueduct, but as always, my mind dreamed the worst and horrible underground monsters began to form in my mind. When I thought of what type of horrible beasts might be brooding down within the darkness of these tunnels, I shuddered with mortal fear. The splashing began to swell so loudly that I could have sworn that the culprit was in the very same corridor as I. I lifted up my sword for confidence and stared into the darkness of the tunnel from which the sound was coming.

The being burst into my sight looking around strangely as if it were trying to hear instead of see. At first sight, the creator of the splashing sounds appeared to be little more than a ghostly skinned man with milky white eyes. I do not believe he could see for he held his hands against the walls as if guiding himself by feel through the murky darkness. His face was gripped with a look of fear as if he were running from something. I had never seen panic in the face of any man or beast like I saw in his. His head turned toward me as if recognizing my breathing patterns, and without warning he rushed toward me with his hands stretched outward. His hands seized my neck as he squeezed his fingers forcefully bringing blood to the surface. My eyes began to bulge from the pressure of his grip and as I could not break free, I began to stab him with my sword. His grip was like iron tightening with each breath I strained to take. Like a boa constrictor his hands slowly tightened their grip before pushing me under the water. The warmth of his blood swirled around us through the cold water with a bitter salty taste as I struggled for air so as not to drown with the crazed man. My sword found its mark many more times before the hands upon my neck gave way and I burst out from the water sucking in the stale air of Gurtique's ancient aqueduct. My throat hurt with each breath I took and my lungs burned from the water I had swallowed.

Who was the strange man I had just killed and how had he found his way beneath Gurtique? Was he a lost dreamer as I or an ancestor from the ancient city above gone into hiding from the gods' wrath or something far from both? His face had been permanently stricken with some sort of grief, and not being able to bear its look, I pushed the blood-riddled body downstream.

Abruptly a chill came upon me and I began to feel the fear of the madman I had just slain. A weird murk came from the tunnel ahead turning the fresh water in which I stood into a foul murk. The next thing I saw is hard to explain, not because of the darkness of the aqueduct, but because of the nature of what I saw. A huge bulking mass oozed out of the same tunnel from which the crazed man had run. As the strange creature came near me I could feel my mind warp unnaturally being filled with a near irresistible urge to ravage and murder those whom did not serve the gods. I could hardly look at the thing, for its ghastly form was unfathomable. It wasn't solid and it didn't have one particular shape, but was more like a free-flowing blob. It was enormous and its form touched both the ceiling and the floor as it passed through the tunnels making a slithering sound. It had a huge round eye, not on its body, but in the center of its clear jelly-like body where it could easily see in all directions. I could also see the bones and bodies of men floating inside of it, men of all sorts, some like myself and others such as I had never seen or dreamed. I ran from it like a madman to escape the effects of its radiated lunacy to avoid permanently losing my sanity. I ran away without constraint navigating the unfamiliar and nearly invisible aqueduct system. In the darkness I bumped my head then faded into unconsciousness.

Epilogue

I awoke to a beam of light peeking through the crack in my curtains. All around me was the familiar scene of my small log cabin. I had returned to the waking world. When I tried to get up out of bed, I was stiff and could hardly walk. I had been asleep for six days.

It has been almost a year since I have last visited the Lands of Dream. That is why I put this account of my travels into words, so that maybe remembering it will help me find it again in my dreams. In between my searches for the beautiful city of Celpahia and the lost ruins of Gurtique I ponder the friends I left in the Lands of Dream. I wonder at times, when I watch the stars, what my gypsy friend is doing and if the other dreamer I met in Gurtique ever drank from the Fountain of Dreams. And what of the man in the ivory tower, does he still travel the edge of Dream in search of new elements to create his wondrous inventions? But even with all these memories I have not forgotten the suffering and death that my desire for the Fountain of Dreams caused. The crew of the lost *Sea Dancer*, the three dead priests of Eidolen, Xanier and the hideous deaths of his men and poor Jarne, all for naught! Maybe it's the wise words of Alzoond that keep me from finding the Gates of Deeper Slumber, or maybe the gods themselves. At present I do not know, but to date my continuous searches bring me nothing but grief.

Over the past year, I have closed myself off from society in fear that its mundane influence might affect my ability to return. My friends have abandoned me as mad and my family has repeatedly tried to have me committed. It seems that forces from both worlds oppose my dream. Be that as it may, this opposition only strengthens my desire to return. To escape the aberration of the waking world I have sold all my worldly possessions and moved to a remote location in the mountains, where I have obtained various drugs, herbs and lost tomes to aid me in my quest. This account of my walk in Celpahia will be my last contact with the waking world. I can only hope this written manuscript can help to revive my memory or help another dreamer find the Fountain of Dreams because for now I must only sleep and dream.

    I once knew a man who had lived an entire lifetime in the Lands of Dream having a wife, many children and grandchildren. Upon dying of old age he awoke from his dream to discover that only one night in the waking world had passed. That very morning he took his life, because he had already lived the life he wanted to live.

Search for a Dreamer

The Counsel of Dream

Part I
The Trail of my Father

As a child I never had the chance to get to know my father on a personal level. He disappeared when I was only five years old and what few memories I have left of him are now nearly gone. What little knowledge I have managed to obtain came from conflicting stories and opinions originating from members of my family and what few of his acquaintances that I could find. Since my uncle was the only surviving family member on my father's side, most of the information I came to know came from my mother's family. I don't mean to insinuate anything about my mother's family, but from what I can tell, no one besides my mother cared very much for him. My late grandfather detested him so much that he outright refused to even mention his name. My grandmother claimed that he was an alcoholic as well as a drug addict, while my mother claimed that he had been mentally sick for several years before his strange disappearance.

I did manage to obtain several official records pertaining to his life, but as is the case with government and business records, they gave little pertinent information. However, I did discover that my father had been arrested several times through political influence from my mother's family and that the year before his disappearance he had been committed to a mental institution by my mother through the advice from both her family and friends. He escaped twice and after his second escape he was never heard from again.

Several years later, when I was nearly twelve years old, some of his belongings as well as a fictional manuscript titled, _A Dream within a Dream_, were found in an abandoned log cabin belonging to another mental patient with whom he had previously escaped. The formerly mentioned manuscript received a great deal of attention from the media after its appearance and was labeled by most as merely the delusional account of a madman. The local media took up the strange story and it was even published for a while as weird fiction, although now nearly ten years later, it is long forgotten by everyone but me. When the accounts of my father's life along with his newly found manuscript were first splashed across the newspapers, my mother sent me off to a boarding school in England to protect me from its effects. I managed to obtain a copy of it for myself as a youth, and after reading it I swore to discover the truth whatever it might be.

Once I successfully finished a stint in college, my mother found me a job at a local law firm in hopes of keeping me close to our family's estate. I took the position out of love and respect for her alone, but I never found it interesting enough to truly devote myself to it as a career. The strange aura around my father's past life and unusual disappearance never truly left my everyday consciousness. I never spoke about my obsession with it for fear that my family might have me committed in much the same manner as my father.

My mother was always willing to talk about him before he became sick whenever I asked her, but she refused to go into any detail about him after his torrent breakdown. He had graduated with honors from Cologne University and had spent nearly three years after his graduation along the coast of France and Italy soaking in the local art and culture. It was on a trip my mother took to Paris that they met for the first time. She said that she immediately fell in love with his zest for both life and art, which at the time he believed were one in the same. The two spent an entire week together, fell in love and returned to the States to be married.

My mother claimed that while in Europe he became interested in a particular type of landscape art produced by a group of young artists who claimed to be part of a new movement known as Dreamscapism. Their work was both strange and beautiful and was recognizable by its bright and deep colors. They claimed that their work was a direct influence of visits to a dream realm beyond the subconscious of man somewhere between reality and fantasy. My father initially became an avid collector of their work, and being an artist, even made a few attempts in producing such works, but he detested the results and later destroyed them by setting his workshop on fire. He claimed that he lacked the passion and understanding of his own dreams to produce such worthwhile work and with the blessings of my mother returned to Italy for a short stay of two months. After he returned, my mother stated that he was happier than she had ever seen him and he began to produce vivid works of art that were absolutely brilliant. My mother claimed that the only thing that kept them from being recognized as works of brilliant art, was their unusual subject matter. Most were nothing more than landscapes, but they were unlike any landscapes of this world. They featured crumbling empires of silver, endless fields of deep purple and peculiar creatures of distorted shapes. My mother absolutely loved their brilliant color and spent a great deal of both her family's money and influence to promote them. She managed to get his work some national attention and even got a national art gallery to schedule an exhibit for his work, but my father vehemently refused to allow the works to be put on display. He claimed to her that they were expressions of beauty and that they were not to be cheapened for financial gain. With each passing day he became more obsessed with his work until it was all he would do or discuss.

My dear mother claimed that he would sometimes stay up two or three days straight to complete some of his works before his "memory" faded. To this day my mother believes that it was his obsession for the artwork of Dreamscapism that slowly drove him mad. He became more and more distant with each passing day and eventually moved out of their house and took up residence in an old barn which he turned into a workshop. Sometimes he would not come out for days at a time and whenever my mother would try to visit him or bring him food he would become furious at her for disturbing his work. During this time his work changed from bright colorful subjects to themes of a dark and hideous nature. Eventually he quit painting altogether and started ranting to her about finding a way to permanently stay in his dreams. It was at this point my mother claimed that his obsession turned into a sickness. It was all he would talk about to anyone and eventually he quit talking to people ignoring them as if they were lifeless shadows. He switched his monetary focus from collecting rare art to collecting materials that dealt with the Lands of Dream. When I asked if any of this material still existed, my mother became perplexed that I would want to have anything to do with the materials that helped drive my own father insane and refused to comment any further.

My desire to have some type of closure with regard to my father's true persona and disappearance finally brought me back to

England to speak with my father's only surviving relative, my uncle. Being my father's only and younger brother, he had corresponded through letters with him throughout his two incarcerations in the Belmount Institution for the Mentally Insane. He had kept all of his letters as well as what little of my father's artworks that he could acquire after his sudden disappearance. I studied each letter more than a hundred times and at their first reading they appeared to be nothing more than the work of a man plunging further and further into madness. They became more intense with each correspondence as well as slowly making less sense. With each reading I became more intent on discovering the cause of my father's demise, if there was one at all!

His final letters were actual maps and geographical locales that made up what he claimed to be the Lands of Dream. Several when connected gave an overlook of the Lands of Dream, which he claimed to have personally known. But it was his final letter that he wrote before he escaped for the second and final time that intrigued me the most. After hundreds of failed attempts and nearly four years of failure, he claimed to have found a passage that a man from the waking world could use to pass into the Lands of Dream. Unfortunately, it didn't give any concrete details to the method of the transition or to the location of such a passage.

I got to study twenty-four pieces of his work and found each piece mesmerizing. The canvasses were caked with thick brush strokes constituting a strange flow as if to lead the eyes of the viewer. At first glance and to the untrained eye they appeared childish and hazy, but when the viewer stopped and stared for long periods of time the colors blended upon the canvas to take shape and form landscapes of astounding beauty and creativity. It was a simple beauty that my father had told my uncle could only come from the world of dreams. He believed that the complexity of our times had stolen such splendor from our own world long ago.

I enjoyed each one of his paintings, but there was one in particular that pulled at my thoughts, seizing me as if in a trance that drew me to it incessantly. It was striking, as were all his early paintings, but it was different from the others in that its subject matter was more than a landscape. In its center stood a tall white tower that glistened from the sun of Amora, as related in a letter to my uncle, and sat upon a mountainside overlooking a small harbor filled with brightly colored ships. Its title was, *A Man and his Ivory Tower*.

My uncle immediately saw my love for it and gave it to me as a parting gift. I begged him to keep it, but he kindly refused. I spent a few more days with him in his small flat out of respect for his kind generosity before leaving for America early one morning.

Afraid that it might get damaged during my travels, I had my father's painting expressed home and caught a flight to Wisconsin to meet an old friend of my father. He had been along with my father during his first escape from the Belmount Institution for the Mentally Insane and was still confined there nearly twenty years later. He was currently on restriction for a recent violent attempt to escape and when I visited he was in the maximum security wing of the hospital. His room was small and white as I might have expected, but it was far from cozy. It consisted of four walls with wall to wall padding and a bench-like seat attached securely to the floor. From its appearance, it appeared to be both his seat and his bed. An attendant chained his hands and feet before leaving to watch our conversation through a small slit in the wall.

"I would like to ask you a few questions, if it is all right with you Mr. Lithglow," I asked kindly.

"You have the look of your father," he said leaning back on his bench ignoring my initial question and starting his own conversation.

"You know who I am?"

"Just as well as you know who I am," he said coldly.

"You knew my father?"

"I knew him for two long and confining years," he responded, "but the only thing I really learned about him, was what that look can do to a man."

"A lot of people say I took after my mother," I responded.

"I'm not talking about your appearance boy," he said, correcting me as if I were a child, "I was talking about the look you have in your eyes. He gave it to me too, damn him! I hate him for that," he said leaning back on his bench.

A bit startled by his last reply, I sat down in a small chair across from him that the attendant had left for me and glanced around his small room. It was as if we were sitting in a plain white box. If a man weren't actually mad, living a lifetime in such a place would certainly make one so.

"Yep, you got it all right. You got it bad," he said breaking the silence around us.

"What look?" I asked.

"The hunger," he answered. "I haven't seen it in another man since I last saw your father. It is going to drive you mad. Right now you just want to know if it is real or not, but soon that won't be enough."

"Hunger?"

"You know very well what I mean, the Lands of Dream!" he answered loudly. "But once you get there it won't be enough. You'll want to go again and again, until visiting is not enough. Your hunger to see it will change to an overwhelming desire to stay, but that is not what will drive you mad. What is going to drive you mad is that every time you get there, the harder it is to return. For its serene beauty to be so close but at the same time to be out of reach is too much for the fragile mind of mankind. I saw it slowly drive your father insane. Oh, he was already beyond the line of insanity when he first came here, but each day he went deeper and deeper until he couldn't stand to dwell in the dull mundane color of our world."

"All I want is to find out what happened to my father," I replied correcting him, "not to see any world of dreams."

He paused and leaned over toward me as if he was trying to keep our conversation a secret.

"I spoke with him last night you know," he said in a raspy whisper.

"Who?"

"Who have we been talking about?" he asked as if my response was ridiculous. "Your father."

From the corner of my eye I could see the attendant was getting antsy and I tried to change the direction of our conversation.

"My father has been missing for nearly twenty years," I explained.

"Not gone," he replied pointing at the floor and pausing for a moment, "just not here."

"Did he come here to see you?" I asked humoring him.

"No," he said looking at me angrily.

"They let you go on visits then?" I asked out of curiosity of the conversation.

"If you're going to keep asking stupid questions, you can go and leave me to finish counting the seams on the walls," he said irritated.

"I'm sorry Mr. Lithglow. Please tell me about your visit with my father," I said apologetically.

"I started visiting him in my dreams about six years ago and would you believe he hasn't aged a day since I last saw him. He's got quite a nice place too! It's kind of small and all, but it's on a really pleasant lot near the river," he said excited. "Yep he's got a really nice place all right… built into the side of a small hill," he said repeating himself and laughing lightly.

"What do the two of you talk about?" I asked, trying to sound as sincere as possible.

"Oh we don't talk much," he said, "instead of wasting time we enjoy it. Words between two people just don't compare to two people experiencing a moment. Usually we gaze at the stars together or watch the river flow by. You know," he said looking in to my eyes, "the hours I spend with your father are the only things I look forward to anymore. It used to be that the only thing that kept me from killing myself was the restraint of these miserable people, but now I live to visit him in my dreams."

His delusional account of visits with my father left me speechless. We both sat in silence for what seemed like eternity and my heart went out to his poor soul. He might have been insane, but no one deserved to be confined in such a way for decades. I reached out and touched his hand. It startled him and he jumped back, almost pulling his hand completely away from me, but once he realized that it was a gesture of kindness he put it back down on the table. I believe that it was the first time anyone had touched him in an act of pure kindness. I turned my head and pretended to cough and quickly wiped away the tears that had suddenly filled my eyes.

"He misses you and your mother you know," said the poor confined man.

"Thank you Mr. Lithglow," I said recomposing myself.

"Please call me Herald. Your father does," he said strangely consoling me.

His pitiful situation and delusional accounts of his visits with my father saddened me and I nearly broke down into tears again, when an attendant interrupted me.

"Mr. Lithglow is very tired and needs his rest," said the attendant standing behind me. I had been so caught up in our conversation that I hadn't even noticed him come in.

"I'm not tired," replied Herald at the top of his voice.

"Now Mr. Lithglow, visiting hours are up for today," replied the attendant as though speaking to a child. "Maybe your friend can return to see you another day."

"I haven't had a visitor in nearly twenty years," replied Herald smartly to the attendant, "you'd think you could give me a little leeway in regard to your stupid visitation hours!"

"Mr. Lithglow," said the attendant as if he was correcting a misbehaving dog, "if you don't calm down, I'll have to give you a sedative."

Herald quieted down as most frightened children do when confronted by an authority figure and I left without incident. The hospital's visitation times were stringent and I was only allowed to see him for one hour each Wednesday afternoon. I had taken residence with a widower by the name of Mrs. Plind north of town for twenty dollars a day, which is steep by anyone's standards, but her home was in the country and away from all the hustle and bustle of the big city and the cost of my room and board included both a homemade breakfast and dinner, as well as taking care of my laundry. Her home was both old and large, but one which had been built with care and taste. It had four tall pointed gables and sat in the middle of nearly 48 acres of rolling hills, pasture and woods. A huge ancient oak tree stood rooted in its front yard, with branches that stretched out in all directions giving cover from the heat of the searing sun. It reminded me of a similar oak tree that I had played under as a child, bringing back memories from my childhood that I had thought were lost forever.

One such memory included my father holding me under an oak tree. He asked me to look out toward the sun as it was falling behind the mountains that ran along the skyline of our property. I remember looking out at it as he had suggested and after seeing nothing unusual began to play. Frustrated at my lack of attention, he stopped my play and asked me what I saw. I told him the sun and began to play again.

"No," he said pointing out toward the mountains, "that is the universe in motion! No matter what we do, no matter how we try to change it, it will continue on moving forever, unaffected by us in any way. We are nothing more than spectators. Sit back and together we will enjoy watching what little part of it we can see."

He picked me up and held me under our old oak tree and we watched the sun move out of sight for what seemed an eon. It was Mrs. Plind's old oak tree that actually convinced me to stay with her during my visits with Mr. Lithglow. It was a decision I would enjoy. Being from a large family she enjoyed the company as well and treated me as if I were a member of her now absent family. She was somewhere in the middle of her seventies and had nearly outlived everyone in her family besides her two remaining sons who rarely visited her. As I stayed with her, I could tell that she was mothering me, but in consideration of her isolation from her family, I allowed her to do so.

My room was upstairs near the far end of the house by itself with only a single window in the corner. It offered a beautiful view and when I wasn't visiting Herald, I was sitting in front of it studying the strange letters of my father that had been given to me by my uncle. His maps were the hardest to cipher, due to the strange way he put them down on paper. Unlike ordinary maps, which are drawn on a two dimensional basis, his were drawn three dimensionally through the use of an x, y and z-axis. So in their study, you not only had to try and track location by going north, south, east or west, but by also going straight up, down or at an angle. It was quite confusing and without a starting location, it seemed impossible. I had first hoped that my visits with Herald might help me better understand the mental stability of my father before he disappeared, but now it seemed that maybe he knew enough about my father's aspirations that he might be able help me to understand his maps and if they might lead to anything.

The week after my first visit with Herald passed quickly and before I knew it, it was time for me to go and see him for a second time. The kind Mrs. Plind asked about my "goings-on" in town, but in fear of her reaction, I told her that I was considering a position at a local law firm. She seemed pleased that I might end up taking permanent residence and packed me a sack lunch before I left. I arrived at the Belmount Institution for the Mentally Insane early that morning and was finally allowed to see Herald about thirty minutes after the start of their only visitation hour. I found him sitting in the same room and in the same position as before, but this time he appeared happy to see me.

"I'm so glad that you decided to come back and see me!" he said excitedly.

"I plan on coming to see you quite a bit," I said sitting down across from him.

"Good," he said reaching out and touching my hand, "because I have a message from your father."

His response shocked me so, that I found myself frozen and unable to physically respond.

He ignored my blank look and continued, "I wish you could have seen his face when I told him that you came to see me last Wednesday. All he did was ask one question after another about you," he said looking at me intently. "I believe that it was the first time we ever wasted time talking about anything that dealt with this world."

Not knowing how to respond I looked at him blankly without offering a response. My lack of a response clearly aggravated him and his aforementioned smile changed into a look of annoyance.

"I see that you do not believe me," he said angrily.

"No Mr. Lithglow… Herald," I said correcting myself, "you just took me by surprise."

"Well I did," he said happily. "I sat down and spoke to him last night in my dreams just as I am sitting here speaking to you right now."

"What exactly did he say?" I asked curiously.

"He would like you to come see him," he said candidly.

"I wouldn't know where to start," I said humoring him.

He leaned forward as far as his restraints would allow and whispered into my ear.

"I can show you the way," he said.

Before I could react two attendants came in and abruptly ended our conversation.

"That will be enough for today," said one of the attendants while gripping my shoulder to alert me that it was time to leave.

"But we just started and there is plenty of time left for visitation," I responded while looking at my watch.

"I am sorry, but you have been asked to leave," said the attendant forcefully.

"By whom?"

"Please," said the attendant looking directly into my eyes.

I got up and began to leave when Mr. Lithglow went into a rage. He jumped up from his seat and began to kick his legs and swing his arms wildly in an attempt to break free. Both of the attendants tried to subdue him, but he was too much for the men. He knocked one out with one of his shackles and managed to get hold of the second one from behind and began to choke him with one of the chains that restrained him to the wall. I stepped back in horror as I watched what had been a calm man turn into a frenzied animal. The attendant while being choked was still able to scream for help and after a few moments several more attendants rushed into the room to join the struggle. A nurse took hold of my hand and led me out of the room and into the hall.

"You're going to have to leave now. Please," she said again after seeing my reluctance, "it is what is best for Mr. Lithglow."

I reluctantly began to walk down the hall, but stopped when he began to scream out to me.

"He told me how to find him!" he screamed.

The nurse took hold of my arm and directed me once again toward the exit.

"Get me out of here!" he yelled again in a deafening tone. "Get me out of here and I will show you."

I drove home that evening and spent the next week doing nothing but thinking about what had occurred and anticipating our next visit. I decided to collect most of my father's maps and writings and take them with me on our next visit in hopes that maybe Herald could shed some light on them, but I was greatly disappointed by my next trip. It had been decided by the hospital administrator that my visits with Mr. Lithglow had undermined his treatment and since I was not actual family, I would not be able to visit him again. I argued with the administrator for nearly an hour, but left without prospect of further any visitations.

That night back at my room I slept uneasily and did something that I rarely ever did or at least remembered, I dreamed. While in my past dreams I could never really recall if they were in color or not, this one was copiously colored. The color in this particular dream expressed itself in rich bright tones as if expressing its zeal for life. The dream itself didn't really seem to have a beginning, but more like I had been thrown right in the middle of it. The first thing I could recollect was that I found myself standing knee deep in a field of long golden grass. Hanging above me was a clear light blue sky that came down and actually seemed to lie upon the tall golden grass as it swayed in the wind. I never felt so relaxed and free from the bonds of our world. It was as if all of my worries blew away with the wind that streaked through my hair. I found myself smiling for no reason but for that of being alive. Off in the distance were tall snow-capped mountains that endlessly stretched along the horizon. I know this is strange, but I could actually feel the warmth of the sun on my face. I was surrounded by nothing but the ground, sky and wind and I relished it! My eyes caught the glimpse of a single bright purple butterfly as it frolicked through the air stopping occasionally to tend a flower and I wondered where it was going in such an infinite field of beauty.

"Wondrous, isn't it son?" said a deep calm voice.

"Yes it is." I said simply, while never taking my eyes off the butterfly that danced an aerial hypnotic dance of pure rhythm.

A man's hand touched my shoulder and rested gently upon it.

"I can still remember the first time I saw the Lands of Dream," said the voice. "It is good to see you have the same appreciation for it that I have. Maybe we are not so different after all."

After several more seconds of quiet appreciation, I turned around and looked at the man who stood next to me in my dream. He had on a long loose sleeved shirt of sunshine yellow that appeared from behind an emerald green velvet vest accented by a purple silk hat with long waving plumes. Although I had only seen a few pictures of him as a child, I immediately knew that from his strong jaw, short beard and gentle demeanor that he was my father.

"Is that you?" I asked him unbelievably.

"I am as real as you at this moment," he said.

"Is it always this peaceful here?" I asked turning my eyes toward the mountains before me once again.

With his hand still on my shoulder he said, "What you are experiencing at this very moment is true content. Your desires and struggles in life have vanished. You are now in harmony with the universe and that is enough." He paused a second and repeated the end of his last sentence, "That is enough."

I felt so happy that my clear sight of the surrounding beauty became muttered with tears. I never wanted to lose the tranquility I felt standing there with my father, and from that moment on, it would be all I lived for. I turned around and embraced my father for the first time in over twenty years. His long arms accepted me and patted my back reassuringly.

"It is a lot to take in the first time," he said laughing and crying at the same time in my ear. He paused a moment holding me tightly, "I'm so sorry that I neglected you as a child. Knowing you never truly had a father has plagued me here since my arrival. It has been the only thing that has kept me from being completely happy."

He held me in silence for several minutes and continued to cry and speak into my ear at same time, breaking the quiet melody around us, "I have been trying to find you in your dreams for so long. To show you why I did what I did. To show you I wasn't insane." He paused again and finished, "To show you the way here."

I stepped back and looked into his eyes. Tears glistened down his check drying away with the wind.

"There is so much more I want to show you," he paused again, "so much I want to share with you."

I didn't know what to say. I had spent most of my life wondering and searching for who and where my father was and once I was standing in front of him I was speechless.

"Help Herald," he said softly. "I have shown him the way."

Suddenly his image began to streak off into the long field getting smaller and smaller till it completely faded away. At first I had thought it was his image that had left the field, but it was I who was stretching violently away from the Lands of Dream. My body began to spin slowly as if I was falling, but instead of down, I was falling across the landscape below. I began to spin faster as my body picked up speed and in a matter of moments I had left the golden fields and was passing over the snow peaked mountains I had admired earlier. My momentum kept increasing exponentially until the color of the countryside melted into a muttered rainbow of colors like the initial image of my father's paintings. I began to feel dizzy and closed my eyes.

When I opened them again I found myself immersed in the dull morning sunlight that seeped into my room through the thin curtains that lined my window. I rose up and swung my legs over to the side of the bed and sat at its end. Had I really stood in front of my father and held him as he spoke to me gently about the Lands of Dream or had my imagination finally manifested a dream to put my curiosity about my father's sanity and whereabouts to rest?

I could hear Mrs. Plind's spatula scrape against an iron skillet downstairs. The aroma of freshly brewed coffee and sizzling sausage crept past the doorway in my room and brought my thoughts back to the waking world. For some reason my mind felt numb as if I hadn't slept at all. I put on a robe that Mrs. Plind had been kind enough to lend me and went downstairs. When I got into the kitchen, she had her back turned toward me and was already hard at work preparing lunch.

"Good morning," she said kindly. "I hope you slept well."

"Actually I didn't," I said groggily. "It seems I dreamed all night"

"Oh," she said apologetically while breaking string beans and placing them into a tall silver pot, "I hope you didn't have a nightmare! All that research you are doing is catching up to you. You need to take it easy for a day or two. I swear I have never seen anyone study things as much as you."

Small snapping sounds of firm fresh green beans breaking continued as she spoke. She paused a minute from her labor and brought me a plate covered with flapjacks, sausage, eggs and a cup of coffee. Then she smartly put a lump of sugar and spoon of cream in my coffee just as I liked it, stirred it and continued.

"Really," she said, "it's not healthy to have your nose stuck in a book from sunup till sundown."

"I know," I replied.

She turned around.

"What is it that haunts you so?" she asked concerned. "I mean you stay up to all hours of the night looking at those papers covered in chicken scratch, instead of going out and living."

She pointed her spatula at me, "You are still a young man. You should be out enjoying yourself instead of being cooped up in here all day. What about a girl? You interested in a particular girl?"

"No girls," I stated quickly to erase any thoughts of local matchmaking, "it's… it's the loss of my father that plagues me so," I said slowly.

She sat down her spatula and removed her apron.

"Oh dear, I am sorry," she said remorsefully. "I did not know."

She pointed at the long comfortable robe I was wearing.

"That was my husband's favorite robe," she laughed lightly. "Although he only wore it a few moments a day, as he worked from when he woke till he slept. See… it's idleness that wears on a man's mind. A man needs work to occupy the time God gave him on this earth."

I leaned back and examined the delicate designs softly displayed in its material.

"I'm sorry," I said regretfully wiping it off unconsciously. "I didn't know."

"Oh it's okay dear. It is just a robe… a mere memory," she said. "After he first died, I kept all his stuff on exhibit, as if this house was a museum dedicated to him, but once I accepted that he was gone, I started letting people use his stuff, to make use of them. It sparks memories of him in me when I see them in use… good memories."

"Well, my father's death was long ago and I have accepted it," I explained. "It was how he died that I have not come to closure with."

"Well I know quite a bit about losing loved ones. I have survived my mother, my father, my sister and two of my four boys so far. It's always hard, but one thing I can tell you," she said, "obsessing about the past does nothing for your future."

A horn sounded outside.

"It looks like Charlie has brought the mail early today," she said while wiping her hands on her apron before going out to speak with the mailman.

She handed him a loaf of bread she had baked with a kind smile. He nodded to her to thank her for her kindness. I could hear them commenting on the weather and other mundane subjects. I took a bite of my breakfast and began to think once again about what had occurred in my dream. It had seemed so real, but here I was moments later eating breakfast in the country. Rationally there was no possible way I could have been in that field talking to my father, but I had never had such a vivid dream in my life.

Following my kind land-lady's advice, I went out onto the front porch and stretched out in a porch swing. It was covered with a deep plush cushion and my tired body sank down into it like hot corn in a stick of butter. A cool breeze similar to the one in my dream blew across my face and awoke my thoughts again. The world I was born should have been enough for me, but it wasn't. The landscape that stretched outside Mrs. Plind's home seemed so dull and gray when compared to the vibrant beauty of the landscape I had stood in with my father. I closed my eyes to shield my thoughts from the inert world that now seemed to be little more than a prison. This world held nothing more for me. I would never know peace again till I found it in the Lands of Dream or through the solitude of death. My father had finally passed his legacy to me, a legacy that threatened to consume me in a fiery passion, just as it had devoured him.

Part II
Incarceration

I knew what I was about to do was going to bring into question the legitimacy of my sanity in the eyes of everyone, including myself. No matter how hard I tried to forget my encounter in the Lands of Dream and any association it had with my father, I could not get it out of my head. I thought about it constantly, and not a moment passed in a day that I wasn't contemplating it in some way or another. My obsession with it consumed me both physically and mentally and crippled my ability to carry on with any type of a normal routine. I couldn't stay focused long enough on anything to hold any kind professional position or even develop personal relationships. I found everything around me including conversations and activities of others pallid at best. It was as if I was a piece of a puzzle in the wrong box.

Not wanting to concern Mrs. Plind, I left late one night under cover of darkness with intentions never to return. All I left her was a small note, so as not to worry her along with a few months rent to help her get along till she found another boarder. Within a few hours of driving, I found myself standing in the dark under a full moon looking through the gates of the Belmount Institution for the Mentally Insane. I knew very well that once I crossed over into its interior, I would also be crossing the thin line between the sane and insane, a place every psychiatrist desired to comprehend. Using a blanket to cover the barbed wire along the top of the fence, I crawled over into the courtyard. Since the fence surrounding its perimeter had been built to keep people in and not out, I had little trouble reaching the front door, and after finding it locked I rang the bell. After a few moments an attendant came to the door in bewilderment.

"Hello," he said looking me over apprehensively.

I could tell from his expressions that he was trying to figure out how I got to the front door so late.

"Hi, Dr. Stills here," I said casually as if my appearance at two o' clock was normal, "I am here to see Mr. Lithglow."

"I am sorry," he said while holding the door open slightly, "but I am not allowed to admit anyone at this hour."

"This is an emergency," I said quickly. "I just received a call from the hospital administrator about a patient who needs immediate medical attention."

"We have a doctor on call here," he said trying to reason out the situation.

"Yes and he was the one that requested me," I said reassuringly. "This is not a matter of general medicine, but one of neurology."

"Stay right here while I go check with Dr. Brennan," he said attempting to close the door.

I put my foot in the door and blocked it from closing. He felt my intrusion when my foot struck the base of the door and he frantically tried to slam the door shut. I managed to get half of my body in before he got a good hold on the door. He pushed it as hard as he could while trying to force me out with his other hand. I took a hold of his hair on the back of his head with my one free hand and pulled his head back enough to squeeze through the closing door. It slammed shut behind me and we began to struggle. I used my grip on his hair to get behind him and using a pair of bolt cutters I brought with me under my coat, I knocked him unconscious. He fell as though lifeless to the floor and for a minute I feared that I might have killed him. After checking his vital signs and finding him alive, I quickly changed out his coat with mine, took his keys and headed toward Mr. Lithglow's room.

There was a series of locked doors and hallways between the front door and Mr. Lithglow's room, but with the attendant's keys I found them of little deterrent. After only a handful of minutes I was standing at end of the long white door-riddled hallway that led to Mr. Lithglow's room. I began to walk down it swiftly, when a door further down the hall opened and an attendant in a long white coat stepped out. I tried to avert my eyes and turn around, but he noticed me immediately.

"Hey you!" he yelled down the hall. "Who are you?"

After I did not answer he reached down and pulled out some kind of a baton and I knew he would not be as easy to dispatch as the last attendant. I took off running back in the direction from which I had come and he began to chase me. I spun the keys between my fingers trying to find the right one before I reached the door and began to jam them forcefully into the key hole one after another in the hope of finding the right one before the attendant caught up to me. The fourth key I tried slid in smoothly and the knob turned. The man's hand grabbed my coat and I bent the key breaking it off into the door just before I slipped out of my coat and slid through the door. I slammed it shut catching his fingers causing him to scream horribly before sealing the door. He began to fumble with his keys in an attempt to open the door, but cursed when he saw that my key had broken inside the lock. I quickly ran down the hall ahead and turned several corners to get out of sight. I began to look for a new way to reach Mr. Lithglow, when red sirens along the wall lit up and began to wail.

I knew I didn't have much time and I ran as fast as I could through door after door looking for anything I might have seen during my visits to gain some type of orientation. Another attendant spotted me and took chase yelling at me frantically. I ran around a corner and spread against the wall, holding my bolt cutters out. He came around the corner so fast that he lost his footing and slid across the floor colliding against the wall opposite. I slammed my bolt cutters down on him and he collapsed into a jumble on the floor. I took hold of his keys and dragged him into a closet so as not reveal where I had been.

The screaming sirens stoked an urgency in me and I began to run once again. As I came to a corner, I tried to stop, but slid into sight of a wire-glassed enclosed office with three attendants inside. They spotted me and began to point in my direction. I turned around and ran back out of sight. I cut from one hallway to another to keep out of their eyesight, but in the meantime I became disoriented and before long I had no idea from where I came. I opened another door and found a long hallway that seemed somewhat familiar and began to walk down it quickly. I got about halfway down the hall when I noticed a bulletin board I had seen several of times during my visits. Realizing where I was, I quickly took a door that led toward Mr. Lithglow's room. Suddenly, I found myself once again in the hallway where I had broken the key off into the door to escape. I took off one of my shoes and propped it in the door to keep it from closing and ran toward his room. I had only gone a few feet when the same attendant I had locked in stepped around the corner at the other end of the hall. He began to run toward me and I turned around to lock him in again when I saw the other three attendants from the office behind me opening the door I had propped open. I began to flip my keys in my hands once again to open a door beside me. In my panic I couldn't get the keys to fit in the small keyhole. When the attendants saw my intentions, they began to run toward me from both sides. I finally got a key to slide in and got the door open, when the four men seized me. I struggled and tried to bring my bolt cutters to bear, but a baton knocked my legs out from under me. Blackness overcame me as four batons rained down upon my arms, legs, body and head.

When I awoke I found myself lying on the floor constrained by a straightjacket in a small padded white room. It was uncomfortable, almost maddening, and I crawled up to the wall like a worm spinning myself up to a sitting position. I sat there for hours nodding in and out of a strange sleep. I found myself in a long black sandy wasteland. All around me swirled a foul smoke that rose from the ground below. The sky was a dark inky blue, churning with storming red clouds. I found that not only was my torso constrained by a straight jacket, but also that my face was covered in a type of tight cloth locking mask. The heat was unbearable and sweat began to roll along my skin under my restraints. Lightning began to strike my surroundings causing black sand to jump up on to me like sand in the wind. One bolt nearly hit me and I could feel its energy surge through every hair on my body.

"Son," said the benevolent voice broadcasting around me as if coming from invisible speakers, "what has happened to you?"

It was the clear booming voice of my father.

"Father," I yelled muffled by my restraints, "I have failed!"

"No, not until your death have you failed," said the voice. "As long as blood courses through you, there is hope."

I lowered my head and another bolt of lightning struck near me almost knocking me over. I looked up to see if I could see from where my father's voice was coming.

"The gods fear your intentions," he said. "They know you are coming. Stay awake. Do not dream till you find me! I fear what they intend to do to you!"

I heard a door click and I snapped back to consciousness to find myself in my small white prison once again. An attendant came into my cell holding a tray of food. It was the attendant whom I had forced myself in on at the front door. He had short blond hair and wore thick black glasses. I noticed a large bandage on the back of his head when he turned around to shut the door. He walked up to me and stood over me without saying a word. His shadow loomed over me uncomfortably. I looked up in time to see him dump my tray of food all over me. The tray crashed on top of my head sending food spiraling all over the room.

"Remember me, you fucker?" he asked angrily. "You're going to get in trouble for knocking that tray over you know."

Instead of responding, I looked at the mess helplessly.

"Oh my god," he said sarcastically, "looks like you had an accident."

He started to unbuttoned his pants and with an evil grin, he began to urinate on top of me.

I tried to roll over to keep it from splashing into my face, with little success.

"Now that is just disgusting," he said kicking me in the side. "A grown man pissing all over himself, the doctors got a lot of work to do with you."

He laughed horribly as he picked up my tray laughing all the way down the hallway from my room. I lay powerlessly in his urine a broken man contemplating what I had become. Had I gone full circle and become what my father had been? Hours passed before anyone came to see me and when they arrived I recognized one as the hospital administrator. He had two other attendants with him; one was the one who had urinated on me a few hours ago. The administrator kneeled down and looked into my face, with a concerned look.

"Get him cleaned up and bring him to my office," said the tall lanky administrator.

The two attendants came over and helped me to my feet.

"And take him out of that jacket. Restraint cuffs will be enough," he ordered before leaving.

I was given a shower under the watchful eyes of two attendants and after receiving some clean clothes was taken to the administrator's office. An attendant led me in, sat me down in a chair across from him and locked my arms in restraint cuffs that were already built onto the arms of the chair.

He looked at me over the rim of his glasses and said, "I am sorry about your accommodations earlier. I assure it will not happen again."

He leaned back into his chair and began to look through a file lying on his desk.

After a few moments of awkward silence he spoke again, "I see from your file that your father was a long term patient here and that Mr. Lithglow had gotten involved with him on several occasions, concluding in a tragic result. I empathize with your desire to understand what happened to your father."

He paused again and the room became as quiet as a black hole.

"That is what this is all about, is it not?" he asked me openly.

I felt a great shame being caught doing something so foolish and avoided his question altogether.

"What have I been charged with?" I asked him bluntly tearing through the silence around me.

"Well nothing at the moment," he replied startled at my response, "we are more concerned about your well-being than prosecuting you for any crimes."

"Fine," I said, "then you won't mind me speaking with a lawyer."

"There is no need for such matters," he said calmly. "Like I said before, we are not charging you with any crimes. We are here to help you."

"I know very well you cannot hold me here without legal representation," I said boldly.

"That has all been taken care of," he said in a low confident tone. "We contacted your mother this morning and she has handled everything."

"What?" I asked raising my voice. "I am an adult! You cannot hold me here against my will! I have not been convicted of anything, yet alone declared legally incompetent!"

"Please," he said soothingly, "calm down. We are here to help you. Judge Edisar has been kind enough to let you stay here, instead of sending you to a state correction facility, until your mother arrives and we can better assess the situation."

"You mean a hearing on my sanity," I said.

"No," he replied promptly, "but I will advise you, that your response to treatment will have a lot to with what will finally be decided."

I dreaded the look that my mother's face would be carrying like heavy baggage, when she arrived. It would be one of sympathy, concern and fear, but mostly it would be one of fear. Fear that I was traveling down a long road of self-destruction, as did my father. I listened to hospital administrator speak to me for nearly twenty more minutes, without a response. All I could do was hide my eyes and the shame they showed. It wasn't being kept chained up like a wild animal or that everyone spoke to me as a child that brought the weight of it on me like a wet towel, it was that my mental stability and sanity were in question, not only to others but also to myself! After a long lecture, I was finally sent back to my cell and placed back under physical restraints. As I was led back, I saw Mr. Lithglow's room down the hall from mine and realized I had been placed in the maximum-security wing, where they kept only the most mentally deranged and dangerous patients.

Over the next week, I learned the weekly routine of a patient in the Belmount Institution for the Mentally Insane firsthand. We were given three meals a day, and although most patients were allowed to eat in the hospital's cafeteria, those of us in the maximum-security wing were fed in our small padded rooms like dogs in a crate. The first thing I noticed was that the man I had attacked didn't bring my food anymore. Instead a larger man who rarely spoke brought my meals. The only time he did speak was when I would ask him a question and then his responses usually ended up being little more than a yes or no and although his silence wore heavily upon my consciousness, at least he wasn't violent.

After my first session with the hospital administrator my straightjacket was removed and although most of the other hospital's patients were assigned one of the hospital's psychiatrists the hospital administrator decided to handle my case personally. I spoke to him for one hour each day at the same time, one o' clock in the afternoon to be exact. I could tell that he was very interested in my case, since I seemed to be suffering from the same derangement as had my father. I pretended to have positive responses to his therapy and I could tell that it pleased him. The one thing I took from these "sessions" was that he was "in charge" much like an older brother over that of a younger brother and as long as I went along with what he said, I received special privileges. He asked a lot of questions about my father and always seemed over frustrated for a man in his position when I would declare to know nothing about him.

  With little to look forward to but mealtime and one hour of therapy a day, the days dragged on terribly and after the first week, I began to long for the dreaded reunion with my mother. For some reason her arrival was delayed and when I inquired about her in one of my therapy sessions, I was simply told that something had come up and although she was still coming it was going to be a little longer than she had first expected. When I began to inquire more into it, I was simply cut off and vehemently informed that I needed to focus on my own well-being and not to allow outside matters interfere with the progress I had been making. Knowing that my mother would never abandon me, I decided not to push the matter any further and went on with my therapy as suggested.

  As the days passed, I began to ponder the strange delay of my mother. I had role-played her response to hearing about my incarceration in my mind numerous times and had imagined how she would frantically rush to see me through the quickest forms of transportation available to man, but to my dismay, several days had already passed such transportation means. With each day that passed I began to feel more displaced from the world outside of my cell almost as if it might not be there anymore having faded away like that of a dream. I began to imagine I was outside once again near the old tree at Mrs. Plind's house. I even tried to recreate the feeling of the wind and the sounds of birds in my mind. A large smile spread across my face and suddenly I was happy again. It was as if my mind had risen from the detention of my cell and carried me to a safe place beyond the reach of its tall walls. Then suddenly I froze in terror. Here I was lying in a small white padded room smiling like an idiot. Was I truly mad or had this place driven me to it? Fearful I might begin to question my own sanity, I quit day-dreaming altogether and gathered my thoughts back to where I really was, confined to a small white room. Although it depressed me, this strategy held my mental stability in check. It was during one of these thoughts about my current situation that a small scraping sound interrupted me. It came from the wall opposite the door to my room. I quickly slid my ear against the padding on the wall and listened. It was faint, but constant. Perhaps I had heard it before and had passed it off as water running through pipes, but now I could tell it was something else, a rat maybe or perhaps some sort of remodeling.

The sound continued throughout the rest of the day and on through most of the night for what seemed like small spurts of thirty minutes or so before it would stop for a short break and continue again. The next day I was careful to see what was behind my cell on my way to my afternoon therapy session, but to no avail. It was all I could think about through my session and I almost brought it up to my therapist, but refrained in fear that whatever it was might be stopped. Besides what if it was a rat or something? Just knowing he was there was some kind of company, something beyond the padding in my wall. In excitement I was led back to my room and locked in, after several moments when I was sure the attendant was gone, I quickly fell back near the wall and intently listened! To my disappointment I heard nothing, but the long ring of silence. At first I fell into a great depression, as if I was trapped alone on a deserted island. I leaned against the wall nearly crying. Whatever it had been, it seemed to have abandoned me much like it seemed that my mother had. I crumpled to the floor and lay still in desolate solitude once again. Several moments of silence passed before a mental picture of how I must have looked imbedded itself in my brain. I quickly regained my composure and began to try to assess the situation from a rational point of view. If it was alive, it had to rest. No man or animal could go on with such activities forever. The thought of it from that point of view relaxed me considerably and gave me another gleam of hope.

The next day to my excitement the sound returned and continued on and off throughout the rest of the day. It got louder with each day and I began to feel an excitement I could hardly control. I nearly shook with exhilaration every time it started and practically collapsed in anxiety during the pauses in between. At that moment in my life I can sadly say it was all I lived for.

The attendant opened the door for me so I could enter the office of the hospital administrator. The tall thin administrator welcomed me in cheerfully pointing at the very same chair I had sat in for one hour each day for the past three weeks as if I needed an invitation to know in which chair to sit. I clumsily rattled with my restraints as I took my seat placing my arms in the cuffs so the attendant could lock me in. As soon as I sat down, the hospital administrator motioned for the employee who had brought me in to leave without locking my restraints.

"You have made excellent progress since your first session."

I sat and listened to him, pretending to hang on his every word knowing it thrilled him whenever I accepted his thoughts and theories. I had learned much like a pet that when I did as I was told, things got easier. If I went along with the therapies I was allowed to sit in my room without constraints, but if I opposed them, then I slept in restraints, and I wasn't sure I could bear another night helplessly locked in a straight jacket.

"I also have some news that might shock you, but I believe if you stay calm after I tell you, we will be able to discuss how it will be beneficial to your overall treatment."

I had never took anything he said seriously, as I only pretended to show interest, but this time there was a different tone in his voice. I rose up from a slouching position so to hear him better. A deep knot swelled into my gut. She wasn't coming! I screamed inside my mind, my own mother had left me here to rot under the care of the same mad doctor with whom she had left my father. Our fates truly were linked, destined one might say, as we both would end our lives in a mental institute.

"Is it about my mother?" I asked nervously. "Is she okay?"

"She is doing fine considering what has recently transpired."

"I don't understand? If you have information about my mother I feel I have the right to know."

"You remember the rules of Belmount, the patients are not in charge and therefore do not demand of those who are," he reminded me sharply.

"Please," I asked kindly so to hear the news, but still allow him to dominate the conversation.

I knew he enjoyed controlling his patients. Nothing brought a smile to his face faster than when I agreed with one of his deductions. Although he might be in charge and control my every move through unlawful imprisonment, I was not without my manipulations. But I had to be very careful and be certain they seemed sincere, for if he ever discovered I was playing along, he might never release me from his horrid prison for the insane.

"The reason for your mother's delay is that the remains of your father were discovered by some hikers a few days ago."

His words rolled over me like a freight train, shattering my already fragile mental state. After years of wondering about my father's strange disappearance the answer was finally thrust upon me leaving me speechless.

"I understand the overwhelming emotions you are feeling, but you must fight the negative ones and embrace the positive ones."

"Positive?" I asked almost in a trance. "You tell me my father is dead and I'm supposed to see the good in that?"

"Yes, with the death of your father comes enlightenment if you so choose it. Your father died tragically here in this world, meaning he is not traipsing around in some imaginary dream world. This was the final piece that was missing from your life. You now can have closure and move on with your own future."

"When is the funeral?" I asked automatically.

"Your mother has decided against having a ceremony. She is going to have him cremated and buried in your family's cemetery."

"I would like to go."

"I'm sorry, but I don't think you leaving during the middle of your treatment would be a good idea."

"You don't think seeing my father laid to rest is a good idea?" I asked cynically.

"It is too soon, you're experiencing too many emotions to cope with by yourself. When your treatment is complete and you leave here, then I assure you… you will be ready."

"How long might that be?"

"That really depends on you."

"You're never going to let me out of here are you?" I asked him.

"Please," he said quickly, "you are doing so well with your treatment. Don't go down the same road of destruction as did your father and try to escape this world through some magical realm inside your subconscious."

I returned to my ominously quiet room in low spirits. Had the remains of my father proven me mad? Had I imagined my dreams with him? Was I, as my mother feared, becoming my father? To contemplate one's own sanity is to question reality. What was real and what had my mind created? Had I imprisoned myself in this padded room by imagining it? At that moment nothing I had ever known seemed real. Was my life real or merely a dream? That night I sat up and rocked back and forth so as not to fall asleep and dream.

Another day passed in the solitude of my cell as might any other day with a white silence orbiting me like white space around a distant and lost planet. Then in the corner of my eye, the padding on the wall moved slightly. It wiggled back and forth causing the entire wall to flow slightly like the tide of an ocean. I gripped my head with my hands trying to make the illusion stop, but to my torment it continued incessantly shaking the wall. It twisted the padding along the wall as well as my mind, threatening to tear through both. Then it happened right before my eyes. A hole poked through a seam in the padding exposing the tip of a finger! The pink tissue on its end wiggled in the free air as if exploring the room in which I sat. I slipped from my bed, slowly crawled up to it to watch it squirm like a worm bursting from the earth. An overwhelming desire to touch it came upon me and without thinking I touched it. Upon doing so, it disappeared back into the padding as if frightened away by my touch. I waited curiously for its return when a muffled voice called out to me from behind the wall's thick stuffing. Unable to hear the sound clearly, I leaned up against the wall and held the rip in the padding open with my hands. Behind the thick cushion was a concrete wall, but near the floor was a small hole about a quarter in diameter. I lowered my head to the floor and peered into the shadowed hole. A green eye peered back at me causing my heart to skip a beat.

"Hello," said an exuberant but muffled voice.

"Hello," I responded still somewhat stunned.

"My name is Gant," said the voice which was then accompanied by a finger poking out the tiny hole.

I shook the finger hooking it with mine before responding with my name.

"Nice to meet you," said the voice more clearly. "It is so wonderful to finally speak with someone after all these months,"

I peered back down into the hole, and this time instead of being greeted by an eye, I encountered a set of stained teeth.

"I have been digging into this concrete wall for months… I think," said the voice slowly reflecting, "surely a year has not passed yet."

"Do you not at least go to daily therapy?"

"No," answered the voice, "I am in solitary confinement and have not heard a sound made by another in months. Those damned attendants are so quiet! They don't even make a noise when they set my food through the door. I swear they wear socks over their shoes so I cannot even have the concession of hearing their feet clank!"

"I'm sorry and I thought I had it bad."

"No worries, we all have our own hells to deal with," Gant said, suddenly composed. "You don't realize how wonderful it is to hear the voice of another, don't these doctors realize that man is like a dog, social. Since the dawn of time men have built communities, not hovelled themselves away like mad hermits!"

"How did you manage to dig through solid concrete?"

"With a lateral… it just fell out one day and I began to use it as a digging tool."

"What is a lateral?" I asked not familiar with dental terms.

"It's a tooth. I've been scraping toward your room for weeks, for the hope of anything that might ease the torture of silence. I believe it has been the sound of my scraping that has kept me sane."

"I didn't realize that a tooth was strong enough to compromise concrete."

"Concrete is merely a hydrated compound easily filed away with friction and saliva."

I paused, amazed by his technical speech and sheer determination to overcome his sentence of silence knowing I would not have done so well.

"So what are you in for?" he asked candidly.

"I believe I'm losing my mind."

"Who told you that, one of the shrinks here?"

"Recently reality has begun to collapse and I'm not quite sure what is real and what is not. What about you?" I asked to steer the conversation away from my sanity. Since this would be my only other outlet besides my daily sessions for conversation, I didn't want to discuss my sanity in it as well.

"I'm here because my train of thought didn't conform to the expectations of society. I saw things differently and in retrospect I see now that I threatened the status quo. That's why they put me here, to keep things all nice and neat."

I sympathized with his situation as it was far worse than my own relating a sense of fortune no matter how slight it might be. We spoke for hours, both excited about the new avenue of conversation opened to our quiet and drab world. Gant spoke like a philosopher discussing the universe and the minor role man played within its boundaries. Whether we conversed through the night or through the day was of little significance as within our walls they were one in the same. Much to my new friend's dismay, after hours of endless conversation where barely a moment passed without a word coming from one of our mouths, I decided to give in to the exhaustion from the excitement of a simple conversation.

That night as I closed my eyes my body fell into a deep slumber weighed down by the heavy burden of fatigue, but my mind churned wildly searching for a door to the Lands of Dream. It was there I thought… my father is not dead. Suddenly I opened my eyes and I was still in my padded room, but I could not move. My limbs lay dead at my sides unable to aid me. What had happened to me? Had my body failed me in my sleep while my mind lived on?

"Son," said a shadowed form standing in the corner of my room, "the fourth dimension is closing in on the gate you must seek. A hemisphere from the Lands of Dream known here as the third hemisphere rolls upon one of our own for one moon cycle every twenty years. That cycle has already begun. If it closes I don't know another way for you to pass over until it rolls through again."

Unable to move my body, I stared at him from the corner of my eye.

"I am imprisoned," I replied hopelessly, "these walls hold back my physical being while Doctor Jentry has chained my mind with confusion. I know not if I am mad or if you are real."

"In the Lands of Dream the keepers of the keys are horrid beasts set down by the gods to oppose those that wish to infest its borders, but here in the world of the waking the keepers are men of reason. The Lands of Dream are beyond reason, therefore they cannot see it. Escape your bondage and free Herald before you waste away your life as I almost did in this waking world of madness. I can see it in the windows of your mind that this world holds nothing for you. Leave it now lest you suffer its predestined fate."

As quickly as the shadow had appeared it disappeared leaving me trapped motionlessly in a world of darkness. Whether I had lost my mind or not, I would not waste away in a dull world driven by pointless finance.

The next morning I leaned down next to the small hole peeking through. Once again I was greeted by an eye.

"Good morning," said a small voice from the hole, "sleep well?"

"No, I dreamed all night."

"You lucky son of a bitch, this place has stolen everything from me, I cannot even dream of Hell for I am already there. What I wouldn't give to visit elsewhere if even for a moment."

We spoke of our past and wished-for futures, but never did we discuss the present as neither wanted any part of reality. Our discussion continued until it was time for my daily session with Doctor Jentry. I was led down the long hall between my cell and the hospital administrator's office and as usual I was left alone with him. He sat across from me with a smug confident smile.

"How did you sleep?" he asked hinting toward my tendency to dream as my dreams were usually our primary focus.

Not daring to tell him of my dream about my father, I lied. "Well."

"Any dreams that you can remember?" he asked quickly getting to the point.

"No."

"That is not necessarily a bad thing," he commented, "maybe the discovery of your father's body has eased the separation anxiety you were experiencing. I'd like to schedule a neurological study and have your brain waves monitored at night. This is a non-invasive procedure so no need to alarm yourself, but it will better help me understand your state of mind while you sleep."

Having little other choice I agreed and late that night I was taken to a secure room where electrodes were placed upon my scalp to study the electrical activity of my brain while I slept. I found it difficult to fall asleep as three men sat and watched me, but after closing my eyes I eventually succumbed to the hazy Wall of Sleep.

My eyes opened not to a dark room with wires attached to my skull, but to a beautiful wooded area with a soft cool breeze. It appeared to be fall for the leaves on the great trees above were boasting beautiful bright colors of deep red, vibrant orange and royal purple. The ground below was covered in the same lucidly colorful leaves which crunched beneath the soles of my feet. I spun around to take in my entire surroundings only to see that I had somehow dreamt into the middle of a deep forest. It must have been a very old forest for the trees stood hundreds of feet tall towering high above blotting out the sky to my mortal eye. I had never held such beauty for even the trunks of the trees seemed to sparkle from the sunlight that filtered through the treetops above.

As I examined the serene forest setting in which I suddenly found myself, I noticed a shadow move off to my right. I spun around just in enough time to see it slide from behind one tree trunk to another. I stared at the trunk where I saw it disappear without allowing myself to blink. The odd creature's head poked out from the side and stared directly at me. It was small and gray standing somewhere between two and three feet tall having large round yellow eyes. Upon seeing me it darted back behind the tree trunk. Unsure what else to do, I headed in the direction where I last saw it to feed my raging curiosity. As I reached the massive tree trunk the small creature leaped from behind it with a long screech. The high pitched sound startled me and I intuitively jumped backward. The strange being turned its head to the side as if to size me up and upon seeing my sudden fear leapt with the agility of a powerful cat landing on my chest and bowling me over backwards. The deep layer of multihued leaves scattered into the air as the beast and I fell to the ground. His tiny sharp fingers began to grip at my neck violently as if trying to steal my life. Being far larger than the small being I stood up in a rain of swirling leaves, broke its grip and instinctively threw it against the tree. The small gray creature recovered its position in mid air bouncing effortlessly of the base of the tree using its legs to spring back at me. It tumbled back into me knocking me backwards again, but this time its small dagger-like claws went directly for my eyes. My hands seized its wrist holding back what surely would have been a blinding and final blow. Its wide mouth opened to reveal a large set of sharp jagged teeth much like that of a shark. Drool dripped from its teeth down upon my face as the thing rose up to strike my exposed face. Suddenly in mid strike it turned its focus from me and shifted its head as if it heard something. With all the strength I possessed I slung the creature into the air twirling it in the process. It stuck to the trunk of a tree with its claws far more firmly than could a cat with its head high into the air listening. The small fiend leaped into the air vanishing from the spot it had clung to leaving an arrow with brilliant green feathers in its place. The arrow's tip sank deep into the base of the tree with a rattling thud barely missing the agile creature. It hissed as I watched it scurry up the trunk of the tree with smooth grace out of sight into the treetop above. I rubbed my neck smearing the trickles of blood upon it thoroughly startled by the entire experience. Suddenly a man dressed in cheerful pantaloons and a long green silk hat ran up toward me carrying a bow armed with another green feathered arrow. He stopped at the base of the tree the small creature had climbed and stared into its top with squinted eyes.

"Ah the little beast is gone for sure now," he said angrily. "Had it not heard me I would have gotten it for sure."

"What was it?" I asked still dazed by the scuffle.

"A wyner," he answered placing his arrow into a quiver on his back.

I noticed he had several arrows, but not all were green as the many bright decorated ends were like a rainbow of color.

"Strange to see one so far from Adesieal," he said appearing confused. "Nasty little winy beasts, let me have a look at your neck."

He pushed my head aside looking at my wounds, "Ah those aren't bad, but you better put some of this on your cuts so they don't get infected. There is no telling where that foul thing's hands have been."

He pulled a crumbled leaf from a small skin pouch hanging on his waist and slapped it into my hand.

"Rub this on it."

I took it and began to rub it over the lesions around my neck.

"So what brings you out here so far into the forest unarmed?" asked the brightly colored man.

"I know not, as I awoke here just a few moments ago," I answered confused.

"You are a dreamer!" he shouted in enthusiasm. "Nice to meet you, don't think I've ever met a dreamer so far in before. Not a lot to do way out here. You're welcome to come back with me and have a bite to eat, but I wouldn't stay out here alone and unarmed if I were you, that thing is watching us as we speak."

Not wanting to tangle with the strange creature again, I accepted the woodman's offer and followed him through the forest. He walked in front of me happily almost with a bounce in his step leading the way through the tall forest. As we walked the trees began to spread out, becoming sparser with each step, until finally we came to the forest's edge. Stretching out before us was a cozy yellow grassed valley lined with small huts of mud and grass with smoking chimneys. Stout men chopped wood echoing the sound of their axe tips through the valley in harmonic rhythm. Young boys and girls played, running between the small huts while shouting happily under the warm sun. I watched mesmerized by the tranquil beauty of both work and play intermingled, something my own world had lost long ago with the stress of deadlines and profits. Here the only concerns were food, lodging and the simple pleasures of company. At that moment I knew I had to find a way to stay or die trying.

My guide led me down toward the tranquil scene and introduced me to men and women carrying on happily with their daily chores as if I were a long lost relative. I spent the night with my host and his wife who was as beautiful a being I had ever seen. She had hair spun of light gold, soft milky skin and green eyes that sparkled under the light of fire like emeralds. All the people of the village were handsome or beautiful in their own right, with none being obese in shape or rude in temper. It seemed they were a part of their environment being as gentle and calm as their surrounding valley. The three of us laughed throughout the night with my two hosts bursting with laughter as I described the idiosyncrasies of the waking world. Both accused me in playful jest of deceit as the things they heard seemed too fantastic and strange to believe.

"You mean to tell me that the people of your world get married and then one day decide to get one of these divorces and act as if it never happened?" asked the hunter who had saved my life earlier.

"Yes," I answered in shame.

"What of the vows they took, did they not mean anything?" he asked, finding what I was saying difficult to believe.

"I'm not sure," I answered, unable to defend my culture.

"What do these vows say, I take this woman until I am tired of her?" he said amused.

"What of the children?" asked his charming wife with wide eyes. "What happens to them?"

"Usually they live with one and visit another."

"They visit their parents?" asked the young hunter curiously trying to get a mental picture of my world. "Who chops the wood to keep the family warm and hunts the food for their bellies?"

"Who cooks and gathers the food if there is only one?" asked the young woman.

"Well the people of my world do not hunt or gather food anymore. We buy it."

"What do you buy it with?" asked the hunter.

"Money."

"Money?" asked the young woman.

"Coin," I answered back quickly to help them understand.

"People give you food, wood and clothing for little pieces of metal?" he inquired in confusion.

"Why yes," I answered as if I had finally gotten my point across.

"What do they do with the coins?" he asked.

"Buy other stuff I guess."

"Where do you get the coins?" asked the young woman.

"From their jobs."

"I thought you said the people of your world didn't do a lot of labor. What kind of jobs do they do?" asked the young man.

"Finance, retail, factory work… it's far too complicated to explain in one night."

"Agreed," said the young man, glad to end his line of questioning, "your world is far too complicated for a simple mind such as mine."

He had kindly ended our conversation blaming the strange complexity of my world upon his inability to comprehend it, when in actuality my world had become too complex for even the simple pleasure of a cool breeze on a hot summer day with nothing to do. The people of Dream worked for basic necessities, food, water and shelter, while the world of the waking worked for greed, so to own and control more of his fellow man.

"Yes," I said as the pieces of our two worlds came together, "that is the problem. It is far too complicated of a world to harbor even the simplest of pleasures. It is for this that we dream to your world and you not to ours."

I spent the remainder of the evening enjoying delicious food and good company. I kept my hosts up as late as they were willing afraid to go to sleep for fear I might wake and never return. I sat outside the small hut as they slept and stared out at the vast cool blanket of stars that hung over the small quiet valley. They glimmered brightly forming constellations I had never seen, revealing that this world was far from my own as I stared at the universe from a different direction. Whether it was real or not I would return, even if it meant dying in my sleep so my last thoughts would be in the Lands of Dream. But when my eyes reopened, I found myself back in the custody of the Belmount Institute for the Mentally Insane. Wires were still strung from my temples and the top of my head hanging against my skin in cold conclusion of dream. Tears formed in my eyes as the dull color of the waking world tormented me once again. Upon my waking two attendants began to remove the wires and the harness I had been strapped with to the table. I was quickly returned to my room and as soon as I knew the attendants were gone, I rushed to the small hole in the wall to let my friend know of my whereabouts.

"Where have you been?" he asked. "I have to admit, I had feared your release."

"I was kept overnight for a sleep cycle study."

"Did they find anything out?" he asked with concern, for I had confided in him about my father and my dreams.

"I don't think so," I said guessing, "but I did visit the world of dreams again."

"Please, I beg you," said the voice from the hole, "tell me everything!"

I related to him my experience happily reliving it once again, describing every plant and person I had come in contact with in great detail. My only friend left in the world lay next to the hole between our cells and listened intently, never saying a word to interrupt my narrative. As I finished my experience, he stayed silent for a moment to savor the moment leaving a long white silence between the two of us before speaking.

"Did you tell them anything?"

"I have not spoken to anyone."

"Don't you tell anyone, especially Doctor Jentry. If anyone can destroy a dream, it is that man. It is because of him that I'm here in solitary confinement."

Knowing first hand that people accused of mental disabilities are commonly defensive about their detention I had not asked him about his own, but since he had brought it up, I asked out of curiosity.

"What could a man do to deserve such a punishment?"

"My condition didn't respond to his treatments as he had hoped and therefore I was labeled as untreatable. I fought his treatments every moment of the day, and I won too… he gave up all right and here I am in utter silence, but I still have my pride," he declared proudly through the tiny hole between our faces. "I don't have anything else, but I still have my pride."

As his finished the word pride, a key slid into the keyhole in the door to my cell. I promptly covered the hole and jumped up trying to look inconspicuous. The attendant looked at me strangely, while I straightened the rags in which I had been fitted, as if he were able to read my mind, and for a moment I feared my secret would be discovered.

"Come on, I know you're busy looking stupid and all, but the doctor wants to talk with you."

It was the attendant I had attacked upon my break-in to the institute and for a moment I feared what he might do. He stood patiently waiting on me, and upon seeing my reluctance he scorned me nicely.

"Come on… unlike you, I don't have all day, I'd like to go home to my family tonight."

I followed him quietly down the hall like a submissive puppy so not to stir his curiosity about my strange appearance upon his entrance, for at that moment my secret friend was all that stood between me and utter madness. He took me to the hospital administrator's office and led me in holding my chains like a master his obedient dog. He left by signal of the administrator and I sat down following his strict protocol. The door shut behind me leaving me alone with the man I would one day become to know as the Mind Stripper.

"Let me ask you a question," he said holding up a stack of forms with wild squiggles, "and let me also remind you that your cooperation is directly linked to the success of your treatment and ultimate release from this facility. What did you experience while sleeping last night?"

His tone insinuated he had some sort of inside knowledge into my dream, but he had not completely broken me yet and I was still capable of resisting his mind picks. I knew he was bluffing, having only a slight suspicion of what I had experienced.

"Nothing unusual," I responded quickly so to appear truthful.

"Nothing abnormal?" he responded as if in disbelief of my statement. "I've literally studied hundreds of EEG patterns and I have only seen one…" he paused as if his tongue had slipped, "and not one looked anything the sort of these."

He threw the stack down before me as if I were qualified to understand their markings. I looked at them curiously as might a monkey a computer.

"The whole damn sheet is mostly beta waves!" He yelled angrily at my lies. "Sleep patterns normally run through five stages with each lasting around thirty minutes with the final stage being that of vivid dream, before repeating itself throughout the night. The average person experiences about different five cycles of these five stages. Your chart shows that once you entered your first stage of REM, your mind never left."

"I don't understand," I responded confused.

"You spent nearly seven hours in one stage of REM, I want to know what you dreamt!"

"I don't remember."

"That was exactly what your father told me when I asked him that same question. He tried to match wits with me just as you're doing right now, but he went mad trying to keep his little secret from me!"

His words sank deep into my heart and a rage of sudden understanding surged into my soul, "What do you mean drove him mad?"

"You forget I am the only one who asks questions here."

"He was never crazy at all was he? You failed with him and now I'm next!" I declared.

I knew my last statement had struck a chord, for he stood up with a red face and white clinching knuckles.

"You forget you're in my world, where I control everything around you. As does the Lord, I can give you light or I can take it away. I hold the key to your life and what little sanity you have left. We can go about this nicely or I'll break you as I did your father!"

I stood up to challenge him but found myself held in check by my chains which had been fastened to the chair.

He laughed at my feeble attempt to stand up and then shouted for an attendant.

"You're about to see the power of an angry god!"

The attendant, who had led me from my cell, came in with a sense of urgency provoked by the urgent scream of the administrator.

"Put him in the box."

A smile appeared on the face of the attendant as he excitedly seized me for the upcoming task.

"Come on, I've got a surprise for you!" he said with an evil delight burning in his eyes.

A chill leapt from his cold eyes into my soul and at that very moment I knew something horrible awaited me. Although I knew in my heart I stood no chance of success I impulsively tried to break free of his grip. He quickly buckled my legs from behind with a baton and then pulled me back up to my feet.

"So you want to hit the box the hard way, eh?"

As he spoke those words, he slammed my face toward the wall. As my arms were chained to my waist, I was unable to lift them high enough to block the incoming concrete wall. My forehead struck it flush and suddenly everything went fuzzy. My legs and arms went limp and I unwillingly fell to the floor in a surreal state. A second set of arms seized me raising me upward. The long hall began to shiver as if the solid structure of its walls had become a cloudy gaseous state. Its straight walls waved in a long frequency as if part of a sound wave drawing me along its corridor. Voices muffled by the cloud in which I hung echoed around me with wicked laughter. My feet began to bounce down flights of stairs as I sank deeper into the depths of the institute in which I had become imprisoned. The walls and the floors transformed in color from white to dingy brown, exponentially gaining color as I was dragged below. Blurry metal beasts bellowed angrily at me bursting steam into the air as I was drug like a sack of trash. Suddenly the two attendants carrying me along dropped me to the floor in a state halfway between consciousness and unconsciousness in front of a grimy door covered in mold and mildew fed by the moisture accumulated from the boilers used to heat the hospital. The door swung inward creaking ominously as it revealed what it had enclosed. My eyes continued to play tricks upon my mind shifting the room wildly as might a quiet earthquake. A dull light bulb hanging from a dirty wire clicked on to illuminate a tiny square room. Black and blue hued tiles flickered like a cold flame as I was dragged and dropped to lie next to a grating. Two pale hands quivered before my eyes unlocking a chain which held the grate to the floor. A cold darkness crept from the hole it exposed crawling onto to my skin and sinking into my pores. Suddenly the chilling murk engulfed my heart and fear seeped into my bloodstream. I wrestled like the madman I had become, kicking and screaming into the cold darkness as the two attendants tried to shove me through the small void in the floor. My teeth sank into the arm of one of the men and he screamed along with me as the three of us struggled in the darkness like a wild three-headed beast gone insane in a battle with itself. Arms, fists, legs and feet struck blindly in all directions as my face came to the edge of the black hole. A darkness matched only by the darkest pits of Hell filled the abyss in which I stared. My head sank in first completely enveloping my senses and taking away my power of sight. I struggled with the edge of the hole gripping its edge, but stomping feet forced me past its rim. I was stuffed into the small enclosure like a person might thrust trash into a can being shoved and kicked until I was engulfed in its darkness. I wrestled with the iron grate as it was slammed down to lock me in with a terrifying click. A small trickle of light beamed onto my face falling into my hole like water disappearing into a pool of darkness.

"Please, have mercy upon me," I begged, "leave the light on."

A man laughed, "Doctors orders," he said, and then with a click, everything went black.

I heard the door shut behind the attendants as they left and for a moment I could hear their footsteps down the hall, then nothing but silence. The small box in which I had been thrown was about three feet tall and three feet wide, a perfect square of sense-numbing darkness. Its inner blackness stole four of my five basic senses, erasing my sight, hearing, smell and taste, leaving only the cold touch of darkness to acknowledge I was alive.

I have no knowledge of how long I sat cramped in that hole as I could not tell when it was night or when it was day. I tried to keep time by counting the times I slept, but each time I awoke from a slumber, I could not be sure if I had been asleep for hours or merely minutes. A small trickle of water dripped in through the grate bringing me my only source of nourishment.

I knew not for sure, as I had been forgotten by the world since my incarceration, if I had been placed here to be broken or simply buried alive. At that moment had Doctor Jentry released me, I believe I would have broken down and told him whatever he wanted, but no such mercy ever came. Instead I was left in the darkness with a hardening heart. Had my father endured this same punishment? An unseen smile appeared within the darkness. My father had beaten him and escaped from this horrid world and I would follow. He could not break me by stealing the stimuli outside my body, for I could reach freedom through my dreams. I closed my eyes and faded into a void even darker than that in which I sat.

When my eyes opened they were no longer cloaked by a cold blanket of darkness and I was no longer confined by damp concrete walls. I found myself in a deep field of thick tangled thorns that rose nearly ten feet from the ground. Bright sunlight gleamed down upon me from the sky which appeared milky in vivid colors including a wavy blue, brown, red and yellow. This sky was not transparent as is the sky of earth, but seemingly dense like wet paint. A black creature the size of an elephant streaked across the sky flapping its wings ever so slightly before going into a long graceful glide underneath the sky's deep colors. It had a long tail almost like that of a rope which flapped behind it majestically guiding it as a rudder might guide a boat through glassy water. It closely resembled a medieval dragon, but what creature it actually was I cannot say for it traveled quickly out of sight to become only a speck in the distant skyline.

Before me were rows of thorny green vines tightly tangled in all directions, but strangely cutting through the nearly impenetrable foliage was a thin but clear path. I followed it shifting through the tight shrubbery willing to go wherever it led happy to be free of the torture I had been placed in below the Belmount Institution for the Mentally Insane.

I looked ahead into the sky whenever the vines thinned enough and in the distance I could see a tall black palace of volcanic stone. Its massive towers loomed closer with every step I took until I stood before a tunnel of thick vines covered in blooms belonging to every stripe in the rainbow. They were tightly woven to create a perfectly round tunnel; so tight were their bonds I was able to walk upon its base as the vegetation channel rose from the ground carrying me high above the thorn garden where I had awakened. The vines creaked as I stepped upon them but never wavered beneath my weight. I rose high into the sky until I was walking among the birds of Dream. They fluttered outside the tunnel chirping at me curiously before lighting gently upon the vines to get a closer look at the newest tourist to the Lands of Dream. Although I was hundreds of feet in the air, the black castle still stood high above me engulfing me in its shadow. The tunnel came to an end at the massive structure's front entrance leaving me standing before its ponderous gates.

The gates were imposing, at least thirty feet high and nearly fifty feet wide, and upon reaching toward their structure I suddenly noticed that they had been built without any way to open them from the outside. My first thought was to knock, but I quickly changed my mind upon wondering what might dwell in such a place. The stone of the strange stronghold was rough and porous, yet solid enough not to be able to see through its structure. From the naked eye it appeared quite brittle and to support or invalidate my assumption I swiftly kicked a jagged piece of the structure's wall as might a child an old broken stump in the sanctity of a hidden forest. It broke away easily, crumbling in several pieces onto the ground, but then to my amazement the wall quickly regenerated forming the rock wall back as it had been within seconds. Out of curiosity, I broke off several other pieces of the mysterious palace and as before, each breakage magically healed itself. I stepped back wondering if the giant structure I stood before was alive, magical or a combination of both. Almost to answer my thoughts, the giant doors slowly opened creaking in invitation. Unsure what else to do, I cautiously entered the black fortress stepping into the darkness like an unknowing mouse into the mouth of a waiting cat.

Inside it would have been completely dark, since there were no windows or openings into the black citadel, if it had not been for the glistening of the interior walls. They were covered in crystal stones which shimmered brightly in blue, red and yellow sparkles turning the interior of the palace into a swirling prism. I touched the glowing stones upon the wall and found them strangely cool to the touch as if reflecting the light from somewhere instead of actually emitting the colorful radiance. The interior ceiling of the structure was so high that I could not see if there was one at all. The walls ran off into the darkness, and from the best I could tell I was standing in a room larger than that of an indoor football stadium from the waking world.

Leading straight through the center was a path of red molten brick, which glowed like hot coals shining a passageway through the revolving colors. I warily tested my bare foot on the radiant pathway and found it as cool to the touch as were the crystals on the wall. I walked through the shadowed edifice with wonder-struck eyes that soaked in everything inside this phenomenal place I had dreamt. The path came to an end at a large archway with a look similar to those in ancient Rome, but its center was more pointed than round. As soon as I stepped through the arch, the lighted path beneath my feet faded to the same color as the rest of the floor. I peeked through the opening and peered down the long rectangular room. It was a massive structure, nearly one hundred feet long with two long fountain-fed pools which stretched down both its sides. Water trickled down the black walls serenely filling the deep pools of water which flowed toward the back of the room toward a tall wooden throne sitting high on a short round pedestal. Sitting upon the throne was a black shadowed figure. From across the great room, I could not tell who or what sat upon the throne, just that it was at least human-like in shape.

"Welcome to Bramble Rock," said the shadow.

I stood silently under the arch without speaking.

"Please come forward, we men of dreams do not have time to waste here."

The shadowed form's words aroused my curiosity. Was he a dreamer as well? His voice sounded familiar, but I couldn't place it. It was certainly not that of my father, but of someone I had spoken with before I thought, maybe in a previous dream. I stepped from under the protection of the arch and began to walk down the long corridor toward the shadow king. He sat in silence, watching my every move. I had walked nearly half the distance when I saw a small form observing me from behind one of the fountain spouts. At first I pretended I had not seen it, watching it from the corner of my eye as I walked. It watched me patiently until I had passed the next fountain before rushing up behind it. I watched its movement and spun around to catch it in the open. My sudden movement startled it causing it to leap backwards against the wall hissing wildly. It was a wyner, either the same or another specimen of the creature that had attacked me in the woods during my dream. It screeched like an angry cat gnashing its jagged teeth. I crouched down holding out my hands, ready to strike at its head if it sprung at me again.

"It will not harm you unless I want it to, and at the moment I do not," stated the shadow upon the throne.

I stepped backward carefully staring down the little beast. Its round yellow eyes watched me hungrily as though it was ready to strike upon the command of its shadow master. I stopped in front of the throne before the cloaked form. Its head lay down slouched into its chest speaking through a closed hood.

"What brings you to my realm dreaming from a black hole in the floor?" it asked with authority.

His statement stunned me, how would a creature of Dream or a dreamer know my place in the waking world?

"Although I'm not a mind reader," said the voice, "I know what you are thinking, because here I am known as the Mind Picker!"

A black gloved hand pulled back the form's hood revealing the face of the hospital administrator of the Belmount Institution for the Mentally Insane, Doctor Jentry.

My heart froze in terror as the very man who had told me my journeys within my dreams were simply delusions was sitting before me on a grand throne of thorns. My tormentor in the waking world had followed me to my last hope of solitude.

"You look like you just walked over your own grave," he said seeing my stunned state.

"I don't understand, you punish and torment those who dream as you?"

"There are no dreamers as I… I am the greatest dreamer the waking world has ever known!" he boasted. "I did not come to this world to consume anomalous liquors or sit upon giant mushrooms and smoke the day away chatting with some alien from across the universe. I have garnered power, wealth… a kingdom that will one day overrun the entire realm of Dream, and I shall rule it an eternal king!"

His words were that of a madman, a madman with the power of a dictator. Dozens of the little creatures I had seen earlier began to congregate around me cutting off any hope of escape. One command from the madcap king before whom I stood could have the horrid beasts shred me apart. What a death in the Lands of Dream meant, I did not know. Whether it held no consequence or would destroy my mind in the waking world I was uncertain.

"What does this all mean?" I asked, unsure what my captor sought. "You are obviously a greater dreamer than I, with far more understanding of this world than I could ever hope to comprehend."

He smiled, soaking in my accolade, "Only one thing stands in the way of all I spoke to you, your father's secret! I have taken in the refuges of Dream who were repelled all across this vast realm after the dead wars of Zeethe. I have befriended the Mongrel King and now I breed his forces hidden away from the many eyes of Dream. My living palace and great forest of thorns protect the goblin, orc, ogre, troll and wyner from the forces of men. They huddle beneath this city as we speak, growing in numbers… preparing for war."

The mad plan sent a shiver down my body as I imagined the inhabitants of Dream answering to such a cruel master.

"What part am I to play in all this; the secret you seek is not mine… it is my father's. If I knew such a secret, do you believe I would be lying trapped in a dark hole in the waking world?"

"It was in my research with those who were perceived to be delusional that I came to know this wonderful sphere. At first I thought them mad as they spoke of marvelous cities made of pearl and waterfalls that flowed upside down, but as I studied their dream patterns, I found those who claimed these experiences had far different readings than those that did not. So being a man of the mind, I studied their cases, becoming a specialist of those who had dream delusions. Then one night I myself awoke in the Lands of Dream! Why it was splendid, I could think of nothing else, so I continued to study those who traveled here learning from their trial and error."

"You knew that none of these men were insane and yet you kept them caged like lunatics!"

"Yes, they became little more than tools to feed my waking lust to return here, and then I met your father," he said pausing with spite. "He had seen and done so much here all the while searching for the secret we all desire... to detach ourselves from the waking world and live here forever. He is the only man who has gotten away from me! But I will prove who is greater here when I rule the Realm of Dream and all within it bow directly to me!"

He looked at me with raw hatred as his abhorrence of my father had transferred directly to me.

"I do not know what you seek."

"You cannot lie to the Mind Picker! I know your father has contacted you, tell me where he is, what he has told you to do and I will show you the mercy of the King of Dreams."

"Mercy..." I yelled up to the throne in anger, "what of the mercy of those you let rot behind the walls of Belmount, separated from their families, their children... their dreams?"

The little creatures began to stir upon the raising of my voice, crawling toward me drooling in anticipation of an ordered slaughter.

"You're a mere ant in comparison to my power. Forget not that I control you in both the waking world and that of dream; there is nowhere for you to escape. I could have you torn apart right here with the snap of a finger. The damage done upon the mind by a death in the Lands of Dream is irreparable. As the mind sees its body die, it ceases to function and leaves its host brain dead. Remember where you really are at this moment, cowering in a black hole in which I can choose to leave you or bring you out."

"Is your power as a dreamer as great as that of my father?"

He stood up from his giant vine formed throne, "It was your father who ran from me, and it is your father that hides in the southern realm of Dream past the Strait of Phylain. I cower before no one here!"

"Why is it that you reside in a black citadel behind a wall of thorns?" I asked to deflate his claim.

His face stiffened and then as if understanding my intent it softened into a smile, "Kings do not argue with peasants. As it is for all dreamers, each trip into the Lands of Dream is more difficult than the last. I cannot become a true king and rule over my lands if I am not here. If you tell me what you know about your father's secret, I will release you from the institute a free and sane man, but if you continue to defy my will, I will break your body and mind down until you divulge all you know and I will leave you behind its bars an empty husk to live out your final days in isolation."

A pain struck my heart and I cowered down like a broken dog. I was frightened of him. How had my father stood up to such a man who struck at a man so ruthlessly through both his heart and mind?

"Tell me!" he ordered, impatient with my slow demeanor.

Although it might mean the end of my own body and mind, I would not betray my father or those who dwelled happily within Dream. Whether it was my own strength or that my father that filled my heart I might never know, but suddenly I stood up with pride, ready to die and sink into madness in the waking world.

"You shall never learn what you seek from me!"

The mad King of Thorns stood up holding a staff of gnarled thorn and commanded my death. The small beasts leaped at me with protruding razor claws and teeth.

Hands gripped my armpits, pulling me from the shadowed hole and dragged me into the dull swinging light above. Two men dumped my body unto slimy tiles outside the hole awakening me from my near death in the Lands of Dream.

"Did a week soften you up a bit?" laughed one of the men.

"You sure Dr. Jentry wants him out?"

"When he ordered us to throw him down here, he said throw him in for a week or so to calm him down."

"But Dr. Jentry isn't even here."

"It's because of your lack of initiative that I'm in charge of you, so shut up and help me drag this sack of shit back to his cell."

Part III
Into the Lands of Dream

The bright light of my cell stunned my eyes stealing away the sight I had not used in over a week. As soon as the door to my cell was latched shut, I crawled blindly toward a wall searching for the small hole which led to my only hope of sanity.

"Hello," I whispered trying to orient myself, "where are you?"

I heard a thump then a cry of direction, "Over here!"

My flaccid muscles struggled to drag my body across the thick padded floor toward the voice.

"Where have you been?" asked the voice as though anxious for a reply, "I feared something horrible had happened to you!"

I slumped down near the voice worn from the strain of fighting cramped muscles.

"It might as well have," I responded hopelessly. "Once Dr. Jentry comes back for me, everything will be finished."

"Maybe not," said the voice, "I remembered what your father told you and in your absence I have been working on a solution."

My eyes opened as might a kitten seeing the world for the first time.

"What?"

"I was able to fashion this from a chain link I broke loose from my bed. I also enlarged the hole between us as well so it will fit through."

My blurry vision struggled to perceive what popped through the tiny hole in the concrete wall and much like a mole I used touch to discover its facade. The object was cold, hard and sharp. I lifted it to the rim of cloudy eyes and squinted.

"When they come back to get you, use it to surprise them, fight like a wild animal… it might be your last chance to ever get out of here."

I fondled the small skinny object which was no more than two and a half inches in length.

"Just promise me you will take me with you," pleaded the voice through the hole. "It was either give it to you or use it to kill myself. Don't leave me here alive. After meeting you, I cannot bear to be alone again."

The selfless gesture brought tears to my eyes as I gripped the potentially deadly weapon. In the hands of a man with nothing to lose and everything to gain it would be as dangerous as a loaded gun. Over the next hour my vision and mind cleared as I focused on what had to be done. Failure would mean death, or worse a life at the mercy of the Thorn King. Either would amount to eternal exile from the Lands of Dream.

I stood firmly staring at my door ready to leap into action. Time churned clicking away the perpetual gears of the universe as I stared blankly at the padded door of my cell. No matter who or how many people came through that door, I would prevail.

Suddenly the door swung open revealing my adversary. It was fitting that it was the very attendant I had attacked upon my entry into the Belmount Institution for the Mentally Insane. It seemed we that were fated for a final struggle. He paused in his entry, surprised to see me staring directly at him.

"Assume the position," he ordered, freeing his baton from a strap on his belt.

Patients were to kneel to the ground upon an entering attendant so as to be easily subdued with hand cuffs, but this time I would not be submitting. He would have to earn it.

"Listen you little bitch," he stated, angered at the defiance of his command, "you better get down before I break you down!"

"I'm not going to kneel down today," I said, knowing that one of us was about to die.

Had he been smart he would have locked me in and gone to get help, but he was proud, too proud to back down from the insubordination of a lunatic. He held his baton high ready to beat me into obedience. Power was very important inside a mental institution as the weak were the insane, the strong the sane, a principle that had to remain in place for the sake of the sane. The hands of time stopped but for a second, as I leaped into motion. My hand drew forth my small sharp claw as I landed upon his body slitting his neck in one swift stroke. Blood squirted from beneath his chin as I withdrew my weapon, squirting into my face. I struck him down in cold blood mutilating his body by striking it continuously as had my ancient forefathers their own enemies until finally he struggled no more. A final breath gurgled from his mouth as I sat over him a victorious predator. The blood of my prey that had splattered upon my hands, face and arms dripped slowly from me as I stood up without remorse. The dead man had stood between life in a padded room and that of the open fields of Dream. The haze of violence I had woven cleared from my mind, and abruptly time flowed quickly again. Seizing his keys and baton, I rushed into the hall frantically searching for my friend's cell.

"Gant... Gant where are you?" I asked pressing against cell doors.

"Here, oh my God, I'm in here!" replied an eager voice from behind a locked door.

I fumbled with the giant key ring knowing that each try might be my last. Finally the lock clicked and I swung the door open to see my friend for the first time. He was tall and lanky standing nearly a foot taller than I, a lean giant by anyone's standards. His eyes were a pale blue, held up upon his face by tired crow's feet. He obviously had seen hard times, times of tortured solitude. As he had told me many times, man was like the dog because he was meant to live in communities for safety and companionship. To lock a man up alone without contact with others is by far the worst punishment ever to fall upon a man since the beginning of time. He smiled a long dirty grin.

"Your destiny is now one with mine," he said.

I dropped the small bloody shank into his palm. He knew as well as I without a word being spoken that anyone who stood in our way would meet death.

"We must free one other as he knows the way...actually, we have to free them all," I stated stalwartly.

"We don't have time," argued Gant.

"What gives us the right to be free over everyone else?" I asked. "Behind each door is a person placed upon this earth with as much right to live free as you or I."

"There is no time!"

"Dozens of patients running around this facility will overrun the staff. It will help to cover our escape."

Instead of wasting more time arguing, he nodded and I commenced opening doors, unleashing the insane upon the sane. Men and women began to run up and down the halls yelling wildly as others shuffled by quietly following us like lost puppies.

"I think he's this way," I stated noticing a cork board upon the wall.

I swung open the heavy door to find my father's friend sitting in a corner with his head between his knees.

"Herald, it's time to get out of here," I paused, watching his face lit up like a lantern of hope, "show us the way to my father."

He jumped to his feet like a child invited to an amusement park, ignorant of the consequences associated with a violent escape from a mental institution. He ran up to me like a dog to his master; if he had had a tail, I swear it would have been wagging.

"Hurry," he said formulating his thoughts, "I spoke with your father last night... we don't have much time."

He rushed into the hall speaking to me as he led the way, "I knew you would come. You have the merit of your father."

He paused, confused by the dozens of inmates in the hall.

"We're taking all of these people?"

"No," I stated turning toward Gant, "just him."

"Does your father know this?" he asked as if I spoke to him daily.

I knew had it not been for Gant any escape attempt would not have been possible. He had a hold of my loyalty.

"Herald... he's coming."

"I don't think he is going to like this..." he looked at my face and saw its determination, "but it doesn't look like changing your mind at this moment holds much feasibility."

"Which way out?" asked Gant.

"Not yet," I said interrupting our escape, "we have one more thing to settle here before we leave this realm.

I knew the way to Doctor Jentry's office by heart, having been led there many times in chains, so I led my two friends and half a dozen mumbling patients toward it with blood on my mind. I knew if I could kill him here, I would do the world of Dream an immeasurable service. In my heart I was afraid of him, but better to face him here and now in the waking world than later with his powers in the Lands of Dream. Our group stormed toward the main door which separated the office and waiting areas from the cells of the inmates. Upon seeing our group, the single attendant in the guard shack sounded the hospital's internal siren. Red rotating lights filled the halls followed by high pitched whining. The half or so dozen patients with us broke into a panic upon hearing the alarm and began to run around madly beating at walls, doors and themselves, while Gant, Herald and I walked straight up to the locked gate. I quickly pulled out my keys and began to try them into the lock. The eyes of the guard on the other side of the gate swelled two times their normal size upon seeing my keys. He quickly rushed to the door and began to push against it. The long thin piece of grooved metal slid effortlessly into the key hole clicking its chambers and freeing the door from its frame. The three of us pushed the guard backward sliding his feet across the slick tiled floor before rushing in and overwhelming him. I seized his baton and knocked him unconscious with three fierce blows. Until my invasion into the Belmount Institution for the Mentally Insane, I had never struck a man, but at that moment I couldn't have cared less if the man I beat lived or died. Patients poured out of the mental ward into the office area leading the assault onto the sane. I wove through the madness finally coming to the door of the office of the man I feared more than anyone in the world. I lifted up my baton determined to murder him in cold blood if he were inside. I swung the door open finding his desk and the chair I had been chained to so many times in the past, but to my relief, I found it empty.

"Hurry," replied Gant tugging at my shoulders, "they have surely contacted the police. We don't have long to get out of here."

I grudgingly pulled away from the office where I had seen so much mental anguish and followed Gant into the hospital's main entrance. Nurses and guests crouched down nervously as patients overran the entrance to the world of the sane, some violently assaulting those they encountered, others simply wanting to talk to their uneasy counterparts. The three of us quickly rushed outside into the bright light, and although we knew the gravity of our escape, each of us stopped, stunned by the bright warmth of the sun. Herald stood staring toward the great ball of fire blocking its harmful rays with his arm, a man who had not seen the sun in over twenty years.

"It's so beautiful," he said mesmerized by its power, "I cannot imagine anything more wonderful."

"Herald," I said covering his eyes, "if you stare into it, you will go blind."

"Oh how glorious such a thing would be!" he replied.

Gant and I pulled him aside before rushing off into the woods surrounding the mental ward. The thick woods blotted out the very sun we all adored as we ran through the tall structures hurriedly putting as much distance as possible between the hospital and ourselves. It would not be long before the local authorities would be out searching for those patients not present, and although we ran frantically, I knew our chance of escape was slight at best. I could only hope the Lands of Dream were not some mental manifestation created by my mind to appease the loss I felt of never truly knowing my father. Even at that moment as I ran away with my father's old friend Herald, who supposedly knew the way to the magical realm of my father, I harbored serious doubts. It was these doubts that threatened to shatter my fragile mental state with the possible truth that I might actually be insane destined to spend my life in a padded room, which was exactly where I would spend the rest of my life if the Lands of Dream were merely a delusion.

The three of us ran on and off as fast as our legs would allow for nearly four hours before we fell into the brush to rest. Spending days on end trapped in a small padded room had done nothing for our endurance. We huffed and puffed while lying on our backs and staring into the brilliant sky above. Soft white clouds calmly streamed above obscuring in spots the clear blue sea hanging above our heads.

"Where are we running?" asked Gant gasping from behind a tree.

"As far away from the institution as we can," I replied light headed.

"And then?" questioned the panting voice again.

"We just need to find civilization again, blend in and let Herald lead us to my father."

Herald sat blissfully in the sunlight completely oblivious to our conversation twiddling a flower between his fingers. Ignorance truly was bliss; if only I could know such simple pleasures, instead of the weight of worry I held in my mind and heart while following one lunatic and leading another.

"Herald...Herald," I said trying to get his attention.

He looked up from the flower twisted about his finger as if awakening from a deep slumber.

"Do you know the way to my father?" I asked to reassure Gant and myself.

"Oh yes, we reviewed the way again last night in my dreams," he said answering confidently. "Your father was very insistent that I knew the way by heart. If you can just get me home, I will know the way."

Although he answered with absolute conviction, his strange mannerisms and blank stares of wonder did not give the reassurance I had hoped to receive. Suddenly I realized that in my zeal to escape the walls of Belmount I didn't have the slightest idea to our destination.

"Where is that, Herald?"

"New Mexico," he stated with the carelessness of a child.

A voice of panic screamed within my head, "Oh my god!" My face turned pale white. What had I done? How would three men wearing yellow jump suits from a mental institution without a penny to their name travel halfway across the country without being captured? I turned my face away from Herald and Gant so as not to disclose my doubt. If we were to make such a trip, we needed money and new clothes. In desperation I turned to the only friend I had left in this world.

We slipped up behind a huge oak tree, hiding underneath its shadows. I poked my head around the tree's massive trunk leaning against an old knotted root which had bowed above the ground. The old country home with four gables sat proudly in the wind which whipped across the old fields in which it stood. I slowly walked up toward the front door ascending its creaky stairs before striding gently across its paint-chipped front porch. The old screen door, which was warped from years of service, rattled on its hinges as I knocked projecting the wood-racked clatter into the interior of the home. I waited patiently, ashamed of what I was about to ask of such a kind person. Footsteps echoed from behind the door coming to rest behind the thin barrier. A kind face peered from behind the off white door.

"Mrs. Plind, I am so sorry to bother."

"My dear, how are you?"

"Not well," I replied, "can we come in?"

"We?" she asked looking behind me strangely.

"I brought some friends."

Two pitiful looking heads popped from behind the oak tree in her front yard.

"You and your friends get in here right now," she stated boldly.

We happily accepted her kind invitation and found ourselves eating a quickly prepared lunch of salty pork, creamed corn, pinto beans and corn bread. Not having eaten for nearly two days, we gulped the food down like wild savages barely breaking it with our teeth. What a bizarre scene it must have been for an old woman from the country to watch three men sitting in her kitchen in yellow jump suits eating her food like a pack of hungry dogs. After eating, I took Mrs. Plind aside and spoke with her in private. I knew how I looked had to be alarming, and barely knowing my kind ex-host, I dreaded what I had to ask.

"I've gotten into some trouble, and although I hate to ask, you're the only person I have left to turn to."

She looked at me with the forgiving eyes of a mother.

"What do you need?"

"We need some money and some clothes to get to New Mexico as soon as possible."

She looked at me for a moment before turning around and straightening her apron.

"I don't have much, but I did save this."

She handed me a small envelope, the very envelope I had left her upon my departure for Belmount. I flipped it open to find all the money I had left her for advance rent.

"Sometimes a kind gesture repays itself," she said.

"Thank you," I said gratefully.

"Now come on, let me get you some of Everett's things."

With our mental patient uniforms gone, the three of us almost looked sane as we stood on the deck and said goodbye to Mrs. Plind. Gant, being close to seven feet tall, looked out of place in the clothes of Mrs. Plind's late husband, with arms and legs sticking out nearly six inches from the cuffs of his shirt and legs of his pants, while Herald being much shorter had to roll up his pant legs and sleeves to be able to use his hands and feet.

"Thank you for everything," I said feeling eternally indebted to her for her kindness.

She took my face in her hands and squeezed it with more love than my own mother had ever done, "Son, I hope you find what you are looking for, just be careful not to pass everything else along the way."

I hugged her before hiking away never to return, whether it would be because I was to pass into the Lands of Dream or because I was to be institutionalized for the remainder of my life.

We bought three bus tickets to Questa, New Mexico, and began our journey across the Mid West. Herald, whose head seemed to already be in the Lands of Dream, stared blankly at the world from which he had been sequestered for over two decades. Gant sat across the row from me casually reading a magazine, and for the first time, I noticed something strange about his actions. While Herald was staring at everything as if for the first time and I nervously looked around unsure of my own mental state, Gant sat calmly reading as if he belonged to the world from which we were hiding. He showed no signs of anxiety although he had just escaped a mental institution with two other men who were leading him to a magical world outside the reality into which he was born. His hands calmly turned the pages in his magazine as if all was right with the world. The best I could make of it was that he must have been falsely accused and was completely sane or that he was so mentally deranged that nothing affected him. Either way, I began to feel a strange uneasiness as if there was something about him I did not know. The bus pulled out of the station carrying along with it three undercover lunatics heading toward either the Lands of Dream or a harsh mental breakdown.

The bus took a rural route leading us from roadside diner to roadside diner along the highways of America's Mid West. We ate heartily upon the last of my money as we would not need it where we were going. Herald smiled every moment of the day as we traveled toward the dream my father had passed along to him in his own dreams. He had wasted most of his life in the land of the waking a prisoner in a padded room, but now he finally had hope. In his excitement it was all he could talk about.

"Occurring right now as we speak in our solar system is a rare constellational alignment known by astrologers as the Jupiter-Saturn

Conjunction," he whispered confidentially while leaning over his eggs so not to let anyone else in the café hear. "This extraordinary positioning has been taking place since the beginning of time in increments of around twenty years. When this occurs, a series of doors between this world, the world of the waking and a completely different dimension, the Lands of Dream, will open across every planet in the solar system connecting the two worlds but for a short time." He paused a moment looking to see if the coast was clear before continuing, "Your father found this door twenty or so years ago, and if his calculations are correct, the very same door is open right now as we sit in this restaurant shoveling down greasy eggs and bacon!"

I sat across from Herald and as I watched him speak with such conviction, he appeared the sanest man I had ever known.

"Where is this door?" asked Gant.

"I assume there are thousands across the earth open right now to allow passage between the two worlds, but the one we are in search is in a cave near my hometown of Questa. I had spent nearly half my life there before being institutionalized, and to believe I was so close to it and yet unaware of such a thing is astounding. It is as if it was meant to be."

"How long do we have before these doors are closed?" questioned Gant again.

"Once Jupiter passes Saturn and Saturn comes out from Jupiter's shadow, the doors will close and not open again for approximately twenty years."

"How long will that be?" I asked, not wanting to miss what might be our last opportunity to escape the world of the waking, because it was certain that not one of us would be able to evade capture for another twenty years.

"Oh we've got time," he said while dipping his toast into yellow egg yolk and chewing it between his teeth, "we've got time."

"I've got to use the bathroom," declared Gant pushing his chair from the table. "I'll be right back."

Herald sat across from me scooping the slimy roadside food into his mouth seemingly thoughtless of Gant's presence. Once Gant walked around the corner out of our sight, my friend's face was taken with a tight look of concern. He leaned toward me again having lost the peaceful look he had as Gant had sat with us.

"Taking him along is a bad idea," he stated, "your father will not approve."

"Herald, it is because of the actions of Gant that we were able to escape," I replied in his defense.

"You do not even know why he was at Belmount. Some of the patients there, especially those in confinement, are there because they have murdered."

"I do not think Gant is a killer."

"You do not think or you know he is not?"

His implication troubled my mind and I sat unsure of what to think about the man I considered my friend. Although I wanted to remain loyal to him for his actions at the institute, Herald was correct in that I knew little or nothing about him or his past.

"We should leave him here," suggested Herald quickly.

Although I was uncertain about Gant's character, I wasn't willing to abandon him yet.

"We will do no such thing. Although we know nothing of his past, we do know about his present and he has done nothing but help us in our quest to escape this world."

"I think it is a really bad idea."

"Do you think it is or do you know?" I replied, turning the tables on Herald.

He smiled a long grin, settling the matter between us before continuing with his breakfast.

"Where is he anyway?" I asked curiously. "Stay right here, my father definitely wouldn't like you coming without me."

I stood up and began to look for Gant. The roadside diner doubled as a truck stop and therefore was quite large having a convenience store, a truck parts department as well as the restaurant itself. I walked around the corner and found the bathroom but to my dismay I did not find Gant. I wandered to the checkout counter and to my surprise I found Gant standing out front talking on a payphone. I stepped backward so he would not see me. He said a few words and then quickly hung up the phone. I rushed back to our table and sat down across from Herald as if I had never left. Herald looked up at me strangely.

Gant came back around the corner and calmly sat down beside me.

"So where did you go?" I asked causally taking a sip of coffee.

"To the bathroom like I said."

"That's it?"

"Yeah, you ought to check out the bathroom, they have showers and all."

I sat back and watched Gant finish his food behind his lie. Who could he have called and why had he chosen to keep it from us? Maybe Herald was right after all; even though I owed my freedom to Gant, he might be too high a risk to take along. The three of us sat happily drinking our coffee while waiting for our bus to pull out of the station with only me pondering how many of us might enter the Lands of Dream.

After a long trip, our bus pulled into the dusty bus station of Questa, New Mexico, leaving three men standing beneath the shadows of the Taos Mountains. Being a small agricultural town, we were the only visitors at the rural station which was really little more than a four wall pen barely larger than a one car garage. It was desolate and lonely, not much different from the small room in which I had been imprisoned at the Belmount Institution for the Mentally Insane. Herald looked up at the mountains of his hometown stating only one word, "Finally."

Having no other way of traveling, we walked along the dusty road trusting the memory of a man who had been absent from the area for nearly thirty years. Our footsteps scraped along the side of the road stirring the dry powdered earth into the surrounding arid atmosphere. I wet my lips with a nearly dry tongue to protect them from the blazing heat of the sun beating down upon us from above. Our forms braved the sun along the long road dragging along three tired shadows until we came upon a broken down old home. It was no more than a one-room hovel with broken windows, a front door hanging from one hinge and a roof that had finally given way to the merciless sun above. Herald walked onto the deck, finally home after being absent for over two decades. The tips of his fingers skimmed the outside of the failing structure soaking in the memories of his past.

He pointed over to the end of the front porch which had partially collapsed with a long grin.

"This is where your father wrote the memoir of his travel in the Lands of Dream. Over there use to be a porch swing," his eyes reformed its image. "Before my wife left me, we use to sit right there and swing for hours."

At the memory of his wife, tears welled into his eyes dripping down upon a jaw of torment that quivered as he spoke, "it was because she left me that I started losing my mind. It was because she left me for my best friend that I was sent to that hell hole."

I put my hand onto his shoulder with a soft reassurance as I knew very well the mental anguish associated with the loss of a close loved one.

"Herald, I understand what you're going through, but now is not the time for a breakdown. We can't make it without you."

He turned around upon my plea wiping the tears from his eyes.

"We screwed up in this world, but only a few miles away is a whole new world where we might have a fresh start."

A smile appeared upon his face and his expressions suddenly changed from depression to glee.

"I'm sorry gentlemen, let me get my things and we'll be on our way."

He turned as if to go into the shamble of wood to collect his things, stopping suddenly upon the realization that there was nothing left for him in this world.

"I've got all I need," he said.

We followed him down a dirt road before entering a wooded thicket. Our eyes widened underneath the cool shade provided by its lofty trees. Herald followed a small overgrown trail batting aside Mesquite tree thorns, thick brush and weeds along the way. Being so close to our final destination, the three of us barely spoke as we rummaged through what had strangely transformed from a blazing desert into a dense forest. Branches, leaves and spider webs tugged at us as if trying to warn of some impending doom. We ignored their warnings and after some time we found ourselves standing before a small rocky hole in the ground. It was barely four feet across and appeared to coil into the earth like a natural staircase.

"Even after three decades, I knew exactly where it was," stated Herald proudly. "This is where I use to come as a child to get away from everybody." He laughed as if coming upon an epiphany.

"How bizarre that I'm returning once again after all these years to get away from the world where I was born."

I leaned over the small earthen orifice finding it cluttered with dirt, rock and broken branches. A long lean hand touched my shoulder.

"Want me to go first?" offered the tall quiet Gant.

"No, this is what I have been searching for all my life. I just didn't know it till now."

Gant had seen the fear in my eyes assuming it was from the dark hole I stood above, but in actuality what I feared was the truth. Below me a few feet below the earth's crust was the truth of my sanity. What if I climbed below to find there was no mystical portal to another dimension which held my father? What if I had imagined it all? What would I do with my life then? I shook my head to erase the thoughts of suicide that plagued my consciousnesss. I stepped down in to the rocky chasm gripping rocks and roots as I slipped into the stone mouth of the earth. The long fissure descended about fifteen feet into the earth before I found the base of the cave below. The floor of the dark cave was made of smooth stone covered in thick mud that had fallen in from above. A small trickle of light glimmered in from the world above barely illuminating the small mineral cavern. Dirt and dust fell onto my head as Gant and Herald followed into the darkness. I stepped from below the hole staring into the utter darkness that engulfed the hidden cavernous world below the earth's surface. Not having a flashlight or torch, I fumbled in the darkness using the cave's smooth stone rock walls as a guide into the dark obscurity. I could feel the wall turning a corner swallowing me into an overpowering darkness. Completelty devoid of light, I blindly stumbled through the cavern turning a blind eye to the risk of falling through an unseen fissure which could tumble me to a death hundreds of feet below. Better a death hundreds of feet into the earth than imprisonment in the light above. I could hear the echoes of Gant and Herald searching for me, but at that moment my only concern was the truth of my sanity. I walked as blindly as I had all my life searching for my fate and to finally be so close sent chill bumps up and down my arms and legs. A strange buzz, similar to the snow of a television at the end of the broadcast day, radiated through the darkness ahead. I staggered after the emitting fuzz following its sound like a bat through the darkness or maybe a moth to a flame. The floor suddenly rose up, a fact I discovered as my nose bashed into its smooth edge. I instinctively rubbed my face, brushing the blood away from my cheek as I climbed up onto the raised area. The world of darkness I had been immersed abruptly disappeared as a dazzling light emitted from a large round hole in the wall of the cave. The air in the small cave sucked past me rushing into the spiraling cavity of cosmic void. I could feel its attraction as my hair and clothes pulled from my body toward its center. I stood near the center of the huge crack in the universe staring out into the cosmos. Stars, comets and planets were barely an arm's length away as if I was a cosmonaut floating through the depths of space. A vivid light radiated into the small cavern directly from the flames of an immense sun crackling through the halls of space. Dozens of brightly colored planets orbited the fierce star circling it in mad delight. Having some interest in astronomy, I recognized the universe before me as not our own, but another holding a different position in the cosmos far away from that of ours. If I stepped into it, would I be blasted into the abyss of space without protection having my very skin stripped from my body or would I come face to face with my father?

Gant and Herald crawled up into the cavern behind me and to my relief, they saw the prodigy before me as well. I know this not by what they said, but by their actions. Both men's faces froze in incredulity before the window in space. Herald stood next to me with his hair standing straight up leaning toward the yawning portal. His mouth moved, but the draining force of the puncture in the universe sucked the sound from his lips, sending his words to some unknown destination. Knowing there was nothing left to do, I stretched out my arms and stepped into the stars.

The molecules in my body began to tear apart right before my eyes. My hands broke apart vanishing into the space and stars as I was irresistibly drawn inward dissolving into the vast cosmos ....

Upon the reformation of my molecular structure my eyes opened in a palette of astounding color. A flowing prismatic rainbow appeared before me in lush grass, swaying trees, colossal flowers and radiant clouds. At first glance the vibrant colors were too much for my mundane eyes and I was forced to close them as might someone who steps into the sunlight for the first time after living in the dark their entire life. I had never seen nor even imagined such splendor could exist. Flowers that stood taller than men with blossoms larger than a man's head rocked gently under influence of the cool wind. Tall snow-peaked mountains shining brightly under the warm morning sun stood nobly in the distance separating a crystal calico sky of blue, red and yellow from a churning royal purple grassy field. I rubbed my eyes vigorously so as not to miss the moment of the dream in which I had awoke. I leaped to my feet in excitement, I had done it. Against all odds, I like my father before me had found the Lands of Dream!

My high spirits quickly changed to concern upon the remembrance of my two friends who were nowhere in sight. Had they chosen not to come upon witnessing my molecular breakdown or had they been transported to a different continent in a world that had no borders? A terrifying scenario paralyzed my thoughts sending a chill down my spine upon a warm summer day. What if they had been torn apart failing to be reassembled as had I while passing through the Jupiter- Saturn Conjunction? If so their bodies might have been scattered across universes lost forever. Other rationales for their failure to appear played out in my mind, but I shut them out because no matter what happened, it was at the moment out of my control. Unsure if I would ever see Herald or Gant again, I decided to carry on and find my father as he might be the only soul I knew in this strange and beautiful world.

The deep purple grass pressed against my knees refusing to expose any paths they might be hiding. Unsure which direction to begin the search of my father, I began to hike toward the mountains in the distance since at least they would give me an objective in which to travel. As I took my first step toward the majestic peaks on the horizon a head rose from the deep grass startling me. I jumped backward upon its appearance, falling into the high grass vanishing from the wonderful world of beauty. I quickly poked my head above the grass line to see Herald holding his eyes as if in pain. Happy not to be alone, I rushed to my father's old friend and held his head in my arms.

"Herald," I yelled merrily, "am I glad to see you."

"The colors hurt my eyes."

"It is okay, friend, the shock of beauty will soon pass. We're use to the dull colors of our world like the grays of pavement and the smoke of pollution, but never again. Never again will we have to suffer the monotonous mediocrity of the waking world… never again."

Herald's eyes reopened with flare soaking in his surroundings as does a phoenix in a fiery rebirth draining the oxygen from the air. He came alive rising from the ground running through the grass and flowers shouting in glee in having finally concluded a twenty plus year journey.

"I'm not crazy!" he cried sobbing, "I'm not crazy!"

We both stretched out our arms and ran through the cool wind as do children mimicking a plane, having found a second childhood and most importantly a world to accommodate it. We searched the field for the remainder of the day without any sign of Gant and decided to spend the night in its center underneath a blanket of stars in case he happened to appear or awaken from its bosom. Full of enthusiasm for my new world, I dared not to sleep and spent the hours of the night studying the constellations of Dream. The stars hanging above my bed of luxuriant purple vegetation shone brightly in the night, seemingly closer and more active than the skies of our own world. Multiple moons, shooting stars and huge nearby planets filled the blackest of black backdrops fluorescently lighting the heavens. I pondered the countless constellations curious about their many formations and identities. With the risings of the suns of Dream, Herald and I gave up on the arrival of our third companion. Maybe he decided to stay in the waking world or maybe he had awakened on the other side of Dream; either way, there was nothing left for us to do than to meet up with my father. Fortunately for us, he had given Herald explicit directions to his location within the Lands of Dream. We began our long trek across Dream searching for a city known as Celpahia.

The very air sparkled as we crossed the countryside searching for signs of civilization. We found many natural wonders and sights that would have been impossible in the world of our birth to include nomadic trees, glowing rocks and singing mushrooms, but not one sign of civilization, not even a simple road to follow. We spent two more nights under the open sky where I had not slept so peacefully since I was an infant in my mother's arms. What was strange about my sleep was that I did not dream at all. Whether it was because I was already living in Dream or that all was well in my mind and I no longer needed dream to escape the life I now lived I do not know. Perhaps once we found my father, he would be able to enlighten me about such things.

On our fourth day, I began to wonder if the Lands of Dream were inhabited at all, when I first saw her image along the horizon. She was riding a sleek ivory unicorn through the purple meadow with yellow blooms as elegantly as might a ballerina in a studio of dance. Her form glided in perfect cadence with the beast upon which she rode appearing almost as one fine-tuned creature rather than two separate entities. Upon seeing us standing in a dry sea of purple and yellow pasture she urged her mount toward us. The elegant pair glided up to us gently without making a sound upon the soil upon which we stood.

"Greetings," she said tenderly with a slight nod of respect.

She, completely nude, sat upon the lovely mystical creature holding a lock of the creature's hair between her fingers. Her skin was as soft and white as cream without any apparent blemishes, not even the slightest freckle, scar or skin discoloration that I could see. I marveled at the woman's beauty having seen none to rival it in all my days in the waking world. Stunned by the presence of such angelic perfection, I stood silent. If I imagined an angel, it would be in her exact likeness. Seemingly confused by our silence, she nudged the mare beneath her circling us with a curiosity almost as apparent as our own.

"Do you not speak?" she asked staring into my eyes.

It was a gentle stare one of purity and kindness, unlike any I had ever seen as the eyes of those from my own world, which always had some element of guilt or weariness in them. I had always believed that the eyes were the windows to a person's soul and if such a statement was true, this woman's clear green eyes were a window to innocence.

"Do you not know where you are?"

"No we do not." I replied in a stumbling manner with far less elegance than that of the person with whom I spoke.

"Might I help you then?"

Herald stood mesmerized as had I been with an open jaw of utter silence.

"Oh, that would be wonderful, we are looking for a city named Celpahia," I replied quickly so not to lose my thoughts again.

"Why that is far away in the southern realm of dreams," she replied, seemingly surprised by the remoteness of our destination.

The unicorn stepped around us again spinning our heads. It was a fascinating creature with large bulging muscles and short tight hair that was bone white in color. Its horn was twisted and bleached white with the slightest streaks of pink in its groves. The wondrous creature snorted and shook its head expressing its discontent with having to stand still during our conversation. Although tamed by the beautiful angelic woman upon it, it was still a wild beast of Dream and it ached to run. A type of vertigo overcame my mind as if I were standing high upon a cliff, unsure whether it had been brought upon me by her encircling us or simply by her astounding loveliness. She giggled upon seeing our puzzlement.

"You cannot reach it by foot either."

"How can you reach it?" I asked curiously.

"By air or sea of course!" she replied as if stating the obvious.

"Forgive our impudence, but we are new here and know nothing of your world."

"Oh forgive me!" she said embarrassed, causing her unicorn to beat its hoofs against the ground. "Let me introduce myself, I am Lady Falasia and this is Karasail my trusted friend and partner." She patted the animal beneath her and it snorted as if greeting us as well.

"We are two simple dreamers, lost in this strange and charming world."

She sat high upon her steed staring down at me curiously. Her hair was a long curly red hanging over her back and shoulders partially covering her naked breast.

"You are only lost if you're somewhere you do not wish to be," she stated firmly as if her statement was common knowledge.

"Then, by God, we are far from lost!"

Upon hearing my statement a deeper look of perplexity overtook her face, "Of which god do you speak?"

A moment of bewilderment overcame me as well as I realized I knew not the name of the god I had been raised as a child to worship.

"It's just an expression," I replied so not to create a religious discussion. "In which way should we travel?"

"You are on the island of Akgaule, a land of simple people with modest needs. There are no roads or ships here as everyone travels their own way."

"What of food and lodging, do you have things such as these?" asked Herald as confused as I.

"Oh yes, we have those things!" she replied cheerfully.

"Where might we find these?" I asked, assuming such a place would lead us to some sort of civilization.

"Why these things are everywhere! The land provides all the food we need and once the light of the sky fades away, we lie down to sleep," she answered with the simplicity of an innocent child.

Being from a material world, her statement did not make any sense, "You have no home?"

"Why yes, this island is my home!"

"Do you not grow your food?" asked Herald assuming all simple lifestyles had to involve some aspect of farming.

"Why would I want to do something the land already does?"

"Do your people have a city or a town?" I inquired trying to find someone who might know a way to Celpahia.

"We do not confine ourselves to the boundaries of one location, for there is so much to see and do elsewhere, if it were not for the great oceans we would travel across all the Lands of Dream."

A bit frustrated with our conversation, I paused a moment remembering I was the alien here and that I needed to be mindful of that fact every day I was in the Lands of Dream.

"A beautiful as your homeland is, we have an engagement that we must keep, is there anyone here we might speak with about leaving this island?"

"Hmm…" she said in deep thought upon her picturesque steed, "that is quite a conundrum as I have never met anyone who has wanted to leave Akgaule before. Maybe Xahep could be some help, as he has not always lived here as I."

"Great… would you mind taking us to this Xahep?"

"I would be glad to," she replied blissfully in the manner in which she replied with all of her responses, but once again she reminded us of another dilemma, "but at the moment I'm not sure where he is."

Herald leaned in close to me and whispered in my ear, "I couldn't stand to be so carefree, it would be too stressful."

"He might be at the forest vineyard, and if you like I would be glad to take you."

Having no other option we agreed, following behind the blithe young woman on foot from whom I could not take my eyes. She rode like a true lady riding sideways with both her legs hanging daintily off the same side of the mare. I watched every inch of her intently from behind studying her tight subtle curves careful only to look away bashfully whenever she looked backwards. She seemed not to care about our stares, showing no signs of modesty as might a child running around naked. Obviously her culture did not share the same shame as did ours in regard to nudity.

Her smooth soft face turned to her side looking down upon me as I walked along side her and her mount, "Why do you cover your body? It is not cold." She questioned trying to make sense of the garments we wore upon our bodies.

"It is part of our culture," I replied simply for I knew no other reason, but that I had been taught to do so since childhood no matter the weather.

"Even when the sun bores down upon you, you wear such things?"

"Why yes."

"Does your body look like mine?" She asked wondering if we were horribly disfigured below our attire.

"Our bodies are of the same species," I replied, "but nothing like yours."

"What do you mean?" she asked with the curiosity of a youthful child.

"We are not as beautiful as you."

Her cheeks turned to the tint of roses as she giggled behind a petite hand.

"Do none of your people wear clothing?"

"We, just as the creatures of the land, do not wear clothing for if we were meant to do so, the gods would have given them to us."

She obviously had a purist attitude toward life taking it as it came, living only for the moment, without concern for tomorrow. The only comparison I could contemplate to equal her temperament was that of a wide-eyed child new to the world.

We traveled through the stunning countryside of Akgaule which left me astounded by one natural wonder after another before we came up upon its central forest vineyard. This was an unusual sight encompassing thousands of small trees about a dozen or so feet tall bunched together and separated by only a few feet from trunk to trunk. Hanging across the tops of the small forest was a web-like network of thick copious vines. Brilliantly red fruit about the size of an average man's fist hung from the twisted vines alluringly calling to those below. Underneath the tangled web of fruit were other men and women with the same soft white skin tone as our guide. Some stood below the vineyard picking produce, while others lay on the ground either napping or chatting with one another, with everyone in sight except Herald and I being completely nude. Falasia slid effortlessly from her mare and stepped up to a group of bare individuals who had congregated together and lay leisurely in the shade beneath a tree with large purple fruit. A handsome young man casually spoke with her before looking over toward Herald and me who stuck out like sore thumbs by being the only

347 | C h a r l e s   C l e m o n s

individuals with clothing. He walked over to us without hurry eyeing us closely as might a dog another. Instinctively I eyed him as well noticing many of the same traits in him as I had seen in Falasia with the first being that he seemed without worry. His face, as was Falasia's, was soft and smooth without wrinkles save those around their mouth where they smiled. He had no bags or lines under his eyes from anxiety or any scars from past injuries for it seemed Akgaule was free of thorn, predator and poison.

"Welcome, come and feast with us underneath this fine Umaleuz tree," he said, inviting us with a calm hand motioning us toward the tree with giant purple fruit hanging from its branches.

The residents of the place seemed in an almost sensual trance beneath the tree's alluring cover.

"Come," he induced with a slight tug upon my arm, "the Umaleuz soothes the mind and body."

I followed the young man and lay down among the naked men and women with the full intention of finding the best way off the island as quickly as possible. Herald followed behind me with a terrified look as if he might be sexually assaulted at any moment by the strange and beautiful people surrounding us. Although I did not share his concern, I understand his fear as in our world mass groups of people did not lie around naked together unless they were mentally ill, and while Herald had spent over twenty years in a mental institution, he was not crazy. He had simply endured a mental breakdown after his wife had left him for his brother and had been sent to Belmount institute to rot way the remainder of his life.

A lovely young woman with light brown curly hair handed me one of the huge purple fruits hanging above my head before lying down and cuddling up beside me. She started to pull my clothes aside so to press her skin against my own, but trying to keep my focus, I pulled the protection of my garments back up.

"Falasia told me the two of you want to leave Akgaule?" asked the young man genuinely trying to understand my plea.

The beautiful young woman's hand began to caress my chest beguilingly, but I pulled her hand away as I did not know the woman and feared if I partook in the pleasures of Akgaule I might choose not to leave as had the rest of its residents.

"Yes, do you know a way off?"

"A way off?" he inquired as if having never thought of such an intention. "Why no one has ever wanted to leave here before."

"Falasia told me you have not always lived here."

He took a deep bite of his fruit squeezing clear bubbling juice down the side of its glossy skin. He sighed with delight lifting it up as a signal for me to do the same with my own. He noticed my apprehension to follow his lead.

"Please, refusing to taste a fruit handed to you by another is outright impolite."

I reluctantly took a bite in the firm skinned fruit. It tenderly squirted into my mouth firing signals of delight from my taste buds. I had never known anything to be so sweet. In comparison, the sweetest of honeys I had ever tasted in the waking world were closer to bread than the fruit I sucked into my mouth. Suddenly I was supremely relaxed with few cares in the world.

"Falasia is correct, I was born in Dtyrl, a land far west of here just south of the gateway to the Land of Lights. It is a delightful place with many comparable wonders, but it was a place of war, so I came here choosing the kindness of love over the victory of murder."

"Is there a port here, where ships bring supplies?" I asked, formulating a way to leave.

"We need no supplies, for all we do is to eat, drink, sleep, make love and live. We follow only the pleasures of life ignoring all other concerns."

My head felt light swooning as I spoke, "How did you arrive here?"

"A wonderful sea creature unlike any I have heard or seen let me ride upon its back to the shore."

"Where is this creature now?"

"I do not think the kind being was from this world, but maybe a dreamer from elsewhere. While we do not have seasons or count years here on Akgaule, this all would have happened fifty or more years ago."

His statement stunned me greatly as the man sitting before me looked younger than I, very close in appearance to someone in their early twenties in the waking world.

"So you're saying there might not be a way off this island?"

He looked at me quietly searching for the meaning to my question, "I never said such a thing. I simply stated that no one I know has thought about it, but I'm sure if that's what you want it can be done. I have seen ships sail by the coast as I walked along the shore searching for sea shells."

My head lowered with heavy eyelids dragging me down into a deep irresistible slumber. I had felt nothing as wonderful as I did during that sleep as my mind soared with pleasure and my body rested in massages from many hands. My eyes reopened under starlight nestled with warm soft naked bodies of careless perfection. A calm breeze rustled the great fruit and leaves above me giving me the tranquil feeling of a cool summer night.

The next morning we followed Falasia upon her grand unicorn Karasail, who traveled as gracefully upon land as did a cutter upon the sea. Our guides had agreed to take us to the coast, a two day journey on foot. We walked alongside our host naked having given in to their culture while carrying our clothes along like a knotted sack. Herald had tied his garments around three of the purple fruits not willing to partake in their pleasure only once in his lifetime, which according to the people of this island and except for a tragedy might be without end. That was a detail no one on the island was sure of, for they had not actually taken the time to ponder the term of their carefree lives.

"Why did you not choose to make love with the women who wanted to do so with you?" Falasia asked me out of the blue breaking the silence our voices had held for several hours.

I looked over at Herald who quickly lowered his head, seemingly ashamed that he had not resisted the women as had I.

"I don't know, where I come from such sex escapades are taboo."

"Taboo?" she asked unfamiliar with the term.

"Yeah, you know immoral," I replied elaborating.

"You mean wrong like killing?"

"Yes."

"Your people compare making love to killing?"

"Sort of, but not exactly," I said somewhat confused about my own world's belief system.

"Here on Akgaule we do not associate natural urges or pleasurable actions as wrong."

"So you have been with many men?" I asked with a new and somewhat tarnished image of our guide.

"Oh no," she responded quickly, "I am a liaison to the creatures of this land as is Karasail to the men and women here. Only the pure can consort with a unicorn. That is why I asked you about those women. I assumed since you did not indulge you must be an envoy between your world and ours."

"No, unfortunately there are no purity requirements for the ambassadors of our world. We are more fugitives than any sort of diplomats."

"Most of those who come here outside of birth are renegades of one sort or another," she replied smoothly trotted upon her mount though the tall grass. "Everyone is welcome here."

That night two men, a woman and a unicorn lay in the depths of a colorfully dark forest without fear of harm from man or animal as man and animal had made peace on this tiny island in the Lands of Dream creating a utopia unlike any I had ever thought or dreamed. Brightly colored fireflies of florescent blue, pink and orange buzzed in the forest treetops creating brilliant streaks of light in the darkness above. Occasionally one would curiously buzz near us illuminating the surrounding darkness with a dazzling display of color. I lay awake throughout the night unwilling to miss the serene light show above, not closing my eyes until the break of dawn.

When Falasia awoke me I felt as rested as I had ever felt, even though I had stayed awake most the night. Our host and her companion melted into the orange morning suns over the horizon to find breakfast. I watched her, hypnotized by a beauty I had never believed possible. I had never longed for a woman as I did at that moment for Falasia. I knew because of who she was, I could never have her, but the mind's knowledge of an impossibility did not wean the longing from the heart. Herald rose with a smile as happy as any being I had ever met.

"I do not think I want to ever leave this island," stated Herald.

"But my father waits for us both in Celpahia."

"I know the Lands of Dream are full of wonder and beauty, but no place could be any better than what we have found here. To leave the Garden of Eden in search of paradise does not make any sense."

"I know Herald, but this is all we know of this world. Once we meet and speak with my father, he can tell us of all this world's wonders and then you and I can choose to go wherever we want. My friend, there is no rush, we now have plenty of time to see everything and everyplace from corner to corner of this fabulous realm."

"I understand that you must go to your father, but I came here to escape the hell I had been born into and now that I have finally made it to heaven, I'm not going to throw it away for the promise of another heaven."

I saw the determination in his eyes and I knew that now that he had partaken of the lust of Akgaule that he would not ever leave its shores, but would remain content to spend an eternity in its fertile fields, wild forest and sandy beaches.

"My father will miss you."

"Thank him for me, for if it were not for his dreams, I would have never realized my own."

Falasia and Karasail rode through the forest as one, coming to a quick stop at our makeshift camp. Falasia leaped from her mount with the grace and agility of a feline goddess holding sparkling red gourds. She snapped off a fruit's top handing both Herald and me one before breaking off one for herself. She took it in the palm of her hand and turned it upward allowing its contents to pour into her throat. Herald and I followed her example gulping down the contents of our own gourds. The juice was thick and filling much like syrup, but not nearly so sweet. I immediately felt rejuvenated as if reborn. I jumped to my feet ready to walk across the Lands of Dream that very moment.

The four of us frolicked through the long fields, rolling hills and brightly colored forests like children on an imaginary journey until we came upon a wide sea of vivid blue. It stretched beyond measure engulfing an infinite world of strange and wonderful terrain, phenomena and people. It was near sunset as we came upon a deep sandy shoreline which surrounded the entirety of the great undeveloped island of Akgaule. Soft tranquil waves washed over the island's shoals splashing playfully at our feet. We lay down at the edge of the sea beneath another blanket of brilliant blue littered with gleaming stars. Herald lay next to me snoring with his head caked in soft sand. Falasia lay on my other side, her shapely naked figure illuminated by the glow of the stars.

"Do Akgaule women ever commit to one man?" I asked.

The moon glistened off her bare breasts as she rolled over toward me.

"Do you mean like marriage?" she asked sweetly.

"Yes," I replied excited that she knew of the institution.

"The children of Akgaule do not commit to each other, as our sole commitment is to life itself."

A wave of disappointment rushed over me as if it had swooped down upon me like a tidal wave from the ocean next to which I lay. Although we lay separated by only a few inches, we were still a world apart, her a child of dream, me a servant of the waking world. Because she was far more observant than anyone I had ever known, I turned over so not to let my facial expressions foretell my true feelings toward her.

"How about you, what do you think of monogamy?" I asked.

Her hand gently caressed my cheek pulling my face upward toward her eyes. They gleamed like pearls under the reflection of light from the moons of Dream. I yearned for her to say yes so I could take her at that very moment.

"Monogamy?" she asked of the word she had never heard.

"In my world when two people fall in love, they choose to be with only one person."

"Forever?"

Her eyes searched into mine as in the Lands of Dream, forever really meant forever not as in my world where many times it meant for now.

"Yes," I lied.

"I could not do that," she said staring at me intently, "for I have chosen the path of liaison between man and animal, and if I lose my innocence, I will no longer be able to speak with the creatures of this land."

I reached out and touched her face caressing it softly. She leaned responding to my touch bringing her lips up to mine. Only the slightest hair of space separated our lips when I reluctantly pulled away. This was her world and I had came to it to meet my father, not destroy those I came in contact with. If I made love to her, it might have fulfilled the lust that swelled with my loins at that moment, but it would change her forever, taking away who she was, and I cared far more for her than that. A look of confusion overcame her gentle features as I pulled away from what would have most certainly been a kiss. Bewildered by my actions she lay back down and looked back up at the stars. I reached out and gripped her hand to comfort us both. I had to find my father first, before I could ever decide what I was going to do in my new home. To date, my life in the Lands of Dream had been just that, a dream, but unfortunately I would soon learn that not everyone dreamed of lively forests, peaceful seas and sweet nectar, especially those that came from the waking world.

The next morning the four of us became children of the sea dancing in its cool refreshing waters and laughing under the warm sun. Falasia ran about much like a kitten curiously playing in spurts which she complemented in between with regular cat naps. I watched her with admiration, almost with jealousy of her blithe lifestyle. She and her people were living life as it was meant to be lived, as children of nature, something I would never be able to completely be a part of. Her perfectly curved body ran along the beach keeping my full attention until in the horizon I spotted a set of deep red sails. The wide red forms stood firmly seated by a gust of wind carrying the lustrous vessel across the great ocean as effortlessly as a skate over ice. I jumped up in excitement waving at the ship in the distance but quickly realizing that such a distant craft would never take notice of such a vague speck along a secluded coastline. Herald ran up next to me shouting in an attempt to signal the far off ship.

"They will never see us this far off and we have no way of signaling them," I replied sadly.

Falasia ran up to us with a sad look as if she was going to miss me.

"It appears you can leave us now."

"I won't be leaving you anytime soon," I said correcting her.

A charming smile appeared on her face upon my statement, but lasted only briefly as she responded dejectedly, "I can signal it… if you want. That is, if you don't want to stay here with me."

I gripped her shoulders and held her close to let her see how I felt.

"I have to do something, but I will come back to you, I promise."

She looked at me intently before snapping her finger to signal her trusted companion Karasail. She spoke into the valiant creature's long ear with a strange chatter unlike any spoken language I had ever heard. The powerful animal reared up onto its back legs at the conclusion of her words, sprinting from the beach and rushing through an ocean of swirling purple tipped grass. Its sleek muscles propelled it at a speed near that of light making it difficult for my eyes to focus upon it as it faded into a distant streak.

I watched the colossal crimson-sailed ship cut slowly along the horizon shrinking further into the depths of Dream taking with it my hopes of seeing my father. In a matter of moments its sails became merely a red speck and with their disappearance I sat down disheartened. How long would it be before another ship passed and without cause actually come to Akgaule. I might never be able to signal one and in effect have reached the Lands of Dream without ever seeing my father. I turned and looked over at the beautiful Falasia, who even at that moment smiled while playing in the sand, apparently heedless of my dismay. As I sat beneath the warm morning suns pondering my destiny, a cool shadow engulfed the three of us. I quickly looked up to see what had blotted out the suns of Dream to see a marvel of astounding grace, size and beauty. A massive creature the size of a modern elephant glided through the air swooping from the mainland and out over the deep blue sea of Dream. It passed over us at the distance of only a few feet giving me a close and delightful view of its amazing splendor. It appeared to be a cross between reptile and bird with a large scaly head and a body of pearlescent silver glimmer. Its wings and long whipping tail were covered in bright blue feathers. A long wailing screech of vigor tore through the sky part wail, part roar, tearing from its beak as its body slashed through the sky. The massive form soared out toward the red speck on the horizon becoming barely a glimmer in the light of the reflecting suns. A peaceful silence surrounded us as we quietly observed the direction in which the captivating creature had vanished. Time crawled to what seemed a halt as we waited to see if the magical being would return. After a time the glistening creature reappeared swelling toward us to massive proportions until we were blotted from the light of the suns once again. A whoosh of wind ripped between us as the flying beast rushed over us to disappear back from wherever it came.

Falasia laughed in glee while clapping her hands in applause of the spectacle we had been so fortunate to witness. Then far off where the sea meets the sky, a minute red speck returned ever so small at first, but then swelled back into the crimson sails I had longed for earlier. The ocean-born dot from the distance materialized into a grand two masted junk. An enormous anchor dropped from the ship's cathead splashing the heavy hook into the cool waters of Akgaule's colorful reef. A skiff was lowered alongside the large vessel upon which several humanoid figures climbed aboard. The rowboat pushed toward us by power of oar, but was still too far out for me to distinguish the features of its crew. As the boat's bow set into place upon the sandy beach I studied both it and its strange crew.

The small rowboat was ornately carved with inspiring faces and symbolic cosmic images. Its wood sparkled an innate green, not like that of painted green, but more as if its structure had been carved from a bright green wood. Its passengers although human in shape, by no means bore any relation to that of human. They were short, about five feet in height and slender almost like eels with inky black damp skin randomly covered with even darker skin blotches that were closer in appearance to actual pitch than that of a skin discoloration. Their heads sprouted long smooth snake-like tentacles that were pinned over the back of their heads with metal rings similar in appearance to braids or dreadlocks, but these were not thin like hair, but thick like flesh. Their eyes were glossy black as if used to see at the bottom of the sea rather than in bright sunshine. Black glossy stains that looked somewhat like tears oozed from their eyes. My first impulse was to turn and run from the horrible beasts and not to do so took all of the fortitude I possessed. Herald stood next to me aghast at the four monsters from the sea that had come ashore apparently for me.

"Which is it of you that wishes to travel with us?" asked one of the sea creatures before us.

Herald, terrified the creatures might mistaken him for me, pointed at me too frightened to speak. Falasia, having never met a stranger, ran up to the strange creatures hugging the one that spoke.

"Welcome to Akgaule!"

The beast looked at her strangely, apparently not impressed by her stunning beauty.

"We have not come for a visit, but were told by the great air serpent that someone here required passage across the seas of Dream."

"I wish to travel to Celpahia," I spoke, regaining some of my courage.

"We are not going that far south, but we could drop you off at another port where you might gain passage there upon another vessel."

I stood silent, unsure if I should go with the bizarre creatures or not, for once I was upon their ship I would be at their mercy, if they had any mercy at all.

"Please, if you want to come, we must go. The sun is hard upon our flesh," stated the being excessively oozing a glossy black resin.

I had come to see my father and I knew that I would have to come to terms with the strange and unordinary if I was to become part of the dream world in which I currently found myself. I hugged both Herald and Falasia telling them both separate goodbyes.

"Herald," I said hugging him, "thank you for bringing me here to my father."

"I will be here if you do not find a place you like better over there," he said, pausing and looking over at Falasia, "I'm sure something will bring you back."

Falasia rushed into my arms hugging me with the uninhibited love of a child not afraid to express her true feelings. She loved everyone in the world of dreams, but I someday hoped she might love me differently. She didn't speak, but only shed a single tear, the first which she had ever known.

I stepped aboard the small vessel and sat in the middle as the four weird sea-men rowed us out to sea. The interior of the tiny wooden vessel was smooth as if made of one piece such as being carved from a larger whole rather than pieced together by small parts such as boards. The interior was as bright a green as the exterior supporting my earlier speculation that it had not been painted, but that it was the material's natural color. Once the smaller craft reached the edge of the main ship I was stunned by the towering marvel next to which I sat. Its hull was made of the same green wood showing no signs of being pieced together as if it had been carved from one giant piece of wood as well. The exterior was adorned with intricately detailed hand carved images of astrological signs, insignias of nature and likenesses of strange sea gods. At the front of the ship was a green bust of Marpuaeliua the Lady of the Sea, a fact I would later learn in my discussions with the strange black seamen.

Giant hooks were lowered down from the great looming ship which the crew of the skiff hooked into small holes along the ship. The small vessel was then hoisted from the surface of the sea and pulled onto the deck of the mighty junk by the manpower of its crew. I looked at the thin almost rubbery arms of the men who had raised us above finding it difficult to believe such slender limbs harbored such raw strength. Upon the barking of a black seaman, who obviously held some form of high rank among his people, the crew pulled the anchor and raised sail pushing us away from the coast of the lovely Akgaule coast. Falasia sat high upon Karasail waving until I could see her no longer. The front sail of the ship was enormous ballooning into a massive sea of red that harnessed the great winds of Dream and thrust us forward into the sunsets dipping into the distant horizon. Once the ship took to sail, the strange sea men began to pull open hatches in the deck and crawl into the darkness below. In a matter of seconds, I found myself standing alone under the fading sun, curious about my fate now that I had placed myself in the hands of such disturbing creatures. Almost as if hearing my thoughts, a hatch a few feet away creaked open to reveal a slimy black hand motioning me below. My heart froze in terror as I visualized what horrors might lie below the wooden floor upon which I stood. Dozens of the horrid black beasts might be waiting below planning who knows what. I knew nothing of this wonderfully strange world and I did not want to end up in the stomachs of predatory pirates. Mental images of my flesh being torn from my bones in the gloom below held me firm in the light above. Although it was little more than a comfort, I felt somewhat safe in the sunlight on deck. The hand returned once again, but this time with greater urgency. The bottom of the first sun of Dream sank into the edge of the sea bathing me in the twilight of Dream. Darkness was soon to engulf me whether I was above or below the emerald deck upon which I stood, and sooner or later I would discover the intentions of the crew whether they be admirable or horrific. I skeptically lifted the heavy door from which the hand had gestured and stepped into the shadows.

A damp murky world veiled my eyes as the sun vanished behind the heavy wooden trapdoor. A black cold hand seized my arm guiding me through the utter darkness below deck. Unable to see, I followed instinctively holding out my arms so as not to bump into anything. The creature held my arm firmly like a vice grip of flesh leading me through a network of twists and turns until I was utterly disoriented. After several moments we stopped and through the image of my hearing I envisioned a door as it groaned open. I was led past a splintering door frame and left to stand alone in the dark as even the hand that had led me through the obscurity abandoned me.

A voice came from the darkness, "Please sit down," it said.

I nervously stood in the black void unsure of the request, for I could see nothing, let alone a chair.

"I'm sorry, I have not dealt directly with a surface dweller for some time."

An ebony hand appeared from the darkness illuminated by a faint flame. The small flickering fire touched a round stone, which suddenly started to glow weakly. A glossy black face emerged under the radiant rock.

"Please sit down," repeated the voice.

I stumbled a moment before finding a small wooden chair behind me. Not wanting to taunt my host any further, I pulled it up and sat down.

"Sorry about the lack of light, being from the depths of the sea, we do not require light to see," explained the ebony face, which appeared to be levitating in the darkness, "it is actually uncomfortable to us."

"Excuse my curiosity, but what brings you and your men above the sea to float upon it like land dwelling men?"

"We are fugitives of the sea, unable to return to the waters of our birth. For any of us to do so would mean certain death as our own people have cast us above to live or die, but never to return. To survive, we endure the dry wind which desiccates our skin and the scorching sun that burns our eyes. It is because of these conditions that our skin slowly bleeds and our eyes glaze over. To ease these pains, we hide below in the day and ride the decks at night. Among the land dwellers who know little about us, we are known as nocturnal navigators."

My mouth opened and a word almost passed my lips when one of the black seamen screamed out, "The suns have sunk and the night is upon us!"

A cascade of cheers rattled through the ship's dark hull followed by footsteps and the creaks of hatches opening above.

"Let us go above and speak more; we do not get the opportunity to speak with others very often."

He kindly led me through the dark ship into the moonlight above as might an adult an irresponsible child through a china shop. On deck the dark glossy men smiled staring out over the ocean which no longer shone clear blue, but a black as sleek as their exterior. My host and I stood at the stern of the ship watching the ocean churn behind the green galley slowly returning to a state of utter calm as we sailed on into the night. Being at the mercy of the undersea men, I dared not ask what deed they had done to be banished from their underwater land through fear of being ill-mannered. My companion did not have the same restraint.

"What brings you from the island of Akgaule? In my time on the surface of the sea, I have heard of people going there, but I have never heard of anyone ever leaving it."

"I am in search of my father whom I have not seen in over twenty years."

"Twenty years is but the twinkle of a star in the Lands of Dream," he stated peacefully. "We have roamed the crest of the seas for two hundred years, lost above our native depths in the blinding light."

"Two hundred years?" I asked stunned. "Surely whatever you have done or are accused of will now be long forgotten."

"What I have done shall never be forgotten among my people," he replied wretchedly. "Our destiny is to roam a world where we do not belong."

As I spoke with my host and discovered he was less of a monster than most men I knew, my curiosity overcame my fear of inquiring about the past of him and his men.

"Might I ask, without being disrespectful, what you did to be exiled from your homeland beneath the sea?"

His black face turned toward me with a grimace of frustration and I wished the words had never left my mouth.

"You may not," he said in a hiss, "but as it has already been done, so I will tell you of my contravention. Many years ago, I fell in love with a Maritaun woman whose beauty was rivaled by only the goddesses of Dream. Her name was Placie and she was the daughter of a great Maritaun noble. We were both young and I loved her with all my heart so I asked her to be mine and to my heart's delight she accepted. I have never known such ecstasy and for a moment I was as happy as has been any heart in all the universe. But I was a commoner, little more than an officer in the Maritaun marines, and although at that time I believed love could conquer all, I was to learn nothing conquers all, not even a dream in the Lands of Dream. Because of my common rank, we were forced to meet in secrecy to express our love, a love I would do anything… a love that I would later destroy. One day I heard the announcement of the Prince of Maritaun's marriage and to my dismay his bride was to be to my Placie. I rushed to her home and upon hearing from her father it was true, I rushed to the castle of King Vauencet to stop the wedding. When I arrived, I found I had been banned from the ceremony. I could hear the music behind the walls of the undersea palace and in a rage fueled by maddening love I went to my men and returned to storm the palace. Taking the guards of the citadel by surprise we gained entry and to my horror I found my beloved Palcie in the arms of Prince Vauencet. She had toyed with my love never meaning to be with me… she had never really loved me, I had only been a distraction to pass time. I had wanted to be with her for all time, and to find out I was to be only a fleeting flash in her life was more than I could stand. In a blind rage, I cut them both down shedding their blood in the very bed where I found them. At that moment I wanted nothing more than to die along with them, but as I raised my sword, my men pulled it from me and carryied me from the city. I live today only because of what my men did for me. It is because of me that they roam without a homeland and until their death I cannot have my own."

The black creature that stood next to me dripping with the ooze that protected his flesh from the dry air was not a monster at all; in actuality he was more human than I for he carried a burden equal only to those that dwelled in Hell, if such a place even existed. Wanting to know the name of the valiant creature I stood next to under the stars, I held out my hand saying my name. He did the same replying with his own, "I am Jaiet, once a Maritaun, now a simple nocturnal navigator forced to roam the seas of Dream without a dream."

His men, although condemned to a life of vagabondage, played underneath the stars of dream, leaping into the water like mermen and returning with great catches of fish and crab. We ate the sea harvest under the stars after cooking it on open fire pits aboard the green ship. The next morning the sea men went below to hide from the rays of the sun and rest as I stayed in the light above soaking in the brilliant warmth provided by the suns of Dream on a cool open sea. Our ship cut through the mighty smooth ocean and for a moment I pondered how the sea-men steered the powerful vessel during the day without watch, but realizing they had done so for centuries, I lay contently upon the bow with a full stomach and napped under the suns of Dream without concern.

When I awoke, the suns stood high in the sky illuminating the great smooth sea of glass upon which our ship sailed. White-blue marbled water crashed against the hull as the vessel cut through the vast ocean rippling an otherwise perfect sheet of blue. My eyes searched the endless blue finding nothing but our ship, the sea and the sky. The cool salty air refreshingly filled my lungs with as much invigoration as it did the sails upon the ship I stood. Standing alone on the deck of the emerald ship upon the wide open sea was as beautiful a moment as I had ever had the pleasure to enjoy. As I soaked in the splendors of Dream, a small speck of green similar to our own ship vaguely appeared over the bow. As it swelled in size, it vastly outgrew the mass of the ship upon which I stood, slowly becoming the tip of a forest-covered continent. I rushed to the nearest ship hatch and slung it open propelling the bright sunlight above into the murky darkness below. My eyes struggled to adjust to the vast light difference leaving me blind in the shadows below deck. A black shiny face found me in the darkness.

"Land," I said as if it were the greatest thing, "land."

"It is the coast of Vastoal. We will take you to the port of Vineying. There you can obtain passage from the northern realm of dreams into the south through the Strait of Phylain. From there across the Cerulean Sea you will find your city of Celpahia."

Our ship sailed round the Horn of Kadusal setting anchor in the wondrous harbor of the miraculous city Vineying. Its towering sight was beyond anything I had ever imagined. The harbor flowed roughly being formed from dozens of giant waterfalls which poured over the vast cliffs surrounding the harbor. A cloud of fine mist created from the bubbling waterfalls cascading into the harbor rushed over our ship covering it in a damp revitalizing sea spray. Hanging from enormous trees soaring hundreds of feet over the rocky cliffs were thick vines two and three feet thick. At the end of each of these giant vines dangling gently in the mist were charming old world cottages.

"This is the land of the elves, the first beings to dream into the Lands of Dream," stated Jaiet. "They are the most powerful race that have dreamt here, with an arcane knowledge of things most do not even know exist. They are a wise people, fierce isolationists who do not meddle in the affairs of others."

"Will they help me?" I asked, mesmerized by the picturesque city.

"They are chivalrous traders. You will have little trouble finding safe passage to your destination."

I lowered my head, "I have nothing to trade."

The hand of my host opened before me to reveal a colossal iridescent pink pearl. It was about the size of a golf ball gleaming opaquely under the sea mist.

"I cannot accept something of such value," I said with a knot in my throat.

"While rare among surface dwellers, such treasures are common for those who can walk the bottom of the sea," he stated holding out his offer. "We survive in your world by trading things we scavenge from the sea."

"But I have done nothing for it."

"It is an offer of kindness, a tribute to our friendship."

He dropped the heavy smooth ball into my hand patting my shoulder before walking down onto the deck to order the docking of his ship. Slimy, black and as ugly as any creature I had ever imagined, I had never met a better or more beautiful person than the poor banished soul Jaiet. The sea-men of the green galley lowered its red sails and dropped anchor beneath a giant dangling circular building, which held position directly in the center of the harbor. A circular center began to descend from the bottom of the round structure supported by four evenly placed thick vines. The thick wooden platform touched the surging water of the harbor coming to rest against the base of the green galley. The black seamen began to load their trade goods aboard the wooden platform, heaving sacks of colorful shells, fish, crab and pearls aboard its railed edge. I stepped aboard with Jaiet and his men gripping my only possession, the marvelous pink pearl. Jaiet tugged on a hanging rope and suddenly the wooden platform rose from the sea expelling water through its railings. I quickly seized the rail so as not to tumble over it into the rough sea waters below. We rose so quickly that my head became light and I closed my eyes in order not to faint. When I reopened them, we were standing in the center of a large spherical building surrounded by walls and had it not been for the water on the floor and the sound of the crashing water outside, I would not have known I was dangling above the ocean.

A slender elegant man with long blond hair and a sloping forehead greeted Jaiet as an old friend. They seized each other's arms enthusiastically smiling happily.

"The elves of Vastoal have awaited your coming for many months as their women whine for your jewels of the sea!" said the refined man. He was the exact opposite of my friend Jaiet, being fair, near ghostly white in complexion, with white eyes and thin pointed ears.

Jaiet, with his glistening black features, returned the greeting, "Thank you, oh great King Shaii, it is good to be among the just and noble elves once again."

"You and your men will stay at my palace and feast with me tonight!" Upon seeing that Jaiet was about to refuse, he cut him off with a stern look, "I insist on this my sea friend."

Jaiet simply nodded before the two hugged and laughed.

"Who is this you travel with?" asked the observant king looking over toward me.

"This is,"

"Say no more," interrupted the king walking toward me. "I do not see many like you," he said as if impressed by my mere appearance in his world.

"Nor I many like you," I responded.

He laughed out loud booming a zest for life throughout the round structure, "I assume not, our people left your world long ago." His face settled from his laughter and turned stern with a grip of seriousness. "I see you no longer dream among us, but are one of us."

I nodded.

"I welcome you, but be wary. There will be others here in Dream that will not do so."

His face returned to its previous state of joy, and all of us by his order followed him to a cable car which we rode across the great harbor over vines to the top of the cliffs. It was a glorious sight, and once again, like Akgaule, I had found a land I wished to never leave. Once upon the mighty cliffs, we stood under the shadow of a great tall forest. Exotic birds, insects and flowers hung all around us. It was a natural city of its own as the trees had windows, stairs and doors, because in fact the elven people of Vastoal lived within the very trees. King Shaii's home was deep within the giant jungle, the largest of the trees within it standing hundreds of feet tall and over one hundred feet wide. It was rumored among the elves that its roots reached and fed off the center of the universe. Its interior was lavish having the finest hand-carved wooden furniture, a commodity known in trade through all realms of Dream. Although Captain Jaiet had over a dozen men, the large home held us all comfortably as we sat within it sipping elven wine in deep discussion. Most of the conversations were of things and places of which I knew little or nothing, and although all I did was listen, it was one of the best conversations in which I had ever been involved. I sat in glorious intoxication listening to the Maritauns and the elf king speak of strange far-off lands and people of which I one day wished to visit myself. They discussed the stubborn dwarves of Rouige who hid within its mountains forever mining rare gems and precious metals, the kind, but mischievous fairies of the Rainbow Isles, the incessant warring men of Dream and the foul ever rising and falling hordes of mongrel. The latter being fecund and brutally unorganized lived in cycles of invasion and retreat against the realm of dreams, but to date had been held in check by the men of southern Dream who loved war as much as they. We smoked and drank out the night passing into slumber early the next morning. Having the least tolerance to the alien intoxicants native to the Lands of Dream I was the last to awaken to the melody of singing jungle birds and harmony of brightly colored buzzing insects. My room was high up the trunk of the tree bored into a giant overhanging branch. I stepped out onto my room's private terrace and gazed over the tree covered soil of Vastoal. Brightly colored tree tops stretched as far as the eye could see, from my viewpoint, not one inch of the continent was without shade. Caring little to rush from the cradle of such raw magnificence I sat down and stretched out under the wind to bear witness to the spectacle of Dream.

A knock at my door awoke me from a day slumber. An elegantly dressed elven gentleman stepped in through the perfectly oval door carrying a tray of freshly picked fruit and nuts and a finely carved wooden bottle of elven sweet wine. I soaked down my breakfast combination of juicy fruits and crunchy nuts with the sweet liquor savoring its tangy taste and tropical aroma. Although a far different cry from the traditional greasy breakfast of my former world, it was both hearty and delicious. The Lands of Dream knew not only how to caress a man's five senses, it knew how to enchant his soul.

It was customary for the elves to take a mid-morning siesta after their breakfast and to keep with their grand traditions I did the same fading into a light snooze under the sun and shade of the Vastoalian forest. One thing about the Lands of Dream I had never considered was that within it I never dreamed. Whether that was a trait of all men within its borders or only those that came from without, I did not know. But if I had to guess, I would assume that dreams were the way creatures from the waking world escaped its borders, while here in dream, no such need was necessary.

A light thud awoke me from my nap of which I was unsure how long I had been asleep. The sun was just overhead and while I knew little of its placement in regards to the day, I assumed it was sometime near noon. At first nothing seemed out of the ordinary, besides that it had become eerily quiet. Before I had fell asleep, my woodland overhang had been a lively orchestra of lighthearted birds and softly buzzing insects. I rose up and turned toward from where I had heard the thump. In the corner a small crystal pot lay on its side still gently rocking. A small obscure shadow crouched behind the translucent object. I sat up so to get a better look at my new and uninvited guest. Assuming it to be some strange woodland creature I curiously leaned toward it freezing in fear upon seeing it more clearly. Two wide bleary yellow eyes stared at me through the crystal pot eyeing me impatiently. It was one of the horrible wyner creatures that had attacked me earlier in the woods and that had followed me during my nefarious visit to the fortress of the Mind Picker. Startled and unarmed, I threw the fur lying upon me as a cover to try and tangle the beast. It easily avoided my throw bouncing from behind the fallen vase against the wall before using it to spring toward me with its teeth and claws stretched outward. I held up my arms before me to protect my vulnerable face and eyes. Its teeth sank into my arm ripping through my flesh. Blood rained down upon my face and body as the creature tied to shred through my arms so to tear into my head and chest. An arrow cut through the air piercing the small creature's skull lifting it off of me and pinning to the wall. The horrid little beast hung lifelessly from the wall like a poorly stuffed trophy left to rot. I spun my head around to see from where the arrow came finding the thin but imposing figure of King Shaii in tight leather armor covered by a long red cloak. Two more magnificently dressed elves stood at his side wearing similar armor with long forest green cloaks.

"I came to see if you might want to go along with us on a hunt, but see you have already found game."

The distinguished king walked up to the creature he killed and pulled it from its place upon the wall. He sniffed it like a dog, before making a foul expression and throwing it at the feet of the other two elves.

"We have wyners amongst us. I want every available hunter out searching the woods. Kill them on sight."

The two regal elves quickly took his command rushing off and leaving us alone with the nasty corpse.

"They are usually little more than vile spies, but this one was more aggressive than any I have ever seen, obviously sent as an assassin," stated the king.

"This is not my first encounter with the little beasts," I replied holding my arms so to stop the blood flow.

The stately king leaned down knowledgably looking over my wounds. Upon seeing their severity, he tore a large piece of red cloth from his fine cloak so to bind my wounds.

"I shall send up a maid to properly dress these wounds, then we shall discuss this matter further," he said solemnly.

Shortly after his departure, a slender young maiden with long straight hair worn in the exact same fashion as the male elves, entered my chamber after a soft knock at the door. Her hair was strawberry hanging down to her curved hips. Her soft white hands delicately smothered my cuts with a brownish salve before deftly wrapping them with damp bark. As she leaned toward me to dress my wounds a pleasant aroma of freshly bloomed flowers embraced my nostrils. She wore only the slightest of jewelry to accent her natural complexion, but I did notice she wore an exquisite deep violet pearl necklace, undoubtedly a trade good of my Maritaun friends. Although she did not speak to me before, during or after dressing my injuries, she beamed a genuine smile that lifted my heart, lightening it almost as if an angel had touched my soul.

I followed my beautiful guide through the immense tree, which served as both King Shaii's palace and residence, to a large meeting room where King Shaii, Captain Jaiet, and several other noble elves sat in conference. Upon my entrance, I was motioned to sit down at a large round table at which they all sat.

"My esteemed comrades, I would like to introduce you all to a grand dreamer who is now a resident of our world," introduced the elven king.

The stately figures at the table rose and bowed in respect. Uncertain of their customs, I did the same which caused each to return to their finely polished wood chairs. The well dressed men wore thin clad leather armor much like King Shaii, but with different color cloaks which must have in some way represented their rank or status. I noticed the guards wore green and that no one I had seen so far wore red as did the king, but what the other colors meant I was unsure. As I sat they continued with their meeting.

"As I stated earlier, with the help of our fairy folk, we have had two more wyner spottings with one escaping our archers. This is very disconcerting as we have not seen such activities since the third Mongrel Wars was cast upon the Lands of Dream several hundred years ago. I as well as many of the men at this table lost many a good friend and countrymen during the bloodshed to repel the monsters back to the deserts of Fathel. I have dispatched couriers to the folks of Vastoal, the dwarves and the Hamse House to warn of what has transpired here today."

"Might this foretell of a possible fourth invasion from the waste of Fathel?" asked an elegantly tall elf with long straight brown hair, partially covered by a silky yellow cloak.

"The men of the south have reported no sightings of troop hordes along the coast of Fathel," answered the King.

"It might be little more than a vendetta against this dreamer," replied another grand looking elf wearing a purple cloak.

"True, but the wyners do not work for money, but solely out of fear or for power," countered the wise elven king.

"The only connection we have with these little beasts are with our guest," implied another of the elves, "maybe he could shed some light where we shuffle through darkness in thought."

Seeing all eyes fall upon me, I stood up and addressed the counsel.

"First let me thank the elven people for the hospitality I have been shown during my short stay here."

The judicious group of individuals nodded kindly upon my introduction easing my anxiety as I continued to speak.

"I know not what these strange creatures want with me, but I do know that they want me as this is not my first encounter. I intend on leaving here as soon as I can affreightment passage beyond the Straight of Phylain. This single action may ease all your concerns."

"My friend," replied the great king of elves, "we have not assembled to judge you as you cannot be held responsible for the actions of others, especially a mongrel, but only to try and understand the events around us. Thousands of years of life within this realm have taught us that everything portends something, from an opening flower to a raging war. Wyners are cunning but lack the aptitude to plan such an assassination attempt. Someone else has sent this into motion and it is this mystery we ponder so."

I thanked him for his kind words and sat down. The meeting quickly ended afterward as the great leaders dispersed back to their lands wary of mongrel movements within their own country. Before I could leave I was addressed by the king.

"I have already secured you passage aboard the Jade Runner one of dream's swiftest sea vessels, but you are as welcome to stay here as you are to leave. Although the elves rarely meddle in the affairs of others, we fiercely defend the borders of the dream folk. You will be as safe here as you will be anywhere in the Lands of Dream."

"Thank you once again, but I feel I have become a burden and wish to trouble you and your people no more." I pulled out the grand pink pearl given to me by Jaiet. "Please take this as payment for the room and board, the finest I have ever had the privilege to enjoy, as well as the passage aboard the Jade Runner."

I dropped its heavy smooth mass into his hands. He eyed it for a moment rubbing its glossy surface.

"Jaiet must think quite a lot of you to give you such a deep sea treasure, why it is as fine as any I have ever seen. Why its value is enough to negotiate ten trips to the southern realm and more than enough to lure a man to slit your throat to possess it. Once you pass through the Strait of Phylain, you will pass beyond the influence of the dream folk and the dwarves into a realm ruled by war as man, mongrel and beast struggle for its domination. Since man and mongrel have dreamed here, they have done nothing but war constantly changing their borders as the land stays the same. Nothing changes upon the shed of their blood. The trees and flowers will still grow in the same place, without care for who claims to own them. If you go there for peace, I fear you may be disappointed."

"I go there to be reunited with my father."

The king tossed the mighty pearl back into my hands refusing its payment.

"Then you will need gear, weapons and clothes as the men of Dream value power more than rights. I shall have you fitted as a baron so that you might be received as well."

I thanked him again, knowing that no amount of gratitude could ever repay his generosity and placed the pearl within my pocket. I was fitted and supplied with traditional elven clothing and gear, but refused the fine sword I was offered. I had no idea of its usage and therefore it would be of little value, but mostly I wanted to be able to live in the Lands of Dream with a clean conscience. Something I could no longer do in the waking world. I parted ways with the wise elven king and the generous Jaiet and after another night upon the great forest continent of Vastoal I found myself at the docks being lowered toward a yellow ship.

It stood on top of the water magnificently sleek in design looking as if it were built to literally cut through the ocean rather than float upon it. Its crew were elven, slender but determined people of dream, most were thousands of years old while appearing as young or younger than I and yet they smiled in their dreary duties upon the wonderful ship as if it were a pleasure to perform. The captain of the grand vessel greeted me whole heartedly assuring me the wood I stood upon was as worthy of any vessel to ever touch the sea. Sails as warm as the yellow the suns overhead lifted outward embracing the swift winds of Dream.

The tall trees of Vastoal faded as our ship cut through the smooth sea at a speed I dreamed unimaginable by a boat without the power of mechanics. As the giant continent of the dream folk became only a memory, I began to wonder if Herald had not chosen more wisely than I to stay upon the untroubled shores of Akgaule with Falasia, while I wandered precariously further into Dream searching for my father. Had I overlooked happiness only to go in search of it? What of Falasia? Was there any hope of a future for us, or was I only dreaming within a dream? I pondered many things as I looked over the side of the ship and in doing so, discovered the origin of the name of the wondrous ship upon I rode. While both its hull and sails were sunshine yellow, when it cut through the deep blue sea, it left a light mirage of green where the hull touched the sea, as if running through liquid jade.

The elven clipper made quick progress propelling across the great seas of Dream upon which I saw many glorious wonders. The portside of our ship passed by the great ash covered volcanic island of Lusete home to the lonely mud people, while our starboard shared with me the rare sighting of a sea-maiden, known by those that live within Dream as the succumbs of the sea. Once a man or male humanoid was beguiled by such a lovely creature he was never heard from again. But even these grandeurs paled in comparison to sight I was fortunate to bear witness to later that night. Under a blanket of radiant constellations our small lantern illuminated ship sailed directly over the brightly lit underwater city of Maritaunia, homeland of Jaiet and his men. Bright blue illuminants pierced the depths of the sea sparkling through its waters dancing upon its surface playfully. Tall twisted spires rose high from the sea floor covered in fluorescent pastel coral. Upon the sight of its glory from above, I knew that Jaiet's heart had been broken twice, once by his love Placie and ultimately by his mother country.

My trip across the massive island riddled and great northern Turquoise Sea initially appeared as little more than a tourist expedition across the northern realm of dreams until an able seaman spotted a black vessel ahead. The small black object quickly grew upon the horizon as our captain stood at the helm steering our agile craft directly toward it.

"It's a mongrel raider!" bellowed an elven seaman.

The black galley under full sail turned its prow rocking toward us at full speed. I rushed up to the captain, "Can we out run it?"

"Aye, there is not a ship on the sea of dreams we cannot outrun," he bragged of the ship he commanded, "but as long as I breathe, no mongrel that I see shall sail the seas."

A great terror overcame me as I saw the captain steer the small Jade Runner directly toward the monstrous black mongrel monstrosity. I backed away from him in the realization that I would never be able to out reason his hatred of the mongrel. Elves rushed from below deck brandishing gleaming sharp weapons of war.

Our captain, whose hair was as white as the salt from the sea, stood high at the helm guiding our ship toward it in an apparent collision course. The greasy black vessel came within the range of my less astute human eyes flying a bright red ensign stamped with a black fist fluttering high upon its flagstaff. Once within attack range of our much smaller vessel, long determined oars dropped from portholes in the black hull rowing violently against the sea. Our captain seemingly without fear continued to steer us toward the looming black hull which stood some ten feet higher than our own. A shroud of darkness fell upon our deck as the giant ship's bronze ram barreled directly at our ship. I rushed to the center mast and seized it holding on for dear life, so not to be thrown into the sea upon the collision of the swift moving ships. When a crash seemed inevitable our composed captain jerked the wheel whipping the sleek Jade Runner alongside the towering vessel. Our prow cut through the black galley's oars upon its portside snapping them like dry twigs.

Elves rose up along the side of the ship firing arrows into the passing ship's portholes with remarkable accuracy mowing down its slave oarsmen in a ratio of roughly one per every two arrows fired. A terrifyingly deadly feat considering that both the shooter and target were moving upon a rocky sea. Our captain determined to send the ship and its crew to the bottom of the sea, quickly turned our ship around to take chase of the wounded orc ship. Suddenly oars dropped from the hull of the Jade Runner thrusting us in feral hatred after the black galley, for the orc and elf were natural enemies bent upon the destruction of one another. The Jade Runner found it quite easy to catch back up to the limping black galley upon which our captain steered toward its starboard so to mow down its last remaining oars. The Jade Runner's oars lifted within its belly just before impact. More wood snapped upon the Jade Runner's sharp bow, leaving the large black ship solely dependent upon the wind, but this time our able captain had made a blunder being both predictable and too close to the giant orc ship. As we passed through its shadow, dozens of bloodthirsty orcs leaped overboard down upon the small elegant elven ship. Some crashed against the side of the ship plummeting helplessly into the sea while others completely missed the swift vessel weighted to the bottom of the sea by heavy armor, but nearly half crashed upon the deck holding long rusty weapons of war. They were fierce warriors nearly twice as large as the thin elven sailors and surely twice as strong. Their black muscles bulged underneath their rope armor which twined around their body to protect against slashing attacks, a favorite weapon of the elf. Unarmed and lacking the experience of the warriors upon deck, I faded backwards as the brave elves around me rushed toward the invaders. Metal clashed aboard the small ship as the Jade Runner's captain steered away from the black galley so to sever the orc's reinforcements. Using brute strength, the massive orcs pushed the first wave of the elf assault backwards rushing into a counter attack. Looking like fair children in comparison to the mighty black orc, I feared my elven friends were greatly overmatched leaving me to stand alone against the merciless mongrel. But as I had much to learn about the Lands of Dream, I would discover I had nearly as much to learn about the oldest race of Dream as well. A volley of elven arrows slowed the orc's initial assault easily piercing their rope armor. While skillfully shot, most of the projectiles did not kill their targets, but yet only slowed down them for the resurge of eleven warriors that swarmed upon them like ants upon massive beetles. Fierce hand to hand combat ensued spreading the blood of both folk and mongrel and to my good fortune when the skirmish ended it was the swift elf that stood victorious. As soon as the last orc fell, our captain turned his attention back to the mighty black ship we had barely escaped.

"Release the elven fireflies!" he ordered from the helm.

Elf congregated onto the ship's center deck dipping the tips of their arrows into a hot wax type substance before igniting their tips in a copper brazier which held a light but constant flame. They lined up upon one side of the ship holding out their flaming arrows out toward the black galley which was struggling to maneuver without its full ensemble of oars. Then by stern command, fire leapt into the air arching down toward the giant black ship. Arrows riddled the deck and sails of the mighty black wooden shadow. To my surprise, the wood on the ship itself did not catch fire as it was apparently covered in an nonflammable grease, but its sails without such protection burst into hot flames. Within minutes the mongrel ship was dead in the water and for a moment I sighed in relief, but once again I would learn the cunning of the citizens of Dream was matched by only the infinity of dreams.

To my amazement three loud consecutive thumps awoke the quiet sea. Three huge net topped catapults set upon the deck of black ship fired launching a barrage of small black projectiles. My first assumption was we were to suffer a volley of projectiles released with intention of sinking us, but I was to discover something far more sinister. The projectiles rocketing toward us were not boulders or even cannon balls, but screaming goblins dressed in heavy armor holding hooks attached to the black galley by long ropes. They crashed into the wood of the hull, onto the decks and into the water falling down upon us in a blanket of strikes like a meteor shower from the sky. The ones that crunched against the ship and sank into the sea died instantly, but those that landed upon the ship quickly attached their great grappling hooks onto the ship's deck, mast and railings. Then to my horror as the goblins aboard deck clashed with elf, mighty orc upon the distant black galley began pulling our tiny ship toward it. More thuds hit our craft as more goblins crashed into our ship as the orc unleashed another volley of live missiles upon us. One landed in the mizzenmast above my head hanging itself in the rope upon it dangling to death after a short struggle. Another goblin landed near the helm crashing into its railings. It quickly recovered from its flight jumping to its feet with a long toothy grin. It apparently had broken one of its arms during its landing because it hung limply at its side as it approached our ship's captain from behind. I screamed to warn him, but failed miserably as the small beast pierced his chest with a long dirty spear. His corpse fell to the deck looking up at me lifelessly. The small creature, only about four feet in height with dirty olive skin, eyed me wildly with the excitement of its next kill. It pulled its weapon free from the captain's back as I backed away helplessly unarmed. Its long nose edged toward me as it poked its spear at me taunting me in rowdy pleasure. The mongrels are a cruel species that enjoy playing with their adversaries, especially when they do not fear or have the upper hand upon such an adversary. Using his broken arm to my advantage, I leaped to his right side barely escaping the long thrust of his spear. He laughed playfully as I dodged his blows feeling confident in the final result of our conflict. As I slowly walked away from him I saw the black shadow of the Black Galley moving toward our tiny ship as its occupants heaved at the thick rope connecting the two. If the two were to touch we would be done for as not even the resilient elf would be able to withstand the onslaught that waited upon its deck. I dove past the small goblin avoiding his spear strike once again so to reach the body of the captain. With my eyes fixed upon a shiny scimitar hanging at his waist, I rolled over to him dodging two more strikes of the goblin's spear. His second strike sunk the tip of his spear deep into the ship's upper deck making him an easy target once I had the shimmering curved blade in my hand. Unable to raise his right arm and use the buckler upon it, I cut him down with one swift blow killing my first creature of Dream. Blood oozed down the glossy blade as the lime skinned creature thudded against the deck never to rise again. As the elf began to finish off the goblin invaders I ran down the side of the deck hacking away the grappling ropes freeing us from the grip of the incoming mongrel ship. Once the ship was free of mongrel, the remaining elf onboard rushed below deck rowing us safely from the looming shadow of death. Finally dead in the water and without goblin squads to launch, our ship circled the xebec firing upon its crew until the decks were clear and then in one fail strike from the razor sharp bow of the Jade Runner, the black galley disappeared beneath the smooth glassy sea of dreams.

It was a hard fought battle that took the lives of two thirds of the Jade Runner's crew along with its able captain. Under watch of the ship's master, we continued south passing through the Strait of Phylain a wondrous strip of sea that separated the seas of the northern realm from that of the south. Standing at its two sides a few hundred feet from the straights two shores, stood two mighty statues towering hundreds of feet into the air like skyscrapers. They were of two wise figures, one a judicious elven noble in a long robe with a scroll, the other a grand looking human in full armor. On the backs of the statues were the exact images of the other making each half-elf, half-human. Of which gods or heroes their image belonged, I was unsure, but to whoever or whatever they exalted they were grand in size, appearance and workmanship and as tall as any structures I had seen in the waking world. As we passed through the long channel to the right was a great dry desert land, while on the left was a deep lush forested territory. From what I could piece together from the elven onboard, the lands belonged to the human race and were therefore chaotic at best. We skirted quickly through the long sea passage emerging into the light blue Cerulean Sea. We spent several more days upon the sea before a signal was made by the ship's master that we were about to make port. It would be the port of Wren-Henji, a large trading port open to all races save that of the impious mongrel. It was a marvelous harbor snuggled before a huge mountain that shadowed the breezy windy port in its cool form. I jumped onto the docks glad to finally get my land legs back. At first I nearly lost my footing on the stable dock having become accustomed to weeks of a swaying sea. All sorts of people in various dress and color roamed the docks laughing and talking of trade and far off lands. The elf, although of a different race of the other sailors, shook the hands of their sea brethren with glee patting each other happily. Several men greeted me as I walked along the dock as if I were a long lost friend with a sincere hospitality only spoken of in the waking world.

A young boy, no older in appearance than eleven or twelve in the waking world rushed up to me asking me a torrent of questions.

"Where did you sail from?" he asked curiously.

"Vastoal," I replied quickly.

He looked at me queerly, "But you are no elf."

"True and yet I look like you, though I am not like you either."

"So you speak in riddles," replied the gregarious boy. "That is how the wizard in the Ivory Tower speaks."

The tower's name brought back memories of the painting by my father I had studied so intently in the waking world.

"Is there such a tower near here?"

"Yes, I have been there... wait, do you know my mother?"

"No," I replied with a laugh. It was good to see that the youth of Dream were mischievous as were the children of my world.

"Well yes then, I have been there," he announced proudly.

"Is it far?"

"If you walk only a few feet from here you can see it."

"Show me," I pleaded.

The young boy, apparently having never known a stranger, took my hand and led me down the docks. Upon reaching the end of the long dock the majestic tower came into sight gleaming high upon top the mountain identical to the picture my father had painted. I stood proud knowing I now stood where my father once had in his dreams. He had not been mad at all. His only crime being that he had been aware of what the rest of the waking world had not.

"How long would it take to hike up there?"

"I know an old goat trail straight to the top. If you had a guide it would only take you a couple of days."

"I only wish I had the time to see it up close," I commended thinking aloud.

"Time… what manner of a man are you to be rushing so? If you want to do something, then do it," said the young boy, teaching me a lesson about the men of Dream. For in the Lands of Dream, men do not fret about things as do men in the waking world.

"My ship leaves port soon," I explained.

The young boy wiser than I in regard to Dream looked past me at the elven ship in which I had arrived.

"That beat-up ship? What did you do, run over a sea monster?"

"We ran into a galley of orc."

"Orcs, have you come from the dark continent of Fathel?"

"No."

"Then where did you encounter these orcs?"

"North of here."

"Mother said not to worry as the mongrel have not come north of Fathel in hundreds of years."

Unsure if I should have spoken of the mongrel or not, I covered my tracks, "I'm new to this world and your mother knows far more than I."

"So do you want me to take you there or not?" asked the boy getting to the point.

"I do not think your mother would approve."

"She would not refuse you the help you require."

It seemed the Lands of Dream were far simpler than the world in which I had been raised.

"Let me speak with the ship's master."

The young boy nodded his head and I quickly walked back down the dock to the Jade Runner. I found its master and learned from him that since his ship was going to take repairs in the harbor, we would be laying over in Wren-Henji for several days. In excitement I rushed back to the boy like a school mate given permission to stay out late with his friends. In order not to worry his mother, the young boy led me back to his home, which was little more than a straw hut built near a clear creek which emptied by waterfall into the harbor of Wren-Henji. I followed the young boy through a field of tall golden grass to a tiny hut where a man was sitting outside the front door whittling a thick piece of wood.

"Father, this man is looking for a guide to the Ivory Tower."

The man, who had light blond hair and a long mustache which hung below his chin on both sides, looked up at the tower on the mountain top. It reflected the sun glittering like a star of its own. He looked back over at me queerly.

"I've never seen a human dress like that," he commented at my traditional tree bark elven armor and brown cloak.

"I'm not from around here."

"I kinda figured that. Then I assume you know the fella that lives up there don't like guests," warned the man whose light blond hair was almost identical in color to that of the golden grass of the field. "As a matter of fact, it is rumored his wolf-dogs eat anyone who comes unannounced."

"I believe he is a friend of my father."

The man looked at me peculiarly once again as if frustrated by his son's request. He sat down his small curved knife and the block of wood which in its beginning stages looked like that of a large hairy bear-like creature.

"I guess I could show you the way up."

"Father," replied the boy quickly, "I'll do it!"

"You'll do no such thing, you don't know the way."

"But I d…" stopped the boy realizing he about told on himself.

His father eyed him with a stern look, "Get in the house and tell your mother we will have a guest for dinner tonight." He looked over at me. "We'll leave first thing in the morning, but first as part of a Zeethe tradition, you must stay overnight and tell us stories of the lands from which you come and where you have been."

I thanked him, wondering if he knew just how far away I had come. Inside I found the small cottage snug and pleasing not as in a treat to the eyes, but more in terms of comfortable to the body. Thick stacks of hay covered with deep soft furs served as both chairs and sleeping places, while a stout fire in the north wall breathed a warm cozy essence into the air. A thin curvy woman wearing a long dress with short sleeves worked at the fire stirring a copper kettle with a thick wooden spoon. As she spoke to me, she threw in oddly-shaped vegetables.

"Welcome," she said with such a fond geniality that I felt she really meant it, unlike most greetings I had become accustomed to during my life in the waking world, which were usually untruthful courtesies.

"Thank you," I said kindly.

"You're just in time for our midday meal."

I thanked her again, and by suggestion of my host I sat down, sinking deep into a fur-covered mound of hay. It was surprisingly comfortable, sinking in around the curvatures of my body while holding in its warmth.

"I've never felt hay so soft."

"It's because Jeisa fluffs it just right," replied the woman's husband.

The pretty young woman looked over with a beaming smile of pride.

I ate like a king and then snoozed the afternoon away with the entire family, which was apparently another tradition of these parts. After our nap, my host and I shared a pipe. My head soared into the stars as he explained to me the simplicity of his people's life. They farmed, hunted, slept, ate, drank and had sex, but there was one thing they did not do, and that was dream. Whether it was because they dwelled within the Lands of Dream already or that they had nothing to desire for such mental creations I was unsure, as was my host. He found my fumbling description of a dream fascinating and we discussed it for quite awhile before I could move the conversation along to something else.

"How long have you lived here?" I asked.

"I have lived here since my birth which was some hundred years ago or so."

"One hundred and ten," corrected his wife who I had thought was asleep over in the corner with the small boy.

The man laughed, "One hundred and ten," said the man correcting himself.

His answer shocked me more than that of the elves who claimed to be thousands of years old for he was human like me and yet he looked as young as I.

"Why you look no older than I!"

"How old are you?" he asked curiously.

"Thirty-six."

Both he and his wife rose from the comfort of their resting places eyeing me strangely.

"You've lived a hard life my lad," commented my host sitting before the hearth.

"Where I am from, we do not live as long as do your people."

"But you look like us," he replied in confusion.

"True, but in my land we have pollution, stress, diseases…"

"Of these things I know only of the word disease, but such things are said to be only brought on to others by dark magic," he said, trying to make sense of my words.

"You have no illnesses?"

"Not any that that I have ever known."

"You or no one in your family ever gets a cold?" I asked unbelievably.

"Oh we get cold sometimes, but we usually just throw another log onto the fire."

"No, I mean sick."

"No," he answered simply.

My head swam again, but this time not from what I had smoked, but from what I had heard.

"Do your people ever die?"

"Of course, if not we would overpopulate even the vast lands of Dream!"

"I had thought everyone here lived forever unless they were killed."

"That would disrupt the order of things as children would grow up to look exactly the same age as their fathers and there would be no urgency to ever do anything because you would have forever to do anything you wanted. We would not have wise elders or old crazy men."

"If you do not mind my asking, how long do your people usually live?"

"My father lived to be two-hundred and four."

"May Mugash have mercy upon me and not let you live so long," laughed his wife.

My guest laughed, "Hush Jeisa, or I will tell him your age!"

Her head rose from its napping place with a delightful smirk, but not a word passed her lips.

I burst into unbound laughter as it seemed the residents of Dream had wonderful senses of humor to go along with their understanding of good living. That night I had a deliciously filling meal of meat mush which was a stew mixture of slowly prepared meat, bread and vegetables.

The next morning I was awakened by my host and his son who was smiling from ear to ear as apparently he had convinced his father to let him tag along. We hiked through the gentle cool morning breeze across the field overlooking the marvelous colorful harbor of Wren-

Henji. It was colorful not in an actual spectrum of color, but in the mingling of the different cultures that anchored within its cove. It echoed with the work of men and the loading of trade goods upon the many ships that waited to sail off into Dream. We crossed dozens of tiny streams which dumped their waters into the bay below before we reached the edge of the mountains. My host led us up a rocky trail that zigzagged toward the top of the mountain when his son tugged at his side urgently.

"Father I know a quicker way."

"The only way up is the way of the obelisk."

"No, father, there is an old goat trail used by the gypsies to trade with the wizard. It is shorter and not nearly as steep."

The man turned around, looking at his son with a disapproving glare.

"How might you know this?"

The young boy's face dropped down as might a dog's tail between its legs when it knew it had done something wrong.

"I've have been up it before."

"To speak with the wizard?"

"Of course not, I wouldn't want him to turn me into a toad! To listen to the tales of the gypsies who have traveled all across Zeethe."

The father smacked the boy on the butt with the palm of his hand and urged him forward, "Then show us the way boy."

The boy smiled because he had escaped any real punishment and was being given the opportunity to lead both his father and guest, an honor for any truehearted boy from any world. He quickly led us to a small grass parted trail which trekked up through the rocks and dry soil of the mighty mountain. Although a well-traveled trail, it was an onerous hike through loose rock and shifting dirt. We spent the night under the cover of bush so not to lose all our body heat to the stars above as we slept soundly on soft furs. The next morning, my joints ached from the frost of the icy mountain air until they warmed with the labor of another long hike upward. Having brought little food, we foraged upon sweet flowers and sour roots, which although they were not all appealing in taste, were filling to the body, soul and mind. As the boy promised we arrived at the top of the mountain in just two days, which must have been an impressive feat for the father praised his son with a happy rubbing of the yellow mop on top his head.

"Here we must part, my friend, for if you choose to stir up the ire of the wizard you are welcome, but we will not test our fate so."

"Thank you both, I wish I had some way of paying you," I said, holding the smooth pink pearl given to me as a gift from Jaiet in my pocket. It would buy a simple farmer much and improve his life far more greatly than it ever could my own. I held it out as an offer to repay his kindness.

"That is a fine pearl, I do not think I have ever had the pleasure to eye a pink one before, but I cannot take that which is not mine."

"Please, you could do much with it."

"My life is as I want it."

"But you have wasted two days leading me up this mountain and surely it will take you nearly as long to return."

"Yes, but we are richer for hearing the strange tales of your land and better off because of your friendship. In the Lands of Dream, the richest man is the one with the most friends."

We gripped each other's arms as I had seen Captain Jaiet and King Shaii do and parted ways, mine toward the Ivory Tower and theirs back toward their small cottage overhanging the wondrous port of Wren-Henji.

"I wish you luck in your travels, my friend, and I hope once you find a place to settle you live as long as the men of Dream."

The man and his boy walked away holding hands without a care in the world. I waved to the two almost with tears in my eyes before continuing over the edge of the mountain looking directly at the bright white glossy exterior of the soaring Ivory Tower. It stood a mile or so beyond the edge of the mountain in the middle of a giant flowering field. Poppy, lotus and cannabis bloomed passionately in a wild mixture of bright flowers stretching as far as the eye could see or the mind could dream. I rubbed my hand upon the tops of the open flowers as I walked through them falling into a type of conscious dreamwalk. My eyelids and limbs grew heavy with an irresistible desire for leisure which brought me gently down to my knees. I slumped over happily giving in to the urge of sleep and closed my eyes before falling into the sweetest slumber I had ever experienced.

When I awoke I found myself not in the flowering fields where I had lain, but inside a small arched room with smooth white marble walls. I reached out to touch the polished surface to know if it were real or dream. The image of a cool hard surface resonated in my brain through my nervous system and I rose up knowing I was indeed awake. The room was very small and by no means elegantly decorated as it hardly contained anything besides me and the bed upon which I had rested. My stomach rumbled cramping as I rose up. I must have slept well leaving me famished as a result, but how I arrived in the room was a mystery I hoped to answer soon. A small bronze door appeared to my eyes as the only other article of interest in the plain chamber. I swung my legs down to the cold floor finding to my dismay that the fine elven boots sewn specially for me by the elven maidens of Vastoal were gone. Without any warning, the bronze door swung open startling me with the image of a badly dressed man. He had wavy white hair along with a patch of white beard on his chin in the form of a goatee and as I mentioned earlier wore clothing that was poorly matched if at all.

"I assume you have rested well?" he asked.

If I had to have guessed his age, I would have placed him somewhere in his seventies, but here in the Lands of Dream, there was no way of knowing his true age without asking.

"How did I get here?"

"My hounds drug you up here, after they found you sleeping in the fields."

I reached back and rubbed the pain in my back. They had obviously dragged me the upstairs without cushion.

"How long have I been asleep?"

"Four days, I have no real way of knowing how long you lay in the fields before my hounds found you. Once they found a man far to the east in it who had been asleep for some several months."

I jumped to my feet alarmed at my time asleep. With the night I had spent with the boy and his family and the other climbing up the Shakh Mountains along with my time in the fields before the strange man's dogs found me, I might have been gone from Wren-Henji well over a week! The Jade Runner would assume me lost by now and be long gone before I returned.

"Why would anyone build a place of residence near such things which cause people to go into such long periods of sleep?"

"I sowed most every plant in that field so to keep away those who might bring me harm."

"Seems irresponsible to me," I replied fuming about being left without passage to the city in which my father dwelled. "What if someone slept out there until they starved to death?"

"I doubt that has happened," he replied, contemplating the suggestion with his hand upon his hairy chin, "my hounds would have surely found the stench."

"How narcissistic that statement just made you sound!" I boomed, still angry at my new found dilemma.

"Did you not hear the rumors about me being a wizard who doesn't like company?"

Realizing I might have overstepped my welcome, I simply nodded to confirm his question without speaking.

"And yet you stumble up here to my home uninvited, for your own selfish reasons no doubt, and yet I'm the self-centered one. I have not seen such uncouth behavior since my days in the waking world. Why I've had advancing armies march upon my tower with more respect."

"Let me apologize for my outburst, I'm distraught about missing a very important passage to the mainland of Deazah."

"My boy," said the wizard from the Ivory Tower, "do you not realize dreamers such as you and I have an eternity for passages to anywhere we want?"

"Eternity?" I asked somewhat confused.

He saw the look of perplexity upon my face and stopped looking at me curiously.

"Why, you have no idea do you? I assumed that since you had cut your soul from the waking world you knew."

"Know what?"

"Please let us go down stairs where the accommodations are a bit more comfortable."

I followed him down a spiraling staircase so very long it seemed to stretch beyond the stars in its length. It twisted downward as into a bottomless pit swaying my mind further out with each step until I was fully gripped by objective vertigo and the base of the stairs elongated beyond my sight causing me to almost fall over the side of the stairwell into the extending abyss. My host seized me at the last moment straightening me up.

"The staircase was built as an optical illusion so that looking directly into it pulls the mind's optical perceptions far apart and you lose all balance. Don't look directly at it," he suggested.

With help from the wizard, I woozily arrived at the bottom of the tower and was offered a small cushioned chair to sit upon which was by no means as comfortable as the farmer's straw chair I had sat on some days earlier. The wizard, who dressed nothing like any magic-user I had imagined, scurried a small mouse away before retrieving a gourd from a dusty shelf. His aged hands humbly poured me a cool elixir which I looked at apprehensively. Although it had been sitting in an open gourd at room temperature, the liquid in my cup was ice cold to the touch. I sniffed it, nervously unsure if I could trust the strange man or not.

"It is not poisoned. I could have murdered you in your sleep or pushed you to your death on the stairs if I wanted you dead."

Since this sounded reasonable, I disregarded my first concerns and took a small sip then after finding it pleasing to the tongue, I drank heavily from my cup as he spoke.

"I am used to receiving uninvited dreamers up here, thanks to that confounded record keeper Alzoond, but not from those who have already discovered the secret to the Lands of Dream."

Almost lost in my drink, I pulled my attention from the cup in my hand, "I search for my father, and I believe you might have met him."

"Ah... a second generation dreamer, your father must be proud." He paused for a moment as if trying to remember something from long ago. "I wish my own son, Randal... had been prone to folly as was I. But enough of me, what is your father's name?"

Upon the mentioning of my father's name, the elderly wizard's eyes lit up like a lamp plugged into a wall inside a dark room.

"Yes, I can proudly say I know your father and can count him as a friend and ally in a world that will never altogether accept us, as the gods who move the forces in this realm both fear and envy us."

"Why would a god be jealous of or fear common men as you and I?"

"They fear our knowledge of science and our gift of unconditional immortality. The gods will only live forever as long as the men of Dream worship them."

"Immortality, what do you mean? I spoke with a farmer here and he led me to believe we will live very long lives, but he never mentioned anything about living forever."

"That is because he is a child of Dream with a body of flesh and blood, so although the children of Dream age more slowly than men from the waking world because this world's cosmic position in space does not pull upon the life force of its inhabitants as strongly as does our homeland, they do not live forever."

"What of the elves? I have met some thousands of years old and yet they looked younger than I."

"The length of a life here, much as in our own world, depends on the strength of the soul. The elf can live five thousand years, the fairy six thousand, the dwarf seven hundred, humans two hundred and fifty, the dragon have yet to show a limit, while those with a small soul like the mongrel might only live for forty years. I've done some extensive study in this field and I believe there is a correlation between soul strength and a race's aptitude toward violence. The most peaceful races, the fairy and the dragon, live the longest, while the mongrel who relish war daily live the shortest lives of all."

"What about us?" I asked, curiously regarding my own life expectancy.

"My son, you have already died," he said frankly. "We have found our eternal heaven."

Upon his declaration my heart froze or at least it felt as if it did, considering I might not even have one. Upon seeing my shock he explained his statement further.

"When you cut your soul off from the waking world to stay here, your soul left your body and came here, leaving your external shell cold and lifeless on the other side."

"But I sweat and get tired here as I always have."

"Your mind has recreated an image of a new body here so that you might touch and taste, live and die."

"Die... but you said we are immortal," I said, correcting him.

"Yes, since we have no body for the forces of time and space to drain, we shall not age here. I am the same age now as when I came here several decades ago, but our minds have physical limitations and if they ever perceive death, our consciousness will shut down and we will simply fade away lost to the weave of space and time for all eternity."

"So neither you or I have a body?"

"I believe, if we could harness the depths of our mind, we might be able to pass through walls or even become immune to death itself."

"Can the gods be killed as you and I?"

"Yes, although their physical limitations are far beyond that of man, a great warrior by the name of Pectus once sought to become as the gods and live among them at the edge of Dream, where they continue to stretch its borders with their thoughts. It is believed by many that the gods of Dream are in actuality the very first dreamers of the universe who carved out this world with their minds near the beginning of space and time, but now they care not to share their secret of immortality with the children of dream." Dry of throat, he paused to take a drink before continuing, "So Pectus set out to take what the gods would not freely give him. He had gained his fame in the first mongrel wars using two fragile but swift razor swords upon his victims by cutting them down with such speed it was said his blades were invisible to even the quick eye of the ancient elf. He challenged the gods to duel him claiming he would entertain the acceptance of any of the gods, whether it be those of war or peace. Not wanting to set a precedent, while having little to gain and much to lose in a duel with a common man, the gods let his calls be unheard. So he journeyed west, far beyond the lands of man, folk and mongrel to the edge of Dream and scaled the monstrous mountains of Zurwuael which are said to make this very mountain look like a dirt mound in comparison to their might. Once a year the priests of the gods travel to these mountains and bring much tithe to their respective gods in livestock, treasure and trade goods so the gods may continue to carve out more strange lands and creatures without concern for idle tasks. Pectus disguised himself as one of these monks and traveled to the ice temple of the once great dream god Dxeegut. There in front of this god's greatest priests Pectus revealed his true identity and challenged him to a duel to the death. Angered by the man's audacity and not wanting to lose the respect of his worshipers, the god accepted his challenge wielding an ice sword twice the length of a normal man's height. Although far stronger than Pectus, the great god underestimated his foe and after a mighty battle fell to the swift razor blades of his opponent before his very servants. So to keep the secret of their mortality from the minds of their servants across the Lands of Dream, instead of exalting Pectus and making him a god as well, they set their fanatical servants upon him and the witnessing monks of Dxeegut slaughtering them like goats on the altar. While the gods killed Pectus and most of the priests of Dxeegut, a few of the enlightened priests escaped and spoke of what transpired."

"I have much to learn," I replied overwhelmed by his insightful theories and fantastic stories.

"Even if you or I embraced an eternal life, the secrets of the cosmos are as vast as the ever expanding universe, making knowledge a perpetual entity. This is the curse of the philosopher for he desires to understand all, an impossible task."

"I hope you do not think me rude after I ask you this, but why do you stay up here alone like a hermit?"

"I shelter myself not from the Lands of Dream, but from the minions of the gods who still seek retribution for the conduct of my own separation of soul. I scorned Phean himself, the god who dreamed mankind here some millenniums ago. See..." he said lecturing me, "men such as you and I are the newest race to enter Dream and to personally do so, I fooled ancient Phean some many years ago and he has never forgotten. It is against his assassins that I have built high upon this lonely mountain top, sowed the flowers that bring on coma, bred giant war hounds to guard my doorstep, created disabling illusions within my own abode and preformed acts of science disguised as magic to cast fear in the hearts of those who might want to bring me harm."

"But does not all this make you a prisoner in the very world you came to be free?"

"I travel all across the Lands of Dream anonymously visiting its wonderful cites and strange new lands, and I have many visitors such as your father, the gypsy king, and who knows, once you find what you are searching for, maybe you'll come see me every once and awhile too."

"Oh most certainly, for it would certainly be like school... with you the professor and me the student."

"Fine, I would be glad to show you what I have learned, but before I retire, what of your father?"

"He led me here through my dreams, but now that I am here, I know but one place where he might be, Celpahia."

"Ah yes, Celpahia. It has always been a favorite of your father's. The last time I spoke with him, he had taken a wife from the folk and built a home along the Manikalra River basin."

"A wife?" I said surprised to hear my father had taken a woman other than my mother as a wife.

"Oh dear," he said concerned, "maybe I shouldn't have said anything and given your father the opportunity to explain it better. She is as mesmerizing as the stars on a cool cloudless night. It was a good match as your father earned the respect and blessing of Shaii the elven king before wooing her with his poetry and paintings. The elf forbid their kind to marry humans since they normally live twenty times their expectations, but dreamers are an exception because our life has no known limits. For a dreamer such as you and I, we should follow the example of the elf and forget about marriage to humans, for its future holds nothing but sorrow."

The talk of marriage brought one image to my mind, the fair and lovely Falasia.

"What of the residents of Akgaule?" I asked, suddenly concerned about the life expectancy of the woman I now knew I loved. "How long do they live?"

"Akgaule? Hmm…" he said pondering the question intently, "they have no specific race of people, but are more immigrants from all over Dream. Every place is different in its aging affects, but I assume the primary factor in such a determination would be their race."

My heart sank, for although she was far more beautiful than any woman I had ever seen in person or picture, she did appear to be human, as without clothes, I got a very good look her… at all of her. My host perceived my sudden look of dismay.

"You have not met someone there you fancy have you?" he asked.

"No," I said lying.

He looked me over as if he didn't believe my answer, "Well good, for as I understand, the people of Akgaule do not pledge themselves to one lover."

"She is different," I answered quickly without thinking.

"The woman you do not like?" he replied playing with me.

"Yes."

Since it was early in the morning, my host went to bed in the top of his tower, while I who had rested enough for several days stayed awake and read through his many journals of Dream. He had traveled to the far east stopping at the Rim of the Unknown, west as deep as the Land of Lights, north to the great cosmic whirlpool and south to the tip of Zeethe. In his travels he had hunted with kings, escaped bizarre monsters, slept as a guest in the finest of palaces and discovered natural wonders never seen by man. He was a proficient writer having filled hundreds of volumes with his studies and travels thus keeping me actively occupied until the suns of Dream brought my host to the base of the tower. As we ate a light breakfast of berries and leaves, I spoke with the wizard earnestly about being a dreamer, something I knew little about.

"If we have no physical body, why must we sleep at all?" I asked, pondering his long night of sleep.

"Just as the body becomes weary with time, so does the mind, soul or conscious… whichever you believe your thoughts to be. Time drains energy and it is through sleep that we revitalize ourselves. It is the pleasures of eating, drinking, sleeping, sex and dream that revive the soul. It is these five things and only these five things that a conscious being needs to be truly content."

We strolled along his mountain which stayed abandoned purely out of respect for his powers by the residents in the harbor below. He was wise, noble and kind, a combination of true royalty and before I left his company, I considered him a friend on which I could depend in the Lands of Dream. Given a small note with a green wax seal, I hiked back down the old goat trail past the harbor of Wren-Henji along a small dirt road leading into the forest of Zeethe. The note I carried was actually a letter of introduction to a man he called the gypsy king. The gypsies of Zeethe lived along a massive mountain range called the Azoul. It was rural with few residents and therefore ideal for the vagabonds that called no specific place but their roaming wagons home.

The sunlight trickled down upon me through the breaks in the trees as I hiked along a rural wooded trail. The long and twisting trail passed through long rocks creating natural tunnels, through cascading waterfalls and under massive tree roots. It was a journey of absolute beauty, one where I nearly fell a hundred times as I stared at the miraculous wonders in delight. I traveled happily through the breathtaking forest with a spring in my step that I had not had since I was a child playing hopscotch. Then suddenly I came upon a man staring at me from the top of a giant rock. He sat like a monkey with his hands dangling between his legs in a crouch watching me intently. He wore a medley of bright clothes that bore color from every stripe of the spectrum. On top of his head he wore a yellow bandanna type cloth.

"Hello," I said, embarrassed to be caught frolicking like a whimsical child.

"Are you one of those mad hermits from the Mhorhaen?"

"No, I'm just come from Wren-Henji," I said, a little sensitive about being called insane after my incarceration in Belmount Institution for the Mentally Insane.

"I see you do not openly carry a weapon," he stated, touching a sword hanging from his belt.

From it hung a brilliantly curved blade with a shiny handle encrusted with bright red rubies. Suddenly a wave of fear rushed over me as I realized he might be a highway bandit or worse an assassin in league with those who wished me harm.

"Most men I've met around here without weapons are sorcerers… you use magic to protect you?"

His line of questioning added to my sudden discomfort and for a moment I thought of bluffing him by claiming to be a great wizard with an arsenal of deadly spells, but knew if he called my bluff I would be unable to muster any sort of pretense to convince him otherwise.

"I'm not looking for any trouble."

"Do you realize you walk through a woodland not far from the Mhorhaen where vicious creatures greater than man still reign?"

"I'm looking for the gypsies."

"The gypsies have few friends outside their own and I do not believe you are counted as one."

"I have a letter," I declared reaching into an inner pocket.

As I reached into my pocket the man leaped from the rock and rushed up to me with a speed of near light bringing the tip of his ruby scimitar at the base of my neck.

"Hold still there…" he ordered looking me over again, "if you speak anything that sounds like an incantation I will gut you."

A lump froze into my throat rising up against the point of the blade leaving my voice paralyzed in terror.

"Hand it to me slowly," he said cautiously.

I pulled the letter out as he ordered and extended it cautiously to a hand that snatched it away. He eyed the seal, then looked at me before opening it and reading the contents. His face changed from suspicion to jubilance as quickly as a blink of an eye.

"My dear friend, let me apologize for my earlier behavior. A gypsy can never be too careful." He rushed up and hugged me as would a long-lost friend. "I know your father well! Come," he urged, "let me take you to our camp for some tall tales, good food and strong drink."

We walked a couple of miles at most before we came upon the lively camp of the gypsies snuggled in a small ravine at the foot of the lofty Azoul Mountains which stood so high into the air they blotted out the warm sun creating a cool-winded valley below. Flickering fires, gaudy wagons and groups of laughing residents filled the sprawling encampment. Gypsies in all sorts of wild dress lay, sat and stood around spaced out fires in happy conversation. Some played games, while others told stories, but all were enjoying a period of rest that all gypsies relished after a long day of travel. I followed my guide and was offered a fine place of rest at the base of a roaring campfire. The warmth that radiated from its flames and hot coals melted the cold mountain air away leaving me in a state of soporific contentment. The man with the yellow head scarf stood up next to the bonfire and introduced me to its residents.

"This is the son of our friend the grand dreamer!"

A round of cheers followed his introduction followed by a flurry of pats on the back and offers to share hardy drinks, food seasoned by open flame and odd-shaped pipes to smoke. Feeling as welcome among the rabble of gypsies as I had with anyone, I drank from several mugs, smoked from three different pipes and gnawed upon a juicy bone with dangling meat.

"Ah!" yelled the man in the scarf, "talk with him now, for after all that in a moment he will not remember a thing!"

Everyone including I, burst out in wild uninhibited laughter until I choked upon the food I was chewing bringing the laughter to roars as tears poured from my eyes. Knowing I was a dreamer, questions of my world overran the residents of the fire at which I sat and before long had them all cackling insanely at my stories of strange cars, metal planes and weird customs. For the first time in my life, I was the life of the party and I loved it. In the waking world, I had always been reserved in social situations and in turn I had always felt myself an outsider. As the tales continued, the night stretched on and the crowd around my fire grew while the world in which I stood distorted. Faces began to melt and everyone began to orbit around the fire like planets around the sun as the fire rose high into the sky biting at the very stars. I collapsed backwards falling into a bouquet of soft hands that caressingly lowered me to the supple earth. Laughter and dancing continued around me as I stared from the ground into the cosmos wondering from which star I had escaped. I had never known such pleasures as those I had experienced in my short time within the splendid Lands of Dream and knowing I had many more ahead left me with a smile planted on my face as I succumbed to the wonder of a dreamless sleep.

A chilly morning dew sat upon the fur that had been thrown over me to protect me from the frosty night. Bundles of furs lay all around the campsite rising and falling slowly with the breaths of those beneath. I pulled my arm out of the warmth of fur and seized a long stick to stir the fire. Red glowing embers came to life radiating an inviting burst of heat upon my face, hand and arm. A hand tugged at my fur signaling me to follow. I stood up and followed the gypsy from the woods inside a tall wagon. He offered me a seat and sat across from me.

"What brings you to us?" he asked.

"The wizard from the Ivory Tower told me I should speak directly to the gypsy king."

"I do not consider myself a king, as the gypsy run more like a pack of wolves, letting the strongest lead it. As long as I am that person, then I shall lead them."

"Forgive me."

He gracefully nodded for me to continue.

"You have met my father?"

"A fine man and a rare outsider who has earned the trust of the gypsy. I have had the pleasure of adventuring with him more than once."

"I have not seen him outside my dreams in many years."

"If you are a third the man your father is, you're fine with me."

"Thank you," I said of his complement to my father because in the waking world I had heard very few of him, "the wizard said you might be able to help me with passage to Celpahia."

"We gypsy have little to do with the sea, but I do have a few friends who live by its law. We're traveling to Carlonien for trade, but after ensuring my people make its outskirts safely, I could lead you to edge of the Emerald Sea and board you upon a vessel heading to port there."

"Oh thank you, that would be wonderful."

"Until then, we could use an extra hand along the way to Carlonien."

"How about two hands?"

He smiled, "But before you can travel with us, the Old Hag must approve of you."

"Old Hag?"

"Hag is a term of endearment to the gypsy for it is believed that the great mother of the gypsy was a sea hag who charmed a man from the land and so we are not men at all, but simply the gypsy. It is because of the blood of our ocean mother that we cannot find one place to make us happy, but roam the land like waves in the sea. To honor this, the title Old Hag is given in respect to the eldest woman. Her place of honor exceeds even mine, for she counsels us all."

We walked through the cool morning breeze to a small wagon at the end of the formation. I waited for the gypsy king to enter, but he stood back motioning me in.

"The words of the Old Hag are only to be heard by those to whom they belong. You must go in alone."

I pushed a thick damp curtain aside and stepped into the dark interior of the old wagon finding it dimly illuminated by long-burnt candles. A rainbow of wax had dripped inside the wagon having collected in clumps like the mineral deposits of a deep subterranean cavern. A very old woman seated behind a small table with sagging bags beneath her eyes peered into my own and I felt a cold chill enter my soul as if she had looked right into it. Her eyes had seen a lot during her life in Dream.

"Let me see your hand," she said firmly.

I put my hand out in front of her and she stared into it deeply feeling the grooves upon my palm with her loose wrinkly fingers. She studied it in complete silence for what seemed like an eon before she spoke.

"You have a good soul, but you have brought a great doom upon the Lands of Dream in your coming, a calamity that might swallow us all in a reign of malicious evil."

"I don't understand. I came here in peace. I mean no one any harm."

"It is already set into motion, whether you stay or go is of no matter," she said dryly.

"What could I have done to bring on this doom? What am I supposed to do to reverse it?"

"Your hand tells me only your fate, not what shaped it or how to alter it."

"So it can be altered?"

"Nothing is set into stone, for even the rocks of the earth can be melted at the core of the world and cooled into a different shape, but it takes much energy and effort. That is all."

Upon her final statement she closed her eyes and lowered he head into her palms becoming motionless like a statue. I stepped from her wagon bewildered by her statement, and upon seeing the gypsy king, I was told I had been accepted by the Old Hag and was now an honorary gypsy. He refused to hear my fortune claiming such an action would result in dire consequences and that I should speak of it to no one, especially a gypsy. How a great doom could be turned into a dire consequence I was unsure, but out of respect to their ways, I said nothing else of it, although it weighed heavily upon my mind.

Over the next two weeks, I learned that although the gypsy had a vivid vest for life and were considered vagabonds, they worked hard during the day earning their nights of folly by firelight. My soft hands knotted up with calluses, while my back ached from the loading and unloading of various gear of the gypsy trade from their many wagons. We traveled by wagon train through the day upon wobbly carts through thick forests and open plains until the fall of night when the gypsy knew how to live a life of leisure. The gypsy survived solely upon a fierce loyalty to their own and the cunning of an inborn wit. They sold trinkets, fortunes and of course entertainment setting up a festival at visiting towns that would have humbled even the greatest of circuses from the waking world.

I spent two weeks in hard labor and spontaneous pleasure working harder than anyone in camp in order to keep my mind from pondering the fortune of the Old Hag. Upon setting up the gypsy carnival on the edge of Carlonien, the capital city of the Yeathon, the gypsy king and I took two mules and left for the coast of Zeethe. The Yeathonian people were known for their cavalry being the greatest horse riders in all of Dream. Powerful men upon great steeds sneered at us as we passed through the great plains of Yeathon upon short mules. My guide laughed happily and waved at each of the great horsemen in good spirits much as does a jester in a king's court. Although whimsical in nature, I had seen firsthand the speed of which he could use a sword and knew while he seemed a harmless fool, he was actually a wise and deadly man.

We traveled as do hobos living on what we had and what the land provided. It seemed the gypsy had few friends but themselves, but as we rode it appeared that this bothered my guide little if at all. On the fourth day, a sheet of smooth blue green appeared in the distance and before long I stood at the shores of Zeethe staring into the clear green waters of the Emerald Sea. Soft red sand separated the land from the sea protecting the rich soil of the mainland from the green waves with their crystal white crests. The gypsy king unraveled a giant yellow flag with strange markings, which he rearranged with clamps, creating odd symbols before attaching the finished product to a long pole he had fashioned out of three rods. Then he jammed the flag's tip into the red sand leaving it to flutter in the wind before lying down on the beach and waiting as if taking a nap. Apparently the flag was to signal passing ships we were looking for passage, which direction we wished to go and how much we were willing to pay. Several vessels passed along the coast in the distance but none stopped or appeared to notice us, and just when I began to fear they could not see our flag, a ship anchored near the coast and dropped a dinghy into the water. Its men paddled to the shore and beached before us. The men were haggard and dirty with scraggly beards and ragged clothing. They appeared as little more than true sea hobos, not anything like the brightly colored and well dressed gypsy, who only lived like tramps. The gypsy king spoke with the men and then pointed at me several times before they parted ways. He walked over to me and spoke with a whisper so the men preparing the small boat could not hear.

"These are buccaneers of the worst sort who make a living upon the sea as best they can. We gypsy have much in common with them, although I do not approve of their methods. They are a superstitious lot and so I have told them you are a great and powerful wizard whom they should not bother." He looked over to be sure our conversation stayed private. "I have already paid for everything… do not show any gratitude or kindness in front of these men," he warned, so I would not thank him for his help. "The less you talk the better, and if you have to, keep it simple, be rude and speak in riddles or something, it will add to your mystique. The trip should only take a couple of days and I doubt they will give you much trouble because I explained to them you turned a group of us into snakes for doubting your powers, but take this just in case." He secretly handed me a curved dagger and a small pouch of powder before bowing before me humbly. "Keep the blade for a final resort, but if they ever doubt your power, throw some of the powder. It is a creation given to me by the wizard of the Ivory Tower."

I hid both in my cloak and then nodded at him slightly before stepping aboard the small grimy ship. I could feel the men's eyes upon me, but whenever I looked over their eyes would quickly avert, but nevertheless, they were there staring into me. I suddenly wished for the oozing black sailors from the underwater city of Maritaunia, for they were a noble people quite unlike the devious men with whom I now consorted. Once upon the deck of the ship, I found it in worse condition than the dinghy being covered in moss, fungus and dirt. The men on deck congregated together for a minute, none willing to look at me until the captain of the ship broke up the group, ordering them to perform their various duties. The men ran along climbing up ropes and sails, and once the anchor was pulled, we set sail for the coast of Deazah, the country that held one of the largest cities in Dream and my destination, Celpahia. I kept to myself most of the first day speaking only to the captain when he spoke to me. I sat in my dirty cabin unable to sleep due to the excitement of being so close to Celpahia, as well as from the filth I sat in and the fear of the men I had taken passage with. So to calm down, I went up onto the deck to get some fresh air and stumbled upon two sailors on watch speaking in the shadows of the prow. I couldn't make out their faces, but I could see one was big and fat, the other short and skinny.

"What of em?" said the skinny man, "he's flesh like the rest of us. Why we've fought nasty orcs, dozens of em wit spears and swords and we didn't cower then. And all of you want to let one man sitting among all us ripe for the pickin go."

"Aye, but them wizards are a crafty lot. They turn you into things and curse you and the sorts," replied the heavy shadow.

"You need to be turned into something. Somthings that's not so cowardly!"

"Ah you talk big when he is below, but I bet you ain't no braver than the rest of us," challenged the big sailor.

"Why, I'd go below right now and cut his throat, but you bunch of bums would claim he fell on my knife," said the little man in his defense.

"Then say something to him tomorrow in front of everyone, we'll see how braves you are then."

Fearing I might be seen or heard, I slinked back to my cabin and boarded the door. It appeared things were getting out of hand and if I wanted to keep them under control I would have to back down the little man if he did choose to challenge me in front of his peers. But since I was only one man, it could not be of a physical deterrence for they outnumbered me thirty to one. The only chance I had was to play against their superstition and strike fear into their hearts with the great magical powers I did not possess.

I knew hiding below would only work for so long, so around midday I went above deck and stood overlooking the prow. The ship upon which I stood while nasty and dirty, sailed over the beautiful Emerald Sea elegantly as might a horse through a virgin field. Suddenly a short skinny sailor with only about half his teeth crawled up onto the fore of the ship with me.

"So, you're a great wizard?" he asked nervously.

I spun around with all the confidence I could muster and spoke toward him as if he were nothing more than an insect.

"Has the captain sent you up here to bring my lunch?" I asked.

Several of his fellow sailors were watching us from ladders leading from the front of the ship, with their eyes barely peeking over the edge so to dodge any spell I might throw in anger. I could hear them laugh when I suggested he was nothing more than an errand boy. He lost his confidence for a moment and might have backed away had his peers not been looking on.

"I think a lot of you wizards are full of it and I ain't speaking of magic," he said touching the hilt of a short sword hanging from his hip.

Things were starting to spin out of control and unless I wanted to be hanging by my neck from the mast I needed to back this man down and quick.

"What curse would you prefer I cast upon you and your family?"

Several of the men below disappeared upon my threat and the little man almost scurried off himself, but he had seen hard times and it appeared it was going to take more than hollow intimidations to send him running.

"I ain't got no family and if you were such a powerful wizard, you'd know that."

"The curse I speak of affects not only the living, but the dead."

He backed up for a moment and then a smirk of evil crossed his face, "ain't no powerful wizard going to take any lip from a grubby sailor like me. I'm beginin to believe you ain't no wizard at all, but one of them rich merchants pretending cause your too cheap to pay for bodyguards."

I fingered a handful of the powder given to me by the gypsy king and prayed to whatever god would listen to let it save me from the trouble I found myself in. To be so close to my father and to end up dead at the hand of dirty pirates would be an ending that would haunt me until the end of time, if there such was an ending to its entity. He pulled the sword from his belt and edged toward me eyeing my hands. It glistened on the dirty ship, being the only thing I had seen that appeared even remotely clean upon it. I lifted up my hand and threw the powder at him screaming a word that had no meaning that I knew save that it sounded somewhat mystical in nature.

"**Zabooza!**"

The powder flew into his face and before me and his comrades, his face and body ignited into blue fire. It roared upon his skin and he screamed in agony and fell over the edge of the prow onto the center deck below. The magical blue fire quickly spread onto the deck flickering up masts and onto ropes. The captain came out of his cabin onto the poop ordering his men to abandon ship. The men ran about screaming in terror, for to die by fire upon a great ocean of water was a great fear of the sailor. Dinghies lowered to the sea below full of terrified men and before I knew what had happened I was standing alone upon the soiled ship which was quickly being engulfed in flames. I ran about looking for another escape boat, but found I had been left to single-handedly deal with the mess I had created. The magic flames ran up over the sails and throughout the ship trapping me on the poop ready to engulf me within it, then suddenly it disappeared leaving everything it had touched unharmed. The skinny man I had thrown it upon first stood up upon the main deck realizing he wasn't dead. I pulled the curved knife from my cloak and rushed to the main deck to finish him before he could come to his senses and defend himself. Upon seeing me coming, he fell to his knees and began to beg for forgiveness.

"Please oh great and mighty wizard, forgive me for ever doubting your magnificent magic! I am but a simple minded man, who knew no better!" he screamed in tears.

Unsure what to do with him, I was tempted to have him jump overboard to his acquaintances, where they might pull him aboard the small craft which were fading into the distance behind the ship we stood, which continued to sail without crew toward Deazah. But I knew nothing of sailing and knew if I was to make it, I would need at least one man of the sea.

"I should shrivel you up into a pile of dung and let you smell yourself for eternity, but in doing so I would have to control this ship by magic, a very tiring task," I bluffed.

"Oh please my lord! Let me do that for you, if you will let me live, I will serve you as long as you wish!"

Knowing I would only be able to trust him as long as he feared me, I said the following, "Steer this ship to the Celpahia and upon making its port, you can have your miserable life and this rotten ship along with it."

"But master," he replied nervously, "I can sail this vessel with some trouble across the great sea, but to navigate down the Manikalra through Nauria's Caverns with only one man as the crew is a task far too great to ask of one even as loyal as I am to you!"

"Just get us to the coast so I may be rid of you and if you give me no more trouble between now and then, I will send you on your way as you look now."

"Oh thank you oh great one!" he yelled in happiness before running to the helm to steer the rickety ship. Another day passed before the welcoming shore of Deazah came upon the horizon. Both the sailor and I gasped in relief upon its appearance hoping we would both part ways without him cutting my throat or me changing him into some strange insect. A good distance from the shore, the man rushed to the front of the prow and dropped anchor. I looked at him strangely as we were still nearly a mile out.

"Take us on in!" I ordered.

"But master, the water is shallow here we will run aground."

"Do we have any smaller crafts left to row ashore?"

"No master," he answered nervously, "they were all taken when the crew ran from your mighty magic." He fumbled with his throat as if too nervous to get the next words out. "Could you not use your magic and fly across?"

I looked at him and then turned around unsure what to say for I did not want him to doubt my powers again.

"Not unless I turn you into a giant bat and ride you across."

He stepped backwards terrified of the thought, afraid to offer any more suggestions that he might become an unwilling part.

"Well since it is such a nice day and I do not wish to drain all my strength, I'll swim to shore, I suppose."

The dirty little man looked at me like I was a crazy fool, but still being fearful of my magic he did not dare speak a word against my plan. Moving as quickly as I could without appearing to be running, I gathered what few belongings I had and jumped overboard into the cool water. The momentum from of leap plummeted my body deep beneath the surface. I struggled against my heavy wet garments swimming upward toward the murky light while painfully holding my breath. I gasped for dear life upon reaching the surface looking up at the little man who watched me curiously. I began to swim toward the coast to hopefully make the shore before the man above me saw my ridiculous situation and decided to call my bluff. My earlier threats must have really scared him, for while I toiled through the ocean treading water like a fool, the little sailor scrambled about on deck of the ship looming over me still trying to escape my wrath. I struggled against the waves trying to hold my head above water, as the shore seemed to recede further back with each stroke I took. The small ship began to scoot away from me as well as its single passenger opened its sails and pulled away to dissolve into the distant open sea. The once smooth ocean began to churn fiercely bubbling up like a massive pool of champagne as the surf crashed into the coral reef below tossing me around like a loose buoy. My arms and legs began to tire from my struggle between life and death, with death gripping at me from below and life taunting me from dry land. My mind urged my failing limbs on as I could not bear the thought of dying only a few feet from the coast of the land my father now called home. Cool salt water rushed into my eyes, ears and mouth trying to smother me from every orifice as my head bobbed up and down, first above and then below the surface until I began to feel myself losing both the physical and mental resources to carry on. The edge of the sandy beach was the last thing I saw when my arms and legs completely quit functioning and I sank to the bottom of the sea which was barely ten feet deep. My feet drifted slowly down as I held the last breath of air my lungs would ever know descending into tangle of bright coral and rock. And so I edged my head backward staring straight up at the murky sky above and let out my last exhalation of breath. Painful salt water rushed into the empty passages of my lungs and so to die peacefully I closed my eyes and bowed my head floating with my arms and legs protruding outward like those of a lifeless scarecrow. As I commenced to fade into whatever waits on the other side of consciousness something rushed underneath me propelling forward like an errant torpedo. I rocketed to the surface feeling the air brush against my face as I glided across the sea without a boat as might a real wizard toward the coast. Between my legs lay a powerful dolphin carrying me through the water like a cowboy would ride a horse upon land. The animal carried me to the beach leaving me gasping for air as I violently vomited the sea from my lungs. Rising from the brink of death, I waved at the kind creature which nodded back with a chirp before vanishing underneath the sea.

Relieved to still dwell among the living, I lay on the beach regaining my strength. It came back slowly as the day wore on replenishing my soul under the cover of night and a constellation as grand as those we as men see in the waking world could only see through a telescope. Strange oddly colored planets, rocketing fire-bearing comets and swirling black holes moved within the cosmos above turning the sky above into a multicolored circus of astronomy.

The next morning I awoke with the suns and I looked inward toward a vast continent, a single man against a mighty unknown. My legs carried me over rolling hillsides, babbling brooks, waving fields and fertile valleys without any sign of civilization. I hiked across the stunningly beautiful continent for seven days in quiet solitude with the only voice I heard being my own as I thought out loud in the attempt not to lose my sanity in the silence I walked. Even as I walked along alone, I would have taken a land of dream where I was the only soul left rather than return to the loud horns, choking pollution and cutthroat business dealings of the waking world. Upon my eighth day on dry land, I found a wide river basin which cut through the land like a winding snake across a tall grass field. Tall weird plants stood high along its rim protecting its banks from the naked eye of man, so I followed it along watching the center of the river to guide my trek. Then what I saw next justified all the travails I had endured so far, wonderfully colored ships of all shapes and sizes navigated up and down its currents creating a highway of astounding cultural exchange as many different races and nations headed to and from the grand trading port of Celpahia. Many of the ships ran flags with strange markings up their masts, but having barely escaped my last journey upon a ship, I thought it best to stay on land so I waved off their offers and continued along the bank on foot. Nine more days of quiet travel and amazing scenery led me to the glamorous glittering city of Celpahia. Its green copper domes and white stone buildings glared in brilliance upon the twisted Manikalra beckoning me to finally reunite with the man I had once called my father.

Part IV
Dreams Change to Nightmares

People moved happily through the streets chatting idly at street corners and waving at me happily as I passed with wide curious eyes. I soaked in the city's residents straining each of my senses to their limits in order not to miss a single word, person or sight along the way. The roads of the bustling city were an extensive network of junctions, forks and alleyways that left my mind boggled with limitless options until I finally gave in to the pleasures of the place stopping at a street bar which had tables along the cobble road to sit and enjoy a drink. A kind woman served me a cold stout which I paid for with a single coin given to me by the gypsy king that I had not lost to the Emerald Sea. The drink sat heavily against my tongue clinging to my taste buds as I gulped it from a tall mug in large swigs as did the other men and women drinking near me.

"Ah, a fellow dreamer, might we sit together and share conversation and drink?" said a voice from a street side table.

I turned to see from where the voice came and upon first glimpse of its originator, my heart nearly fell into my stomach. His appearance was so bizarre that it was beyond anything that I could have imagined. His skin was pale, bordering on being transparent and even from a distance of about twenty feet, I could see some of his internal organs. From what I could tell from his exposed skin, his body was completely hairless, but what made him the strangest being that I had ever seen, was that he didn't have any external features, such as eyes, ears, a mouth or nose. His face was completely round and covered with several random orifices. He seemed a nice enough fellow from his demeanor, but after I met him, I was glad that he didn't have eyes to see my initial reaction when he first approached me.

"Might I buy you another one?" he asked.

I nodded, unsure what else to do and in response to my quiet reply, he raised two fingers to a young lady in a full-bodied dress and then sat down across from me. Since he did not have eyes, I was unsure how he knew I had nodded my head or that a waitress stood near us so that he could place an order. While he did not appear to have any optical organs, he sat down with a grace equivalent to that of a sighted person. Two more drinks appeared upon our table and after a coin left his hand we were alone once again.

"Thank you," I said to my new friend.

"It has been many a year since I have had the opportunity to speak with someone from your world," he said, raising my curiosity even further.

"You know where I am from by just sitting near me?"

"I can tell you are not familiar with dreamers from my solar system."

"I have not had the pleasure."

"We do not receive stimuli through sensory organs, but by displacement. Through waves radiated by my tissue I can see all around you. I can perceive everything whether it is behind me, or in front, behind something or in the open."

"What of sound?" I asked, intrigued by my strange companion's unusual physiology.

"My external tissue acts as a complete organ that receives sound from rebounding radiation created by myself and others. It is quite sensitive. I can hear faint sounds such as heartbeats from many yards away, but as you are a dreamer, you have no such functions."

"What do you mean?"

"You have no heartbeat."

I reached down and clasped my chest, and felt a faint but constant beat, "you are mistaken."

He laughed with a roar, and no matter how hard I concentrated I could not decipher from where it came.

"You are a young dreamer," he said laughing. "Your mind fabricates everything about your body to comfort itself. Your subconscious has been programmed to believe it must have bodily functions to survive, but here as a dreamer your only true presence is your soul or essence of life."

"Do many from your world dream here as well?"

"There are not many dreamers in the cosmos anymore. All minds of higher consciousness have two aspects, one part technological and one part imaginative. Young races use the imaginative facet the most, creating mythologies, traditions, religions, art and poetry, while older races tend to depend upon their technological side using it to understand and control everything with tools and inventions. As a species becomes older less and less of its people dream here as I have seen with yours."

"You have spoken with many?"

"Why yes, I have dreamt here off and on for many years enjoying the great diversities of the universe. I spoke with another dreamer from your world a few years back. He mentioned something about your entire world being at war with itself."

I leaned backward knowing of the great war he spoke, that between the Axis and the Allies.

"This man unfortunately spoke the truth of my world."

"Strange to imagine an entire world at war with itself, but he explained to me that in your world multitudes of cities band together to create something he called a country."

"Yes this is also true."

"How could a leader or such country satisfy the needs of such a large area with so many people with so many needs?"

"It is quite a complicated subject, but I can say in most cases the majority dominate the minority."

"Ah, I can see from your lack of defense you had little love for it."

"Little," I replied caring not to speak of the monochrome waking world I had been born in and escaped from.

"Ah, understood," he said changing the subject. "To answer your earlier question, much as in your world, my people have discovered much in technologies and have lost interest in the arcane, but you will begin to see more soon as I live on a dying world. As this realization becomes a reality and their technologies are powerless to save them, future generations of my people will seek out the sanctity of Dream as have you and I."

"Your world is dying?"

"Yes, the center of our solar system in its old age has swelled into a red supergiant that will one day become a supernova destroying everything my people have learned and accomplished throughout their history. Only those that escape to here will remain to keep those memories alive."

"You are a very interesting person," I said. "Maybe the most interesting person I have ever had the privilege to meet."

"To good company and good drink!" he said in a happy toast. "May the troubles of both our worlds stay where they are and never pass into that of dream!"

I raised my mug and took a deep swig with my fellow dreamer. We drank our drinks and then parted ways, he searching for a way to stay, I in search of my father. Although he did not know my father or where he might live within Celpahia, he did give me a name of a local sage who was renowned for his knowledge of Dream and whatever transpired within its wide-spread borders. I followed his directions finding the small establishment with little trouble as the residents of Celpahia were very kind, and after a few pointed fingers I stood below a crooked sign that read; *Alzoond the Storyteller*. The door creaked open slowly to reveal an elderly man reading a stack of papers that stood a good foot high. He rumbled through them madly as if in some type of hurry.

"Hello," I said to get his attention.

"The man continued to look through his papers shifting them like a whirlwind turning what had been a mess into that of a greater one.

"Hello," I said again.

The papers stopped shifting a moment as two eyes peered at me through tiny lenses.

"Sorry, I'm closed."

I stood backward and looked at the door which had an open sign hanging in it.

"The sign says you're open."

"Did it say that to you or did you read that?" he replied smartly.

"Sorry, I read it."

"If you could take it down on your way out," he said in a half-order, half-request tone.

Not wanting to irritate a man with the reputation of the great Alzoond, I decided to press the matter as kindly as possible.

"I'm sorry, I can see you are busy, but I assure you that answering my question will not take long."

A pointed chin with a gray beard bobbed up from the mass of papers hanging below two eyes full of frustration. He spread out his hands emphasizing the massive volumes of rolled scrolls, dusty books and flat piles of papyrus.

"Do you believe I know all the knowledge of dreams by heart? If such a statement were true do you believe I would waste my time here in Dream scribbling it down from dusk to dawn? If your question is of any significance, research shall be required, besides I am too busy. I have been receiving strange reports from other scholars across the realms of

Dream of significant events that along with times and locations are pieces of a larger whole of noteworthy significance that I have not been able to piece together."

"Please, I am looking for a man who lives here in town; surely such a question would not take you long to divulge."

"Such impatience from a grand dreamer such as yourself? How did you find the secret of Dream with such impulsiveness?" said the wise sage who seemed to always to speak in questions. "Of my time here I have records of only five men from the waking world who have discovered the secret of Dream, such as you. You make six."

"I brought another with me."

His eyes lit up like trees struck by lightning bolts upon hearing of unrecorded knowledge, because the wise Alzoond lived for nothing but to learn and inscribe it for others. He pulled a feather free from a tall vial and put its sharp tip against a blank piece of paper. I stood quietly staring at him blankly as if I did not know what he wanted.

"Well go on, all knowledge must be recorded!" he said quickly.

"Now who is impatient?" I said turning the tables on the wise scholar.

"You have made your point, if I have the knowledge you seek, I will trade it for the knowledge you possess."

"His name is Herald and he now lives on the idyllic island of Akgaule."

He wrote in a rush as if trying to write down everything before he died. The paper beneath his quill crinkled under the fury of manic writing.

"He comes from your world?"

"Yes."

He placed his quill back into its holder and looked up at me seriously, "Tell me of the man you seek, I will tell you all my records hold."

I spoke my father's name and I could tell from the way his face lifted that he would not have to look up my father's whereabouts.

"You have taken on more than merely your father's appearance. Your father is a man I know well... he and I still speak on occasions. I'll not hold you any longer. Your father has taken up residence a short distance upstream on the south side of the river."

I spun around feeling as light as a cloud as nervous energy surged through my body.

"Tell him his story keeps getting more interesting every day," said the old librarian.

I rushed out into the street running to the river through crowds of people like a child rushing to win a race against his peers. I quickly found the Manikalra River which flowed through the center of the city providing fresh clear water to its residents who swam, fished and drank directly from it without any concerns of pollution or contamination. Its currents pour directly from the center of Dream created by the minds of the gods who still preserve the Lands of Dream in reverie. While I should have walked lazily along the bank as if on a Sunday afternoon stroll, I did not. Instead of ambling carelessly, I moved with a purpose in my step, for with any one I might come upon my father, a man I had not seen in nearly thirty years. I quick stepped along the river for about half an hour when a small bungalow with a long red sloping roof and a veranda facing the river came into view. The home sat next to a hill to offer shelter from high winds and keep cool on summer days under its shade. A pillar of white smoke rose from the chimney high into the air where it slowly faded away into the distant sky. Stacks of wood lay along the building's east side stacked up perfectly to the bottom of its windows so not to restrict view of the rolling fields in which the little but beautiful home sat. Unlike most country homes of small size, this one was not made of wood, mud, or stone, but of large marvelously sparkling green and white marble blocks. Outside roamed all sorts of grazing herd animals, some like those of the waking world, others like nothing I had ever seen. While as beautiful as any palace I had ever had the fortune to look upon, its simplicity made me wonder why great dreamers such as my father and the man from the Ivory Tower had chosen to live simple lives rather than amass great power. And then it came to me with a simple clarity, they had come here to live their lives, not to exalt themselves.

A silhouette came out from the home and stepped out from the veranda into the sun staring at me. Upon seeing me, the person rushed to me like a child to see his own father and embraced me with all his strength. His eyes wept and his mouth laughed great booms of delight as we hugged each other in person instead of dream for the first time in decades. He was as I remembered him, tall and lanky, yet muscular and graceful at the same time. His upper face was smooth showing little age while his lower jaw was covered with a short full beard with touches of salt and pepper. He appeared no more than thirty five or forty years old, making him appear more that of a sibling than my father. I seized him back tightly and laughed with him like I had never laughed before. We looked each over intently, each hardly believing the other was not a dream.

"Of all the wonders I have seen in Dream, none have brought me as much happiness as seeing you after all this time," he replied happily.

"It has been a long journey."

"Please come in, I'd like you to…" the smile fell from his face as if he had said something terrible.

I knew what secret he concealed, the secret that he had taken someone besides my mother as his wife.

"Father, I know of your marriage to a woman of the folk."

"You must understand, I love your mother, but she does not share my devotion to the splendor of Dream. I tried to reach her in her dreams, but she is a creature of the waking world, not open to the follies of dream and I could not reach her."

"I did not come here to judge you, but to find where I belong. I never fit into the waking world, but here I have finally found unadulterated happiness."

The smile returned to his face and he hugged me once again, "I am so happy! Please come in and meet Genuasah."

As we walked toward the secluded home in the country alongside the great Manikalra River, a divine woman about five feet tall with long black flowing hair down to her waist stepped out in the tall grass barefoot in a yellow sun dress. Everything about her was elegant, her features, her bodily curves, even her demeanor. She had by nature all the characteristics that the women of the waking world vainly struggle to possess through cosmetics, surgeries, drugs, exercise and diets. Being as exceptional in mind as in body she need not be told who I was.

"The son of the great dreamer has come, a grand dreamer in his own right."

I nodded with a blush and she seized me in a tight hug as had my father. We went into their home, where I was treated as a guest with fine food, interesting talk and a peaceful atmosphere. Fire crackled warmly in the fireplace, which was built in the center of the home like a fire pit, while my father and I caught up on old times and discussed my future in the Lands of Dream. We spoke throughout the evening and into the night, still unable to catch up with the time we had lost from each other while separated. The next morning we were awakened by a knock at the door that mystified my father because he rarely received visitors. He went to the door and opened it to encounter a grand looking elven soldier in full shiny armor with a long flowing orange cloak. Knowing a little about elven tradition from my visit to Vastoal, I understood that it was their cloak that denoted their standing but I still remained unsure of his status. From the look of the soldier's fine armor and weaponry which hung from his gear, he was of some substantial rank. He and my father spoke quietly for a moment at the door before my father turned around with an astonished look.

"You and I have been summoned to the court of King Shaii," he said in a vexed tone.

Outside docked in the Manikalra River was an elegant red streamlined sea vessel bearing bright white sails that hovered over a formation of valiant elven warriors. That very evening my father, his elven wife and I boarded a massive elven war galley with a full crew of sailors, a detachment of strikingly equipped elven soldiers and the wise Alzoond who greeted us warmly. The red ship, which I was told was the color of elven war vessels, sailed agilely down the twisted Manikalra passing the beautifully lit city of Celpahia. The city's lanterns glowed invitingly to my father and I, but our summoning had been of the direst importance according to the orders of the distinguished King Shaii. Being accomplished sailors, the elven crew maneuvered the giant war galley at an alarming rate down the river through the gusty black passages of Nauria's Caverns. We traveled by memory through the darkness as much as we did with lantern light until we burst into the light of day and emerged out into the vast Cerulean Sea. I had barely arrived upon the coast of Deazah before I had been whisked away back nearly to where I had started my trip in the Lands of Dream.

Day and night rolled by in succession as the crew riotously steered us toward the great forested continent of Vastoal with an urgency that seemed to lack nothing less than desperate determination. While the men of the ship sent to retrieve us knew nothing of why, they did know a counsel of great importance was assembling in the court of the elven king and that we had been summoned to be seated as well. Such a demand gave me a feeling of great importance since I had not been in the Lands of Dream for long and yet I already was being summoned to meetings with great kings.

After many days of travel, our ship docked in the wondrous waterfall-fed port of Vastoal beneath its great hanging docks. I stood next to my father as we were pulled upward by enormous turning cranks into the belly of the buildings above. An unarmed elf wearing a long light blue flowing cloak met us as we docked within.

"You are just in time, please follow me," he said leading us into a sky cart.

The small wooden structure carried the three of us over the vast and busy port which now harbored hundreds of ships of all shapes, types and lands. One was about the size of a modern battleship, and unlike all the others which were made of wood, this one was made of bolted metal. Small stocky men with long black beards roamed its topside, but from the great distance where I sat I could not make much else of their appearance. Upon reaching the cliffs of Vastoal, we were taken to a great hall built in the base of a giant tree which stood hundreds of feet wide and from my point of view, appeared to be thousands of feet tall. Its roots must have run into the center of Dream to hold such a structure upright. Inside were smoothly polished living thrones of wood which still bore leaves and fruit. Sitting in and around, for those beings who were too large or small for the chairs, were kings and queens of all races and creatures of Dream. In attendance was King Shaii The Grand Druid of the Elf, Lord Gruem The Mine Master of the Dwarf, King Hamse the Fourth Ruler of Zeethe, King Nahl Head Trader of Deazah, Queen Lai Steward of the Fairy, the noble Rangers Quertu, a centaur, and Witg, a satyr, who represented the woodland creatures of Dream, Baron Earuy Chief of the Gnome, Patriarch Whushi Grand Wizard of Uthal, an ancient silver dragon from the northern peaks of Kuish named Omauk-Et, The man from the Ivory Tower and Alzoond the relentless scribe. Hosting the affair, King Shaii sat at the head of the circle and stood to address us all.

"All of you have been summoned to Vastoal to discuss several dire events that have taken place in the Lands of Dream over the past few weeks," he announced. "Mongrel spies and vessels have been spotted in all corners of Dream. Today we have received word by messenger sea hawks that the great Kings of Narefick and Gruedell have fallen to mongrel forces."

The whole meeting hall burst into an uproar as its participants grumbled in shock of the statement. Man, elf, dwarf, fairy and woodland creatures rose to their feet in hot debate.

"No such force could have passed from Fathel through the gate between the north and the south without my watchmen reporting it," countered the great King Hamse the Fourth taking the suggestion as an insult to his watch. His great continent of men, Zeethe, sat north of the massive mongrel wasteland, and for him to let such an event pass without report made him appear incompetent before all convened.

"The invasion of mongrel did not come from the shores of Fathel, but from the Isle of Thorn ruled by the wicked Mind Picker, who desires to exalt himself to the King of Dreams."

"The mongrel could attack any of us from either of these points. Why are we here and not at home defending our homelands?" asked King Nahl.

"Forget that, I say we forge in after the slime and crush them where they breed!" announced Lord Gruem of the dwarves.

"Both wise decisions in their own right, but there is more to consider," declared the elven king. "The men of Narefick and Gruedell have been cultures of wars for centuries and did not fall easily, but they fell to a new mongrel field general, an anti-hero who is said to be immortal. He goes by the name Gant. It is also believed that the Mind Picker has discovered the way to stay in Dream and now lives eternal in his fortress of thorn."

The name struck icy fear into my heart freezing the blood in my veins. Dizzily I fell backwards into my chair white as a ghost. Dr. Jentry had fooled me all along as Gant had been merely a plant to help me escape and lead them both to the Lands of Dream. All the events taking place were the direct result of my actions. I had put everything I loved, including my father's dream in jeopardy.

"While every race here has made sacrifices throughout all the mongrel wars, it has been the five chief continents which belong to man, dwarf and elf that have held the balance of power in the Lands of Dream. With one continent conquered, they will undoubtedly choose another as their next attack, whether it be Zeethe or Deazah in the south or Drugin or Vastoal in the north I cannot say, but with the fourth mongrel war upon us, it is safe to say there will be much bloodshed. Each mongrel war takes a heavy toll upon the older races who do not replenish as do the fecund mongrel species. It is because of this inevitability that I proclaim we do not defend against the mongrel and drive them from our homelands, but divide into two forces and invade the Isle of Thorn and Fathel itself to destroy the mongrel breeding pits forever!"

The aggressive plan stunned all in attendance, for no one but mongrel had ever entered the dark continent of Fathel and returned.

"Invade the wastelands of Fathel? Such talk is nothing but a glorious way to perform mass suicide!" declared King Nahl.

"I desire to destroy the mongrel as much as any other, but to do so would leave our homelands defenseless, and if we failed, all of Dream would fall into the dirty hands of the mongrel king and his strange new ally the Mind Picker," stated a human general.

"It will be a gamble, but one that can be minimized if all our peoples abandon their cities and go into hiding, those of Zeethe into the vast Mhorhaen, the dwarf into their deepest mines, my people into the trees," countered the great elf king.

"Such a command would give our lands to the invading mongrels," replied King Hamse the Fourth, deeply concerned.

Omauk-Et, the eldest of the dragon who was nearly eight thousand years old, spoke with a booming voice defending a plan he had wisely help devise, "It has always been the mongrel that attack, it has always been the mongrel who invade… they will leave little to protect their own lands and once they invade elsewhere, they will be too far distant from their homelands to return to its defense in time. With the demise of their breeding pits, we can ensure many a millennium of safety from the threat of mongrel. The sacrifices made in this war will not only be by the humanoids, but by the dragon as well."

As the dragon were as wise as rare, the room fell into silence upon his response, understanding the magnitude of the ancient beings words. At first conception, only the dwarf were ready to wade into the bowels of mongrel land, but with direction and sworn support of the dragons of Dream, a great alliance was struck to face against what would be the greatest of all the mongrel wars to date. The armies of King Hamse, King Nahl, Lord Gruem, along with the sparse but specialized support of the fairy, gnome, centaur and satyr would land on the shores of Fathel and march to its core to destroy the unknown mongrel king's black citadel and sprawling breeding pits, while the elf and dragon would swoop into the Isle of Thorns to stop the Mind Picker and his mongrel forces. It was a solid plan, but risky, for if they failed in the assaults upon the mongrel strongholds, there would no one left to return to the great continents of Zeethe, Deazah, Vastoal or Drugin to defend them and the good citizens of Dream would be enslaved by the ruthless mongrel.

Feeling responsible for the rise of the Mind Picker, I wanted to be a part of my new home's defense and stood up in front of the council before it departed to prepare for its daring strategy.

"Great kings and queens of Dream," I said bowing humbly, "it is with great shame that I declare it was I who unwittingly led the Mind Picker and his hero Gant into Dream making them whole here as you and I. I place my life in your hands, but if you see fit, I wish to join you in your assault upon the Mind Picker."

"I as no one else in the Lands of Dream have the right to take a life they did not give unless they do so in self-defense," said King Shaii nobly, "but we cannot use you in this war, for fear of losing favor of the gods."

His rejection struck deeper into my heart than could have any blade forged in Dream. It was a cold but wise decision.

"While this war must be fought without your aid, we could use your advice as a dreamer. It is said that in the battle upon the continent of Jhertyl the weapons of the men from Narefick and Gruedell passed through the anti-hero Gant as if he were an apparition," said the Elven King standing in full elven battle gear, which was as hard as modern steel, but as light as thick cloth. "Can such a thing be true?"

My father stood up taking the floor to address the counsel, "It is only possible to have flesh upon the dimension you were born. As dreamers, we are conscious spirits who have the potential to be as powerful as the gods of Dream. It is this enlightenment that makes the gods fear us so."

"Bah!" screamed the mighty dwarven lord swinging his great axe into the thick wooden table between us. Its thick mighty blade sank half a foot into the robust table making the entire room rumble as the table rose from the floor and bounced back with an earth-shattering boom. "You expect us to fear ghosts? The mountain forged weapons of the dwarf will bring down this Gant and his pathetic mongrel army!"

"It is true that the dwarven forged weapons are as fine as any in Dream, but even they will not be able to harm the Mind Picker and Gant if they have discovered the secret of spirit materialization."

Being workers of the earth, dwarves hold the elements of its soil in the highest regard, trusting their very lives with the mighty weapons they forge from its bosom. The dwarf lord, distrustful of arcane magic, challenged my father's allegation with a booming laugh.

"No man or creature can take a direct hit from a dwarven forged axe and go unharmed!" he boasted.

"Strike me with your axe," dared my father boldly.

The dwarves being a fiercely proud race, historically never backed down from a challenge, and the eminent lord of the dwarves was not about to be the first. The powerful king unhooked a massive iron war axe forged from the deepest mines of Drugin wielding the heavy object with tight knotted muscles as if it were weightless. He lifted the axe of his father whose bloodline has ruled the continent of Drugin for millenniums high into the air and bore its razor head above my father to encompass him in its shadow. I saw the great dwarf lord's muscles tighten as he brought forward the hammer toward my father who stood fearless underneath its massive oncoming strike. Fearing I might lose my father again, I leapt across the room with a speed impossible by human standard, almost turning into pure energy. I struck the stout muscular king in his side bouncing off him like wind off a mountain and slid against the wall with a thud. The axe blade passed through my father striking the stone floor below him cracking it with a loud clap of thunder. The once confident king gaped at his great weapon which had harmlessly passed through my father who stood motionless with a long sly smile.

"See, noble lord, dreamers are not from this world, so we are not subject to its laws."

Then he reached out and lifted the dwarven lord's beard high into the air above his head showing he could dematerialize and materialize his own body at will. The entire room burst into laughter at the comical situation, embarrassing the great dwarven lord. He knocked my father's hand from his beard cursing at him for the lesson given to the counsel at his expense.

"How might we strike down a dreamer with these powers?" asked King Shaii.

"Mortal weapons are forged to strike down the body, not the soul," replied my father, "but the weapons forged by the gods of Dream, who were once dreamers themselves can strike down both the body and the soul."

"The gods barely concern themselves with the fate of humanoids, never would one risk all to aid us in battle against the mongrel," avowed King Hamse the Fourth.

"He is not speaking of summoning the gods, but of retrieving a weapon forged by a god that sits in the Ruins of Abka," corrected the wise Alzoond. "When the Lands of Dream were formed by those who dreamed in the universe first, the gods created the races of Dream to worship and increase their own power with the major gods creating the elf, dwarf, man and mongrel. The lesser gods, on the other hand, unable to form intelligent races, created monsters to deify themselves. Serzie-Ju, a human god, passed down a black sword forged in the mountains of the gods to a fabled human hero as reward for defeating a rival god's champion in battle. This sword, which is known by the name Evoker, is buried in the tomb of the fallen human hero Yxwuth."

"The black sword Evoker is nothing more than a legend," declared King Nahl, "that leads fools to their death within the grip of the Bloom!"

"Aye, the Bloom was placed by the gods after Yxwuth's death destroying an entire kingdom in its lust so the sword would not fall into the hands of another, because within its blade is the power to kill a god, but I assure you it is no myth," stated Alzoond firmly.

"Then we must send a force to claim it and wield its power against the Mind Picker and his forces," declared King Hamse the Fourth.

"It is true that our only hope lies with this weapon, but in its reclaiming numbers are of no consequence as the aroma of the Death Bloom affects all as well as one," said my father.

"Who might take on this cause?" asked King Shaii now leading the proceedings.

"I offer my blade's service!" announced the dwarf lord.

"This ruin is within a realm I declare as my own, I will personally take on this task," offered King Hamse the Fourth who was a king with a long heritage of heroic men in his blood.

Each king and queen of the counsel offered someone of service, either themselves or a hero from their land, but it was my father's proposal that shocked me the most.

"I offer the services of my son, a grand dreamer in his own right."

"Father," I replied nervously, "I know nothing of this Bloom!"

"You expect us to leave the fate of Dream to someone who hardly knows its boundaries?" asked Baron Earuy Chief of the Gnome.

"You saw how quickly he moved against the gallant Lord Gruem. Could anyone one of you or your champions move with the speed of lightning? Can any of you dematerialize your body at will?"

No one spoke.

"It is settled then," said the noble King Shaii, "but to ensure our attack is an utter surprise we must make our assault even without the sword before the mongrel can regroup. I will send with you a sentinel of elf as fine as any that have ever taken breath in Dream. May we have chosen wisely."

And so without scarcely saying a word the fate of dreams had been placed upon me, a man who just a few weeks ago had doubted his own sanity. As the kings and queens of Dream prepared to assault the lands of the mongrel, I rushed to my father pleading for him to change his mind.

"Father, why not you? I might fail. I do not know the secrets of my mind as do you."

"It is by no means a guaranteed success for anyone. You saw how quickly you moved when you came to my defense? You can do anything you want, as your only limit is your mind."

"We can go together and claim the sword as father and son," I pleaded.

"Son, I know you feel guilty for what the Mind Picker has done, but you are not at fault. It is because of me that the Mind Picker is here. Had it not been for me leading you here in your dreams he would have never found the way. If I do not go with the dragon and elf, they will be at his mercy. I can't get the sword and stop the Mind Picker at the same time," he said holding my shoulders with a firm grip from each hand, "I finally found my way here so I can spend eternity in the splendor of Dream with you, we cannot let this man who represents everything wrong with the waking world turn the Lands of Dream into a realm of nightmare. I never told anyone this, but when I first began to search for the secret of Dream, I found a pool formed from the dreams of the great Phean himself that when gazed into revealed parts of a man's future. I had to know if I would succeed in my aspirations to stay here and in my observation I saw that fate of Dream would not fall into my own hands, but into those of my only son. This is why I searched so desperately for you, because your fate and that of Dream are one! If you fail in claiming the sword, all of Dream might fall. Remember this… the Death Bloom allures the flesh, which you are no part. Focus your mind, and it cannot entice you."

In haste to surprise their foe, thousands of soldiers in hundreds of ships sailed from the port of Vastoal across the seas of Dream to meet the fourth mongrel wars head on. I stood once again upon the bow of the Jade Runner, the swiftest ship in all of Dream. I waved goodbye to my father who rode along with King Shaii and his army of elf warriors upon the backs of the great silver dragons of Kevight. They shone like mirrors under the suns of Dream fading away into the horizon toward the Isle of Thorns. The Jade Runner's bow cut through the sea toward the southern realm of Dream bound for the southern tip of Zeethe which had been abandoned many centuries ago by man as the Death Bloom rose from the earth at the command of the gods beguiling those who did not escape in time in an orgy of carnal lust ordained for divine starvation.

We quickly reached the Strait of Phylain and passed through the shadows of its guardian statues. The stone eyes bore down upon our small ship and its skeleton crew as we continued on our desperate mission to retrieve the ancient Evoker, the sword of the gods. As we passed along Zeethe its grand cities, villages and ports sat empty like ghost towns having received word by messenger sea hawks that mongrel armies were approaching and that no armies would arrive to defend them. The people had taken heed and had gone into hiding disappearing into the woods and mountains in desperate flight. Even the bustling trading port of Wren-Henji sat without a single ship in its harbor with its waters rocking ominously bare. The splendor of Dream had faded under the weight of dire circumstances in which I had played a significant part. With my own body partially decayed in the waking world by now, I had little option other than to fight for the new world I loved so dearly. I would not let it fall under the heartless rule of Dr. Jentry while my mind still roamed the Lands of Dream.

We sailed around the southern tip of Zeethe passing the native Islands of Jheanb, a tribal civilization that still lived as had man at the beginning of time, having no greater technologies than that of stone tools and fire. Outlandishly painted men stood along the shores watching us pass without the slightest sign of emotion. Their heads were shaven save for a tall black pony tail that stood straight up on the top of their brown heads. Wild colors had been painted onto their bodies covering them in painted eyes which made it appear as if hundreds of eyes were watching from a single man. The elves upon our ship explained that the untamed fierceness of these people had kept them a free and unchanged culture for thousands upon thousands of years.

"Ships ahoy!" screamed a watchman from the tiny crow's nest high upon the main mast.

The Jade Runner's crew swarmed on top its deck like busy ants preparing for whatever awaited ahead. I ran to the bow fearing the worst, expecting to see an attack fleet of invading black mongrel galleys, but what greeted me was not a horde of mongrel infested ships, but a vast graveyard of broken and sunken ships. Hundreds of ships stood quietly still in the distance broken apart and sitting upon sharp jagged rocks having all strangely run aground as if pulled to this location by some navigational magnet. Bloated and rotting bodies drifted in the water aimlessly encircling our ship as we sailed through the sea necropolis nimbly avoiding ships which seemed to have carelessly run aground. I could see the concern in the stern sea-worn eyes of our captain as he tried to comprehend what could have caused so many captains to foolishly guide their ships to self-destruct against the jagged rocks throughout what appeared to be a smooth and easily navigable bay.

As we approached the mainland, a soft caressing aroma drifted over the deck of our ship bringing the entire crew including myself to its edge with our heads lifted high into the air. My mind lifted in gentle delight as the fragrance surrounded me in a supple embrace. At that moment I had never known such wondrous delight. It called to me like an addictive drug drawing me toward its source. Suddenly some of the ship's crew began to leap overboard crashing into the water frantically swimming toward the shore. Our captain, under the same allure, steered over his own men knocking them beneath the surface of the bay to reach the shore from whence the aroma came. An irresistible urge overcame me and at that moment I cared for nothing or nobody, not even myself for all that mattered was whatever produced the divine scent. The closer we got to land, the more fanatical we grew becoming nearly unable to function consciously.

Then it happened, the beautiful Jade Runner ran around splitting its hull upon a large serrated rock. Seeing the ship no longer moving toward shore, I as well as the rest of the ship's crew leapt overboard into the still bay swimming violently toward the shore as do swimmers in the last leg of a race. Arms and legs kicked against me as I fought with the elven sailors to reach shore first. My arms stung with pain threatening to fail and drown me beneath the sea if I did not rest, but I bore through the water with my mind ignoring my body's pleas. I pushed the bodies of the floating dead aside like simple nuisances. Finally my feet were able to touch bottom and I began to run toward the call of the nectarous scent. My eyes lit up with pleasure upon seeing large crimson and yellow flowers hovering on top of tall light brownish-green stalks. They fluttered teasingly in the wind waving me in to share in their carnal lust. Those of the elven crew that did not drown rushed with me to the deep fields of tall flowers crashing into their stalks. I instinctively broke open one of the tall stalks and drank the sweet fluid within. My senses surged with unearthly pleasure. Under its influence I had become a god! We played under the shade of the seven-foot stalks laughing madly at the simplest things. When one would start laughing, we would all start laughing uncontrollably caring not for our fallen comrades only a few feet away until our stomachs hurt and our eyes watered. Upon hearing us, more people of all different colors and species who lived in the fields came out to play with us. They were skinny, almost skeleton like in nature, but at that moment I did not seem to see anything unusual for I had found the universe's true nirvana! I seized a beautifully curved blue-skinned woman and began to make wild passionate love to her as if we were long-time lovers. We caressed each other fervently making love like it were our first time caring not who saw us in the act. More women came and the crew and I spent the remainder of the day and night, drinking the splendid nectar, making love to strangers we did not know and frolicking through the bloom like mindless fairies till we collapsed into unconsciousness.

Two hands began to rub my face and I awoke to a man wearing a damp cloth over his nose and mouth. His eyes appeared familiar, but at that moment all that I thought was of the Bloom. I reached up ignoring him and broke a stalk hanging over me in half. Its sweet syrupy goo poured out toward my mouth but a quick hand slapped it away. I scuffled for it, but the man pulled me away from it dragging me backwards by my ankle. I fought with him violently trying to break free of his grip, but a sudden blow upon the back of my head sent me back into unconsciousness.

When I awoke again, I was tied to the back of a donkey being led away from the Bloom which still called to me from the distance. I struggled against my bonds screaming and crying for the call of the Death Bloom. I begged the man imploring him to free me and when that did not work, I tried to bribe and finally threatened him. He silently ignored my pleas pulling his donkey further away until I collapsed in a stupor of dismay. I had never felt such loss, and if I could not have the Bloom I would kill myself for there was no life worth living without it.

My captor carried me beyond the frangrance and tied me to a tree next to which he built a roaring fire. He offered me food and water, which tasted bland and which I spat onto the ground in anger. I would murder him, rip his very eyes out of his skull for taking me away from the wondrous pleasures of the Bloom once I got free, I thought. He would suffer dearly as I was suffering at that very moment. But the next morning the anger I felt had left my body and was replaced by a commanding nausea over which I had no control. I vomited uncontrollably feeling seasick upon land being woozy and faint. My body shook in withdrawal from the Bloom and all I wanted was to die and fall again into its cold calm embrace. As my senses began to return, my tormentor finally removed his mask to reveal the face of the man I knew only as the gypsy king.

"My friend," I begged shaking in torment, "if you have any compassion, you will let me return to the call of the Bloom! It screams to me! If I cannot return, strike me down right here!"

"You know not what you say," said the gypsy king.

"I have never thought so clearly! Everything else is simply a waste of time in comparison to the love of the Bloom!"

"Did you not see those you were cavorting? They were skin and bones, and happily starving to death. The Bloom does not love you; it doesn't even know you exist. It simply feeds of the corpses of the dead."

"It does love me," I argued not wanting to hear the truth, "it spoke to me, in my mind!"

"It is a mindless plant placed by the gods to protect the sword you seek. These plants create a sweet syrup that lure men and women to their fields to drink and play until they die of starvation and fertilize the ground on which they grow. The thick nectar of the Bloom has no nutritional value and once it enters your stomach, it sits heavily and you lack hunger while you indulge in the pleasures of love, dream and sleep until you starve to death."

"It's not true!" I said, knowing very well he spoke the truth.

"Do you dare defend a mindless plant over your friend?"

I fell in a stupor of tears, "Cut me down right here. I beg you. I have been nothing more than a blight upon the Lands of Dream!"

"If I did so, I would rob Dream of its last chance to repel the rule of mongrel and its ensuing nightmare. The Old Hag has told me that it is your destiny to stand against it and that we all must live by your success or failure."

"I will fail you. If I go anywhere near the Bloom I will succumb to its allure. I cannot resist it. You are much stronger than I. Go claim the Evoker and use it to cut down the foul Mind Picker."

"Whether you believe it or not, you are much stronger than I. If I were to lay claim to the sword and be cut down by a mongrel, it would fall into the wrong hands and doom us all to a new age of terror and slavery, but you… you can hold that sword and walk by the mongrel without a scratch and expel the soul of the Mind Picker with one mighty swoop."

"How will we get near the sword with it being so close to the Bloom?"

"The Old Hag has brewed a concoction that is so foul that when placed upon a cloth you cannot smell the call of the Bloom."

He pulled a round purple glass vial from a pouch dipping two rags into it one at a time. He tied one around his face to cover his mouth and nose and then handed the other to me.

"Normally we would wait until you completely recovered from the effects of the Bloom, but right now thousands of lives are in the balance as wars have engulfed the once peaceful realm of Dream."

I placed the oily cloth over my face and began to gag from the horrible stench. I cannot explain its horrid odor, but I can say that the stink of raw defecation would have been an improvement. We pushed tall brush aside moving in toward the overgrown city of Abka from the north to avoid as much of the Bloom as we could. Ahead, through unkempt gardens and overrun courtyards, sat the crumbling palace of the once great king of Abka, and to my anguish surrounding it were the swaying purple and yellow fields of Bloom. I shook with a compelling craving to rip my mask aside and rush into its sea of pleasure, but I shivered instead, terrified of the godly plant's power. We walked into the ruined city, now a ghost town of starved dead who littered its streets like worthless trash. Their eyes and faces sunken against bone with cold smiles stretched across their face. They had willingly and happily died under the influence of the alluring fragrance, now serving it in death through nourishing the stalks of the plants they once consumed. I turned a corner and stepped directly into a patch of the tall purple and yellow flowers. They touched my skin visually calling to me where they could not call through scent. I touched one lovingly caressing it like a woman, when a firm hand pulled me away from its velvet stalk. Firm eyes glared at me forebodingly over a yellow-stained cloth. I pulled away like a child scolded for inadvertently touching an electrical socket. We walked through the streets of Abka and once I noticed one of the elven sailors with whom I had come lying in a corner making love to a near-dead skeleton of a woman. I moved forward to help him, but was cautioned once again by my friend and ally of Dream.

"We do not have time to save him," he said, his voice muffled through the oily concocted cloth of the Old Hag. "We must claim the sword."

A tall crumbling palace stood high in the center of the city, and it was through its high towers that we were able to navigate the old city's labyrinth of streets. Then like a bolt from the sky, the blue woman I had first met in the Bloom rushed up to me and tried to pull my mask away to kiss me. Her hand pulled my mask down only slightly, but it was enough. My eyes glazed over in delight and I reached out and pulled her naked body against mine ready to take her in the middle of the street. The gypsy king flung the woman to the ground and quickly pulled my mask back up blocking the enchanting aroma once again. I shook my head trying to regain my composure as the young woman rose up and ran away like a child ready to play with another.

We reached the steps of the grand Abka palace staring into its ruins. Stairs of marble and statues of rainbow stone were slowly collapsing under the strain of time, giving way to the fields of Bloom. We cautiously entered through the palace's front gates, which would have been surely guarded by powerful warriors during this civilization's peak, finding a now dark lifeless chamber that had once been the grand throne room of the great human hero Yxwuth. A loyal servant of the god Serzie-Ju, he later became king of Abka under the power of the sword known to the gods as the Evoker. He ruled it in a golden age of peace until his death when the gods cursed his people for fear of the weapon his gluttonous son inherited with the kingdom of Abka.

In the center of the circular throne room sat a tall sarcophagus carved from a single immense gemstone. It glimmered dully under shadow and dust as I walked up to its base and stared into its center. The tomb was a deep orange being quartz in likeness allowing me to see directly through it. In its center was encased the body of the once hero king. We lifted the heavy coffin lid aside and gazed upon the body of the dead king. His corpse had shrunk to that of a scrawny mummy, but his massive armor still held its place indicating the once great strength of the hero who wore it into battle. Lying prone upon the king's chest between two tightly closed hands was the black sword Evoker. It did not shine, but instead seemed dull in color as if a piece not for display, but for use. Getting a nod of approval from the gypsy king, I pulled it free from the hands of the man who had possessed it since it had been forged by the gods centuries ago. The king's hands and arms crumbled to dust releasing the fabled blade. The blade rose into the air light as a feather allowing me to wield it as if it were a thin stick. It hummed through the air cutting it as finely as a reed in a wind instrument, except that this was an instrument forged to create the ultimate death, the evocation of the soul. It had perfect balance, and to test its strength, I swung it against stone, which it cut through like butter. No armor, flesh or soul would be able to resist its strike, but with the Isle of Thorn located far north past

Having lost our only means of transportation, we traveled north from Abka and the lure of Bloom on foot along hidden trails known only to thieves, beggars and the gypsy. We moved as such staying within the shadows of the forest evading the eyes of the mongrel patrols that roamed freely across the countryside burning and pillaging all within their path. Finding few victims, the mongrel took out their frustrations upon the structures of man burning them with extreme prejudice leaving nothing but black smoke and piles of rubble as reminders of what had once been. We followed the coastline for hope of spotting a friendly ship but to our dismay the only sea vessels we saw were of those of mongrel raiding ships. We ran like mad spirits through the trees knowing that as we did the whole realm of Dream had become engulfed in a final struggle that would determine whether my new world would stay one of dream or become infected with that of nightmare.

Upon reaching the port of Wren-Henji we found but a single green ship floating in its harbor. My eyes broadened in excitement of seeing the Maritaun craft rocking quietly in the marina. I knew very well from its markings to whom it belonged and I greeted my black slimy friend on its deck as warmly as I would my own father.

"Jaiet, you fool, what brings you to an abandoned port?" I asked, after releasing him from a warm embrace.

"We have come for the wizard, who we recently learned was under siege by the mongrel," he said slapping my arm with his wet sticky hand.

I quickly looked atop the Shakh Mountains and to my distress the peaceful scene of a glistening ivory tower under the light of sparkling suns, which had been so elegantly represented in my father's painting, had been replaced by the haze of rising black smoke.

"They're burning the fields surrounding the tower," reported the black sea captain sadly. "We had hoped to get here in time, but it appears we have failed."

The gypsy king stepped from behind me and greeted the melancholic captain with a tight arm shake, "My sea brethren, we are on a desperate mission that might bring an end to this war, but for us to do so, you must take us to the Isle of Thorn!"

"What of the wizard?" I asked. "We can't abandon him."

"It is here that our paths must part once again," stated the gypsy king. "You must go to your destiny and I to mine."

"But," I argued being interrupted by the gypsy king.

"Your destiny lies to the north, just as mine lies with the aid of dreamers. First your father, then you and now it seems I am meant to save another," he said valiantly. "Fulfill your destiny for it seems all of Dream is tied to you. I will get the wizard out, have no fear of that.

I nodded and found myself, as the ship I stood upon pulled out of port, watching the gypsy king's bright clothes disappear into the edge of the Shakh Mountains toward the destruction that lay waste to its top. I could only hope that he would succeed.

"Worry not my friend, no mongrel will ever have the pleasure of killing him," said Jaiet with a smile that would have been at home on the face of a catfish.

I learned from the black seamen with whom I rode that the mongrel from the Isle of Thorn had chosen Drugin, the mountain continent of the dwarf, as their northern exploit. I knew that the determined and stubborn dwarf would give the mongrel hell within the mountain ranges of Drugin, but without an army, they would be lost as would all the others of Dream in time. The residents of Dream could only hope that the men, dwarf and folk of Dream in the south could dispatch of the Mongrel King, while the elf and dragon did the same on the Isle of Thorn to return and finish off the mongrel forces ravaging their homelands. I would have to play a larger part than I wished to make such a victory come to pass. As our green ship beneath my feet sailed full speed toward the Isle of Thorn, I held the mighty sword Evoker and eyed its structure. Just holding it brought confidence to one's soul as if it knew what to do and that I was merely a tool in its grip.

Days upon the seas of Dream passed as our ship cut through the smooth surface, but while I held the evoker I did not sleep. Instead I stood on the bow watching our progress without saying a word to Jaiet or his men. The crew of the ship did not attempt to speak to me even once, leaving me in solitude to contemplate what had to be done, but I was not alone for the Evoker spoke to my heart. It knew what I desired and it too desired the same, to cut down and erase the blemish of the Mind Picker and his hero Gant from the Lands of Dream forever. Upon reaching the shores of the Isle of Thorn, a haze of black smoke arose from the island as dragons flew above shooting breaths of fire into the thick intertwined thorns below. Fire burned widely out of control atop the thick thorn. Elves stood upon ships surrounding the island killing any mongrel foolish enough to emerge onto the beach with swift arrows, but even after weeks of siege, the elf and dragon had not been able to take the beaches, for inside the thorn stood thousand of mongrel led by an anti-hero who would not die. Out in the open brandishing two swords dripping in blood stood the tall slender Gant taunting the elven upon the besieging ships to come ashore so that he might slay them. Wearing nothing but pants and covered in the dried blood of his enemies, he appeared a far different man than the one I once knew back in the Belmount Institution for the Mentally Insane. Arrows passed through him as if he were a mirage leaving him laughing madly at his enemies. His immortality and the lives he had taken while here in the Lands of Dream were part of my challenge to escape the waking world, and as I rushed upon the beach I knew what I had to do. Being a single man rushing up the beach, I attracted dozens of waiting mongrel who rushed toward me holding mighty weapons of death. Orc, goblin, troll and ogre came at me with gnashing teeth and swinging weapons only to see their weapons pass through me harmlessly. I could dematerialize and materialize at will cutting down those I felt inclined and passing through those I cared not to be bothered with. Gant lifted his swords and screamed out into the sky a death cry.

"Arhhhhhhh," he screamed, rushing up to meet me in battle, "so the fool has returned! I expected to have to hunt you down cowering somewhere in Dream like the coward you are! Here let me thank you for making me a god!"

I hated him for the lies he had told, the deception of false friendship and for allying himself with the man who had nearly destroyed both my father and me. I did not want to hear another word from his mendacious lips. His swords cut agilely through the air coming at me with swift intention. Caring not for drama, I let them pass through me and then as he stood in shock, I cut him in half with the black blade of the Evoker. His face distorted and twisted in pain as the Evoker erased his soul, banishing it from the cosmos forever to vanish into nothingness. Possessed with the will of the Evoker, I became a wraith, storming through the mighty thorn maze materializing as I passed through thorn ignoring its twisted paths to head directly for its center and the fortress of the Mind Picker. The mongrel that stood in my way fell under the spirit of the Evoker which cut through flesh and armor as if they were simply air. Upon seeing that their weapons could not harm me, the mongrel forces within the thorn began to panic upon seeing me running away like scared children.

"AGKKEAR!" they screamed being the word for "mad spirit" to the mongrel as they fled into caves and holes leading into the ground below.

High on the horizon stood the black castle of the Mind Picker which I had visited once earlier in a dream. This time things would be different. Upon seeing me, a tide of mongrel rushed to the gate of the black citadel banging on its giant doors pleading to their master to be let in.

"Your master cannot protect you now," I cried, unleashing Evoker upon their terrified faces.

I quickly cut down the poor nasty souls stealing their souls upon which the black sword Evoker fed growing stronger with each life it took. It now glowed with power having tasted a multitude of mongrel flesh and soul. Unable to restrain me, I passed through the mighty castle's doors a transparent ghost appearing inside the black citadel lusting for more death. A snarling wyner sat in the corner like a stone gargoyle watching my every move. He leapt toward me ready to strike me down, but passed through me harmlessly crashing in to the wall. It rose up and shook its head, barely escaping a blow from my divine sword. It ran across the wall like a spider landing on the floor and running away toward the throne room where I had once stood a prisoner. I slowly followed it into the fountain-lined room seeing at the end a tall cloaked figure sitting upon a throne of thorns. He sat quietly staring at me, showing no signs of movement.

"So, you have returned a great dreamer ready to strike the master down," he said, seemingly unafraid.

"I have come to finish the tragedy in which I played a part," I said, gripping the hilt of Evoker for courage. Even then when I held a sword of the gods I trembled inside fearful of the man who knew how to twist and mold a psyche like a cheap pretzel. But he would dissolve under the blade of the Evoker as had Gant, I thought to myself.

Dozens of wyners, masters of stealth, began to appear from the surrounding shadows encircling me as before. They could not touch me I thought, they could not touch me I thought again for good measure. Their teeth snarled dripping salvia in expectation of a kill that would not come. I raised the Evoker and began to approach the stationary figure upon the throne.

"So you think you have it all figured out," he said laughing as he had during our psychological sessions in the waking world, "but again I am one step ahead of you and your father. I knew you were his weakness and I used you to have him bring me here and now that I'm here, he shall serve me as will every living soul. It is just too bad you will not have that same privilege."

I continued to steadily walk up to the throne holding my sword out, while his minions followed, ignoring his words so that I might concentrate as I cut him down.

"Remember, to cut me down you must materialize, if even for a second, so that my little servants can rip you apart."

I stopped about three feet away from him while the wyners at my feet began to bite and claw at my image waiting for the moment I might materialized. Their razor sharp teeth and claws passed through me harmlessly awaiting the chance to rip and consume flesh.

"We have a stalemate, as while your sword steals my soul you will be whole and they will shred you into a pulp, but as always I have a fair solution I believe we can all live under."

I raised the black sword of the gods ready to cut him in half. Wyners, dozens at a time, began to leap through me trying to hit my soft neck so to deal an instant death blow.

He held up his hand, "you don't want to lose an eternity with your father now that you have finally found him. Join me and help me rule this world, we can be kings, and once you are with me, your father will join us as well and we all can be kings of a world!"

He was more insane than any of the patients in the hospital he ran in the waking world, and I knew what kind of rule he spoke, one of terror and hatred as mongrel swept over all its lands destroying the beauty of the world in which I wanted to stay. If I could not cut him down while holding the sword, then I would not hold it. I faked a strike causing his minions to leap at me and pass through me harmlessly, then with all my might I materialized for but a moment and slung the great black sword of the gods. It spun but once in the air with its point coming down directly at its target. The Evoker knew death and how to serve it. It sank into the dark one's chest exploding his soul into a billion particles fading away in a scream of agony that could only be experienced in the disintegration of one's essential being. His bloodthirsty servants struck at me one last time and upon seeing they could not harm me, disappeared into the surrounding darkness. They would need their powers of camouflage if they were to survive the onslaught of elf and dragon that would soon come to wipe them out.

With the fall of the Mind Picker and his anti-hero, elven forces supported by dragon fire rushed into the thorn thickets sending the broken mongrel forces on the isle to the brink of extinction. As the northern mongrel base fell, the elf and dragon forces rushed to Drugin to trap the mongrel forces between sea and mountain and crush them into a full rout. The Evoker wielded by me took many a life that day and consumed souls by the hundreds in the wars that followed all across Dream. The southern forces who invaded Fathel succeeded as well, crushing the black mongrel citadel under the weight of man, dwarf and folk sending the mongrel king and the remainder of his forces into hiding. King Hamse returned to Zeethe to expel the mongrel there and free his lands once again. Over the next year, the forces of elf, dwarf and man hunted mongrel into the mountains, caves, forests and seas until their numbers were so insignificant they would not be a concern for another millennium. Peace and tranquility reined in the Lands of Dream once again as its people returned to a life of necessary chores and simple leisure.

The gypsy king who had saved both my father and I had done the same for the Man in the Ivory Tower before returning to lead his caravans a humble hero caring nothing for recognition or glory. To this day, I believe it is he to whom the Lands of Dream owe the greatest of debts. My father and I returned for a while to the glittering city of Celpahia where I came to know him for who he really was, a dreamer who had finally found his true reality. In all my time in the waking world or that of Dream, I still have never met a happier soul. After living a year with my father, I struck out on my own labeled a human hero by the kings of Dream as was the man who wielded the Evoker before me. After the fourth mongrel war, I offered to relinquish the sacred weapon to the kings of Dream, but they wisely refused as being immortal, it could not be in safer hands. It hungered for blood, urging me to use it, a request I normally refused unless it be that of the mongrel race.

One day as I traveled across the many Lands of Dream, a young dreamer bursting with the very excitement I held upon my first visit to Dream approached me.

"Oh please sir," he said politely, "might you pass on your secret of dreamwalking?"

"Young dreamer," I said kindly, "your destiny is yours alone."

"But all I seek is to share in the wonders you have achieved, and to refuse me would be purely an act of selfishness."

"I have seen what can occur when a malevolent soul from the waking world comes here with his own self interest at heart. I know you not and therefore cannot in good conscience tell you what you seek."

"Do I not deserve a chance?"

"Yes, this world is for all who are willing to love and share, but only for those who can truly appreciate its wonders. Do you see me striking you down or trying to stop you?"

"When I had heard of your great deeds from the people of Dream, I had expected to find a man of understanding and compassion, not callousness and spite."

"I wish you no ill will."

"Then tell me what I seek or I will run you through!"

He pulled a small concealed sword from his belt and placed it against my neck. I took hold of his sword and ran it into my chest falling to the ground in pain. He leaped backward and threw his sword aside eying me curiously. Then as he reached down for the Evoker I took hold of his hand and stood up.

"You are not ready. You still hold the hatred of your world in your heart. Until you can free your heart of your world, you cannot bring your soul here."

I left him standing alone, hoping in my heart if he was a good soul that he would one day find his way into Dream as had I. Having an eternity to explore the Lands of Dream, my journeys took me to the great cosmic whirlpool where it is said the souls of the dead from Dream go to be reincarnated. I saw and passed through the glittering gates of the Lands of Lights to meet souls of pure energy that can travel to anywhere in the cosmos with one simple thought. I also trekked far east to the Rim of the Unknown charting a third realm of Dream discovering new cultures and strange unfathomable phenomena. All these things I have seen and yet I have seen almost nothing of what our dreams have to offer because the Lands of Dream touch every star in the cosmos. Where there is life in space, there are worlds here for those souls to dream. It is your soul that is the window to Dream. So search your heart and find your own path to the Lands of Dream, so we might see these things together.

As for me, my soul has been vacant of my body some twenty years and although I grieve for the pain my mother must have felt upon finding my body, I miss nothing of the waking world, for my soul has always belonged in Dream. I think one day, after I have explored deeper into the dreams of alien creation, I might return to Akgaule to pay a visit to my old friend Herald and see if Falasia might consider becoming my wife. If not, then I might journey to the Hall of the Gods with the divine blade Evoker and carve out my own realm of Dream as a god, but that will be another story in itself.

Poems

| Charles Clemons

Knowledge

Knowledge is like water
as it flows freely.
Trap it in a bowl
and it will evaporate.
Seal it in a container,
and it will perspire.
Limited only by its holder,
it can enrich the world
or simply destroy it.
Knowledge is not good or evil,
nor has it bounds or masters
as its use depends solely upon its user.

The Simplicity of Life

What is a flower?
What is its purpose?
A flower is life.
It has no meaning.
No destiny.
It is simply there to enjoy,
for those few who can appreciate it.

The Sacrificial Rock

Since the beginning of time
has stood the Sacrificial Rock.
In the days of darkness
when the gods were many
man came to the rock and worshipped.

Today the rock stands alone
forgotten and forsaken,
by those who follow
a single god,
but as the earth it is eternal.

Everything that rises must fall
and so shall our civilization.
When the world begins to decline
men shall return and worship once again
at the Sacrificial Rock.

A JOURNEY

Life is a journey
one of experiences, growth and learning in which
characters appear, interact, disappear and reappear.
Wins, losses and draws occur along the way
as experiences fade to mere memories
and when the journey comes to an end
there is nothing but what had been.

A Glossary of Dreams

Noteworthy bloodlines, geographic locations, heroes, gods and species
put to parchment by the able pen of
Alzoond, the Record Keeper.

Abka- The first human city to be built in the Lands of Dream
being erected some seven thousand years ago. Its first king,
King Otekue, raised an army of men pushing aside the land's
first inhabitants and in several swift victories ran the mongrel
south to the dark continent of Fathel carving out a place for
man in Dream. As time passed, Abka became the principal
city of man serving as its capital when there was only one
country for mankind. During this first era of man, Abka
became a cultural center serving both man and god until the
gods of Dream themselves warred for religious rights over the
races. During the deity wars, the races of Dream were pitted
against one another based upon their selection of worship
bringing most of Dream into war. A human hero named
Yxwuth who worshiped Serzie-Ju won many victories
increasing his god's territory tenfold and as reward the young
warrior was given the Evoker a sword capable of killing even
a god. The fabled warrior later became king of Abka ruling it
until his death, which also marked the death of the great city
as the gods sent the Death Bloom to protect the sword from
anyone who might use it against them.

Aguija- The third province of Haenic that borders the
Emerald Sea along Zeethe's western coastline. Its people are
known as both great farmers and sailors, but are hailed
throughout the Lands of Dream for their fleet foot soldiers.

Akgaule- A carefree island in the northern realm of Dream, which has no cities, laws, roads or rule as its people are as free as animals to wander and explore for food, sleep and love.

Alboules- The sixteenth and largest province of Haenic and northernmost country of the great central continent Zeethe. Surrounded by the dark Mhorhaen, its only connection to civilization beyond its own is now through a small guarded road that cuts cut through the center of the Mhorhaen of which man dares only to travel during the day.

King Babahl- The royal bloodline of the Narefickian people a country on the western half of the human continent Jhertyl.

Barqua- A great human dreamer known throughout Dream as its greatest explorer. It has been scribed that he was the first to pass beyond the Rim of the Unknown of which he never returned.

The Bright Sea- A sea that gets its name from its bright white sea floor which reflects the suns of Dream giving the enclosed sea within the continent of Zeethe a radiant glow.

Broden- A country in the south of Zeethe between the borders of the Kthaer and the country Oceika. The fifth province of Haenic, its people are known primarily for the light horsemen who roams its borders as have its people for thousands of years.

The Bubbling Sea- A hazy sea that borders The Rim of the Unknown that boils at its center creating a wall of steam making navigating it only possible through blind sail. Legend says that near the beginning of Dream, an active star fell into the vast sea's center and boils the great sea to this day. Whether it be star, volcanoes or the wrath of the gods, its great heat does not allow the passage of normal ships.

Celpahia- A city built along the massive Manikalra River basin that serves as both a trade port to the Lands of Dream and an entry point for dreamers from across the cosmos. Although built in eastern Deazah the kingdom of the great human King Nahl, it is an independent city state that owes no loyalty to anyone but its residents.

Cerulean Sea- The third largest sea of Dream which sits between the great continents of Deazah, Zeethe and The Alekain.

Citadel of Dragetryn- The palace of the once great orc king Dragetryn who ruled western Zeethe before the mongrel were pushed from their homelands and forced to dwell in dark Fathel under one king.

The Cosmic Sea- A rough and unforgiving sea in the northernmost realm of Dream. Many a ship have lost the wind and been sucked into the Great Cosmic Whirlpool never to be heard from again while trying to navigate its dangerous waters.

King Darl- A human king and royal bloodline of the country Gruedell.

Deazah- A continent in the southern realm of Dream predominantly inhabited by humans. Most of its territory fall under the rule of King Nahl except for the eastern city state of Celpahia.

Dreagar- A species of organisms, the second to dream from the cosmos into Dream, are usually short and stout to include the races of dwarf, gnome and the lesser known halfling. While the gnome is the most inventive of the three, all are great blacksmiths and prefer living within the earth, instead of on its surface as do most land dwelling races.

Dreamer- Can be of any species within the cosmos of space, but is considered anyone in the Lands of Dream not born within its boundaries. Most dreamers come and go among the cities, fields, seas and forests of Dream unable to stay beyond a single night of dreamwalking, but some desire to stay, a great controversy among the gods and residents of Dream for dreamers are immortal in life expectancy and do not fall under the same physics as do the residents of Dream.

Drugin- The mountainous continent of the stout dwarven people riddled with deep mines and perilous icy cliff tops that form a continuous fortress only those of Dreagar blood could love.

Dtyrl- An island belonging to a sea raiding people who have become quite rich upon the spoils of their pirate fleets.

Dwarf- The dwarf is a short stocky order belonging to the species Dreagar. They average no more than four and a half feet but usually weigh at least two hundred pounds. They have a thick bone structure and are known for their great feats of strength. They are natural miners, blacksmiths and warriors, knowing nothing of magic. They are usually stubborn, hardworking and care little for the affairs of those outside their own people. All adults, both male and female, have full beards and it is said that dwarves can tell the age of other dwarves by the length of their beards.

Baron Earuy- Chief of the gnome and the underworld of Dream.

Egaulé- The great and illustrious human hero who crawled into the pits of Xeadliow and slew the daemon Uqiot upon his own throne.

Eidolen- The All-Knowing, The Watchful Eye, perhaps the most powerful god of the Dark Peaks. His followers are the races of the mongrel and human that lust for necromantic power.

Elf- The first race to dream within the realm of Dream forming the first continent some fifty thousand years ago. A long lived race with a life span of nearly five thousand years, the elf is a woodland creature known for their skills of archery and tracking. Although small, standing about five feet on average and weighing around one hundred and thirty pounds, the elven race is strong in demeanor and has risen many times to quell the rise of the stronger mongrel races. Both the male and the female wear their hair long usually in intricate braids and neither can grow a beard or facial hair of any type.

The Emerald Sea- The great sea between the continents of Zeethe and Deazah.

Fairy- Although considered one of the folk, the fairy care little for the affairs of others and spend most of their time exploring and frolicking carelessly through Dream. One of the longest living races, reaching ages of around six thousand, the fairy is small being about a foot and a half in height and rarely weigh much more than twenty pounds. Females of the race have butterfly type wings, while the males have wings similar to that of a dragonfly. All are beautiful in both appearance and heart and while many live on the continent of Vastoal with the elf, they have no particular homeland and can be found all over the realms of Dream.

Fathel- The southernmost continent of Dream. A vast wasteland of desert, sand and bare mountains serving as home and last refuse for the mongrel species.

Folk- The oldest races of Dream to include the woodland peoples of the elf, fairy, satyr, brownie and centaur.

Garl- A centralized human country of Zeethe, currently the second province of Haenic known for its residents many trade skills.

Gnome- The gnome are of the dreagar species, but unlike their cousins are far different in that they dwell entirely beneath the earth unlike the dwarf who works and lives within and out. The gnome, male and female, wear short beards and are short and stout being somewhere between a dwarf and a halfling in both height and weight. The gnome can see in the dark hundreds of miles beneath the ground without the slightest tint of light as might a man in the day and therefore bother not with borders for everything below belongs to the great gnome king.

Goblin- Of the mongrel breed with an average height of four and a half feet and weigh about one hundred pounds. Quick masters of stealth used primarily as assassins and light cavalry atop wolves by the mongrel army. Short lived with a life span no longer than thirty years, although few ever live to see a natural death.

Great Cosmic Whirlpool- At the furthest northern known point of the Lands of Dream swirls a great whirlpool that drinks in the great seas. Many philosophers believe it might be a portal to another realm of Dream, while others believe the great whirlpool collects the souls of those that die within Dream and distributes their essence of life back to the universe where it might be reincarnated. Many a ship and sailor has dared to finds it end, but none where ever found or heard from again.

Lord Gruem- Mine Master of the Dwarf and sole royal bloodline of the dreagar. A dreagar of great strength, valor and obduracy that relishes war, the treasures of the earth and stout hairy women.

Gurtique- A once flourishing city where the gods of Dream dwelled in counsel, but later cursed as its residents became decadent and declared themselves gods. As punishment the gods perverted the city's residents into bloodthirsty monsters to guard their secrets.

Haenic- A centralized country in Zeethe that gave birth to the royal Hamse bloodline. Under the rule of the Hamse kings, Haenic has become the most powerful human country in all of Dream ruling an empire to include all of Zeethe, save the eastern most edge of the continent where black magic holds the forces of men at bay.

Halfling- The halfling are of the dreagar, but avoid the concerns of others. Small of stature, being between two and three feet tall, they average about eighty pounds and are experts of camouflage and stealth. They live in small holes in the ground burrowing them with their bare hands like that of badgers. Rarely seen by others save their own, halflings stay out of the affairs of others and therefore few residents of Dream have ever had the privilege of such a glimpse.

Hall of the Gods- A massive construction of absolute splendor unlike any seen by the eyes of man or creature, this fortress is believed to be the dwelling of the gods of justice built high upon the mountains of Zurwuael, beyond the reach and dreams of man and beast.

King Hamse- The king of the largest empire within the known Lands of Dream and royal bloodline of Haenic.

Heiftal- The God of Smolder, The Black Flame, a great god of the Dark Peaks whose primary worshippers are those of war. When he appears to his worshippers or those that rile his anger, he appears in the form of a swirling black cloud. Legend says Heiftal took an orc princess into his bed during a drunken stupor and the result was the large and powerful Ogre, but such claims are violently refuted by the worshippers of his temples.

Human- The youngest race of Dream and seemingly a balance between the peace loving folk and war mongering mongrel. Upon the coming of man nearly seven thousand years ago, the lands of Dream belonged to the folk, dreagar and mongrel, but now man holds his own place a type of buffer between the hatred of the three. Humans hold the widest variety of size and shape among all the races of Dream being anywhere from five to seven foot tall and weighing anywhere from one hundred to three hundred pounds and are known to wear both long and short hair and to both have beards and clean shaven faces. The life expectancy of a human in the Lands of Dream is somewhere between two hundred and two hundred and fifty years.

Islands of Jheanb- A chain of islands in the southern realm of Dream that sits directly between the Emerald and Mordal Seas. Its inhabitants are men, but not like modern men, being more that of man's early ancestors the Cro-Magnon. It is believed they were the first men to dream to Lands of Dream and to this date have not changed their ways since that of early man following the ways of the tribe, fire and nature.

Isle of Thorn- A northeastern island covered in thick thorn patches that cover the entire island and make it uninhabitable by any civilized culture.

Jejir- A legendary creature of immense stature known for its fierce hunting of man. Believed to be a cousin to the long lost Yeti of the waking world, the jejir still lives wild within the Lands of Dream ready to turn dream into nightmare with its brutal stalking of man.

Jhertyl- The northernmost continent of men that has been divided between the kingdoms of Gruedell and Narefick in a war that has lasted centuries.

Karghuial- A northwestern country of Zeethe and eighth province of the kingdom Haenic. Its kings are known for their servitude of justice and worship of Regiah the god of true justice. Great knights of law and order rise from this country questing all across the Lands of Dream.

Kiutryl- The capital city port of the buccaneer nation Dtyrl.

Kthaerian Waste- A great dry wasteland and the fifteenth province of Haenic, home to the mighty tribal warriors the Kthaer Barbarian known for their fearless nature and great strength, which is matched only by the wild beasts of the earth.

King Shaii- Grand Druid of the Elf, ninth solemn king of the elf.

Queen Lai- Steward of the Fairy, Queen over the Rainbow Isles and a well known magus of Dream.

The Land of Lights- A world of pure energy where the mind can flow freely without the limitations of the body. Inhabited by a species of intelligent energy, those of flesh must be careful for such freedom of thought has been known to warp those of a fragile mind leaving them mad upon return.

Leasden- Keeper of Knowledge, The Learned, a god of great knowledge who resides in the Hall of the Gods. A peaceful god whose followers usually include scholars as well as great wizards.

Ljegh- Goddess of Love and Art who dwells in the Hall of the Gods. It is believed it was the talent and understanding of her beauty that spawned the lovely fairy from her dreams.

Lusete- An ash and lava covered volcanic island in the northern realm of Dream belonging to the fire immune mud people. It is rumored that the island's many volcanoes are portals to the Underworld of Dream.

Maritaunia- The underwater city and capital of the Maritaun people located at the bottom of the Turquoise Sea. Ruled by King Vauencet, the Maritaun people do not mettle in the affairs of those above the seas of Dream.

Marpuaeliua- The Lady of the Sea, Goddess of the Sea, a patron of the sailor and all creatures of the sea. Unlike most the gods of justice, she does not dwell within the Hall of the Gods, but her very essence is within the sea itself.

Lord Martoex- King over the sea raiding nation Dtyrl and great pirate in his own right, Lord Martoex has few allies and therefore more to plunder.

The Mhorhaen Forest- A vast nearly impenetrable forest still ruled by wild creature rather than the civilized races of Dream that divides northern and southern Zeethe.

Mogeiah- The First Mongrel, The True Mongrel, believed to be the first mongrel to dream into the Lands of Dream and therefore creator of much of the southern realm. Although it is believed he visits Fathel quite often to upstart the mongrel wars, he dwells within the Dark Peaks with the gods of bedlam.

The Mongrel- A young and violent species of Dream to include the Orc, Ogre, Goblin, Wyner and Troll species.

Mordal Sea- The southernmost sea of Dream which separates the forces of man and mongrel. Many call this wide sea, the Sea of Death, as many naval battles between the residents of Dream have taken place here sending thousands of ships and lives to its bottom.

King Nahl- Head Trader of Deazah and royal bloodline of the peoples of the southern human continent Deazah. Although known for his great skills in diplomacy, it was his skills of war that held back the forces of Haenic during the Emerald Sea Wars keeping the continent of Deazah free of Hamse rule.

Captain Nauria- A great sea captain, the first humanoid to discover the far off Lands of Light. Upon finding its discovery, he and his crew sailed past its massive lighthouses into the realm of light to dwell among its strange inhabitants. Upon their return, both the captain and crew's mind had somehow become distorted becoming suicidal and most of the crew later killed themselves. Captain Nauria became a rogue seaman challenging the sea whenever and wherever he could until he was lost within the depths of Nauria's Caverns.

Nthark- A northern wooded country of Zeethe that borders the southern edge of the Mhorhaen Forest. A country of farmers and natural hunters and the fourth province of Haenic. Its woodmen are known throughout Dream for their skills in archery and tracking.

Oceika- A coastal country upon southern coast of Zeethe that is known for its mighty seamen and war galleys who besiege the coast of Fathel against mongrel invaders. The sixth province of Haenic, it is Oceika's navy that give the Hamse armies sea superiority over their many foes of Dream.

Ogre- Of the mongrel breed, average height seven foot, average weight about four hundred pounds. Believed to be a cross between the orc and the god Heiftal during a drunken stupor, the ogre are used by the mongrel army as pure muscle to batter doors and break the lines of enemy armies.

Omauk-Et- Eldest of the old and wise silver dragons of Dream. A being of neutrality who rarely appears unless times of imbalance grip the realms of Dream.

Orc- Of the mongrel breed, average height six foot, average weight two hundred and fifty pounds. Males have prominent lower tusk that rise up aside their snouts. Short lived, with a life span of about forty years, the orc lives in a structured pecking order where the strong rule and the weak serve.

Phylain- A common human sailor who during the Second Mongrel Wars rallied the flag ship upon the fall of its captain and under his command, a small flotilla held a fleet of mongrel ships at bay in the Straight of Phylain until the fleets of the folk and dreagar could arrive and sink the mongrel navy.

Plazius- The Unknown God, Anonymous Dreamer, believed to have created the western realm of Dream a vast world that alters daily, so that no map or being can chart its territory.

Quandrus- The wandering king who sacrificed his kingdom for solitary immortality.

The Rainbow Isles- A chain of small tropical islands in the northernmost realm of Dream that serves home to the gentle fairy and many other woodland races of the folk.

The Rim of the Unknown- To the far east of Dream past the realms of folk, mongrel and man stands a large rock barrier that rises from the depths of the sea surrounded by a jagged barrier reef impassable by ship alone. Many believe it is a natural boundary that separates the third realm of Dream from that of the north and south.

Seirdu- An island country to the west of Drugin that was cursed with mass idiocy by the Patriarch Whushi, Grand Wizard of Uthal, for a failed attempt upon his life. Being an entire nation suffering from a contagious form of lunacy, its ports have long been forgotten by the residents of Dream leaving it a wasteland of madmen.

Shroom Isle- An island covered with various forms of harmless, toxic, edible and hallucinogenic fungus that is home to an odd species of dreamers known as Sporelugs or mushroom men. They have made no known attempt to communicate which anyone outside their own and usually attack foreigners upon sight. Many of the mushrooms on the islands are in great demand and many a sea raider have perished picking them for their trade value.

Sudal- The first province of Zeethe, a wooded area nestled between the soaring Azoul Mountains and the thick forest of the Mhorhaen. Known for its hunters, woodsmen and fine harvested furs.

Troll- The troll is a tall slender creature belonging to the species of mongrel. The first mongrel King Xeikgh sacrificed fifty thousand goblins to the old and dark mongrel god Mogeiah and it is believed his reward for such a great sacrifice was the hardly troll which can regenerate wounds within minutes and even full limbs in a matter of days. They are tall usually around six and a half feet, but slender weighing about 200 pounds on average. Wounds caused by magic, fire and acid are the only ones they cannot regenerate as trolls have been known to regenerate to full capacity when wounded by other means from that of only a head.

Turquoise Sea- The second largest sea of Dream which is peppered with islands, continents, natural and unnatural phenomena.

Uthal- A castle of mist that serves as home to the mysterious wizard Whushi. It is said that it never rests in the same place twice fading away with each dusk only to reappear at dawn somewhere else in the Lands of Dream making it only accessible during the hours of daylight.

Vaguk- The Seeping Madness, Lucid Death, the darkest and most vile of all the gods. Little is known about this mad being as not even the gods have dealings with one of such a dark and hideous nature and he dwells not with the gods of justice or bedlam. Of what solar system this being dreamt or for how long it has done so is unknown. This god has few worshippers as psychosis is the gift of following the great madness of Vaguk.

Vastoal- The first continent of Dream created when time began dreamt by the oldest life forms in the cosmos, the elven people. With their own world lost through that of a black hole, the last of the elven people will dwell in Dream until the last click of time.

Vineying- The capital city and only sea port of the vast of the forested elven continent Vastoal.

Wren Henji- A sea port on the western coast of Zeethe that serves as a way point for ships sailing between the Northern and Southern realms of Dream. One of Dreams few remaining independent city states.

Patriarch Whushi, Grand Wizard of Uthal- A sorcerer of great power, who many believe rivals the power of the gods themselves.

Wyner- A small agile creature, usually gray, black or dull brown, of the species of mongrel. The wyner, being around two and a half feet tall and rarely weighing over fifty pounds has large round eyes in proportion to its head and can climb trees as easily as can a squirrel. Too small to be effective in battle, the wyner rarely uses a weapon and is primarily employed by the mongrel as a spy or silent assassin.

Xanub- The Worm God, a dreaming entity from the Betelgeuse system that bores through the core of Dream creating large underground kingdoms.

Yeathon- The seventh province of Haenic that lies in the west of the great continent of Zeethe south of the Azoul Mountains. Yeathon is best known for its heavy horsemen and wild fighting style upon which all its soldiers use.

Zeethe- The central and largest continent in the southern realm of Dreams.

Available from Portal Press Books

Cosmic Contemplations

The collected science fiction of Charles Clemons containing the novel *Intergalactic Eden*, the short stories *Suspended Hell*, *The Genetic Game* and *Death to the Queen* as well as the poem Intergalactic Dimensions. ISBN-13-: 9780615142876, 200 pages, available in paperback 6"x9" ($12.00) and hardback 6"x9" signed and limited to 100 copies ($23.00).

Funky Shrooms and Other Exquisite Delights

The second book by the fantastic author Charles Clemons. Includes the introduction Strange has a New Name, the full length apocalyptic zombie novel *The Final Infection*, the short stories *Autobiography of a Necromancer*, *The Other Side of the Blackened Mirror*, *Primordial Beast*, the interview *Satan's Side of the Story* and six poems. ISBN-13-: 9780615174679, 436 pages, available in paperback 6"x9" ($16.00) and hardback 6"x9" signed and limited to 100 copies ($28.00).

The Time Chronicles

Collects the time travel tales of the legendary science fiction author H.G. Wells. Includes his first tale of time *The Chronic Argonauts*, published in 1888, and what many consider the greatest science fiction novels of all time, *The Time Machine*. ISBN-13-: 978-1-4357-3543-9, 128 page, available in paperback 6"x9" ($10.00) and hardback 6"x9" ($21.00).

Dreams Assembled: The Collected Early Dreams of Lord Dunsany Volume I

This compilation collects Lord Dunsany's first three books of dream, *The Gods of Pegāna* (1905), *Time and the Gods* (1906) and *The Sword of Welleran and Other Stories* (1908). ISBN-13-: 978-1-4357-5974-9, 6"x9" paperback ($18.00) and 8.25" X 10.75" hardback ($26.00).

About the author:

Charles Clemons lives in Chattanooga Tennessee with his wife Joy and his son Alex writing short stories, poems, novels, essays and screenplays. A Desert Shield/Storm veteran and constant student, Charles spends his days in the beautiful mountains of Tennessee and nights "pecking" at a keyboard.

I once knew a man who had lived an entire lifetime in the Lands of Dream having a wife, many children and grandchildren. Upon dying of old age he awoke from his dream to discover that only one night in the waking world had passed. That very morning he took his life, because he had already lived the life he wanted to live.